The Sound Post

Fordon James

THE SOUND POST

This is a work of fiction. All of the characters, names, incidents, organizations, and dialogue in this novel are either the products of the author's imagination or are used fictitiously.

iUniverse books may be ordered through booksellers or by contacting:

iUniverse
1663 Liberty Drive
Bloomington, IN 47403
www.iuniverse.com
1-800-Authors (1-800-288-4677)

Because of the dynamic nature of the Internet, any web addresses or links contained in this book may have changed since publication and may no longer be valid. The views expressed in this work are solely those of the author and do not necessarily reflect the views of the publisher, and the publisher hereby disclaims any responsibility for them.

Any people depicted in stock imagery provided by Getty Images are models, and such images are being used for illustrative purposes only. Certain stock imagery © Getty Images.

ISBN: 978-1-5320-5430-3 (sc)
ISBN: 978-1-5320-5431-0 (e)

Library of Congress Control Number: 2018908923

Print information available on the last page.

iUniverse rev. date: 08/22/2018

"To that old street violinist playing to himself tremulously on a certain bleak day in a certain forgotten town."
V. Nabokov

***

Sundays you worked alone. The others were either getting ready for church or still in bed from the drinking of the night before. In the funerary silence of dawn, you could hear the sedate clucking of the chickens as soon as you hit the top of the gravel road leading down to the property. Nary a rooster crow. Nor the moo of a cow. Nor the bay of a goat. Maybe the yap of the old mangy dog that hung around the dressing shed. But not much else aside from the sedate clucking of the chickens, waiting in the dark with no concept of what had become of dawn. Waiting to eat, waiting to die. Born in darkness, fed in darkness, separated from their heads in darkness. And the doors to the sheds were secured with well-oiled padlocks. How easy the worn down keys slid into the loose keyholes. How easy the huge doors slid on well-oiled tracks and wheels. Yet eternal and perpetual confinement. When the hens in the front coops were caught in the fresh flood of sunlight, many would try to produce a fit of panic, but it wouldn't last long. Lethargic and fat, in a minute or two they settled back into sedate clucking. Blind in the dark and blind in the light. Bred out of flight. Bred to get fat and squat. The smell of wet feather, of excrement, of rot, candied the air with a sickening sweetness. The hypnotic drone of the overhead ventilation fans stopped time. The crunch of the split dry feed under foot like crushing fragile bones. And the sedate clucking, clucking, clucking of birds too fat to stand, with nothing to do but pluck themselves raw with clipped beaks and blank stares.

In black oversized rubber boots and black rubber gloves that you pulled up to your elbows, -gloves that never completely dried after washing the night before, you cleaned the water troughs clogged with the acidic squirt of excrement. You poured endless flows of dry feed. You swept the feathers from the dirt. Pulled heads from nooks. Claws from cracks. Wings from wire mesh. And you collected the limp carcasses in a red wheelbarrow. And as those that had succumbed to the crush of the fold piled higher and higher, you'd always try to remember the words to that poem you once read about a red wheelbarrow, but you couldn't quite remember all of it, or who wrote it. So much depends upon a red wheelbarrow, something something something, beside the white chickens, you'd say as you pour Kerosene in the oil barrels to burn the dead chickens. The sweet stench of fire-singed chicken skin clinging to your clothes, filling up your nose, causing your eyes to water as you got in close with a metal boat paddle to churn the dead into ash. So many casualties. And so much ash. What was it? One in twenty. One in forty. The squawk of futility echoed in your ears, long after you had already started walking home. An unmarked ribbon of black top, still hot, dusk a purple mist settling in to the fields, a covey of firefly.

It wasn't as though you were hiding, either. Everyone knew where you were in the old barn on your dead great uncle's land. In particular, your parents knew. But they thought you'd eventually 'come to your senses'. They stubbornly waited for you to come home and admit you were wrong. Especially with winter coming. But you stuck it out. You worked a job nobody with any sort of choice would ever otherwise work. You lived in a barn. You ate things from cans. You fried things in a skillet on a camp stove. You left the bail door ajar, in the night, to let in what light the stars could offer. And then winter did come. Winter was not like the summer, winter cut at your resolve with a dull cross saw, almost cut you in two. But you stuck it out.

Yellow school bus, all full of heat and vinyl seats. Kids full of juice bouncing on board with the squeak of tennis shoes and bubble gum, smelling of shampoo and fluoride. The excitement ripped like Velcro up and down the aisles. Until you climbed onboard and everything went to hush and it would takes several miles of bouncy school bus for the overall mood to self-restore. For the most part you would avoid your siblings, usually try sitting way in the back, but sometimes they would come back and ask: When are you coming home? And you'd see in their faces, not so much concern as curiosity. And you'd ask, Are they going to make me. And they'd say, no, don't see how they can. And you'd say, Well, then no, I am not.

In a small rural town like this most kids ride the bus, first grade through senior year. So everyone knew your story. And likewise, everyone believed the problem was you. But it was your senior year, and there was no sense quitting, you knew that much. But more importantly, school meant a warm yellow bus and a cafeteria and hot meals. It meant electric lights and clean toilets and sinks with running water. And it meant Mrs. Langham. She believed in you. She had harbored you during the worst of the storm. Without her, you wouldn't have had much of a chance. Without her, you would have never made it through to graduation. Without her, you might have given up. But you stuck it out.

At night, when you were alone, an oil lamp burning dimly on minimum wage, you often considered giving up. But just when you thought you couldn't stand the stench of rotten hay and dank decay any longer. Just when you thought you couldn't possibly stand another sponge bath in ironwater. Just when you thought you might literally go mad from scratching yourself under discarded quilts and old horse blankets. Each time you woke to find that evil, pink-faced possum staring down at you from an overhead rafter, sending a paralyzing wave of fear and vulnerability through your body. Each time you came back from school or from work and entered this dark, cold, lonely place, you seriously thought about giving up. But you didn't. You would go to your instrument case, pop its tiny little latches and lay back the lid. And then everything would be all right. Your heart would fill up with warmth from the mere sight. Your dearest friend, this battered old violin. Everyone but Mrs. Langham thought you were crazy. Sometimes even you thought you were crazy. Sometimes when you couldn't figure out you, you'd hear yourself say,

Well fiddle me Jim, what I am doing? as if borrowing from the local vernacular, and, depending on the mood you were in, you'd either laugh at yourself ironically or freeze up in terror. But this violin had something to say to you. In its fragile construct of wood and strings there was someone whispering to you. Like the old can and string trick played in the dark, you knew there was someone on the opposite end trying to communicate to you. Someone lost from you. Every time you took up that bow and drew it across those strings you woke up not just yourself but generations of you going back through grandfathers and great grandmothers, back across states, countries, continents, kingdoms and clans and cairns of rock on barren islands battered by sea and storm and war and famine. You could hear in those vibrating strings the clamor, and the murmur, the babies crying and the mothers singing, the men roaring, and the canons firing, flags and hearts flying, the cacophony of the coils upon tightly wound genetics coils of you, twisting deep into the pre-time, to the very first hunched, stick yielding stumble of you. Before you could even play a single note, these stings sang to you and you had to listen. You simply had to...

Part I

I

It is midnight and a Greyhound motorcoach pulls into terminal. New Orleans, Louisiana, its final destination, enveloped in the steam of an oppressive August heat. A sullen black man jerks luggage from below the bus. Passengers spill out into the depot, gathering their bags, reuniting with friends and family, hugging and kissing and laughing. James Buck stands clutching a blistering black violin case with a look on his face of all the severity of a young artist, an unlikely name for such an unlikely person and no one is here to greet his unlikely arrival.

He finds his limp duffel among the various suitcases and cardboard boxes and ice chests duct-taped shut and labeled with tags revealing their origins in code—St. Louis, Chicago, Memphis, Nashville. The mythical cities along the Mississippi, which people who ride interstate buses use as a reference to where they are from, mostly the small indistinguishable suburbs or decrepit towns in between, which have all but been forgotten, peopled by those who still rode buses, while the rest of the world took to the skies in airplanes or roared across the country in their automobiles along impertinent, unapologetic superhigways.

Buck hits the empty street, uninspired by the oppressive heat, weak from the gut wrenching fear tearing up his insides. He has wanted this moment, now, for longer than he can remember. But now the moment is here, the immeasurable weight of all his expectations is crushing him. He is desperate for something to happen, to pull him free from the past, and into the now, but here now he stands in the street in a dark, lachrymal section of town that makes him second guess his one way ticket, until a streetcar comes rumbling out of the darkness, glowing like a lantern, riding high and dignified. A strange and beautiful visual cue that he isn't in Missouri, anymore; his journey is unmistakably underway. He spots a newspaper vendor chained to a streetlamp. It takes his quarters with an empty rattle. He folds out a paper to the classifieds and runs his gaze along the columns of small print. There is only one entry in his price range. ROOMS, CLEAN, CLOSE TO QUARTER, $95per WK&up. He goes to a payphone and calls. He takes an address.

Off Julia Street, he rents a small and filthy room on the second floor, no bigger than the mattress itself, tobacco smoke stained papered walls. He throws down his canvas bag and sits on the low mattress. He kicks off his red clay-smudged bucks and pulls off his musky socks, airs his sweaty feet, expanding his toes in the shag carpet, feeling cool bits of gravel deep in the pile. He opens his violin case and removes a battered, but picturesque, violin. He puts the instrument under his chin and begins to play; he selects Bartok's *Melodia* thinking it will comfort him, one of dozens of songs he has learned solely by ear, so not perfect, cut rough from the cloth, hand sewn, loose fitted. He pulls down the bow, and a beautiful voice begins to sing. The busy cockroaches filing along the baseboards momentarily stop. In the faint moonlight coming through the small window, a strange drama is beginning to unfold, and the opening monologue begins like this: I'm here. Maybe I should go out now and look around. No, there's no hurry. Tomorrow. How much money will I make? If I spend half the day playing I could make . . . I have no idea. I don't have the remotest idea. Maybe nothing. He stops playing, unable to move beyond this thought. He realizes he is tired, so he curls into bed in his clothes.

He dreams about flying. Like a bird. The changing wind under his arms like wings. He banks on gusts, soars over the clouds on thermals, alights on treetops and roof ridges, peers down on the obtemperating activity of humanity sole-slapping the pavement of inscape oblivion. The air is clean, the world is in hyper color, his movements are fast and unrestricted. It is no wonder in the morning, he feels good. He is full of happiness that his good dreams have returned. In the weeks before his departure, they were dark, tormented, episodic, taking him on fruitless pursuits, involving him in hostile struggles, and many times causing that he would just barely miss some desired outcome by moments, inches, by the narrowest of margins. He is glad to have these good dreams back. Dreams that he has long determined to be his greatest assets; dreams that have served to motivate him, inspire him to keep moving forward, upward, when all around him is dead or dying.

He takes his shower in an enormous community bathroom where the toilet has been removed, a scrap of plywood placed over the hole. He drapes his towel over a tall, rusted radiator. The showerhead is crusted with calcium deposits and spits a discolored water into the stained tub. He washes his thin hair and oily face with shampoo. The water is warm even with the warm-water knob turned off. He bathes quickly so as not to let the foul water wash away his good spirit. He knows the day will be long and there will be very few agents to restore it until he can get back to his other reality -his subconscious imagination, where, for the most part, things worked in his favor and the indifference or the wrongdoings or the general ignorance of other people had the least affect on him. Where things broken inside are repaired. Where emotions long withered and dead, sprout and open in bloom. Where his heart still races when he sees a familiar face. Where feelings well up into his throat. Where he can embrace a sibling or a parent and quiver with love and grow hot with tears. Where many things were which are not in reality. He knows what has wounded him, but not again, so he bathes quickly, embracing what his dreams have offered. He snaps the towel from the radiator, causing it to ring long, while the showerhead drips, tap tee tap, tap tee tap, tee tap. He leaves the hotel, humming. A new life for him is beginning!

He is starving, as he leaves the hotel, called the Hamlet's Bird, a once beautiful Second Empire street front single, long neglected and ridden into irreversible disrepair. He walks St. Charles Avenue, thick with humidity, to the French Quarter.

Canal Street bustles. The Mississippi River lies to his right. He crosses the wide, divided street, takes Chartres to St. Peters, St. Peters to Decatur. He goes directly into Cafe Beignet and gets a table in the open air cafe near the back railing along St. Peters where the street climbs the levee along the river. This café is straight out of a Hemingway novel; he quite expects to overhear the conversations of an artist and poet and a chain-smoking heiress. A thin, brown waiter comes, and James orders black coffee, and it is brought to him rapidly along with a glass of iced water. The ice is already melting, and he pays the waiter, and the waiter drops the coin remainder in the pool of condensation on the cool marble table around the glass, insinuating a tip. Buck drinks the waterglass empty and then draws a sip of coffee and leans back and tries to act as though everything is business as usual, but it isn't. He hasn't ever been in a place like this; it is beautiful and foreign. He could be in Paris or Milan; it is so different from anything he's ever seen. People shuffle by on broken sidewalks. Horse-drawn carriages pull into the curb, the drivers singing bold solicitations. The smell of painted wood, decayed leaves, muddy water, and coffee hangs in the air. The waiter's musk floats by regularly, with a whiff of perspiration. If the wind moves, he can smell fresh fruit, car tire rubber road travel hot, tobacco smoke and the sweet smell of stale alcohol. He enjoys the sounds; the sounds of a city as heard from an open cafe. The beep of a horn. The snort of a horse. A passing truck. Sidewalks being swept or hosed with water. The clatter of heavy porcelain cups and saucers. The chirp of a toddling girl and the tap tap, tap tap of her shiny black shoes on the granite flagstones. Little ribbons of music drifting in from somewhere.

II

Outside the black iron fence surrounding Jackson Square, painters, portrait artists, tarot-card readers, magicians, and various other street entertainers, even a poet selling a rhyme for a dollar and any three words you could conjure, are thick like merchants at a bazaar. Inside the perimeter of the fence, Andrew Jackson stands high and alone on his horse, his stone face oblivious to immemorial wrongs, flowers around his pedestal blazing in the forenoon sun. Large oak trees cast slat-backed benches into shade. It is a stifling ninety degrees by eleven. Buck enters the square through the Chartres street entrance and takes shade. He has now his first impression of how very dense the Quarter is, which he likes. But he has the dissatisfaction of not knowing anything about his surroundings and, at the same time, a great anticipation to discover it. He wants to know the city. He wants intimacy immediately. He wants to be six months or a year into his new life. He watches through the fat bars of the fence a street magician make a red silk handkerchief disappear into his fisted hand, then pull it from a playing card, which he has rolled into a tight cylinder with open hands. Buck warns himself: It may be difficult to please the crowds. Will they want more than I have to give? These long ignored solos I've learned by ear.

He gets up from the bench and leaves the square through the Decatur gates as a carriage departs with light clops on silent wheels. The blazing sidewalk smells of French bread and cooking grease, of beer and seafood plates, of mustard and horseradish. At a restaurant called Maspero's, a pretty young waitress seats him at a table, and she is friendly, and Buck wishes he were the type that could make an advance and openly show his admiration, without feeling it is unwanted. He asks her for a glass of iced water while he makes a choice from the menu. The heavy pitcher beads with sweat as she pours him a glass. A ceiling fan ineffectually rotates overhead. He orders half a muffuletta and sucks the water from the glass and fills it again himself. After a great wait, during which time he consumes most of the water in the pitcher, the large sandwich comes out on a thick, white plate, big and round and stacked heavy with hams, cheeses, salamis, olives, and vegetables. He can barely finish it. He is the only person in the restaurant. The waitress hurries out his check to be done with him, to return to the paper back novel she reads at the bar. He washes his hands and face in the bathroom and then leaves the restaurant, walks along Decatur to Conti Street, turns up over the levee and finds a park. The wind moves over the river here, and he sits down on the lawn and lays back for a nap.

When he wakes, it is four o'clock in the afternoon, and he walks through the city back to the hotel and goes up to his room. He takes out his instrument and sits down on the bed. It is hot, and he cannot play but only sweat and think about where he will play the next day. He envisions himself nervously in several different spots. I mustn't play near the open cafes where people can sit for long periods. I'm not ready for that. He closes his violin into its case and grips it by the handle and reasons to go on a walk to find a spot where he can play.

Along Royal Street, near a bistro, leaning on the tan stucco wall of a building with a neglected balcony threatening to fall from the second story, is a man playing the saxophone. James Buck slows to pass. The sax player watches him over his swollen cheeks, his eyes squinting. He has found great acoustics in the deep street. James pulls coins from his pocket and tosses them into the musician's open case. He walks on slowly, listening to the instrument's generous voice. He thinks it is a good instrument. It has a broad range of moods. Maybe, someday, one day, I will explore it. He is about to think about it more, then stops himself and says to himself, I don't play the saxophone; I play the violin. I need to learn to play this one very well first.

On the corner of Toulouse and Chartres, he backs against the wall of a building and takes out his violin. It is growing dark and the streets are being swallowed in that darkness, and he tries to think what this place is like in the day. He becomes wide-eyed seeing the sunlit figure of himself bowing his violin in his mind's eye. Then he places the violin under his chin and begins by warming himself with little exercises, freely and effortlessly. Then he moves to playing Chopin's *Nocturne in C Minor.* He continues to think of it being daytime. How will I hold my face to the people passing by? Should I thank those who put money into my case? Maybe nod, modestly? Something that says I appreciate your appreciation of me. An older man walks by -a burnt out hippie, probably a street performer himself. He smiles as if hearing something unexpected and says:

"If you place dollar bills in your case, it'll look better." He tosses change into the open case. James looks down at the two quarters, a glint of distant lamplight turning them into a foreign currency. He does not put more money into the case; he wants to marvel his first earnings.

He plays until about eight o'clock, and he grows very tired standing and playing the same set of songs over and over. He takes the money up from the case, and it counts to four dollars. He feels good and wants to buy a beer. But he will not. He knows his money is tight. He starts walking back to his room, thinking how good it would be to sit inside one of the bars without walls on a stool, drinking a dark beer that would be cold and the air cool, and people would be milling about contentedly drinking and talking and smiling like people do in beer commercials. But he reminds himself that in the beer commercials the beer is water made to look especially thirst-quenching, and the people are paid just to be there because they look good, and they probably don't live in a filthy, roach infested room, with sheets so stained and smelly they are obligated to sleep in their clothes. In beer commercials, as in commercials for cleaning products, the world is mostly very, very clean, and what dirt does sometimes show up can be eliminated in a single sanitary swipe. So when he gets into his room, he does not think about what he could have done with the four dollars, because he knows one beer or twenty, none of this will go away. Instead he tries to think about what he will do tomorrow. All those many nights while imagining being here, nervously impatient to embark on this big adventure, it never occurred to him that a clean, modest room would be well out of his budget. How could he have known? Who could have told him? What access did he have to the outside world? He was just fortunate enough to have a Greyhound bus stop in town; and not a station either, just the familiar sign with the greyhound in full sprint and a bench, at a gas station, and luckily the woman who sold him his ticket two weeks in advance hadn't lived in town long enough to know his unannounced 1am departure would get at least half of contents of the dinky town into a delightfully awful little stir. So what could he have known? Very little, and so this is what he has to deal with, and he has to be patient. He lies down and tries to get to sleep. He rolls over and over a dozen times trying to get comfortable, to allow sleep to steal over him. He remains still with his feet apart and his arms at his sides, looking up at the stained ceiling. He hears the paint cracking, each flake whispering farewell before free falling, tumbling down. He hears rats wheezing in the un-insulated walls. He hears the fencing antennae of the roaches' den. He invites sleep consciously, but it will not come. He knew it never came invited. It always stole over you when you were not aware. So he lies there for hours, trying not to be aware. Finally, it comes and takes over him, though intermittently.

III

Morning is broiling. There is no wind to move the humid air around. James Buck gets out of bed and is tacky with the humidity settled all night on his body. He showers and leaves his room with his violin in its case. The air outside the hotel stands around irritated and bored like a doorman that hates his job but will not see about getting another.

The humid air sits on the tops of his ears and his high forehead, and he beads with perspiration under it. He is thinking of his spot. He is excited about playing. It is seven thirty in the morning, and he does not want to start this early. He goes to Cafe Beignet.

For his breakfast, he orders coffee, this time with cream because the coffee is so strong, and a saucer of beignets. They are thick with confectioner's sugar and, with each bite, his breath dusts the tabletop around the small saucer with sweet powder. Through the iron railing around the cafe he sees a wood-wheeled cart pushed by a stringy-haired artisan go by and he is, now, feeling urged to eat quickly and go to his spot. He does not want to start too early, for to endure a good portion of the day, but the anxiety of losing his spot compels him, finding a spot with the right acoustics is tantamount to the playing itself, this much he knows instinctively. By nine o' clock, he is leaned up against the peeling wall of the building at the corner of Chartres and Toulouse with his violin under his chin and two folded one-dollar bills and loose change in his case.

He plays steadily until noon, collecting several dollar bills and a lot of change but not knowing how much, feeling too self-conscious to kneel down to count it. He wants to break for lunch, but there are many people out grazing the old streets. He is tempted to go to a grocer around the corner, but losing his spot is a greater concern. He made many laps of the Quarter on his first day and he feels confident believing some places are just simply better than others, for their combined acoustics and exposure. He decides to stay and continue to play. The temperature is still rising. Sweat rolls down from under his armpits and off his forehead or along the bridge of his nose. His chin is wet on the tailpiece of the violin. His feet hurt and are hot and damp in his brown leather shoes. His legs ache from ankle to thigh. He is playing poorly, thinking about food and rest. He endures two separate sets of hunger pains and knows he will not be very hungry when he finally goes to eat, which will be at 4 pm.

He sits down on the sidewalk with his back against the wall. He is very tired, but knows that he cannot sit long because it will make it hard to get up again. So he stands up and something about getting up, with violin in hand, and the realization that he is in the French Quarter, New Orleans, playing his violin on the street (as though it is just now occurring to him), makes him strong and proud. He starts to play with a renewed energy, and shortly thereafter, a very beautiful lady strolls by and drops into his case a clean one-dollar bill. He plays another two hours.

IV

He sits on a bench along the backside of Jackson Square to count his money. He puts the one-dollar bills back to back and counts them and then folds them into his pocket. Seven dollars. He makes one-dollar stacks of the quarters. There are also dimes and nickels and pennies, which he leaves in the case. He stuffs five dollars and seventy-five cents in quarters into both front pockets and they make an uncomfortable pair of lumps.

He didn't think he would have made this much money the first day playing. A lot of people had dropped money in passing and did not listen to the music long. This does not bother him, but he thinks it can mean unstable earnings. He worries about location. What if I can't always get a good spot? But he stops thinking, immediately. He knows he will have to worry about that soon enough. He goes to find someplace to eat, though he isn't very hungry; having gone all day without eating, his stomach has shrunk. He thinks about the large sandwich of the day before, and it makes him nauseous thinking of eating something so heavy. He steps into a cafe with a flagstone courtyard under the canopy of palmetto fronds. He drinks a coffee slowly and watches the people of the street. Listening. So many sounds he wants to identify. The strange Southern accents, for instance, not all of which are the same, he is quick to notice. Some are muddier, monotonic, and rounded. "th" becomes "d", *Where dat o'boy had dat house down on da by-you.* Others are a buttered, pleasantly dandled lilt, *well bless your heart.* There is this use of "yat", he catches in his ear, *where y'at?* Once and again there's a twangy enunciation, slow and *matta fact,* not entirely too dissimilar to that heard around his own hometown, but more slack.

Then there's the jazz in the café, there's banjo somewhere from further up the street. Every once in a while the Natchez blows a deep whale's bellow through its organ whistle. There's shutters thrown open with a clack. Walls complain of their age, and termites. The stucco cracks. Stone workers are repairing an arch, their trowels make a scraping tinny sound through the sanded mortar. Horns meep. A dog barks. Like the fox finds the vole hidden under the snow, his keen ears can hear the rats whisper in rubbish bins. Oleander tell of lizard and butterfly. Parakeets in the palmettos, gurgling, chirping, squeaking, -their language of clicks and clatters, the dry fronds papering as they flit and quarrel. The robin on the railing warbles a little differently than the robin on the copper guttering, beak full of twigs for nest making. Jingle, jangle, brass bell on the door, cash register drawer. Slurp of coffee, tines to porcelain, ice tinkles in a glass of cold water.

*

In dark, but early evening, he finds a grocer and buys two apples and bread rolls from the in-store bakery, and a can of pork and beans. He goes to the park along the river and sits at a bench near a tall lamppost and has his dinner. He uses his Swiss knife, which he keeps in his violin case, to open the can of beans, and he eats the sweet beans by raking them onto a roll. He enjoys his meal, and sometimes a gentle breeze comes off the river, giving him some relief from the heat.

He lies on the grass for a nap. The sky is dark and almost green. The streets themselves are dark and empty and so quiet he can hear the traffic lights buzz. He is thinking about tomorrow. He is poor. He isn't even twenty years old, has nothing and no one in the world, but right now he is happy.

V

The next morning, he showers and gets out of the hotel at seven. It is not outrageously hot or humid yet, the air still sweet. He walks into the Quarter along Decatur and comes to an open air cafe called Cafe du Monde. The menu is adhered to a stainless steel napkin dispenser on the table of white marble. A short Vietnamese waiter in jerk hat and black bowtie comes and takes his order. Most of the chairs are still overturned on the tabletops. The flagstones wet from the morning hosing. He drinks his coffee and rubs sleep from his eyes. He looks around and thinks about whether he should go to his spot again to play, or find another. He thinks about it awhile, but decides he should not waste time finding another.

Down St. Ann Street and then along the flagstoned esplanade, where people sit in iron benches with pigeons clustered about their feet, past the St. Louis Cathedral and the Cabildo, and one block up Chartres Street, he finds his spot unoccupied. The air still cool in the little shade afforded here, the curb swept and damp. He puts dollar bills in with the change already in the case. He begins to play some lively Tchaikovsky segments. There aren't many people out. After a few minutes, he sits down, looking at his violin in his lap. What's the use, there's no one out, he thinks. But then that's no way to think. Someone could be listening in some apartment with the doors open onto the balcony. There could be people just around the corner, out of sight, but not out of earshot. It can't only be about the money. He gets up and continues to play. This makes him feel good. So good, he attempts some bold improvisations of Mozart, picks up its pace, draws out some of the notes, drops others, corrupting the sonata into something beyond recognition, yet beautiful in context to his new foreign surroundings.

VI

In the afternoon, it rains. The rain is warm and comes down on James through the gaps between the dry boards of the balcony overhead. It soaks his sweaty collar. A bar called Kueiffer's stands on the opposite corner. He wants to use the rain as an excuse to get a beer, but instead goes inside to ask the barmaid where he can find a library. She has absolutely no idea. A young man sitting up at the bar in black and white uniform suggests he try looking on Loyal Street and Common, but he isn't certain. He points into the general direction, says:

"Or is that the post office I'm thinking of?"

James thanks him either way and with great luck finds the library quickly. He is drenched from the rain and the librarian behind an eggshell colored monitor helps him get a library card; he can see she's insulted that he should obligate her for assistance in his dripping wet condition.

He sits in the library for two hours listening to tapes of music from the classic composers: Mozart, Beethoven, Bach. He happens on Aram Khachaturian's "Spartacus." It lures him in with its initial mystery, its suspense, then like morning fog concealing the uneventful day, it evaporates before his eyes, sickly rays of dull sunlight penetrating. It becomes overdramatic, drop-of-a-dime sentimental and whimsical, all together a variety pack of emotion, wholesale. He plays Mozart's *Piano Concerto No. 13* in A-major. It is a serious and brooding introspection. He plays Ludwig Van Beethoven's *Piano Sonata Op. 27 #2 Moonlight*. On a scrap of paper, he writes the names of all these pieces and their composers. He is also compelled to write: This is the music of a part of my life I haven't yet experienced, but know I will, and though, at the time I will be sad, I now long for the sincerity and richness of emotion, and afterwards will always remember the time with elegant melancholy, if only because of the beautiful sounds, the music of my depressed soul singing to comfort itself. He re-reads what he has written, and he can't stand it, strikes it out with heavy lines. Often, he embarrasses himself with such ridiculous thoughts.

When the rain stops, he walks back to his corner. He plays until nine o'clock in the evening.

VII

For supper, he eats a vine of grapes and a can of sardines covered with mustard from a small packet he stole from the Lucky Dog stand, ducking in under a couple of drunk young men and taking a packet from the condiment bowl trying not to be seen not buying a hot dog. The drunk young men were about his own age, buying themselves enormous dogs, loaded with all the toppings, laying down a crisp bill freshly crumpled on the bags of buns; they couldn't even bother handing the money to the vendor and waiting for change. They then stood in the street, gorging, as though they had not eaten in weeks, heavy eyes falling shut as they chewed, a big ball of food extending the skin of their cheeks, swaying as the alcohol continued to have its desired effect. They wore the expensive *casual wear* he has seen in advertisements, cotton hoodies with Greek symbols on the front and oversized cargo shorts with an utterly useless quantity of empty crumpled pockets. Leather flip-flops, and well-worn faded college-issued ball caps with bills bent nearly into cylinders. He is at the park eating his supper and he thinks about these boys, or rather the abundance of them when night came on. Are these the kind of passers-by that will put money into my case? Or are these the passers-by that will consider me a bum, another beggar, another uninvited joker in the king's court of revelers. The river, faintly gurgling, glistens under the moon like a giant serpent, digesting the storm drain and run-off of most of the bulk of the heartland, the pig shit and the pesticides, the piss and sewer water, the deluge of the burgeoning Bible Belt. Any discarded thing, light and useless, picked up in the wind and dropped in a creek can make its way here. What dregs and detritus, what scum and flotsam has already washed upon these shores? The feeling of being unwanted, a feeling he has suffered most of his life, starts to creep in again. He tries to hold it off, tries to shut down the little hate machine that's always ready to kick on inside his head in the face of uncertainty; like a little fear driven generator. He eats slowly, carefully, imagining that he can somehow surgically remove this little machine. He knows who put it there. What he doesn't know is how to get it out. He sits watching the sky and the river and the four red lights blinking atop the two bridges spanning the stealthy river, side by side, blinking steadily like the EKG lights for a four-hearted alien asleep in the intensive care of iron traction. There's a light, infrequent wind blowing onto the park, making it only slightly less intolerable.

He returns to his room at eleven thirty and he takes a long shower, a very long shower; masturbating passionately, because it is a drug. It is always there for him. It is free. It is unconditional, it does not care what he looks like or where he's from or what clothes he doesn't wear or how much money he doesn't have. It gives much and it takes nothing, except a little of his self-esteem when he allows himself to feel guilty about it. His head rushes full of chemicals that flush out the heat and sooth him, calm him, comfort him, make him feel as though he is in love. He lies down to sleep satisfied but apprehensive. In moderation, he has promised himself. In moderation. He goes to sleep trying to convince himself he has the discipline to maintain control.

At eight the next morning, he goes out. He made only eight dollars the previous day, but has the rain to blame. It is Friday. Over his coffee, he thinks about his filthy room. He knows because of deposits, even the cheapest rent would initially cost him a great amount. If he can find an apartment to rent for two hundred, he needs four hundred to move in. He had had five hundred before he bought his ticket to New Orleans, one way, eighty-nine dollars, fourteen days in advance. He had paid a hundred and ten for a week at the hotel, because of course 'the only rooms left' rented for one ten, not ninety five as advertised. He hasn't spent any more on food than he has earned busking. He has about three hundred dollars. He will need about a hundred or a hundred and fifty more to get an apartment. He knows he could tolerate the hotel room, because he is good at tolerating what he does not like and cannot change; i.e. most of the life he's lived. It's a question of thinking ahead. He has only so much money. He will have unstable income. If he can produce enough money upfront he can reduce his rent by half. He will maybe have to scrape to eat, and it will certainly be an empty, comfortless place, but anything would be better than the foul cell he sleeps in now.

He can work, if he has to, to get money faster. Or, and it seems rational, he can go without a roof over his head for a period of time. Be homeless. Save money. He knows that getting an apartment is wise. It will be a worthwhile sacrifice. He will have a goal, and he can persevere with as much. Homeless does not mean laying out in the street, in a puddle of your own piss with a dirty hand out for change. I can find a place out of sight for a few days. Urban camping during the interval, he rationalizes. He takes his time over his coffee, looking through the classifieds. At ten thirty, he finds his spot under the wood and iron balcony and starts to play and plays until eleven o clock with many breaks and no lunch. He makes seventeen dollars.

As early as dusk and through the evening, he made his money from young and middle-aged people out for a good time barhopping in the Quarter. Men with women under their arms came by with drinks in their hands singing or yelling, saying things like, "play me something mister" or "look it's Beethoven" or "hey, do you do requests?" James would not say anything to them, only smile. They were all mostly drunk, and they would put dollar bills in his case. Almost always the women would put more money than the men, unless the men were so drunk the women had too much trouble handling them.

He takes the long way back to the hotel, along Bourbon Street. The whole street smells like an open-bar banquet hall the day after a big party. People stagger through the streets, yelling or looking sleepy, hanging off each other. The curbs are soaked with spilt drinks, and heaps of litter choke the sewer gates. Gay men are gathered in immaculate bars. Straight men with stiff haired girlfriends drink sweet daiquiris in the popular bars that are crowded and filthy. Strip joints lure gaggles of men to their open doors with explicit neon signs or picture collages mounted on the exterior walls—raunchy, Polaroid-quality photographs of whores tangled in orgy or spread eagle, fingering their naked crevices, tattoos discoloring their limbs, and dim expressions, vague smiles and drug-heavy, painted eyes ironically succeeding in suggesting great pleasure and deeply satisfying ecstasy. Teenage boys peer through open windows with red and green shutters thrown open, and they can see the skinny, ugly dancers on the catwalk, and they are impossibly beautiful twisting and swaying trance-like in the ghost white flickering of lights. James is as much disgusted, as he is aroused. He can smell the unmistakable musk of lust and a monstrous appetite for sex starts to gnaw at his guts. Like two separate persons, his sense of decency and good taste, and his insatiable hunger for sexual gratification, soft and sweet or raw and sloppy, are at war. But his economy and public timidity suppress the urge to gawk at the nasty spectacle. He walks on to Canal Street, absorbing scenes in glances and in peripheral vision, ears attuned to everything. The cacophony roars in the street, fills it up. The magic of being able to learn music by ear, comes at a price, the world can also make an ugly noise, hard to get out of the head.

He is in his room, now, lying in bed, and he cannot go to sleep. Visions of women he has never met flash across his mind. They straddle him and moan as he penetrates deep into them or they are kneeled at his feet, two at a time, swallowing and suckling. He is so hard he feels like he will split, and, yet, the swelling continues, throbbing, as if tearing the skin. He cannot take it any longer. He had made a pact with himself leaving Missouri. He would start fresh, a new life, a new person. Incessant masturbation would be a part of the life he left behind. He does not want it here. He wants to get control of it. Use it in moderation. As one would a drug. But he is defeated. The pain is too unbearable. He goes at it with both hands and passionately. When he explodes, it runs down over both hands and between his thighs and drips onto the sweaty sheets.

VIII

Saturday starts damp from a light shower before sunrise. Thunderstorms crack in the sky, heavy with dark clouds with flat, black bottoms. He does not get up from bed until nine o'clock. He showers and brushes his teeth with Ivory soap and washes the taste from his mouth with several mouthfuls of cold water, and he thinks, living without a home for a while won't be too bad. I don't mind working for something. I will certainly appreciate the apartment after having slept on the streets awhile. But I don't have to sleep on the streets. There are plenty of places I can find to sleep, where people don't have to walk over me. Why do the bums sleep on hard sidewalks and benches, anyway? The benches are so hard and cramped. Surely there are better places. Under a tree, on the grass. But then rain! If it rained, I would not want to be on the ground, especially without something between myself and the damp ground.

He goes down to the lobby. At the front desk, a skinny black haired woman sits, delicately peeling little flakes of dead skin from a fresh tattoo of tentacles reaching up out of the flat crest of her chest to strangle her by the neck. She is irritated by the interruption. James says:

"Good morning. I wanted to tell you that I plan to check out Monday evening."

The woman says:

"Yeah." She doesn't give two shits when he checks out, and by the evil in her glare, can't believe he is disturbing her at all, especially with such a sickeningly polite manner of speech, as though his naïve mannerism is born of simpleness, which she considers pathetic. He walks out the hotel saying goodbye, politely. She sits behind the desk, her bone white arm up, picking at the scabby graffiti below her chin. He buys a paper from a coin-operated vendor on the street side.

He spends the remainder of the morning smudging the print of his paper with his oily fingers, drinking his coffee. Every listing requires a deposit. He thinks, maybe, he should look for work. He scans the help wanted columns. His eyes skim as though what he is looking for will show itself like a shining coin, and his eye will succinctly fall on it. He can work a few weeks to make the money needed to get an apartment. He can play out at nights. Work on new pieces, if he likes, which will be great. He envisions steady, peaceful days of hard work, imagines the sedate satisfaction of spending money without frugality. The camaraderie of occupation. Other than tending chickens, which he's vowed to never do again, carpentry is the only trade he knows—the after-school and weekend occupation of a strong boy in a crowded and impoverished family, whose father was in that line of work. He has no tools, nor work boots. It isn't exactly a glimmering medallion, but his pertinent eye catches this listing: Roust-about. Local contractor, possible weekends. Must be willing to work. He rolls the paper into a baton and takes a quarter from the waiter's tip and finds a payphone. He has nothing to write with. A Midwestern accent gives him directions as though he is writing them down. He says he'll be there. Monday, first thing. 1812 Napoleon Avenue. In order to remember this address, he puts it in the form of a question: Was Napoleon alive in 1812? Yes, I believe he campaigned against Russia in that year.

In the spot James has now begun to consider his, a magician, a slender, oily creature, is performing behind a small table draped with red felt and gold tassels. A volunteer designates a card, which gets lost in a shuffle and then found, only this time defaced by a black marker. After a quick accordion shuffle, he asks the volunteer to sift the deck for it, when it can't be found he withdraws it from his mouth as a tight cylinder with the exact marking. Magic, everyone loves a magic trick!

James finds an out-of-the-way spot on North Peters Street behind long rows of novelty shops. He takes a place near a statue of a thin woman sitting on the edge of a water fountain with her long, beautiful bronze legs stretched out, leaning back, her long hair frozen in cascade over the water bowl. The place is peaceful. There is little pedestrian traffic and he knows he will not make any money here. He opens his case to tips, but does not think about it. People, the few that pass, smile at him and walk by, or stop and sit on benches for a moment before moving on, listening. He wishes he could play better for them. He wishes his music were magic and could turn him into a great musician. But he thinks surely he will become better, practicing and learning new material, building confidence, in time composing his own material. He plays for several hours while evening and contentment settle on him.

IX

He decides to drink with the few dollars he has earned. On Toulouse, he enters the courtyard of O'Flaherty's Pub at the end of a low, dark, stone passageway. The barmaid comes out through narrow, arched, wooden doors. From within the barroom, he can hear the reeds of a folksinger's harmonica quiver; the withdrawn air vibrating. The caramel-colored wainscoting absorbs much of the song of the trembling guitar strings, except when the narrow doors fling open and a few cords blow out. Through the door's small panes of glass, like a dozen wood-framed portraits, he can see the people sitting close together at small tables, animated, drinking from tall glasses. He envies their closeness, their merriment and friendship, but tries to convince himself he does not long for it, but he also knows he does, but rationalizes thus; I need time to build myself up. What would I be in a group of people right now, but a pauper, a gypsy, a dull country boy, a drudge at the nickel and dime vaudeville?

The large runcinate leaves of the courtyard have a plastic shine and catch the light from the outdoor lamps on black poles or the lights from inside the barroom. The large flagstones under foot are graybrown and serious. The music from inside makes him feel like he is approaching a festival, in an old Irish town, a celebration, and he wants it this way. The nearing feeling and the excitement, not actually being there, afraid, as if it were, that having a thing might not be as good as wanting a thing.

X

Again, James dreams about flying. He flies over expansive fields of tall, green or yellow grasses. For miles he flies over the fields, soaring in the soft blue, warm sky, banking right then left at whim, bending up, climbing, then slowing at the zenith and flipping over, he races towards the earth. He comes down fast, feeling the wind in his face and the air pressure under his arms, as though they are wings. He wakes up invigorated.

A large coffee house sits on the corner of Rue de la Levee and Rue St. Philip with a double-trunked tree growing out of the sidewalk with floppy leaves of a yellower green than summer. Under the tree, a slim woman adjusts the strap of her heeled sandal. She swings her brunette hair and catches James' stare and sparkles her awareness of him with her hazel eyes. He is seated up on a raised platform at a wide window, an old upright piano to his right. The sill of the window is deep like a bar top. He has spread out his paper and is reading his three favorite comic strips; Calvin and Hobbes, Garfield, and Non Sequitur.

The brunette, her hair a deep bourbon color, sways into the cafe in her shiny lead colored skirt; there is twenty inches of brown-skinned leg from her skirt's hem to the top strap of her sandal. Her passing smile is enormous. She orders her coffee with the characteristic, but polite haste of an affluent cosmopolitan. She takes a chair a window down from him. She smiles, closed lips, as she sits and looks at him. Her voice when she speaks is breathy and sexy.

"Haven't I seen you playing the violin?"

"Yes, you may have."

"You play very well."

James Buck knows he does not play that well. He wonders what she means. Does she not know the difference? Or does she have her own intentions. He isn't sure how to reply. She asks:

"You're not playing today?"

"I was going out after breakfast."

"Is this where you always come?"

"I really haven't been in town that long."

She isn't interested in how long or where from. She crosses her long brown legs, leans forward placing her elbows on her knees. She holds her cup of coffee in both hands like scooping water from a stream. She turns her foot amorously. She says:

"This is a wonderful cafe. Do you like it? I like it because it reminds me of South America. It is very old and full of character. You'll meet very interesting people here." He is sipping from his coffee mug. "Isn't the coffee great?" she asks.

"Yes. Yes, all the coffee in this town is excellent."

Her shoulders are forward. She turns her head to look out the wide window, creating an irresistible image of elegant sexuality. She volleys her eyes back and takes a slightly exasperated breath, then says:

"So, I have to fly. I hope I see you out."

"Yes, that would be great."

She stands, her heels knock on the hollow platform. She extends her hand.

"Damarie."

"James." He takes her slim, manicured hand. And then she leaves on a gorgeous stride.

His day will be changed. This brief, but generous act elevates his spirit. As though this stranger -this beautiful young woman were the only person alive in the world. As though everyone else were nothing more than piñatas dangling on strings, their shadows dancing across the pavement and if he wanted to get anything out of them he would have to strike them with a stick. He sits long in the cafe, feeling now, more so than at any moment since he arrived, that he, in fact, has arrived and more importantly, is welcome. Afterwards, he takes his violin to the levee along the river. It feels good playing today. The sounds rising into the air and reinventing it.

XI

The next morning he wakes at fifteen after five. It is growing light out, so he gets in and out of the shower, quickly, and is soon waiting for the streetcar. He is wearing his oldest pair of jeans and his buckskin shoes; they are the only strong pair he has. He's not really dressed for physical labor, but there isn't much he can do about it. He jumps on the streetcar across from the hotel, and it carries him down the avenue in the warm morning air and it knocks hollowly under him. The breeze blows in through the open windows and the trees of the street are green and close to the open windows. The conductor cranks the lever of the electric motor to move forward or to disconnect the charge so that he can break and slow the car at an intersection or to pick up passengers. He rides over busy avenues and small streets alike. He can see the white on blue street sign from a great distance: Napoleon Avenue. He gets off and walks until he comes to the right address. Several men are standing around new and old trucks. James asks where he can find Leo. A bigheaded man with a big chest and short legs says he'll be out soon. James waits, leaning against one of the trucks. He is nervous about his inappropriate dress.

A young man, about twenty-four or five, sun browned, small and fair-haired, but rugged in his general form and dress, strides down the drive. He announces:

"All right you lazy drunks, let's get." The men load into their trucks. He sees James and says:

"Jump in on the other side."

Leo backs from the driveway, rapidly. The other trucks fall behind as Leo speeds along the narrow street. One truck takes off in the other direction. Leo pulls a cigarette from a pack from the dashboard, offers one, asks:

"Smoke?"

"Sometimes, when I'm drinking. Never this early."

"We're goin' out to Kenner this morning. Got some soffit work needs done on the house. The boys will work on that. Need you to pick up the trash around," he says, and James can tell he has no interest in taking authority over people, and he doesn't have the New Orleans accent, more like that of his home state.

"Damn traffic gets worse every morning," Leo says, turning the stereo knob and smoking his cigarette, weaving through traffic with little concern. After a long freeway ride, they come to an ugly suburban house near the international airport. Tools are unloaded, but unlike the driving, the men don't begin work speedily. The air has already become oppressive, to the point where James can feel the skin of the back of his neck sting. He immediately begins picking up trash from the yard and placing it into the bed of one of the trucks backed into the yard for this reason. Leo stands in the yard a moment, looking at the progress, then he says:

"Now I better go get them other heathens started before they get to horsen' around."

He peels off in his truck, hurriedly.

At 10 am Leo returns with doughnuts for the crew, and they all stop working and sit to eat and talk of the difficulty they face with this problem or that, and Leo tells them to do this and that thing and it will work. They just listen and nod, men much older than the easygoing supervisor. They all smoke cigarettes, which Leo loans out, generously. They go back to work in half an hour. Leo says nothing to James before he leaves, and James wonders if he is doing a satisfactory job. He works with determination, but thinks maybe it isn't as fast as it can otherwise be done by someone else, this chronic self-doubt the only thing he learned from unapproachable parents that occasionally serves him well, raised as he was on the utter extreme from the 'you're perfect just the way you are, and there's no one in the world like you' Apple Jacks shoveled into the gullets of many in his generation. So he picks up every last stick and nail, cleans the lawn with a fine-toothed comb. He is weary from the heat, but the yard is as clean as golfing greens when Leo arrives at lunchtime. Leo compliments the quality of his efforts. After lunch he and Leo climb into the truck and pick up the freeway to go to another work site.

Leo drives a relatively new vehicle, but badly neglected. The cab is like a bachelor's apartment. The carpet is red and filthy with gravel, paint, dirt and dried mud. The dashboard is cluttered with empty cigarette boxes, tape measures, old and new tools -some still in the plastic packaging. On the bench seat, between them, sits a stack of manila folders fingerprinted with white and gray paint, stuffed with white papers, lumberyard receipts and yellow invoices. Leo opens a folder and cocks his head down to look into it. He reads off the top page and then flips the folder back closed. He has not said anything since they left. Then he says:

"Get'n damned hot out."

"Yeah."

Leo rolls his window up and switches the air conditioner on. James rolls his window up as well. Leo asks:

"You have any other shoes than those?"

"No, I left most my clothes and stuff." He worries himself immediately about this response, but Leo does not pursue it. He says:

"I got a pair in the toolbox back there you can use, if they'll fit ya."

"What size are they?"

"Nines."

"That'll fit."

"They're s'old as hell, but they're strong shoes." James looks at Leo's broken boots. He sees something very noble and truthful in them.

They turn into a gas station on the I 10 service road. The gas station is closed down, and the large windows are covered with sheets of plywood. A white, Ford pickup truck with a black emblem on the door reading City of Metairie Gas and Water Department is parked up close to the rear of the station. Leo parks next to the truck and climbs out. He instructs James to get a hammer and a crowbar and those work boots from the tool chest, then throws him the keys. Leo walks around to the backside of the station. James gets the tools and the boots, which are damp, loose fitting, and one has a hole in the top, which his big toe wants to stick out through. He puts his own shoes in the cab of the truck and goes around to the backside of the station.

Leo is kneeling next to a man lying on his side with his head under a raised register hinged to the wall. Leo says to James:

"Jack needs some help. He can drive you home after. Can't you Jack? I'll mark down your time tomorrow, so if you work late, let me know."

"Okay."

"Okay, good."

"I think it'll need a few pipes replaced," Jack says, from under the register.

"All right, well, I'm get'n, so . . ."

"All right," James replies.

Leo gets into his truck and drives off. Jack comes from under the register.

"So we need to get at this pipe here, but first we need to pry off this register. We don't need to keep it, so don't worry about breaking it, then we'll break up the sidewalk here."

They heave together; James down and Jack up, until the hardware on both sides snaps and the register hits the ground with a clang.

Jack is twenty-something. He has that brown complexion of someone who gets daily sun. His frame is not big and muscular, but lean and evenly balanced. He wears a T-shirt, which is clean and white, except where it is matted wet against his sweating back and sweat-soaked under arms. His hair is brown and short and thick like an animal's. He has a handsome face with dark brows. He could easily be on the cover of a magazine. He says:

"The water's just a trickle in this place."

"Hmm," James is trying to seem interested in the problem.

"They had a plumber out here, and he said that it was somewhere with the pipes from the ground. So they sent me out. So, it could be right here." He points at the cement below his feet. We'll work our way back."

They get into the trap side by side fitting wrenches on pipes, pulling, straining, sweating, busting thumbs and fingers, bruising muscles and getting irritated by the work. They call it quits at 6 p.m. They load the tools into the city truck. Jack says:

"We'll probably need to bring a couple more wrenches out tomorrow. Or maybe we'll just use a torch."

"Okay, whatever you think will work."

"Thirsty?"

"Sure."

There's a working soda can machine on the front side of the building. Jack gets two cans of cold drink and offers James a can and a ride home. He lets him out at Julia and Poydras, from there he walks to the hotel.

After a cool shower, he towel dries impatiently and catches his reflection in the shattered mirror hung in an aluminum frame to the wall. He doesn't often think about his appearance, but when he does, it always produces some sadness, he just isn't a handsome young man, or so *he* thinks, and that's that, excepting his beautiful green eyes, the only thing anyone has ever complimented about his features. He is surprised at how thin he appears, just now, as compared to these men he has met today. He hasn't looked at his upper body in the mirror in what seems like years. He's used to the small shaving mirror hung on a chain over the washbasin in the barn where he got ready for school and work. He has a good body, some natural muscular definition, maybe wanting of a couple pushes on the tire pump. Black, course hair has begun to accumulate in an asymmetrical patch on his chest. With a newly burned farmer's tan, his arms, face and neck are like someone else's carefully attached to the pale torso of his own. The heat is heavy on his back, neck and forehead, and the damp shower air condenses against the red brown skin.

He will have to get out of the hotel tonight. He worries it is not a good decision. He weighs against it the wages he'll be making. He walks back to his room slowly, dirt accumulating on the pads of his clean feet. He sits on his bed on his towel. I'll be sunburned and tired and needing proper rest if I continue to work. He is content to remain unclothed a moment in thought. I don't have the necessity now. It may be foolish to suffer when I can avoid it and still get the same end. I'm not afraid. I could do it if it was still the only choice. I have swapped my sacrifice: nights on the streets for days working in the heat. He pulls on clean undershorts that hold him firmly. He slips on cut-off pants. I am not resigning. I'm not compromising. He pulls on a cotton-thin, white T-shirt. He flips on thread-loose canvas shoes. He grabs his violin and leaves the room, finds the lobby empty.

He comes upon a large fountain, near the ferry terminal; it's water gushing nearly ten feet into the air. The blue tiles of the bottom are rich with coins, which he has half a mind to collect. He needs it more than the fountain. It feels good here, the water saturating the humid air with negative ions. Around the inset fountain dish is a circle of high-backed, tiled thrones, decorated with various Spanish Coats of Arms. He withdraws his violin from its case. He lays down the bow high on the strings and gives a sharp pull. He turns one of the little, wide-headed pegs. He does this to another. He places the bow over the sound hole on the strings and pulls down slowly, sustaining a long, tragic wail that dissolves into the sound of the water rushing up out of the fountainhead. Maybe not the best place acoustically, but with the sound of the water it is never-the-less pleasing. He pushes the bow back up, and bending it outward a fraction, produces a similar long cry, only an octave higher. The sound stirs the organs in his chest, and they become warm. He comes back down, fingering slowly, with concentrative movements. He works a series of cries into a sorrowful story. Rough and clumsy, inarticulate, much like the very pages of his own life. A fragmented concerto a solo, which if anything, just needs to escape. To a trained musician, an ugly porridge of regurgitated Mozart and Bartok.

He moves slowly into a delicate sound, for a moment, and then into a crescendo he knows well. His hands and fingers yield themselves to the music and he begins to think separate thoughts that soar much higher than the small wooden instrument he holds under his chin.

He plays until nine o'clock. He walks into the Quarter and comes upon a small restaurant, where he eats a large roast beef po-boy with fresh tomatoes and finely shredded lettuce, on French bread soft as a grandmother's kindness. The fried potatoes are hearty, until he becomes full, then they are heavy. He walks back to the hotel and speaks apologetically with the desk clerk to arrange another week.

She suppresses her unnecessary irritation. James lays awake in bed, sticky with humidity, listening to a mosquito buzz about the small room.

XII

Leo delivers James to the gas station, and Jack sits in the company truck doing paperwork on a clipboard with neat, rounded print. They start into their work as soon as the tools are laid out. Dripping with sweat two hours later, Jack leans back against the brick wall of the back of the station. He says:

"Humidity's rough, isn't it?"

"Yes, definitely. I'm not used to it."

"Where ya from?"

"Missouri."

"Really, that's where I'm from; St. Louis."

"I was born in St. Louis. I lived about a hundred miles south of the city."

"You like New Orleans?"

"It's nice, I think, so far."

"What brought you here?"

James does not like questions about himself. He does not know how to explain himself to other people. He has no skill for it. He would rather disrobe for a stranger, than talk to stranger about himself. He says:

"I wanted to see what it was like in the French Quarter. I heard it was very interesting, and I came." Which had nothing to do with the truth.

"Just like that?"

"Sure."

"Well, good. You plan staying?"

"I don't know. I would think . . . I mean, I intend to, but I'll see."

"Cool," Jack says, casually and unconditionally. Then:

"Well, let's see if we can't make some progress."

This is how they speak, this is how many speak. To fabricate something more interesting is to lie.

They work until noon, then break for lunch. Jack has to work elsewhere after dinner, so James finds himself back at the house near the airport, collecting rubbish from the backyard. He is not interested in the task, only the result. He cleans thoroughly. Meticulously restoring the grass to health. It is more interesting to clean it well, than to just clean it. Takes pride in the return of the green grass blades. He is drenched in a prolific sweat. It pours from his face and head and stings his eyes and soaks his clothes. It has a sour sweet odor when it cools in the fabric. When the men knock off, they drive back to the big, disorderly house on Napoleon Avenue. Leo is here, and he offers James a ride home. He declines, but Leo insists, claims that he has to go that way anyway. James accepts and climbs into the truck. Leo says:

"You and Jack get finished up out there?"

"Almost. Maybe we'll finish tomorrow before lunch."

"Good."

"What do you have for me after the house near the airport?"

"Oh, couple jobs, around. If I could keep the old lady from spending all the money, I'd like to pick up this set of table and chairs and work on them. I could get you to stripping 'em."

"Antiques?"

"Nineteen ten stuff."

"That's pretty old."

"Yeah, that old stuff is so much better than anything they make these days. You can't buy anything anymore not made of pressed board. Everything's crap. That damned wife of mine wanted a TV center for the living room and keep bugging me to make one. I was too damned busy; what she do? Goes out and buys one at Wal-Mart. With the TV and VCR loaded on it, I'm afraid to change the channel in fear of it collapsing. Nothing but a piece of shit. And she spent a hundred-something dollars on it."

"Yeah?"

"I told her I was goin' to get some oak and make a real entertainment center." He brightens, thinking out loud. "With doors that swing open and make the shelves custom to the TV and stuff, and little slots for the VCR tapes. Then I was goin' a put a stereo system right next to that. It'd be like a movie theater. But that damned thing just couldn't wait."

They are approaching Lee Circle.

"Isn't it right up here?"

"No, no, it's past the circle, up a little more. You can drop me here if you want."

"No, I'll drive you there, no problem."

"I can walk from here." Imposing on other people, another skill he does not have, nor does he want.

"No, I'll get ya up there."

"Thanks, I appreciate it."

"It's no problem."

"So you think you'll get those antiques?"

"Probably not, money's always tight, and I'll need to get that garage cleared, to have room to work on them. Always too much needs get done just to get by and little time for anything else," Leo says. If James closed his eyes he might think he was talking to someone twice Leo's age.

He is in the shower immediately and it is fresh. He is glad that he is mildly fatigued and content and does not need to masturbate. He leaves the hotel with his violin. He buys bread rolls, pickled sausages, a pear and a quarter-pound packet of sliced turkey breast from the grocer on Royal Street. There is the strange and very real sensation of being someone else tonight. This new mysterious person -violinist/ adventurer, is a vague acquaintance to the simple country boy he has always considered himself to be, who when at work with Leo, he is reminded of with much conflicted emotion. The soiled blue collar. The anonymous stick in the proletarian woodpile fueling the rich man's weenie roast.

XIII

He wakes warm from yesterday's sun, and again the morning is hot. His back drips warm sweat, soaking his shirt as he walks down Napoleon. Jack is waiting for him and they ride out to the station. James asks:

"Why does Leo have me helping you, you work for the city and we're working on city pipes?"

"Because he knows how the city is. There isn't enough help. He knows they won't send me any help to do a two-man job. It's worth his while to just pay you to help me get it done with quickly, so he can start working on the place."

"Really, then why are there so many people standing around doing nothing?"

"City's full of drunks and drug heads and lazy niggers?" Jack says, casually.

Such talk is not new to James, not at all, especially in a small rural town, where except for the drunks, the other two are rare and the subject is still raw. In Missouri, there's a passion, a rage almost, against drug users, and lazy niggers, each in their respective category, but also kind of lumped together with liberals and atheists, the typical *us versus them* meme. There's a determination in tone, as though there is something that can be done about it, and the time is nigh, except they say it private, never publically. In the right company, they get themselves into a sermon, as though a "lazy nigger" can just wake up one day and be a person who just happens to have dark skin and everything is fine and dandy, an endowment of oppression and discrimination recoiled. As though a drug user can be somehow convinced by an impassioned sermon to drop the pipe and get high on the word of the Lord Jesus Christ, and miraculously forget about the shitty world as such cast. This from Jack is dry and hopeless. This is matter of fact, same as if he would have said, 'sure is humid out' or 'can't believe it's tax time already'.

Then Jack says:

"Hey, you pack a lunch?"

"No. Should I of?"

"No, I didn't either, but I know this great place to get red beans and rice."

*

He climbs the steps of the house on Napolean to the upper door and knocks. He is let into the house by a young boy with fair blonde hair who looks like Leo's miniature. The boy says:

"Mom, a guy is here." His voice is dry and impatient. He is an unenthusiastic boy. Mrs. Kodovbe, obviously Leo's mother, comes around the unfinished partition (a project forever in the works) that separates the kitchen from the large living room. She carries a towel wadded in both hands, drying them. She is not an old woman, middle forties. James imagined her to be much older. She has a long face, pocked from lifelong acne, like the hood of a car after a hail storm, made up poorly; too much rouge. She says:

"Yes. What can I do for you?"

"I was looking for Leo."

"He's out with his father."

"Do you know where?" he asks, and Mrs. Kodovbe does not like his abruptness; her smile weakens. She answers obligatorily:

"At a job sight."

"I don't want to brother you, I . . . " and this lightens her instantly, as he figures it would. She says:

"He'll be home for lunch in a minute."

"I just came from a job. I need to know what to do next."

"I'll beep him."

"Could you? That would be very helpful."

The phone hangs on a wall over a desk overwhelmed with papers and folders. She pages him and then she says:

"He'll call back in a minute. Would you like something to drink? Are you hungry?"

"Well no, I. . ."

"Here, come in the kitchen."

He follows her into the kitchen, and she pulls down a large glass from the cabinet and fills it with iced tea.

"Here take a seat. Let me get you something to eat."

He sits at a waist-high counter, on a wooden stool facing the stove. The iced tea is very sweet and cold, and the glass is dripping with sweat. Large stewpots steam on the stove, as if quietly gossiping, and the steam is sucked straight into the hood over the gas range. The phone rings.

"Hello." Mrs. Kodovbe listens almost half a minute. Then her tone is sharp. "Well, a fella is here, looking for you . . . yes . . . you heard what your father said, these men need to be . . . yes . . . " She turns to James, "What's your name?" "James," he says. "James," she says, "okay, but are . . . I know, well? Then are you coming home for dinner? I know she ain't got anything fixed up for you. Well, you should hear how you talk to your mother, it's terrible. Yes. Yes, of course, all right, but you better come home and eat some of this food I got cooked here, all right, here he is," and she stretches the phone on its cord to him.

"Hello. Yes. Yes he said he would. Okay, yes, that's no problem. Sure, what time. No, that's all right, yep, see you." He gives the phone to Mrs. Kodovbe, and she hangs it on the wall. She asks:

"He got some more work for you?"

"No, he said I could go home for the day."

"I don't know how he expects men to stay on if he don't give them steady work. His father's the same damned way. They just think on one track. It's a damned wonder they get anyone to work for them. You got to get on their asses all the time. Do you want some lunch?"

"No, that's all right, I had some red beans."

"It don't look like them heathens is coming in. I don't know why I let him talk to me the way he does. You should hear how he talks to me, like I was dirt." Then, and without provocation, she becomes joyful and warm like some character on a television drama. She is obviously unstable. She says:

"We've got plenty."

"No, thanks. I just…"

"I've got some stew with taters and carrots and a whole mess of food here." She opens the icebox, takes out a heavy tub of butter. "I got this big dish of strawberry shortcake." James can smell the syrupy sweet strawberries from the barstool. She says:

"I am so used to cooking for a large family that I always have too much. All the other kids have abandoned me. I never hear a word from them. I miss having the whole bunch; they used to be eight of us here. You're more than welcome to stay."

James says, and Mrs. Kodovbe is perplexed:

"I really don't care for any. I appreciate it, though."

"Well here, let me fix you a sandwich," and she pulls slices of bread from a sleeve and starts spooning cubes of roast beef heavy with gravy. She folds the two slices together and puts the sandwich on a plate. She says:

"Here have this with your tea."

His mouth begins to water before he can protest. He bites into the sandwich, the tender chucks dissolving in the warm gravy. He washes it down with a pull from his glass of candy-sweet iced tea. He says:

"This is very good. I haven't had anything this good in quite a while now." The smell of the kitchen: sweet corn, smashed potato, wild greens, tub of Crisco between the burner always warm, a kind of soapstone cleanliness, yet saw dust; it smells of the kitchens he knew in Missouri. He is comforted by it, but is reluctant to embrace it, as though in doing so he will betray his new self. He does not want to stay. He says:

"I hope you don't mind me leaving so quick?"

"No. Go on, enjoy the day off, since you have it."

"Yes, I . . ."

"No, the boys are always wanting time off. They'd wish that they were you. It is a shame that he couldn't find something for you, though. They should have all kinds of work. They've been pretty busy, lately. I'm sure you want the money. You have a wife?"

James is standing, ready to leave. He involuntarily looks over her shoulder at the big pot brimming with stewed beef. Mrs. Kodovbe catches this look. Before he can answer, she asks:

"You sure you don't want another sandwich? Here let me make you one to take with you."

"No, really." She is already building another.

"It don't take but a minute. I've got plenty. It'll probably soar, anyhow, before it gets eat. I got to learn to cook smaller portions." She wraps the sandwich in a paper towel. He can feel the heat and moisture through the paper. He is uncomfortable with the thought of walking out of the house with a fat, juicy sandwich soaking in a paper towel, dripping down his arm. He hopes she will not tell Leo. Leo will not know his reluctance. He wants Leo to know he is not a freeloader. Thus the branding iron leaves its mark.

XIV

A cool, long, trickling shower, indulgent; streams of soap lather run down the insides of both of his thighs. He wanted to shower quickly. Wash his face, his hair, bush his teeth and get out. Clean. Fresh. But then his mind started to lobby against him. How does it hurt? It's all you have. You have no wife, no girlfriend, no television, no radio, no friends. Don't be so hard on yourself. Life is short, enjoy it. You don't do drugs. You hardly drink. You work hard. You're a good person. He's unable to resist. He leaves the hotel feeling uneasy and blasphemous. It is showers like these that always leave him this way—guilty and vulgar. When he goes in determined to have control and soon realizes he is powerless.

He carries his violin for repentance. Past Jackson Square, down Decatur Street, beyond the coffee houses. He's looking for a quiet place. He strides along shaded shop fronts, under balconies; the shopfronts stone gray or brick brown or red. The curb slabs broken. He sees a sign in the window of a tall, narrow painted door: ROOMMATE WANTED. The black crayon print is shaky. This would be a good idea, he thinks. Make it that much easier. A much needed distraction from himself. An opportunity to meet other people. He swings the door open and crosses the dusty threshold, and a tall young man stands behind a counter made of boxes of vinyl records. James asks about the sign. The young man is lanky and his hair is long, stringy and orange. He speaks slowly and politely and continuously drops glances on the violin case, surveys the case with the same slyness a man uses to size up a women's chest or the gap between her legs. They agree to meet at five that evening, outside the record shop. James plays at a bench along the river's edge above the sheds of the Farmer's market, where he buys a fresh turnip and peels it with his Swiss knife.

He returns to the record shop at five. The clerk is locking the doors. He introduces himself.

"David."

"James." They clasp hands, not strong, not long.

"I'm going down for a beer, want one."

They pace unmatching strides along pocked, gray curbs littered with cigarette butts. David leads them into a foul-smelling place, which smells better at the furthest end near the popcorn machine popping fresh kernels. Long-necked domestic beers are ordered. David's behavior is modestly young mannish, starkly contrasting his appearance. He says:

"So anyway, man, if you don't have a place, right now, you can stay at my parents' house, until we can find a place. That'd be cool with me. But I want something in the Quarter, of course." The bar top is dry and tender, it's varnish worn away and the wood is taking on a rosy gloss under their sweating beer bottles. James Buck asks:

"When would you like to look?"

"Hell, we can start right now. I'll get a paper." He takes coins from the shallow depth of a torn jean pocket and he looks at James before turning away, as if for approval. He's dressing the part of post-hair band, dirty rock, the long dirty hair, the nose ring, tobacco yellow teeth, a worn-out, concert T-shirt, a black leather jacket, stubbed, wallet on a chain. He appears to have the angst, the disdain, until you look into his eye; his eyes reveal something else. They are clean and softened by blonde lashes, and they are young and honest. And then there is something else. Eagerness. James has seen the vagabonds in St. Louis. On the bus coming down here. Roustabouts who have passed through town and worked a week or two for his old man, usually until the first paycheck and then never seen again. There was a sadness, a fear, a hopelessness in those eyes. Even when they tried to hide it, in order to land the job. But with David, his eyes are still alive; they are bright and eager the way only someone with choices could be bright and eager.

David spreads out a *Times-Picayune* before them. James asks:

"Why don't you want to find someone more like yourself? I must admit I'm fairly conservative compared to you."

"I couldn't give a shit. That's fine by me. Besides, you look like someone I can trust. I'm getting another beer. Want one?"

The barmaid places two long necks before them. They spend several minutes looking up and down the columns. They do not know where many of the places are. David lives in Metairie, he says. Says his girlfriend lives uptown. James has a working map of the Quarter in his brainpan. He has sketched it during his walks. He starts reading off some options. David says:

"Fuck man, I don't give a shit what kind of place it is, I just got to get out of my fucking parent's house."

James knows the feeling, but suspects it isn't for quite the same reasons he had to get out. They circle several listings in the right price range. David says unfortunately he has to get going and so they agree to meet the next evening at seven. James goes to Spanish Plaza where the water from the fountainhead is lit by the yellow and green flood lamps. He begins to play, and he plays well. He feels smooth inside.

He wakes at five next morning. He works with Leo. They joke and smoke cigarettes, at least Leo does, and drink a blue sports drink from a big water cooler Mr. Kodovbe purchased from a warehouse wholesaler that Leo filled with ice and then water from the garden hose, but it tasted like it flowed right from a drain pipe out of Dupont, so they drained it and refilled it with gallons of Gatoraide. At lunch,

James and Leo eat at the big house on Napoleon, where Leo lives with his wife and two children on the ground floor. Mr. and Mrs. Kodovbe, his mother and father, live above, with their two youngest sons, Leo's younger brothers.

Leo's wife has boiled hotdogs, which bob swollen and split in cloudy water on the stovetop. A bag of stale buns sits on the countertop, and the mouth of the ketchup bottle is choked with brown ketchup. She does not serve them. She rocks the smallest boy in her arms and starts talking coldly to Leo about things she needs to purchase for her or the child, and Leo tells her they will talk about it later. Leo comes home to eat as seldom as possible. Mostly he eats upstairs or eats out. He eats two hotdogs quickly and drinks several tall glasses of milk. James drinks generic canned soda, which though sweet, tastes much like the can, which is ironic. Don't you drink soda for the taste? Where can a fella get just plain *delicious* water? Then they sit out on the stoop where Leo can smoke a cigarette.

After several, long, crackling pulls on the filtered tobacoo, Leo says, quietly:

"Well, it doesn't look like I'm gonna need you tomorrow. Sort of in between projects. I'll make the day up maybe one day next week."

James realizes with some disappointment that it is because he has no tools and no vehicle. But as it is, he needs the time off.

"That's all right. I don't mind. In fact, I need a little time to get some things done. Me and this fellow are renting an apartment; there's a lot of things I'll need to do."

"'This fellow'," Leo asks, knowing James has traveled to New Orleans alone. James says:

"He put a sign in the window of the record shop where he works. I thought it would be easier to get a place if I went in with another person. So . . ."

"You better watch yourself. This is a crazy town. There's a lot of crazy-ass people around here."

"He doesn't look crazy. I mean, he dresses much like most the young people do these days, a metal object hung out of something, tattoos everywhere, and clothing that looks day old from a bar fight, but he seems pretty sane."

"You better be damn careful. There's more freaks out there than you can shoot in a lifetime."

"I think this guy's okay. I'm not worried any."

"Just be smart or you'll end up dead or worse. Have all your shit stolen."

James says:

"I don't have any shit to steal. And besides you don't do too much complaining dead."

Leo flicks his cigarette in the shrub in the yard and shakes his head and smiles. He says:

"Well there's an interesting way to put it."

XV

He is on his way to meet David in the Quarter. On Burgundy Street, a quiet, mostly residential street of walls of azalea pinks and pale blues and the greens and yellows of tropical fish, he approaches a corner bar, called the Corner Pocket, which he thinks is a pool hall. Two blondes sashay out. They are embraced and their movements sweet for each other. They salute him with brave falsetto: the damsel and the sailor. They walk past, waving their asses in tiny tasseled jean shorts; their hairy, sickly, skinny legs sweeping the sidewalk in matching Doc Martins. Buck is disgusted by what he sees. He has never been this close to homosexual behavior. Finds it repulsive and, profoundly, unnatural, and there's a shamelessness about it, it seems to him, like seeing a fat woman dressed in clothes too small for her. As though they couldn't give a cheap bracelet how repulsive they appear. Their behavior is voluntarily flagrant, immodest, a waving in the face, or rather, a rubbing one's nose in it, bad puppy! So looky here everybody, we are gay and we are here to make it everybody's business because not only is it normal, it's fabulous! Is it fabulous, he thinks, more fabulous than opposite's attracting? Isn't fornicating with your gender copy just masturbation once removed? Something you should have every right to do, but hopefully in moderation, and certainly nothing very glamorous. Is airing a half naked ass in the street like a fresh baked muffin, a sign of a species in ascent? If the farmer found the cocks only interested in each other, what then of the hens, and in time there'd be no chickens at all. Is this genetic message cause to celebrate? Why is this so infuriating?

Tolerance is an acquired trait, he knows that. Unlike fear or confusion or repulsion, which come naturally. He has seen homosexuals on television. Heard about the homosexual behavior of pop stars. But these aren't pop stars. These are sickly, thin, pale strangers; their boney legs rubbing together; their cologne strong enough to ignite. He turns back for a second look with a mixture of disgust and curiosity, why does this have to exist at all, he ponders, yet it does. Why does it bother him so, yet it does. Why does a dog lick his balls? Because he can. As they turn the corner, they see he has turned to look back at them and they blow him a kiss, which he can't help but find mildly amusing. He walks past Bourbon Street, then turns onto Royal Street and walks along the galleries, novelty stores and souvenir shops. He enters the bar called Kueiffer's at fifteen after six. He asks the barmaid for change for a paper, and she gives him hers. He thanks her and folds it out to the classifieds and orders a beer. He circles a couple listings. After twenty minutes and David has not shown, he turns to the headlines; they are of little interest to him, the whole world is of little interest to him, just a giant Super Center of cheap plastic shit and violence and literally everyone seems crazy. Murder, rape, war, abduction, recession, inflation, courtroom, boardroom, Wall Street, Meryl Streep gets another award for pretending to be yet another person she's not. Soda pop and silly hair-do's and 100 dollar running shoes. Throwing this sized ball into this hoop, and that sized ball into that direction. He doesn't care about Democrats or Republicans, it's all pandering anyway. He doesn't care about Savings and Loans. Rich people stealing from less rich people who are afraid to get old and die. The country's in recession, so what! He can't even afford the beer he's drinking, so he can hardly give a shit the Dow is off a few points. No tax plan will right the world, nor democracy! How could he care about home prices and mortgage rates and six year trends? He almost has a low grade hate for everything, except that he doesn't care enough to hate. Hate is too much work. He's got himself to think about and that nearly wears him out. There's an article in the Arts & Entertainment section about a book by Annie Proulx called The Shipping News that sounds interesting, but he'll have to wait until it's available in the library, he can't afford to buy a book. At six forty, David finally comes in. James is not upset, doesn't really care. But David is cautious, at first. And this James thinks is decent, shows some resepct. David pulls up a chair and calls the barmaid by name and very politely requests a couple Rolling Rocks. Then he says:

"Sorry, I'm late; had to let the manager slarve on the horn."

"Slarve the horn?" he asks, raising an eyebrow at this interesting sniglet.

"After stressful days, she likes to gurgle a load."

"Really?" James says in a low tone, fascinated but skeptical, his gaze turning up from the paper.

"It's pretty cool, she lets me cum all over her face and shit, and then slips me a twenty." He beams.

"I wonder if that was in the job description," James says dismissively, thinking, it's official everyone *is* fucking crazy.

David laughs, then turns his interest to the paper. He says:

"Find anything?"

"I circled a few here."

"Let's see," and he pulls at the edge of the paper to bring it in front of him. James says:

"Look at this one here. On Orleans Street. It's only two streets over from here."

"Hmm."

"But the address is high."

"Yeah, and I think Orleans goes right through the middle of a project, past Rampart."

"Oh?"

"Yeah, that's no good, not in this town. Damned niggers will steal everything you own."

James looks round the barroom. Nervously. There isn't a single black person, in a town with a mostly black population. The comment is easy and matter of fact. David continues:

"But, if it's inside the Quarter, it'd be great."

"It's only 285 a month."

"That's a good price."

"Is it?"

"Yes. And it's probably in the Quarter, because if it was in the projects it'd definitely be in the low twos or high one hundreds."

"Why don't I call the number?" James says and David offers a quarter.

The landlord tells him they can see the place now, if they have twenty dollars to put down as a key deposit, David just happens to have twenty dollars. The landlord lives on Governor Nicholls and Royal. On the landlord's directions, they find the apartment easily. It is a white and yellow wooden house, a shotgun with a decaying front porch. No front yard, the stoop right up on the sidewalk. Hardwood flooring in the front room, painted plywood through the rest, with the exception of the bathroom, which is white tile, of the turn-of-the-century variety. The place isn't particularly clean. But has plenty of light. High ceilings. The bathroom large, with a long, deep cast iron tub with no showerhead. There is a courtyard, out back, a young honey locust hung with seed, a couple gnatcatchers gleaning its thorny limbs. There's some junk lying among the elephant ear. The neighbor's laundry is strung across the left hand corner. They don't have to think about it. They agree to take it with zero debate. Why bother looking? What else could they want? A fresh coat of paint and a good sterilizing, maybe, but a better location? There isn't one. They are no more than a few blocks to all the bars David frequents. The projects are on the other side of Rampart, so they're clear of that. No parking for David's car, but no one gets parking in the Quarter. When they return the key, they inform the landlord of their intention to rent.

Back at Kueiffer's, they drink celebratory rounds of beers. They talk finances, share stories for a while, try to get to know each other better, now that they'll be sharing an apartment, seems like the thing to do. A friend of David's, whose head wants to wobble on his neck, comes into the bar and sits with them, he mostly digs at scabs on his arms. David and James talk excitedly about the new place. During a second round of drinks, David goes to the phone. When he returns he says he has to make a quick departure. James does not want to stay any longer in the bar with the other young man, with whom conversation is almost impossible, so he also leaves.

During his small dinner that evening, he looks over the columns in the newspaper. The print is small and blurred and means nothing, as easily read as the surface of a cinder block. He decides the place they have chosen is as good a place as any and will do, who are they to expect more on their budget. He does not think about it any longer. He walks the long way back to the hotel. He goes to bed after a long, very long, shower.

The next day, the sun already angry about this part of the world, he lingers in the coffee house until ten am to avoid it. With its tall ceilings and its location in the narrow street, it defies the forenoon heat. Then he walks Decatur to the record shop, just now opened. The tall and thin shop manager is loading a CD into a disc player, her hair dyed the blackest of blacks, her long nails painted black, wearing all black, her lips painted a bright red, her skin like old soap. The speakers hung in the rafters start to tremble, a death march of drums and violent bass, electric guitar tearing heads off babies, and a hissing, growling, tortured eruption of mostly incomprehensible lyrics. Not exactly how he would start his day, but it does have a lot of energy in it. He notices there are no cassette tapes, only compact disc. When did his happened, he asks the manager? She explains with hard to place dismay, how soon everything went to CD; they won't even make tapes anymore, she telling him just as David comes through the double doors. David says:

"Fucking good, too, tapes suck."

"It's all I've ever used," James says.

"That's cause you're a fucking backwoods country boy, who plays the fiddle and goes to square dances and shit."

"How was the shelter last night? They have a cot available for you? Or did you have to sleep in the gutter again?" James replies sarcastically. The freedom to poke fun of each other is as clear sign of an easy friendship to come.

"Fuck you, let me get you some money so you can get us a fucking apartment."

"Get on it, then. Morning's a small stack of wood."

David corners the manager. James cannot hear what David asks. They go into the back rooms, momentarily. Then David comes out and hands James a fold of large bills like extending a stick of chewing gum. He says:

"I didn't have it on me. Had to loan it from my manager."

"Excellent. I'm sure she'll find ways for you to pay it back."

"Hope so. If you need anything else, I'll be here until six tonight."

"Like what?"

"Fuck, I don't know, I've never rented an apartment before. Take the number of the store with you, just in case."

He has everything arranged by four o'clock. He returns to the hotel for a shower to wash off the day's stickiness from the intense humidity. He leaves his room with his violin and finds Spanish Plaza unoccupied. As he plays he can hear the distant revolving doors of the Riverwalk, like the plastic wheels of a cassette player turning stiffly, as if recording. He plays blindly, half an hour. Then strolls with his thoughts entertaining him to a restaurant on St. Peters, where he orders the cheapest thing on the menu. He pays for it with the silver change he has just earned. The air cools down considerably under a continent of gray clouds that have come up from the river with a narrow head like an anteater's leaning down from the sky over the French Quarter to lick up people from the streets. It'll rain soon.

James finds David waiting outside the closed record shop at fifteen after six. David steps off the curb and meets him in the street, asks:

"Everything work out fine?"

"Sure. Everything's ready."

"Cool, man, so you wanta go out to my parent's house and get some mattresses? You don't have a mattress do you?"

"No, I don't."

David drives a red Japanese two door, pretty roughed up. He removes a parking ticket from under the wiper, looks over it rapidly, not reading it, then tosses it on the dashboard along with many others, then leans over to unlock the passenger door. David impatiently dislodges the vehicle from between two Fords. He takes the nearest ramp out of the Quarter and speeds down the Interstate into Metaire. The small car trembles against the velocity, and then sinks into suburbia quivering, mitigating the forward momentum. They turn one identical corner after another. James, whose sense of direction has seldom let him down, is lost. There are no suburbs in rural Missouri. Country folk might be dumb, he thinks, but they're seldom lost. They climb from the car in front a stack of sandstone bricks with plastic shutters and what looks like plastic grass. David says:

"Home sweet home, but not for long!"

James feels embarrassed for David by the house, and maybe sorry as well. He can almost start to sympathize David's need to get out. Where's the porch? Where's the shade tree? What's with the wooden barricades behind his and everyone else's backyard. Why aren't any of the windows open? Is anyone home? Anywhere. A sprawling neighborhood of flat, quiet houses, systematically separated by the exact prescribed paces, cars out front, and not a person in sight. Suburbia is a brand new phenomenon to him. It had not yet infected the landscape of his piece of the Missouri countryside. He had seen it under construction on a school field trip into St. Louis, in passing, from the Interstate. Having never seen the finished product, it has never seemed to be a real place. More like the set of a movie about teenagers who parents feed them but never beat them, or a sitcom where children carry as much importance in the house as the parents who make it all possible. On the television, he could almost believe he could like to live in such a place. But where are the haybarns to hide out in, the creeks to wade, the dusty country road to walk in summer, crickets screaming in the scorching heat as if on the same skillet your great aunt's frying gizzards and green tomatoes? He'd spent the last year *living in* a barn and it seems now more inhabitable than these storage facilities. It's so unnatural, so fabricated. Banal is the word he'll use once he learns it.

When the Brady's unload crisp bags of groceries from the station wagon in the backyard, the colors are soft and fuzzy. Here, the colors are faded and dim, variations of tan and sand. Everywhere asphalt and cement. And dull, flat houses. Lots of dull flat houses. Houses the architects rendered so dreamily on paper, like Baptist churches, God forsaken in reality. Houses conceived with total disregard to nature and geography. But the lush little squares of thick grass! They you go, everyone's happy! Grass so green it looks plastic. Little ten by twenty allotments of nature. Nature rations. Fake nature at that. There's a peculiar sensation here of having and longing all at the same time.

Nobody's home. The floors are carpeted in cream, the walls are plastered in cream, the furniture is upholstered in cream and it is hypnotically quiet, and cool, too cool now that the clouds have come in. The air-condition quietly sucking currency straight out David's parent's bank account. David finds a note stuck to the icebox: Went to the store, be back soon, Mom. He digs into the icebox and drags out a sleeve of bread, a mustard bottle, a giant jar of Hellman's, and a plastic package of square and sliced processed ham, a tall pitcher of iced sweet tea. They build thin sandwiches and sit around the breakfast bar eating potato chips and drinking the sweet tea. When someone comes through the front door, a sweet voice asks:

"David are you here?"

David answers the question with a question:

"Where are those mattress that we have?" He takes the potato chip bag into the hall.

"They're in the guest room, why?"

"I taking them, we got our apartment."

"Okay, but how are you going to get them there?"

"On top the car." He turns back to James. "Let's find some rope."

They use the kitchen door to the garage, and David immediately mashes the garage door opener, which automatically turns on the light. The door begins to open loudly, and his mother's car sits in the drive, sand colored. Then the rain falls from the sky. It falls as if he has turned it on. David bursts into profanity. His mother comes in to see what the trouble is, and she tells him to watch his language. He doesn't, of course, goes on ranting. His mother says:

"It's all right, you can take them out tomorrow. You both can stay here tonight."

"Like hell." He turns into the kitchen.

"You can't well take those mattresses out in this rain."

David does not reply. He comes out from his own bedroom with a bundle of blankets. His mother asks what he plans on doing, sleeping on the floor? His eyes say yes. He asks James, while they are in the car climbing onto the Interstate with the back seat full of blankets and pillows, if he minds sleeping on the floor, as though the question still relevant.

"No, not at all, not like I haven't before and wouldn't again."

They dash through the rain to the covered stoop. They throw the pile of blankets and pillows onto the floor. David asks:

"When do we get a phone?"

"I haven't dealt with those people yet."

"Anyways, I've got to call my girlfriend. I'm going around the corner to call. You want to come? Probably going out afterwards."

"Sure, but I need to go to the hotel to get all my stuff."

"Sure, no problem. I'll drive you over."

"No, I didn't mean it like that. You don't have to drive me. I can take the trolley. I don't have that much."

"Forget it. Besides it's raining. I'll take you over, it'll be quicker."

David double parks the car in front the hotel. James retrieves his canvas duffel and places the keys on the front desk under the clerk's long nose. She gives him evil attention, as if she quite literally despises him for a just reason, asks if he has borrowed any towels. He says no. She says that he has. He assures her he has not. She says her records show that he has, at which time he sees a sign that reads Ten-Dollar Deposit for Towels. He says:

"Then you can keep my deposit." She looks at him with heat radiating from her ugly eyes. She is looking down at her ledger. Her face might actually be quivering now. What is the problem with this person? He is thinking. He turns away from the vile woman and passively walks out the front doors. Starts to wonder for a moment where things went so horribly wrong. Which of the twenty words he exchanged with her set her afire? He places the bag into the back seat, and David peels away, dramatically, a screeching of tires. James looks at David, thinking, what's with *all* of these people and their inexplicable behavior. He asks David:

"Was that necessary? I didn't rob the place?"

"They probably robbed you, more like it."

"No, but the woman working the desk, I just don't understand. What an awful human being." He tells David about her behavior. David doesn't find it as incredulous. Says:

"People are just fucked up, dude, get used to it. There is no explanation."

Around the corner from their apartment, with its doors actually on the corner, is a bar called the Silversmith. David is on the payphone. The bar is empty at eight thirty. The bartenders are fresh, but bored. James is nursing a beer. David comes from the phone booth and sits up at the bar. James asks:

"Get a hold of her?"

"Nope."

"Try her again, later?"

"Nah, probably not."

"Well."

"This place will fill up pretty shortly."

At ten o'clock a tide of urban materiality rises to the doors. The defected, thrown out in the waste water of some sort of youth processing machine, floods the barroom. Mean or sad or scared or shy, but mostly all young faces in a sea of red, green, purple, blue, white, black, orange and banana yellow hair. A box of abused, or in some cases, self-abused, crayons wrapped in khakis and browns, or denims and cottons or leather and chains. In a group of ten, just as many pairs of sole-thin combat boots as broken bucks. Next to a boy who looks as though he'd spent the last evening sleeping on the curb, is a young man who just double parked his BMW out front and simply doesn't care, his private school education is already paid for. It is an odd and lively, loud and heavy-drinking crowd.

Some hours later, James is at a small table with David and friends of David's and one young girl. People press against them continuously. The music is an invisible liquid metal that dulls the senses and at the same time induces rage and hysterics. The young girl throws herself into the mob on the dance floor where she is tossed in the surf of post-pubescent muscle spasm. She comes out dry mouthed and goes to the bar, carries back a beer and a test tube of tequila. She rejoins the group with the company of another young girl devastated by an explosion of acne. She stands next to James while her friend and David scream in each other's ears over the industry of noise, infectious hate lyrics not so much sung but screamed, sexy in their impudence. The next song takes a spirited though manic turn towards taciturn melody requited with a ferocious rawness, which Buck knows, it has taken over the radio like a plague, and he hates that he can't hate it, the naked baby swims for the dollar, we're all here now, outraged by its absurdity, and the barroom erupts at the first pulse, and James and the girl are pressed together in the crush for the dance floor. She fondles him as a gesture to dance. This popular piece of angst rock is already a classic, excites a common nerve. Everyone leaps, as a whole, into the air, and the house undulates and churns and heaves like a skid of bait shrimp. Some propel themselves into the air and then land on unsuspecting heads. The nucleus begins to revolve, first slowly, then rapidly until it erupts into a warlike frenzy of pushing and shoving, as though a fight has broken out. Being on the perimeter, James is pulled into the agitated center, a whirlpool, and is sucked deep into the eye of the storm and knocked down, trampled, kicked, grabbed, pulled back up and spun around. David comes flying at him and shoves him and sends him backwards so hard he would have hit the floor had not a tall, thick boy served the purpose of a wall. As soon as his balance is checked, a small girl is thrown into him. He catches her fall, and undeterred, she immediately tears into the crowd with great energy and intention. When the music changes, many people disperse, flock to the bar, dripping with sweat, shirts entirely wet. James finds the two girls around David. Every one is as happy as if they collectively took down the first woolly mammoth ever killed by the hand of man. David orders a rack of test tubes of tequila. Another song explode across the room. Repeat. It's raw, and ugly, and angry, but everyone is enjoying themselves with an animal lust.

He walks to the new place in the fuzzy night. Drunks stagger along the streets. Police sit on car hoods or horseback, smoking cigarettes or drinking from Styrofoam cups. He takes a bath because his eyes burn, and his neck and face are sticky from the humidity. He lies hard on the blankets on the floor, but he is tired and cool, so sleep comes quickly. Some hour in the morning, David comes through the door. He isn't alone. James hears the voice of a young girl, and she is very drunk; her words are slurred. He looks at his watch in the faint moonlight, but can't tell the time. David and the girl fall into heavy breathing. James tries to return to sleep, but his imagination is provoked. He hears the rustling of clothing. The breathing. Then the slow, low moaning. He can hear the gentle pat of David against her and thinks he can smell her, or it might be his own imagination. He imagines the skin of the inside of her legs.

XVI

He walks into the Faurbourg Marginy by Chartres Street. It is six in the evening. His neck is burnt from the afternoon painting balustrades in the sun. He comes to a flea market at Elysian Fields. The thrift store is large, dusty and disorderly, and the air stale. He buys two plates, a pan, utensils and glasses for four dollars and fifty cents; the plates kind of greasy and the utensils bent. On his walk back to the apartment, he purchases dishwashing soap and Comet from the grocer.

Washing the pot and plates, he thinks he should stop and sit out on the back steps and play the violin. He feels a stiff guilt, but nevertheless doesn't stop washing, dries the wares, then goes into the bathroom and washes the tub. His hands are chilled by the cold water. The grit of the cleaning agent under his palm. A cool sweat on his forehead from applying steady elbow grease to the yellow watermark. His feet bare and cool. He wants to play his violin with this same involvement. He thinks he should go out immediately, but can't think of an appropriate place to go. The levee? The back stoop was tight, the neighbors' proximity vulgar. Waldonburg? He begins to feel closed in, and his thoughts grow stiff, pressure builds on his temples. He begins to believe he cannot play. Maybe never really could, and never would. He sits down on the bathroom floor with pads of dirt on his feet and his hands puckered and white. He cannot remember what piece he played better than any other. He feels hopelessness settle over him like a light sheet; it's lightness and his inability to grasp it maddening. He shakes his head as if to loosen his eyes stiff in their sockets. There is obviously something wrong with his brain. He draws a cool tub of water. He slides into the deep bath. He watches his hands like hands on a television set, they are not his, until they are well into the job and then the pleasure is great enough to fuse body and thought. And they are inseparably one. Climax is an epiphany, for a moment everything is perfect and so very simple. If only that feeling could ever last for longer than just a moment.

While he is preparing dinner, David comes through the front door dragging a mattress by its cord handle. They determine who will take the front room and who will take the second. The house does not have a hall; the front room enters into the second and then into the kitchen. They eat dinner on the back steps. David smokes several cigarettes as he highlights last night's events. He explains the girl:

"Shit no, she's bat shit crazy, just a little hot tart I like to sink a fork in, occasionally."

"Really?" James isn't entirely convinced of David's "no big deal" disposition.

"I call it squirrel, nut, zipper. Buy 'em a few beers, give them a little bump, and then take 'em home and fuck the shit out of them."

"Interesting." James says, not quite sure what a bump is but is pretty certain it's a drug.

They pile the dishes into the sink and stroll around to the Silversmith.

*

They do not wake from their semicomfortable floor mattresses until past eleven. They go to a cafe without walls, just floor to ceiling French doors, all flung open, sluggish and hungry, and the thin steam that is the morning air carries the smell of coffee across the tables. After breakfast, they ride Uptown on St. Charles, oaks and elms bulge from the sidewalks, and large homes sit back off the street: white, turned balustrades along the front sides, narrow windows a story tall and hurricane shutters laid open; as many colors as flowers lit in sunbeams penetrating the thick canopy of the ancient trees, and the lush greens glaring, each home a story book of architecture for the generations to read. David turns into a narrow, over-parked residential street. He turns again on a narrower street and pulls along the grassy curb of a tall contemporary house with a cleft roof ridge. He's disappointed by what he sees. And why? Why is he bothered by this contemporary design? This abomination in a neighborhood of architectural treasures. Aside from the obvious fact that it's as full of detail as a cardboard box, lid opened. It's so unnatural. Why is everything *contemporary* so unnatural? The more he sees of it the less he likes it, 70's, 80's, brand new, all of it. It suggests the temperament of a nameless slumlord hell bent to banish beauty in the name of profit, under the guise of *design*. It repulses him at an instinctual level. What if Nature worked this way? Made trees like telephone poles. Did away with flowers and birds and sunsets were just flicks of the power switch. Light to dark. No inbetween. No reverence. Seashells just turd colored stones and the oceans full of mullet and jelly fish. If she had always done it that way, none would be the wiser. But to just start of a sudden, you'd feel gypped. He feels gypped, not even his house. He's afraid he's not going to like these people, as they climb cedar steps to a large sun deck. David pounds on a featureless slab of door. A forty-something woman answers, and David asks for Virginia. She says the girls are coming out in a moment, and she steps out onto the deck. A tall girl, not yet twenty, steps out behind her, makeup applied like stucco on her cheeks. *So unnatural!* She yells into the house:

"Virginia, David's out here."

James is leaning on the railing, watching the door. Virginia comes out from the darkness in the house. Everything he's just been condemning in his brain vanishes like a cloth pulled from under the table setting. She is absolutely gorgeous. Dark skinned. Her face is conspicuously beautiful, beauty mark on her cheek, an enormous smile of perfect teeth. Green eyes like the shallow part of the creek where it runs over the rocks on a summer day. His heart leaps. She might be the most beautiful girl is has ever seen, in the flesh, not in a magazine. She could be on the cover of a magazine! Her heeled shoes rap on the wood planks as she steps over the threshold. She says to David, in good humor:

"You should call more often."

"I tried calling you yesterday, but . . ."

"Do you know how to leave a message?"

He doesn't reply to this, asks:

"You want to come see our place?"

"Well, we're going to practice right now, which you should know."

"Okay, how long are you gonna be there?"

"Several hours." She says, her tone is light and amused.

"Then I'll come by later."

"Fine," she says with easiness, with a smile, with a flutter of her lashes.

"Oh, this is James. My new roommate."

"Virginia. Nice to meet you."

Her greeting so formally executed he is certain she has curtsied.

"James Buck, nice to meet you."

"David has told me a lot about you. He says you play the violin?"

"That's right."

"Wonderful," she says, and she really makes it sound wonderful. She is not condescending, says:

"I tried the violin once, remember mom," smiling at her mother. Her mother is stiff, beautiful, she only smiles in acknowledgement. Virginia says:

"Then I changed to the piano."

"Nice choice. I love the piano, but you can't carry it around in a case."

"No you can't." Virginia agrees.

"I want to hear you play sometime."

"Sure."

She says to David:

"Are you going to give me the address, or do I have to get it from James?"

She touches him on the hand, confirm her playfulness. Then she gives David a kiss on the cheek, as she passes, says:

"Call me after eight, we'll make a house warming date."

The three women drive away in an imported, soft-cornered, white sedan.

David and James purchase a large quantity of groceries in a warehouse grocer the size of an Olympic gymnasium, and just as well lit. The building sits inside a perimeter of deepcreekwater green pines on lower Tchoupitoulas. Some of the largest people he's ever seen push shopping carts big enough to cage lions, and you'd think they *were* feeding a lion back at home. Wrapped trays of red meat as long as your arm, half-gallon cans of vegetables, or beans, 50 pound bags of rice. Hundred count bags of bite sized Snickers Bars, and Halloween is months away. There's a frenzy to the shopping. As if the store had granted shopping sprees, but only as much as you can grab in a half hour. The cashier rings their purchases with wrist supports on both arms. She is simple and graceful, almost separate. He wants to take her from the checkout line, speak to her intimately and sincerely and look her steadily in the eyes. He is feeling contented, possibly because of Virginia. He wants to show this hard working check girl his impoverished, but rich life. He helps the bagboy, a black boy, and the boy is nearly shocked, suspicious. She moves her small hands quickly and watches the infrared closely, as though shyly. He splits the grocery bill with David. Never finds an opportunity to speak to her. Thinks about leaving a tip for her, a mute expression of admiration, but realizes the sheer ridiculousness of such an act. It's just that now he wants what David has. A woman to love him. He can imagine her leaning happily against the wall of the kitchen while he cooks dinner. A big worn wood table in a beautiful and aged apartment. They are poor but as rich as any because they are in love, and because other people have been in love before them, and more will be in love after them. The world is simply a beautiful place, and love is the only reason the whole planet exploded into existence. He can get very romantic like with his fantasies.

They sit on the kitchen floor to eat their meal; David eats from his lap, and James capsizes a five-gallon bucket and presses his back against the wall. After dinner, James sits on his bed thinking of the young grocery clerk, her fair skin, her delicate hands. He wants feelings for her to well up in him like hot air in a balloon and carry him off somewhere. He wants to do something, immediately. Compose a melody and wait in the lot until she leaves work in the evening, play it for her. What he really wants is Virginia. But she is with David, as outrageous as that is. He rubs the front and back of his violin to a glossy patina with a t-shirt. David's flipping through a Rollingstone, one of the unsold copies with the cover torn off, which he brings home from work, says:

"Can't believe you play the violin."

"Why?"

"I don't know. It's odd to know someone my age playing an instrument like that."

"People of all ages have played violin for ages."

"That's just it. Why not an electric guitar, drums, a horn even. Something modern."

"Then who'd play the violin?"

"Nobody. You can't make any noise with a violin. It's too . . . whiny."

"Yes, it can be, I guess" he says, staring at the instrument, unoffended, the voice of the instrument loud in his mind. He continues, "as decorous accompaniment to other instruments, but alone it's much different. In fact, unlike any instrument I know, its more infinite and perfect in its versatility."

David raised brows suggest he is skeptical. James Buck adds, in way of mitigating the pretentiousness of he statement:

"That is, if I knew how to play it to its potential. Still have a lot to learn."

"How long have you been playing?"

"Not very long," he protectively lies, should David think he does not play well, he doesn't want him to know that he has been playing for almost four years.

"So, I mean, what are you planning doing at it? Get in an orchestra. They don't hire off the street."

"Don't they? Not sure, I haven't thought it though really. I just took to it, just instinctual, it wasn't conscious."

"No man, I get that, music is like that. But we do need to get you up to speed. There's great music out there."

"I wouldn't know. Sure the hell ain't anything on the radio, especially where I'm from. Aside from country and church talk, there's just new country and oldies and candy pop. Not much else. And commercials. Nothing but commercials."

"Fuck the radio, not shit on it. Dick hurting pussy pop, is what I call it, same twenty songs too, all marketed to teenage girls. Can't go to the radio for good music."

"I go to the library and listen to tapes, but it's all old stuff, very old stuff, never anything new in the library, least not our school, and the town I lived in didn't even have a library. It didn't have anthing really. For that matter. No record shop. Fast food drive thru's, nothing. Doesn't even have traffic lights."

"Damn! But kind of cool, I guess."

"Yeah. Maybe, but when mainstreet is still a dirt road and there's only a gas station, a junk store, and a general store that's also the post office and the owner is the mayor, so it's also town hall, you get the feeling there's a whole lot your missing out on."

David pulls on his cigarette, tries to wrap his brain around that kind of reality. In a moment asks:

"Buck? Any relation to Peter Buck?"

"Not sure. Who is he?"

*

Fans whirl quietly in the lofty rafters. The air is cool and unused. The contemporary, unquestionably expensive furniture, likewise, appears unused. They are at Virginia' s house. David slouches in a couch. James sits cross-legged and shallow in the opposite end, favoring the armrest. Virginia, back straight, in an adjacent armchair. She asks, like she is interviewing guests on a talk show:

"So how's the new place?"

"Great." They both say.

"Have you had time to fix the place up any?"

David doesn't answer. Of course they haven't. He is quick to become impatient with her formality. James says:

"No, not really, but we got some great mattresses."

She smiles at James, and he is overwhelmed. He realized the first instant he met her she was beautiful. Now, though, he is captivated. She is magically beautiful and smart and like no one he has ever known personally. Her etiquette. Her posture. Her attention. She is aware that David is not pleased.

"So, my mother will be back, soon."

"So," David says.

"So, I thought you would like to know," she says, sanctimoniously.

"Is your dad coming up?" David says.

"Nope," the word a little bubblegum bubble popping. "He's not coming up for a week. But he and my mother are still at it."

"Well."

"Well," she repeats, with amusement. She has no makeup, nothing on her lips yet they have color, nothing in her variegated hair, no jewelry except for a single, intricate silver ring around the index finger of her right hand. She looks at James, smiling. She says:

"So you came from Missouri?"

"Yes."

"Nice. How do you like New Orleans?"

"Good, very good."

"What do you do, I mean, other than play the violin?"

James looks exaggeratedly doubtful, with a scratchy hum in his mouth as though trying to articulate a foreign word. She sees he does not have a ready answer.

"Why did you come to New Orleans? Just to play the violin?"

"Yeah?"

"But why New Orleans?" she asks, as though New York, or San Francisco, or hell Paris were just as likely options.

"I don't know, bus fair was cheap and I thought it would be nice."

"Just thought it would be nice?"

"Yes. And well I read some Hemingway, and New Orleans seemed the best America could offer as far as anything like Paris or places in Spain."

"It must *be* nice to think going someplace would be nice and just go." Her smile is genuine, makes him feel like they are easily good friends. David quickly says:

"So, do you want to go to my new pad?"

"Sure," she says. "Why not?" She smiles, shrugs her shoulders, then runs up a large set of spiraling stairs. David watches her and then looks at James quickly, to read what impression Virginia has made on him. Curious as to whether James finds her behavior as artificial as he does. And he doesn't, he is enamored. In fact, so much so, he realizes it might be obvious, and therefore adjusts his disposition, suppressing any enthusiasm that might have shown in his face. When she returns, she wears a different shirt and black flats, and her purse on her hip hung to a leather strap across her torso, accentuating the size of her large breasts. It takes the young male James Buck an enormous effort not to salivate. Virginia locks the big oak door behind them and they climb into David's car. Virginia takes the passenger seat and James in the rear. She makes small talk with James the quick ride into the Quarter. She turns in her seat to make eye contact. David drives recklessly and never uses the rearview mirror to look back. He has the radio blaring, so it hard to hear her really, he just smiles and enjoys looking at her magically beautiful face.

David gives Virginia a thorough tour of the small, shotgun apartment. She shows undue excitement in the spartan dwelling. She says, repeatedly:

"This is a very nice apartment. You guys are lucky. God, I'm so envious."

David tells her about all the little things he wants to do in the place, as they pass through James's room. She sees his violin case. She asks him:

"Oh, this must be your violin? Can I see it?"

"Sure."

She kneels in front of it. James kneels beside her.

"Wow, terrific. What do you play?"

"Well, just a few songs. I'm working on some more."

David says, very dryly:

"He plays on the streets."

"Really. You didn't tell me that part."

"Sorry, it didn't occur to me, but yes."

She becomes luminous in reflection.

"I think I remember seeing you. Did you play for a couple days at the Cathedral?"

"I have played very near it, yes."

"I saw you, in fact, I think I put money into your case."

"Wow," he says, lowly, with checked exhilaration in front of David.

"Do you remember?"

He tries to; but there are a lot of faces now gone by, an endless river of them. He wants to believe he would have noticed hers, wishes he could remember her and see what she was wearing so that he can bring it back and have it now. Virginia says to David:

"It was when Alice and I were coming to see you at work, remember?"

David can't remember. Virginia says:

"Play something for us?"

"No, I can't play that well, like that, on request."

"Oh come on, sure you can."

"Not really. You see I only know a few songs. On the streets it doesn't matter because people are always walking by. They just hear a few notes."

"Oh, don't be silly, play something for us. I'll make you a deal. If you play your violin for me, I'll play the piano for you next time you're at my house, and I'm horrible, so it'll be very embarrassing for me"

James raises his brows. David says:

"She actually can play the piano pretty good."

"Really?"

"Yes."

"I bet not nearly as good as you can play your violin," she adds.

"I doubt that."

"I don't practice a lot, not as much as I should, but I'm willing to embarrass myself in front of you."

"All right, then," and he takes the instrument from the case, puts it under his chin, checks for tune. Virginia stands perfectly straight, her shoulders straight, a large smile across her dark-skinned face, eyes large with excitement, one hand resting on her purse and the other holding the thin leather strap. David slouches against the wall and runs his yellow-nailed fingers through his orange hair.

He begins with high notes that he knows as the middle of a song. He plays them poorly. Stops. Plays them again and continues with the piece. He feels at the same time uncomfortable with the close audience and flattered by Virginia's interest. He wishes he had the anonymity of a painter or a book writer, where his work could be experienced without him present, to not be personally on display. Or rather he wishes he could play so well the music took all attention away from him. Or rather he wishes he wasn't so damned insecure. He cuts short on a mistake. Virginia claps enthusiastically, which obligates a half-hearted clap from David, worse than not clapping at all. He puts the instrument away and tries acting like he is not completely embarrassed. He thrusts his hands into his pockets and leans against the doorjamb. Virginia looks at him, trying to see in his eyes his unique person. She is genuinely impressed. He could never know just how impressed. She might have decided she loved him right then. He looks away from her innocent, consuming stare.

They drive back to Virginia's house, where they meet a meatless, black-haired girl named Alice. They all sit out on the deck drinking iced coffee as it grows dark. Late in the evening David and James drive into the Quarter and park the car on the street near the apartment and walk to the Silversmith. David sits at the bar buying drinks for a pair of young girls who look like identical twins. James is drinking a Scotch and Coke. The bar is tight within a half-hour. The crowd revolves from the dance floor to the bar and back again. David takes great amusement seeing James staggering drunk as the clock licks at 1 a.m. and he vaguely realizes he can no longer stand up in the mosh pit and leaves the bar. He tells two strangers, one of which he thinks is David standing next to him, that he is walking home. They nod at the drunk. As he walks the street, one of the girls who'd spent much of the evening allowing David to intoxicate, follows him out the door. She approaches him rapidly. She catches his fading attention. She asks him where he is going, so early. He slurs when he speaks. She asks if he needs help walking home. He says he doesn't, that he lives around the corner. She insists she should help him home. Locks his arm in hers. Several times he staggers widely unbalanced, and she braces him. At his front door, he tries to find his keys. She reaches into his back pocket to find them; she presses her chest against his and slides her small hands into either pocket to find them, as she does, their lips meet. He can smell on her breath the alcohol and smoke and something very fecund. She takes the keys from his back pocket and unlocks the door. They land on David's bed in the first room.

Very late in the morning, David comes home alone. He finds two unclothed bodies tangled in his bedsheets. He goes to the icebox and takes a long drink from the water jug and then falls back on James's bed to sleep.

XVII

No one in the house wakes until after noon the next day, Sunday. After the girl leaves, James spends the whole day without anyone's company. He gives very little thought to the girl, when there's no chemistry, there's no chemistry. But he does think about his lack of control. He disregards this event, because he was very drunk. He spends the day taciturn. He has become an intensely private individual, but he hasn't always been this way, but spend enough time burning dead chickens and sleeping in a barn and it changes you. He is never overzealous or giddy, now. Although sometimes, very unexpectedly happy, which he takes quietly, just the same. For the most part, he is a very thoughtful person—that is, he is full of thought, not sentimentality. He likes his quiet and his thinking uninterrupted, just as much as good company. Though sometimes, it can lead to a lot of self-abuse. So far, he finds himself an odd ball, in a town full of odd balls, but his is different. Unlike Ignatius Riley, whose debt service to colossal absurdity was absurdity, he is trying to draw some insight from an account of insufficient currency.

This day, he spends it's entirety out walking or playing his instrument, recording sights and sounds to memory, there is some horn in a dark drinking hall, there's some chords on the guitar in this open air restaurant, there's piano on the square. Late that evening, there's pigeons cooing, glass empties crashing in steel dumpsters, there's the first of the street sweepers. He makes himself dinner and takes a long bath, not resisting playing with his nonmusical instrument, which he doesn't have the smallest guilt about, and then he puts on a thin t-shirt and his cut-off Dickies, and he plays violin in the back court, in his bare feet watching it grow dark, doves perched quietly on the neighbors eaves listening. He does not hear David come in at night. He sleeps hard through the night.

Part II

I

It's September, and work with Leo is slow. He's playing out more, at night or when he works half days and on days off. Cohabitation with David is peaceable. He has met plenty of David's friends, whom he mostly can't connect with, phatic and casual, and obscenely interested in only the current particular flavor of culture from which they guzzle, flannel shirts showing up under their leather jackets. He spends random evenings in the Silversmith or Kagan's bar or Kueiffer's drinking moderately and shooting pool. He ran into Jack and his girlfriend the first Monday of the month, and they had drinks in the HalfMoon on Magazine Street. Her name is Kay. She is an average girl, of average height, average looks, a little overweight, and absolutely nothing interesting to say. She has dark blonde hair and skin the color of goat cheese. She is a sentimental, stay at home kind of girl. On his own Jack is okay, sensible, not super talkative, but genuine and easily humored, together with Kay, he's different, they are about as enjoyable as a butter sandwich. So not much to talk about there.

Virginia and David have begun to quarrel, or rather they continue to quarrel, as he is now aware is their habit, and after one particular conversation on the phone, David punches a hole in the plaster wall. This upsets James, because it not only shows lack of control and immaturity on David's part, but more practically, half the deposit is his, and he does not want to forfeit it. He does not say anything to David; reasons to let David fix the hole at his own time and expense, since the lease is for one year. On this particular evening, of course, they are at it, again, on the phone. James does not want to stay in the apartment. He goes to the Theatre Maringy for an amateur production of the classic *Inherit the Wind*. He sits in an mostly empty in hall. There aren't but a half-dozen in attendance. He enjoys the intimate theatre, but is very disappointed with the cast, the men too boisterous and dark eyed and the ladies overdramatic, probably why there are so few in attendance. He goes into the theatre content, and he comes out depressed, feeling especially lonely, not completely due to the performance, and not completely due to the fact that logic and reason were on trial, as they will always be on trial. When he returns to the apartment, he finds David still on the phone. He takes a long, quiet bath. He listens intently to what David is saying to Virginia. He wishes he could hear her side of the argument.

*

He's out with his violin the next afternoon when dark clouds move in over the city quickly. An unexpected rain comes down on him at Spanish Plaza. It pounds the cement. He dashes into the doors of the Riverwalk and stands inside, looking out at the rain coming down hard on the Plaza, into the fountain and onto the surface of the river, as if a tropical storm has blown in from the Gulf. Everything becomes different shades of gray. He turns away and walks along the franchise shops. He has made no tips, but has a few dollars in his pocket, and when he comes to a coffee shop, he takes a seat near the large, plateglass windows. He can see the heavy rain on the mud gray river. Black and brown barges, obscured in the downpour, drift by slowly. Algiers is a dark green blur in the gray.

He notices a familiar face in the cafe. She is the generic-faced girlfriend of Jack's, Kay. She is with two older people, both obese, with coffees in to-go cups, in their paws. When she recognizes him, she approaches. Her parents do not. Not until she says something, as though they need her approval, then they are cheery, and join her at her side. She says:

"Hi, what are you doing?"

"Came in out of the rain," he says, looking up from his coffee at the three; his thin hair matted onto his forehead and the thicker hair on the top is not so matted, causing a sloping forward on his head.

"Yeah, Dad can't remember if he rolled the windows up."

"Shouldn't you go check?"

"Nah, it's the old truck. Besides it'll stop soon. It's just a squall. It'll quit here pretty quick."

"Shopping?" James asks, noticing the bags they hold.

"Yah," they say in the same laughing ejaculation. Kay says:

"Jack's birthday is tomorrow."

"Really?" he says, feigning real concern.

"Yep, he's getting old," her mother says in a well-rehearsed quip. "We're giving him a party at the house," she adds. She has a large, bland face with flesh like the inside of a cow's thigh and straight, dirty blonde hair. Kay says:

"You're more than welcome to come, if you want. Jack doesn't know what we are doing; it's supposed to be a surprise, though I'm sure he knows we're doing something."

"Sure, I guess I'll come."

"Why sure you'll come," her father booms; gut like he swallowed a medicine ball; his gray hair quivers a moment while he chuckles at himself.

"We could come pick you up." Kay offers. She knows James does not have a vehicle.

"No, I can get over there. I've got a friend who can give me a ride."

"Are you sure? 'Cause it wouldn't be any trouble."

"No, I'll make it. What time?"

"About five. We're barbecuing."

"Excellent."

The conversation instantly dies. The fat parents look offended, inexplicably, and James wants to turn away from them; he isn't quite comfortable with their obesity, but also something else, something disingenuous, though he can't quite put a word on it. It doesn't occur to him that they might be sensitive enough to notice that he is uncomfortable with their obesity. He can't help it, it is just so unnatural, so 'right there in plain sight' wrong. There was only one fat man in the town that he grew up in, Mr. Pouk, okay two, his son Mickey, but they were Falstafian, round and agile, and full of cheer, they could do a cartwheel with a glass of beer and not spill a drop. These people seem bloated, off-color, as if sour in content. Shouldn't they have browned skin in all this Louisiana sun? Kay breaks the awkward silence:

"Well, we have to get going. Here's our number if you can't get a ride."

She fishes her handbag for a pen and then writes out her number. He wonders if he should buy a gift. He does not ask.

Next day. He takes a short bath after an eight-hour day of light construction. He persuades David to drive him to Kay's parent's house, in Westwego, an absolutely despicable rash of human infestation eating away the wetlands above Lake Cataouatche. If a hurricane wiped it clean, the better for all, except it'd grow back like mold by the fall. The house could be brand new or twenty years old, there's no way to tell. It looks like it was delivered on a truck and sat down on pallets. He finds Jack on a low couch of dirt colored tweed, and Kay is laid across him with her back slung over the couch arm. Jack has his arms folded behind his ears. They are watching a program filmed in a sort of high-grade, home-video quality. The television is almost as long as the couch and twice as high. Jack has a twelve-inch remote control in his hand and he jumps to the football game quickly, checks the score and then jumps back to the program. Relatively young adults are talking directly and intimately into the camera. As though actually talking to the viewer. Jack says:

"It's about time you get here."

"I didn't think you'd even be expecting me," James asks?

"Kay told me she invited you."

Hardly a surprise, then, he thinks.

"Would you like something to eat?" Kay asks.

"Maybe later."

"Later?" Jack says, "There's no later around here."

James sits in an armchair and does not lean back, instantly uncomfortable with his surroundings. Enormous, white suburbanites traffic the house with smiles pinned to their fat cheeks, and in their clumsy hands jumbo Dixie cups and paper plates piled high with food: the paper of the plates so thin five or six plates serve to create scarcely enough rigidity to constitute an eating surface. They continuously come in through and out through the spring loaded sliding glass doors. Some burst into giant guffaws when passing each other, but not much is really being spoken. Outside, smoke billows from a grill on the uncovered patio. It is still light out. The yard is full of people, most of whom are laid back ponderously in grossly out-matched folding lawn chairs. It is a large group, evidencing little awareness of the cause for celebration. It is hard for James to conceal his condemnation, of which, he has plenty. He just can't fucking help it. How could so many people be so visibly outside a healthy weight to height ratio and yet sit there with four-high racks of barbecued ribs on their knees and gallon-sized cup of soda pop as though absolutely nothing were the matter? Two banquet tables of food, and where's the army? James says:

"Pretty large turn out, Jack."

Neither Jack nor Kay even blink over his slight emphasis on the word large. Kay says:

"Yeah, pretty much everyone's here. Come on let's get you something to eat."

She jumps up and takes him out to fill a plate. She takes a great pride in what there is to offer. Grilled sausages. Chicken thighs. Beef variants. Vats of potato and bean salads, slaws, casseroles. Gallon jars of things pickled. Skins and chips and puddings and pies. Igloo coolers of iced soda can and cold cuts and chocolate bars. Each guest is over portioned with food by the power of five.

Then comes the cakewalk, the singing, the candle blowing, and as James sees it, the obligatory, almost insincere congratulations, he's thinking, while the cake is whittled by thick slices to crumbs, he's never really had a birthday party. His sister once made him a cake. Which makes him think of his sister and not without a touch of pain. But then what is all the fuss, anyhow, he tries to justify. The anniversary of one's birth, as though we live in a time of cholera. Each year a great victory over death? Hardly! Aren't there billions of us? If you know enough people you'd eat cake and and ice cream every day. There is a silliness to it all, but people sure love their cake and ice cream. He takes a tiny slice, is scolded about it. A single dollop of ice cream.

People begin to leave in groups after the ice cream is served. Jack, James, and Kay wander into the garage and beat a plastic ball on a green table with wooden paddles. While the plastic ball pops, James feels good about his distance, watches the intimacy of Kay and Jack with a cynical eye. Are they really happy? Is this really entertaining? I can't imagine how it can be. I would rather be doing nothing at all than doing this doing nothing. He asks where the bathroom is. Standing at the toilet, the frosted window is open. In the back yard by the trampoline, a small boy shoves a small girl and she sets into a balling and a mother comes in a hot fury. She grabs the boy by the hair and yanks him over the springs and stands him up and smacks his face. I've told you to stop treating your sister like that, if I have to fuss you again, I'll take you home. The sight fires his brain, the clumps of his fine hair would fall from his mother's angry grip. He wants to intervene. It's not his place. He finds Jack and asks for a ride back into the Quarter.

Traffic is light, and they speed into the Quarter rapidly. Jack and Kay grow quiet once they enter the city. They nervously lock the car doors with the auto lock button. They intently try not to stare at the bums and freaks and blacks on the streets. James talks them into coming in for a moment. They are not comfortable. They stand in the empty kitchen. They talk so little the humming refrigerator becomes an annoyance.

They might just as well be King and Queen obliged to visit the hovel of a villein, though their own kingdom hath an abundance of no richness. Buck walks them to their car and wishes them a good evening. Sad, sad that *they* are who they are, though they mean well, but they who they are, where does he figure?

*

Leo lets him go after lunch. He climbs off the streetcar and cashes his check at the bank on St. Charles. It is a lovely day. Bright and warm, and people are out in the Quarter. He walks back to the apartment to pick up his violin. He doesn't think David is home and unlocks the door and enters without announcement. David and Virginia are in the front room on the mattress. They are engaged in what could probably qualify as foreplay. James exclaims:

"Woah!"

Virginia comes up abruptly, as if a wind fills her sail: her back straight, legs in black stockings together again, ladylike. David rolls back on the mattress, leaving his lower body towards Virginia, concealing the product of their passion. They are completely dressed, but by the look of their garments they have both been well fondled. David's white face flushes and Virginia's chest heaves as she tries to appear unflustered. James says:

"Hey, I'm sorry!"

"No problem, we were going to be leaving in a few minutes anyway. I thought you worked till five or so?"

"Not today. Leo had no work. I'm sorry I busted in on you."

"We were about to leave anyway," Virginia says with great, convincing honesty.

What can he really say to this? Not much. He goes into the second room and takes cotton shorts and underpants from the closet. He draws a tub of cool water in the bathroom. He sits in the tub as it fills, soaping his face. He cannot stop thinking about Virginia. He is jealous, and also just as much sad. But he knows he could never tell her what he knows about David. He lathers his face and body, working on the chest with circular movements, thinking how disastrous that would turn out, if he did. He has walked from the Canal-Carondelet streetcar stop, and in the bath his legs are firm from that excursion. A knock comes upon the bathroom door. David says through the door:

"We're gonna go."

"Okay, sorry about that."

"Hey, no problem."

The water pressure is low and the tub fills slowly. He lies back and the cool water creeps up his horizontal figure. It comes up half his thickness and touches anxiously and steadily and tickles his skin. He soaps his hair and tries thinking about anything other than Virginia and the stimulus caused by the rising water. He cannot think of anything else, of course, but Virginia.

II

Evening, sweltering. The apartment has no air-conditioning. James Buck goes out for a walk without his violin. He is uneasy, and his head is maddeningly muddled. It is a night white hot from the long, humid day. He walks to the esplanade behind Jackson Square and takes a bench in front of the Presbyter. He watches the dark prevail, sinister with his mind like this, the pigeons light and lift off the large flagstones, the white squirt of shit left behind, the polyhedral standards burn an ineffectual existence, the white complexion of the St. Louis Cathedral ashen, the trees become black bruises against the purple of a sky full of thunderstorm. He sits in thread-loose shorts and canvas shoes that are old and decrepit. Shoes worn wadding streams for miles through the forested hills of Missouri, washed of their color, color of old sail cloth now. He wears a cotton t-shirt, and it sticks to his back with light perspiration against the slats of the bench. With one arm thrown over the benchback, he watches the pedestrians pass. Old men and women with their heads forward or if they are more healthy, they walk arm in arm, or with a leisurely gait, hands folded behind their backs. Young men pass, staggering drunk. Twenty-something young women alone are rare. A particularly attractive brunette passes him and oddly, nervously, makes eye contact. He immediately smiles a straight, disinterested smile, but it is dishonest, an involuntary lie, because he is very interested. Interested in her beauty. But how uncomfortable he feels! How can he smile his curious, desirous, *needful* smile? Because that's it, needful. He wants his smile to say, I see that you are there, and I realize that you are a beautiful woman and walk alone. But I'm not a threat to you. I'm harmless and, though I sit here alone in the growing evening, dressed like a bum, I am not a bum, nor a killer. He watches her now, unnoticed, as she has moved past him. He's no fool, the world has remained a violent place, there's just more news coverage. People are afraid of strangers. They judge as fast as they can by what they see. Like coming across a snake in the woods. He sees her chest from the side as her breasts, full and round, bounce with a heaviness and gentleness that provoke in him a desire to hold her, put his face against her chest and breathe the intoxication of her skin. Her every little gentle movement stirs him passionately. He wonders how the curves and the movements and the smells of the female body could drive him so. Cause a great physical suffering wanting it so badly. The female body is a soft, clean, fragrant place, a palace, a paradise, a refuge of the ugly world. He feels like he's in a cage, seeing it through the bars. And it is so hot and dark and hard this cage. His bones are weary from wanting. Not just her sex, either.

Her love, her kindness, some tenderness to alleviate some of the pain of sentience.

Another female, young and smartly built, comes to pass, and he watches her profile in passing and he follows her walk by regarding where her legs meet; the smooth half-spheres of her small butt and the gentle movement of the material against her supple body. He can imagine her soft skin, clean, white. The dry pubic hair and how soft it would feel against his cheek or hand and the heat would radiate into his palm if he pressed against it, cupping it. Her nipples soft, growing firm. The scent of her heavy hair on her shoulders and the warm in her breath, the sound of her voice in the morning before it's tuned for conversation.

He stands up, quickly, as if to shake the self of a moment ago free from the self he determines he will now be, resolute and unaffected. The sky is the color of grape juice and a herd of smoke gray clouds move in from the northeast. He wishes for rain to cool the air. He decides to put this longing beneath him; he is stronger than that and will not let it affect him. He walks Pirates Alley between the Cathedral and the Cabildo. He turns right at the rear of the citadel and left onto Orleans and walks the street passing his roommate's vehicle. Knowing David is home, he knocks before he enters. He wishes to find Virginia visiting, to enjoy her company. But she is not here. David is on the bed watching a television show. Referring to the television, Buck asks:

"Where did you get that?"

"From home."

"Great, all you need now is a couch."

"Reception's pretty good."

"You'll be a mattress potato, instead," he jokes, watches the show a moment, then asks:

"We have anything to eat?"

"I think there are some dogs."

"Good."

He goes into the kitchen and from the icebox takes a torn packet of wieners. He fills the loose-handled pot with water and sits it on the stovetop. The blue flames come up around the bottom of the pot, the metal blushes. He throws in a dog and waits until it rolls in the boiling water and either end splits. He folds it into a slice of white bread, some ketch up, then a knock comes upon the door. David yells out to the visitor. The visitor bursts in, shoving the heavily painted door open, which drags on the floor, years of coming and going eroding a quarter circle sweep. The young man stands in the doorway wild eyed like a pursued fugitive. James comes into the room from the kitchen eating his hotdog. The visitor exclaims:

"Man, I just ran over a nigger!"

"What the fuck?" David jumps up, exclaiming.

"Yeah. On Rampart, some guy riding a bike. I didn't see him until he came fucking rolling over the hood."

"Jesus! Was he hurt?"

"I don't really know. I was about to get out and see how he was doing, but then all these negroids started coming out of nowhere, gathering around and fucking yelling at me and the guy was rolling back and forth on the street holding his stomach."

"I'm surprised you didn't kill him," David says.

"I know! Hell. I opened my door and heard him wailing and shit, but all these other niggers started coming out of nowhere, all fucking gangsta walking towards the car and I said fuck this, bra, I'm getting my white ass out of here. Out on fucking Rampart Street? That shit aint no joke!"

"Fuck no, someone's shot in those fucking projects every night."

"Are you going to call the police?" James asks, amazed by the story, but instantly suspicious of the details.

"Hell no! I just hope they didn't get my license plate number."

"You might want to call the police, and explain yourself."

The fugitive continues as though he doesn't hear this:

"I drove off as fast as I could and parked way over on Magazine, then walked here."

"Where on Rampart were you?" David asks.

"At Esplanade."

"Man, I don't know," David becomes more apprehensive, "I think you should report it. Save yourself from the possibility of getting stuck with a hit-and-run offense."

"Shit, if I don't do anything, nothing's gonna happen. The cops ain't gonna waste their time, fuck no! But if I save them the trouble, then they'll slap me with the book. They can't ignore it at that point. I'd get a 'hit and run' charge," he starts tallying on his fingers, "probably reckless driving and no telling what else and because he's black and I'm white they'll drag some shit in; they'll make up some N double A C P racist infringement of Constitutional Rights bullshit; I'll get sued for every fucking thing I own and will ever own for the rest of my life. Fuck no I'm not reporting anything. I'll take my chances on this one."

David is easily convinced. James not so much. David looks at him, says:

"Yeah, he might be right. These fucking cops around here are as crooked as they get. He's probably making the right call. They're not gonna do one thing about it. But if he went to them, especially if the cop happens to be black; Hell they'd be fucking laughing at what a fucking idiot he is and throw the whole book in his face, because then they don't have a choice." They both lather themselves with this justification. Who can say if they are right?

"I was going to stay awhile," the outlaw admits, "but I don't think I want to keep my car in this area right now. Just to be on the safe side. I wonder if it's *even* safe to walk back to the car."

"Did they get a look at you?"

"I don't fuckin' know."

David offers him a skillet, which he takes. David asks if he should walk back with him. As they walk out the front door, David says to James over his shoulder:

"If I don't return in about fifteen minutes, call the national guard, there's a riot in progress."

"Yeah you right," the other can be heard saying as he walks out into the street armed with David's mother's well-seasoned skillet.

When David comes back into the apartment, he and James talk about the deep shit Scott could be in. David explains how he met Francis Scott two years ago when he sold his electric guitar to him, and they'd been friends ever since, turns out they went to the same high school. Says Scott's a 'pretty cool dude', using that exact phrase. Says he has the prettiest, little girlfriend you've ever seen. James tries to be reasonable. Asks if they might be exaggerating the outcome just a little. David gets somewhat irritated, Mississippi's Burning style. He barks:

"You don't have a fucking clue, dude. Shit's fucked up around here; like you wouldn't believe. He's doing the right thing."

It's uncomfortable now. What does James know? He does not respond. Conversation stops. The television broadcasts the news. David turns it up, as though something about the accident might come on; there's nothing but morning showers in the forecast.

James wakes to a morning rain. Heavy and cool and sweet before the sun. The rain envelops the house, and the kitchen is cool and dark. The large elephant ears in the courtyard glow green. He makes pancakes and eats them on the back steps. He drinks a glass of milk. Streams of rainwater come off the roof above the steps through the gutter and splash at his feet onto the slab of cement, smooth dented from the years of rainwater convincing it. Occasionally, a glassy pearl of water clings to a hair on his leg and its weight bends the strand of hair slowly. The skin tickles with anticipation before the droplet loses its grip and falls down on the shin, knocking around the hairs on its stream down. He does not finish both the large pancakes. He sits the plate down beside him and puts his jaw into both hands with his elbows on his knees, watching the drops of water flung near his toes thin on the flatness of the steps or amass into welts. This tranquility overwhelms him. Buckets of beer cans sing on the back steps of the neighbor's, the elephant ears tap staccato, the dry seeds in the locust pods provide a whisper of percussion, the rain pelts the tin roofs as the neighbor's sheets and towels worry the clothes line in their saturation.

When the rain stops in an hour, it leaves everything shining like new, vibrant, and the sky clear. It will now be a humid day. The phone begins to ring. It rings many times, and David does not wake up to answer it, so James gets up to answers it. It is Virginia, and she is delighted that he has answered, does not ask for David:

"How are you this morning?"

"Fine, fine. I just had my breakfast."

"Good. How's everything else?"

"It is all very good, I guess."

"Yeah?"

"Yes."

"How's your playing coming?"

"Pretty good."

"Playing out today?"

"Sure."

"It's great practice."

"Yes, but . . ."

She waits to hear him conclude, but he does not. After a silence, she says:

"How's work?"

"Slow."

"Really, well then you have no excuse not to play your violin more often."

"I guess."

David comes into the room, eyes estranged from sleep, lips dry and white, and hair tasseled on the one side and matted against his head on the other side, a crease in his face from sleeping face down. James says:

"David just got up, here he is."

"I'll talk to you later," he hears her say as the phone travels through the air towards David. David takes the phone and his voice is dry, then smooth and apologetic. James takes his plate and glass and washes them in the sink. He goes into the bathroom, brushes his teeth, kind of angry with himself that he treated Virginia so indifferently, but what choice does he have? Also, he angry she's even with David. Not that David isn't a nice enough guy, just has not class. He thinks about this pretty girl he had a crush on in high school, she dated the shittiest guy in the whole school. He had a truck and wore expensive jeans and had great hair, but an absolute douche bag. Funny what woman can see in men and what they can't. He gives himself a sink shampooing, towels off, tries to make something of his shitty dirty blonde hair. Then David leans in against the doorframe. He has finished talking to Virginia. James goes to the corner in which he keeps his clothes neatly piled. David says he is driving to Hammond for a crawfish boil with Virginia, and Virginia asked if he'd like to come as well. James declines:

"No thanks. I' d rather not." Although, he would absolutely love too, but knows it would be torture.

"You sure?"

"Yes."

"Anyhows, I saw you had pancakes. How'd you make those?"

III

David comes through the door just before noon on Sunday. It was nice having David out of the house, but he's glad to have company again. He goes straight to the icebox and takes out the milk jug and turns it upside down above his head, pulling gulps out quickly: the jug breathing in deeply and noisily. James is on his mattress playing his violin, experimenting. He asks David:

"How was the picnic?"

"We got in a wreck," David says, brings down the jug, breathing, swallowing, talking, brings up the jug again.

"You got into a wreck?"

"Yep."

"A bad one?"

"No, just a little one. Smashed the front a little and knocked off the front wheel."

"Completely off?"

"Yep."

"How'd you manage that?"

"I ran into a high shoulder coming off the expressway. It tore the front wheel off. No one got hurt."

"Where's the car?"

"Still on the side of the road. We got a cab to Virginia's. I stayed there last night."

"Have you looked at it today?"

"Nope. I'm fixing to call the folks."

"What'd Virginia say?"

"Nothing really. She was very calm about the whole thing."

David rings up Scott, calling him Frank. James listens to him explain the wreck with unmistakable relish. One might actually think for a moment it was done intentionally, similar to a kid wrecking cars on a Tyco racetrack. Gunning it around the corners trying to see how far off the track they can fly. Over and over, until the cars are broken. Pencil in some new racecars on the Christmas List. Mom, can I get some more Snackables in here! He imagines David just before the accident drinking from a dented beer can driving 90, tuning the radio, smoking a cigarette, flipping back his stringy hair to see Virginia' s cleavage, passing speeding vehicles down the off-ramp. After David relates the full story, he listens to Scott for a moment then hangs up the phone and goes into the bathroom and starts talking to James from on the commode with the door ajar.

"Hey, Scott's coming over in a few minutes. We're going over to the Westbank, you want to come?"

"Sure, yeah, but what about your car?" James asks.

"What about it? It's Sunday, the folks are in church, and I don't have enough money for a tow," the toilet flushes, and James can hear something about David not knowing where he would have it taken anyway. David comes into the front room, his room, takes off his T-shirt and picks up another one from his pile of clothes, not a clean one necessarily, he smells it, it's clean enough, pulls it over his head.

Scott's car is cold from the air conditioner blowing like a draft from a deep freezer. David slides a CD into the player and plays it loud -the woofers breaking in the packaging loud! Piranha feeding, caged animals gnashing, machine guns spraying a gorgeous destruction, air siren, windows smashed in, a man howls:

I believe them bones are me
Some say we're born into the grave
I feel so alone
Gonna end up a big ole pile a them bones

It seduces while it isolates, and no one tries to penetrate it with conversation. It is an angry noise, and it tempts you to love to want to be angry, without provocation except that it feels natural to be angry, there's no need to identify a source, much less articulate one, there's a plenty to be angry about, so be angry. In a cultural bankruptcy as upon us, then, an instinct as inalienable as anger can be misguided, harnessed to no particular end, all for the price of a compact disc. Before they can cross the Mississippi, he has an incredible headache.

After many monotonous turns down one indistinguishable street after another, they come to a house of blonde brick and sand brown shingles. A tall woman with vivid green eyes lets them into the house with overjoy and points Scott in the undoubtedly well-known direction to her daughter's room; there's actually a path worn into the pile of the carpet. The young girl is folding satiny panties on her large bed into a large chest of drawers. She is thin and pretty and has healthy, blonde hair that slips around her thin shoulders like silk. She has the complexion of salt; her dollish face suffocates under a burdensome fard of cosmetics. Scott closes the door. He says:

"What's up?"

He gives her a kiss, and she walks to the chest to lay a stack of undergarments into the drawer. She is noticeably melancholy. Probably from the incident between Scott and the bicycling black man. She says, with forced interest:

"What are you guys up to?"

"I just got into a huge wreck." David announces with characteristic pride, it becomes clear to James that David intends not to be outdone. James sits down in an armchair and watches a large fish hang bloated in green water in a large tank in the corner of the room. He notices the length which the car drags alongside the cement shoulder is increased. The cascade of shattered glass is more menacing. David and Scott are now jousting for attention, retelling relative bits of their embellished stories. Scott' s girlfriend occasionally glances at James, whom she's never met, until Scott thinks to introduce him during a silence after David's prophetic encounter with his parents when he has to call them this evening. David suggests that they go out for beers. Scott looks at his girlfriend with a shrug. David is charged, also adds:

"But we need to call some girls."

Scott's girlfriend, her name is Jenny; she looks at David and at James. James imagines Jenny knows David's Virginia and is embarrassed by David's suggestion. But she doesn't say anything. She phones two girls she knows from community college. At dusk the six are arranged closely in Scott's car, burning its red taillights in the traffic turning into the bowling alley. James has a bare thigh on either side of him, skin like silk and the color of caramel. They throw heavy balls down slick, glossy lanes. The girls giggle and slip and fall on their little asses and twist their little fingers and need immediate attention. David's gigantic feet cramp in the rented shoes, so he bowls in his socks. Scott and Jenny wander off to the pool hall and never return. Everyone is drinking cheap bottled beer. The girl with the upturned lip and brown hair and brown eyes is receptive to James' flirtation, as subtle as it is. She moves her hips freely and touches his hand or shoulder or sits down closely next to him. He wishes he could like the girl. She is beautiful by birth and gender, but ugly by her choices. The chemicals she uses in her hair and on her face. The clothes she wears. The things she says. She reminds James of this loud and rude little slut from New Jersey he screwed in high school with a hall pass and a lack of interest in Algebra. He didn't like her either, her casual, vulgar, and rebellious ways, but they shared something in common, they were both obviously not like everyone else in the small rural school. No one liked her for her rebellion was grotesque. She was the pariah, where he was the ghost. They both stood outside the patriotic crush of the adolescent pep rally.

Everything about her was disposable. Her style, her foul mouth, her virginity, her integrity. Same for this girl except she rebels nothing, supports nothing, believes in nothing, except God, a God she knows nothing about. She is reproduced a hundred times, a thousand times, a million times over. He could hit a girl just like her with a gumball blindfolded in a mall parking lot. He wishes there was a place where they could go. He also wishes he didn't want to go somewhere alone with her. But the simplicity is too attractive. The possibility of sex too persuasive. When she speaks her shallow thoughts in atrophied English, he is strong and withdrawn. When she places her two small hands around the ball, smiles back at him anxiously, swings her hips on the run and bends forward on the toss, he is weak, crazed and taunted.

At the first hour of the morning, as if by school bus, the three young ladies are being dropped off at their respective houses. The brunette gives James a kiss at the corner of his closed mouth, and she is beaming, excited, thinking this is something new. James is sad because he knows it is nothing, and he is amused because she doesn't realize this.

*

It rains hard in the morning, and James and Leo work inside a mobile home in Metaire. They are ripping paper-thin paneling from the flexible walls. One misguided half swing with a hammer would break through to the outside. Why would Leo take such a job? The resident is a single mom and a relation of Leo's wife's. Possibly Leo will not charge her. She is ugly, now. Maybe, once, was pretty. James is sad for her, her reality. An ugly, fat squalling brat strapped in a baby chair, smelling of shit and old cereal milk. A house like packaging in a treeless parking lot and a three hundred-dollar-a-month electric bill air conditioning the place like a walk-in cooler. The whole morning has been deliciously cool and still the air condition blows. The artificial cold, the darkness from the thick curtains and the aluminum foil on the windows create a cave. Maybe the pale, dirty-faced child hasn't seen the light of day since last winter. He thinks about the girl with the upturned lip; this could be her. A pinhole in his prophylactic. Catholic girl most certainly. Would never abort. He is glad how the night went. But also disappointed knowing that had opportunity undressed herself, he'd have had no control over the outcome.

When they're loading the construction debris in the back of the truck, Leo busts his thumb in the tailgate of his truck. Therefore, they break early for lunch. James drives, which is quite comical as the tractor at the poultry farm is the only thing he's ever driven aside from a bicycle. Leo's gripping the base of the stricken digit as blood oozes from the bashed nail. He is calm and inspects the grisly wound with much curiosity. They arrive at the big, white house quickly. Leo's wife is on the sofa with the telephone against her blemished face, the cord twisted in her toes, the television set flipping dark scenes. She gets up and ends the conversation seeing her husband's thumb as he unwraps it from a T-shirt. It is bloody like fresh killed game, the blood dark and warm and dirty and the blackness setting in and the shirt is soaked in blood, and the nail is scarcely discernible, busted deep into the flesh of the thumb. Leo is casual as though it's a blister from swinging a hammer. His wife takes a chair at the oval dinner table, and she takes his hand to examine the wound closely. She runs to the bathroom and gathers supplies: bandages, scissors, peroxide, and a tube of ointment. He runs water over the thumb from the tap, which pours heavy on the sensitive tissues and agitated fragments of thumbnail. His wife is mildly hysterical, begins to beg him to go to the hospital. Leo says he's fine.

"Leo, don't be fucking stupid. We've got to go to the hospital. You've got to get stitches. Look at this?" She's holds his hand up to his face as though he has not seen it yet. Leo says:

"Stitches, what's to stitch together? The nail is smashed. I'll be fine."

"How are you going to work now? Let's go to Charity."

"And wait ten hours just to see the nurse."

"We'll go to the emergency room."

"Are you kidding me? Remember when Billy shot his hand off. The janitor asked him to stand outside in the grass by the doors, because he got tried of mopping up the blood. You think this is going to get me in there any quicker?"

"Fine, we'll go to Torro."

"We can't afford to go to Torro. So just cool out, it'll..."

Then Leo's son bursts through the door, screaming madly, tears flinging out his eyes in both directions, arms straight out in front of him, fingers down and the balls of his palms upthrust, scraped and bleeding. His mother nearly dives on him, swooping him up into her arms, rushing him into the bathroom. The child's screams and the mother's entreaties to clean the wounds come hushed from the end of the hall. Leo's littlest brother, maybe eight or nine, stands in the door and explains to Leo with seriousness that he had fallen off his bicycle. Leo stands leaning against the counter, holding a gauze around the thumb, looking at the little boy standing, hair fair in the sunlight coming through the open door with big, grave, blue eyes uplooking. Leo says:

"Well, close the door, you're lettin' all the air-conditioning out."

Two for one special on little misfortunes.

Obviously, Leo lets James off for the day. Says he'll give him a few hours after lunch, but not to mention it to the old man. James thanks him, but insists that he does not have to; or at least he could return to work without him. "Don't worry about it," Leo says.

David is home when James comes in. He is on the phone with his mother discussing the car. The talk goes fast, and David is angry. He slams the phone on the hook and comes into the kitchen. James sits in a plastic chair pouring a bowl of cold cereal at a plastic table.

"Like the furniture?" David sounds like a different person, very pleasant all the sudden.

"Much better than eating on the floor."

"It was my grandfather's patio furniture. Mom brought it over today."

"Good."

"It's dirty as hell."

"It'll wash." He pours ice-cold milk over bran and raisins. "So what's the story with your car?"

"Twenty-five hundred in damages."

"It's insured though, right?"

"Yeah, but a big deductible."

"What are you going to do?"

"I was trying to get my mom to give me my Christmas and birthday money in advance." James actually has to suppress a grin. He's findings this pretty ridiculous, almost funny. Ridiculous and unbelievable, but funny, "in advance'. He asks:

"Will she?"

"No, but I could get some from my grandparents, probably on both sides."

"I've got a little I could loan to you." He offers, but prays that David won't take him up on it.

"No, that's cool. I'll get it."

The phone rings. It is Virginia. David talks to her:

"Why don't you call a cab? None, nowhere? Well . . . yeah, I . . . Does the streetcar run that way? Where? Yeah? Yeah, yeah, fine okay. All right, see you in a bit."

David explains. He was supposed to drive her to rehearsal today. Her mother's not home, and the streetcar does not reach the address. He is going over so she doesn't have to ride the bus by herself. James draws some warm, soapy water in the sink to wash the plastic table and chairs. David bolts out the front door.

IV

Tuesday and Wednesday evaporate, leaving a powder salt on the skin. He works long hours on a roof, tar sticky hot, climbing again and again a thirty foot ladder, sixty-pound bundle of shingles on his shoulder; the dripping sweat burnt off by the sun. In the evening it feels good not to stand, his muscles tired. He sleeps well.

David is short the money he needs for his car. He coerces cash from his grandmothers, but his parents refuse to give any. Nevertheless, Thursday he and James go to the Silversmith. James has a large check from the long hours on the roof job, and he buys David several drinks. David introduces him to two twentyish girls who are good friends of his. James takes an immediate interest in the brunette. Her face is soft and like a child's, sunny and pleasant and without blemish. Her hair is short and straight and contrasts beautifully with her skin, which has a self-illuminating radiance, as the descending seraph might in a hallucination. And with exacting artistic moderation, she wears a solitary silver loop in her right nostril. This simple accent changes the language of her expression entirely. She shoots tequila like a caballero, but she holds her bottled beer like a schoolgirl holds a bottle of 7-Up. She says to James:

"How do you know David?"

"I met him at the record shop. He was looking for a roommate."

She, then, affectionately surveys him. Says:

"Are you gay?"

"Of course not! Why would you even ask?"

"You have a certain manner about you. Ostentatiously proper."

James doesn't know what 'ostentatiously' actually means, but understands just the same. He is more impressed with her use of the word, then insulted by the assessment. He glances around and then replies:

"I'm not from around here."

She thinks he is being clever and laughs. She pulls a flattened sleeve of chewing gum from her pocket and puts a piece in her mouth, folding it onto her tongue as she pushes it in -very 1980s like. She asks:

"Want to go outside awhile?"

The street air is teakettle steam that clings to the face, thick and white under the sky, grayed. The girl sits across the street on a low transition with one foot on the brick steps, the other swung over. The humid night isolates the girl and the corner of the old blue building from the rest of existence. She has managed to get out of the bar sooner than he. He crosses the street to her and says:

"Couldn't seem to cut a path out of there."

She stands up, smoking a cigarette. James remarks her aloofness. This is part of a newly evolved ritual. She knows she is doing something her mother could have never done. It emboldens her. She says:

"Hot in there?"

"Yes, and hot out here as well."

"Isn't your apartment near here?"

"Yes, around the corner."

"Do you want to go there?"

Her smile is casual, but almost sly.

"Sure."

"Do you have something to drink there?"

"Yes. I think we've got milk and water and ice cubes." She sees that he is serious and her eyes become easy and amused. They don't talk much as they walk to the apartment. The events begin abruptly at the door and go uninterrupted, abundantly and deliciously. She is very elegant and tireless and when James wakes the next morning, she is half under a sheet and half on the floor off the bed, wearing one of his cotton shirts.

David is knotted in his bed sheets with a pale, long-legged girl from the bar. James goes into the kitchen and drinks from the water jug, splashing water onto his chin and chest and bloated stomach. The drinking of the night before has left him exceedingly dry of mouth. He lowers the jug from his mouth and with his left hand scratches his penis in loose undershorts; he smells sex and prophylactic. He soaps heavily during his slow, hot bath and lays back to sweat off the alcohol.

V

On Friday night, third week of September, Buck is walking up to the apartment just as David burst out the front door of the apartment. He leaps in gigantic strides off the stoop. Virginia is at the opened door of a pick-up truck and she sees James approaching. She yells:

"Hey good looking, you need a ride?"

"I guess it depends how far you're going?"

She says, playfully, beautifully, "All the way, baby." Alice lets out a long *oh yeah baby that's right*. David says:

"Hey, we're going to a party, you want to come?"

"Sure. Give me a minute."

He leaps into the apartment, wipes his neck and face clean with a cool hand cloth and pulls on one of David's cotton shirts. They are still standing outside the truck door, Virginia and David, when he comes out. She lets David climb in and then she climbs in and James sits next her, pushes his elbow out the opened window. They fly over the West Bank high on the expressway. The wind whips their hair and dilutes the loud music, which David controls, straddling the stick shift. Virginia is holding her short, tasseled locks out of her eyes and smiling. Alice is driving intently, and James is gazing out over the black city of yellow flares. Alice says:

"I'm sorry I had to bring the truck."

"It's cool; kind of feel like a bunch of Mexican laborers," David says.

James surfs his hand through the fast moving air, has a flash back of some Mexican laborers that his father hired once to dig a hole for the outhouse at the back of the cornfield. It was one of the few times anyone was every hired to do work on the property. Usually he and his siblings did whatever needed to be done. But they where all so young then! So fair haired and innocent, then. He remembers how the two Mexicans couldn't speak but four words of English, would not eat on the screened-in porch with everyone else, out of respect maybe, being so dirty from the job. They would take their plates to the bench out beside the garden shed. The truck might just as well be a time machine now. So easily was he back there in that moment. The screened-in porch. The ham and white beans. Cleaning the mason jars. The cut paths through the tall grasses; you couldn't cut all the grass; there was just too much of it. This was the summer one of the boys broke the window out of the pick-up. And no one would admit it. He and each of his brothers cut their own switches, many switches, until someone confessed, as someone had to confess, his father would have no less. James could never understand why whoever did it wouldn't just admit it. Especially, after the first, then the second -dinner break- and then the third round of switchings. Maybe it was one of the Mexicans, hit it with the shovel by accident. No it couldn't have been, they were already long finished with the toilet by that time. They had to wear long pants for the rest of the summer to hide the marks on the backs of their legs. Re-visiting any of his good childhood memories always comes with the price tag of an unpleasant one.

"Is that David's?" Virginia asks, bringing him back to the now. She is referring the T-shirt he is wearing.

"Yes."

"Wow, you're wearing it?"

"I washed it for David the other day and accidentally shrunk it."

"I've been trying to get David to give it to me."

"Why won't you give it to her," Alice asks?

"Yeah," Virginia buttresses.

"It would have been too big for you," David says, "You'll have to get it from him now."

"Still want it?" James ventures, smiling.

"Sure," she says.

"Now?"

"Sure."

"What will I wear?"

"My shirt," Virginia says, referring to her white Hanes.

"Fine."

"Fine, give me yours first."

He removes his shirt and gives it to her, then waits for her to take hers off. She examines the shirt, a particular band's logo silk-screened across it, which she had wanted from David for some time. She drops the shirt in her lap.

"All right, here's mine," and begins to pull up the tails of the shirt, looking at James with a great smile, well aware of how much he wants to see her beautiful skin against the cool satin of her full brassiere. But then she stops. "I don't think so," and wags her head tauntingly. She pulls David's shirt over her head and then removes her shirt from under it and gives it to James. He pulls it over his head.

The truck comes down off the high-rise, slowing and leaving the right side of James's face numb and tingling, and his hair coarse and dry. They pull into a gas station and buy beers to take to the house. Shortly after they leave the glaring white light of the station, they pull to the curb of a suburban house sitting back on a dark lawn, a handkerchief tree stands in heart break over a broken bench swing, the lawn and porch are empty. They come in through the front door, and music fills the house with its roar like a chain saw does a forest. It plays from a tall, black stereo behind a tinted glass door. The kitchen is the only room lit in the entire house, and the stereo is right near it. Sink full of dirty plates and pans and beer cans. Electric oven open with a black pizza cold within. Microwave door ajar, mustard splattered all over it. A man passes James and Virginia. He is friendly and welcomes them, saying he did not hear them come in, tells them where they can find cold beers. James hears him greet Alice in the other room.

Virginia takes from the icebox two cans of cheap, American beer, giving James a look of pleasurable guilt. He takes the can she offers, opens it and drinks a long pull because he is very thirsty. He brings the can down, belches quietly with sealed lips. As Alice comes into the kitchen, Virginia says:

"Look at this mess. It's terrible."

David comes into the room. He says:

"All right, someone open the refrigerator." He carries the beers from the truck. Virginia watches him open a beer can, embarrassed of his actions, or rather the on-going nature of all his actions. She puts her fingernail under the pull-tab of her own can, gives a little effort to pull it up. David walks out of the kitchen and does not offer to help her open it. James takes the can from her as she holds it out to him in askance. He opens it and she looks at him with tender satisfaction, her goal achieved.

An Indian girl comes into the house through sliding doors, inviting everyone out to the patio. There's a large group of people outside by the pool. David turns up the music so it can penetrate the spring loaded sliding glass doors. Mosquitoes and lovebugs zigzag and swirl like giddy lent particles illuminated over the swimming pool. No wind moves through the trees in the back yard. It is a warm evening. The sound of the music comes through the walls loudly, but the hushed quietness of the neighborhood is nevertheless prevalent. In wood lawn furniture, they sit in a loose circle. David finds an old friend he's not seen in a while, booms:

"Chris, you bastard, I hear you're in a fucking band?"

"U.S.P.S."

"That's fucking cool. How in the hell did you manage that?"

"They were looking for a drummer and a friend of mine is David Spy's girlfriends brother."

"No shit. Man that's cooler than fuck. They need anything else. A technician or roadie or any fucking thing, a fucking blowjob."

The drummer smiles and stares with intense eyes, habitually intense eyes, they never blink. He drinks from his beer can, then says:

"Nah, man, I think we're all set. In fact we're about ready to hit the road for a big rock festival on the East Coast."

"That's fucking great. First time to go on the road with them?"

"Yeah."

James asks:

"I'm not familiar with the band. What does U.S.P.S. stand for?"

Everyone looks at him as though he is a retard who'd babbled some incoherent statement.

"Well, lately we've been joking around about it meaning U Sick Perverted pSychos. But originally it stands for United States Postal Service."

David adds:

"Or the U. S. Pussy Service, more like it."

Virginia stands up, not humored. She asks:

"Can I get a beer for anyone?"

David says he'll take one, tips the one he holds back and empties it. The drummer says he'll take one since she is offering. She asks James. There is something in her voice. Something sweet.

"No, I'm fine, but thanks."

Alice follows her into the house. Virginia doesn't return. Alice delivers the beers. James sits quietly, pressing a jagged-toothed pull-tab to his thumb, more fascinated by how it holds itself to the pad of his thumb than anything else going on. He wants to go in to see Virginia. David appears not to have noticed that she did not return. James gets up and goes inside. He finds Virginia disinterestedly cleaning up the mess. She says:

"I thought you didn't want another beer?"

"This one's kinda warm, actually."

"It's like urine when it gets warm."

"You need some help?"

"Oh, no. I'm just picking up a few things, that way Alice doesn't have so much to clean in the morning."

"This place certainly is a mess."

"Well they've been having a party in this house for three days straight now. Alice's parents are on vacation."

"Oh, I see."

"God, that music is giving me a headache." She goes into the living room to turn it down. James hears the sliding door open, its power spring pushing it closed again. The volume of the music goes back up again. James is in the dining room adjacent to the kitchen, looking into a tall china cabinet full of useless crap, wondering why people have china cabinets and why they collect useless crap to put on display in them. Then he sees Virginia walk past the dining room door that opens to the stair hall, and she turns up the stairs. Alice comes into the house, asks James where Virginia has gone. She goes upstairs to find her. James returns to the living room and finds it unoccupied. He feels the slight need to piss and decides asking Alice where the bathroom is is a good excuse to go upstairs. He climbs the stairs. The whisper of female voices can be heard coming from the dark bedroom. He knocks on the door and it swings open slightly more. Alice welcomes him in. They are stretched out lengthwise on the bed, flat on their stomachs, heads turned to each other, talking. James says:

"I was wondering where I could find a bathroom." He cannot see clearly who is who until his eyes dilate and then he can see the thinness of Alice on the right. She says:

"The door on the left. But hey," James is turning away, "what's going on down there?"

"Nothing." He feels a little silly even answering the question. What could have changed in the last ten minutes?

"Are they all still outside?"

"Yes."

"Good."

"What's David doing? Still acting stupid," Virginia says.

"I don't know."

"I'm gonna go back down there," Alice says and slips off the bed. He becomes nervous about being alone with Virginia. He turns to the door as Alice goes out. He says:

"I have to use the bathroom."

"Right here," Alice says, insinuating the door on her left. Alice slips down the steps like light people do, like a breeze, and James goes into the bathroom, takes a long piss, examines his face in the mirror, searches his face, hoping to find something encouraging. Nothing. When he comes out, he finds the bedroom empty and then descends the stairs to the living room. The radio has been turned off. He sits on the couch listlessly and picks up the remote control of the television set, turns it on and aimlessly flips through the channels. David comes in through the sliding doors, goes into the kitchen and then returns with a beer, pops the top and pours it into his mouth, splashing foam on his chin. He says:

"What's up? Getting drunk?"

"Slowly."

"You need another beer?"

"No, I got a full one."

"Hey, whyn't you come out and join us."

"I might do that in a moment."

David pulls the sliding door, exits, it slides itself shut. Every little banal detail, movement, and comment is excruciatingly boring, if he jumped off the GNO right now he probably wouldn't regret it on the way down. And he is stuck here, with no way out. He's about to start wondering why he's the only one who seems to be having a problem with it, but then Virginia comes into the living room. She smiles at him, sits down on the sofa next to him. She asks:

"What are you watching?"

"Nothing, just flipping."

"Oh."

He turns off the television set. Virginia sits back and pushes her head against the plush headrest. Her hair pushes forward on the sides of her head, and she smiles a large, clean, gorgeous smile. He looks at her, and she never alters her smile. She is determined to reveal her interest in him. An infatuation for her swells like fear in him, and he cannot look at her any longer. Alice comes into the room, and it is a relief.

"Some of those guys are going to be leaving soon."

"Who?"

"James, can you help me carry this stereo back up to my room?"

"Sure."

"Who's leaving?" Virginia asks, again.

"Almost everyone, except some guy talking about guitars with David," Alice says.

"Did David say he wanted to leave?"

"No." Alice says to Virginia. Virginia follows them, holding the cords up the stairs like the tails of a king's gown. They place it in Alice's dark bedroom and begin down the stairs again. James notices photographs on the walls and asks Alice if one in particular isn't her as a baby. He laughs at her infant picture and says he cannot see any resemblance but for the eyes. Virginia looks closely at the eyes in the picture, then into Alice's eyes. Then she looks into James's eyes. Or at least she tries to, this makes his eyes water. She says:

"You know, we've got the same color eyes."

"I don't think so."

"Yes. Look at my eyes." He sees beautiful three-shaded green eyes: a shade of green like summer grass; a shade of green like a creek; and a shade like the deep side of the same creek.

"Maybe."

"Alice, what do you think?"

She looks into both their eyes. James says:

"The light is very poor in this hall, you can't really tell."

Virginia stands a step below him and she says:

"That's not the only thing we have in common."

"Really?"

"Yes, we're both musicians. And look at our skin color, it's practically the same."

"That's not a whole lot of similarities." He tries to descend the stairs.

"What instrument do you play?" Alice asks.

James doesn't answer; he doesn't like the attention, or at least doesn't know how to respond to it. Finds it a touch contrived. Virginia says:

"He plays the violin."

"Wow."

"Very well, too."

"You and him could play something together sometime," Alice says.

"Yes, we could," Virginia says, excited, eyes asparkle.

James does not answer, but smiles slightly, secretly flattered.

"But see all the things we have in common?"

"Yes, it's incredible," he says a bit sarcastically.

Alice runs into her bedroom and puts a tape into the stereo and lowers the volume from what it was set at in the living room. The sound is a melodious, simple, dream-like continuum, lush and hypnotic. Virginia hears the sound and says she loves this band, an English band called The Cure, and goes up the stairs and into the bedroom, insisting James come with her, taking his hand. Alice is laid back on the bed. Virginia pulls him onto the bed. Virginia is excited. She asks:

"Why can't guys be more like you?"

James raises his eyebrows.

"Yeah," Alice says, rising up on her elbows.

"What do you mean?"

"You're very polite, but not in a suckass kind of way. You're very masculine, but also very sensitive. Like you think about everything and how you should treat it."

She doesn't sound gratuitous.

"You don't stare at my breasts when you talk to me. And you never talk vulgarly."

"Yes, but I'm just quiet, that's all."

"But it's a secure quiet . . . you've confidence in yourself," Virginia says, "and you're handsome."

"See, I almost started to believe you, but now I know you're talking nonsense."

"No, I think you're pretty handsome, myself," Alice says.

"And I think it's too dark in here."

"No, we're being serious. And why don't you have a Missouri accent?"

"Why don't either of you have southern accents?"

"We don't?"

"Not really, very slight."

"I guess so is yours, now that I think about it."

Streetlight through a filigree of trees cast distorted webs of shadow onto the ceiling. The music is breathing slowly, now. They are laid out across the bed, James in the middle.

"And you've got a nice butt, too," Virginia says. She puts her hand against his hip. He feels it and does not move and almost speaks, but thinks against it. He will not say anything so that Alice will not know about it, and it can ever come from her to David. It will be between Virginia and himself. Virginia says:

"And you have beautiful lips." She moves closer to him; her foot strokes his leg.

She slides her stockinged foot up and down his leg and cups her hand firmly under his butt. She rolls onto him, bodily, resting her upper torso onto his right arm, one breast atop him pressing firmly and the other just lower, pressing more firmly under her weight on his biceps. She kisses the corner of his closed mouth. The warmth in her lips wholly affects him. It is metamorphic. It is by the truest definition, magic. Everything changes in this touch of her lips against his. The room is now cooler. The coverings of the bed more pliant. His entire body is more solid, a more perfect thing. Information travels from his feet, his hands, back side of the knees, from everywhere in a fraction of a split second. He feels now not like a shoddy construct of brittle bones and tightly twisted arteries spitting cold or feverish blood without rhyme or reason. Everything under the skin and above seems one. Solid and cool. Like a stone shaped by the current of the river. He does not turn his head and he says, very lowly, slowly:

"What are you doing?"

"Nothing," and she breathes the word into his mouth. Alice climbs out of the bed and leaves the room, closing out the sliver of hall light. Virginia places her lips on him again in the darkness, her skin glowing with the green moon and her scent cottony and warm. She is seducing him with the silk of her lips and the stroke of her foot along the length of his leg.

But he is perplexed now, though, knowing he has the control to stop it all. With her breasts firmly against him and her breath in his mouth, he should be about ready to spilt. But he is not. He moves his mouth by turning his head away from hers and says:

"You should stop, you are drunk."

"I'm not. I want to do this," she whispers.

"Right, but what about David?"

"What about David?"

"He right below us."

"Does that bother you?"

"Yeah, and it should bother you."

"I don't care about him. I'm interested in you."

She is undeterred, and raises her head above his, starts for his neck. The door opens and a blade of glaring light cuts the darkness in two halves that fall away and reveal them clearly to Alice. She is matter-of-fact.

"David's looking for you."

"So go tell him something."

"I did; he thinks you're in the bathroom."

"Where is he?" James asks; he does not want trouble.

"He is downstairs on the couch."

"You better go down and see what he wants."

"Does he know James is up here?"

"He did not ask."

Virginia slides out the bed and goes down the stairs. Alice sits down on the bed and slides up alongside, like a close friend.

"So what happened?"

"Nothing."

"Did she tell you anything?"

"No."

"Did you want to make love to her?"

"I don't know. Why, did she want me to?"

"I don't know, couldn't you tell?"

"No."

"So did you want to?"

"That's beside the point. She's David's girlfriend and he's down the stairs."

"Yes, that's true, but what if he wasn't?"

"I don't know."

Alice is quiet a moment, then hastily, possibly to avoid nervousness, but still quietly, says:

"Well, I'm here."

"Yes."

"What about me?"

"I don't know, what about you?"

"Would you like me? I'm here with no boyfriend down the stairs."

This is all that is necessary. He puts his lips to hers, and she puts her arms around him and her legs around him. He holds the small of her back with one hand and the nape of her neck with the other, her shoulder-length hair cool on his hand. She removes his shirt inconveniently, and he slides hers over her small head. She wears a bra, which glows in the darkness, satin white, and she unclasps it from the front, straddling him, revealing that she really need not wear a bra, her huge nipples become erect. He is erect and ready for her and he rolls her over and pulls her jeans down her thighs and grabs her soaking wet crotch and his fingers plunge into her. She releases a low moan, and her back arches up, and she trembles a little. She locks her arms around his neck and draws his ear near, to whisper:

"Have you got a condom?"

"No, actually, I don't"

"No?" She is disappointed.

"No, do you?" he ventures.

"No."

"Well?"

"Well, I don't want to do anything if you don't have protection."

James rolls on his back.

"We don't have to stop doing what we were doing, do we?" she asks.

"Well, it's hard to do this without finishing the project," he says.

"I'm sorry, but I just . . ."

"No, no, that's all right," and he sees how she really wants him. "It's fine."

"But you don't have to stop this, though," and she places her hand over his hand over the soaking mound of pubic hair and she smells like vanilla and sweat, and he wants to give her this, so continues for her sake. She whispers:

"You do me and I'll do you."

Then pulls him out of his underwear with her hand.

He is falling into sleep now. The thin, young girl's arm is laid over his stomach, her hair so silky against his shoulder. He pulls a heavy, knitted spread over them and falls into sleep.

VI

At some small hour in the morning, much before dawn, James wakes hearing what sounds like sobbing outside the bedroom door. He goes to the door ajar and peers into the blinding hall light. He is concealed in the darkness of the room behind the door, and he sees Virginia come up the stairs naked but for a towel, and she is crying. He does not move or breathe. Virginia passes into the bathroom at the end of the hall. She closes the door and goes into the shower; he hears the water come on.

He climbs into the bed beside Alice, and she wakes with his bouncing the bed. He tells her what he has seen and she goes out and knocks on the bathroom door. Virginia lets her in, and James cannot hear their voices over the hushed hiss of the showerhead. He falls asleep, and he does not wake with Alice's thin body slipping back into the bed.

VII

The next morning Alice gets up from bed before James and dresses and goes downstairs and finds David on the sofa in the living room, snoring open mouthed. The house is a foul-smelling disaster. She finds Virginia in the master bedroom, which is on the ground floor, curled in the heavy coverings and she climbs into the bed with her, and they talk and nap intermittently like sibling cats until they hear David and James scavenging the kitchen dry of mouth and hungry. They search the icebox and pantries. They find a sleeve of crackers and the three beers that survived the evening. When the two girls come into the kitchen, Virginia is hard and closed to David and gives James a look of full of questions.

Around dreary curb corners, they swing slowly through cheerless suburbia like on a somber stroll through a cemetery of low, shingled mausoleums. Alice pulls the wide truck into a tight slot in the parking lot of an overcrowded franchise restaurant. They stand silent and uncomfortable among the herd corralled at the host's podium. Smoking or non, as though it makes a difference? Families of four fill booths like when you break a tube of instant biscuits. There are a lot of mouths in motion, but very little conversation, just the sounds of mastication, flat wear hitting dish ware, the bustle in the kitchen sliding out plates full of breakfast items of nearly indiscernible variances of color and temperature. Virginia looks at James often, humored by his condescending expressions. She gets it. Nobody else seems too. Of course not. And even if they did, what would they do about it? Dislodge themselves from between the vinyl and Formica and take a brisk stroll? Raise a few hens and scramble their own eggs? Take their frittata on china at a table-clothed affair from a jacketed server? Actually have a conversation? Impossible! This is not only what they do, but probably all they can do. He and Virginia are quietly bonding over this. She sits next to Alice in the booth, directly across from James and their feet are close together under the table. He bumps her foot when he reaches for the menu. She gives him a decipherable look, a look in askance about last night. She doesn't think she sees any sort of answer from him. When the waitress is present, she touches her foot to his, again, and they hold intense eye contact in those seconds David is preoccupied with the laminated menu. Alice takes no particular interest in James; if anything, she is a bit mischievous. When breakfast is served, she temperamentally refuses to pass the pepper and when James shakes it over his eggs, she chides him how much he takes.

The breakfast makes him uneasy. The eggs watery, the ham watery, as though injected with it, probably is, and the toast cold. Virginia could have been served a cut of raw horse, she doesn't look ten seconds at her plate from watching David to find a moment to watch James. She smiles pleasantly.

David and Alice smoke cigarettes and flick their ashes in the plates that never get bussed from the tables. With his stomach upset by breakfast, he is impatient and unsatisfied. He can't talk openly with Virginia. He finds nothing interesting about the retelling of the highlights of the marathon house party now coming to a close. He has to sit and be patient. Anonymous humanity, the insatiable feeder, looks foul, smells foul and sits big in their booths all around him, swelling with want with each passing second. He feels alienated. David or all of mankind, it makes no difference; an obstacle standing in the way of what he wants. It fatigues his heart and agitates his brain. Love, which he thinks is at the table, has faint fragrance—splash of honey in pig fat. He knows something new was made last night, and he wants to be excited about it. But happiness requires pre-conditioning. It requires previous experience.

Virginia's hair is short and many colored: burnt cinnamon, caramel, locks the color of coconut shell, some golden hues. Her hair is thin and soft like infant's, like the hair of a Yorkshire Terrier. Riding in the truck to the ferry landing, he glances over to look at the side of her face, trying to remember her of the night before. How her lips felt against his. How her breast pressed against his chest. Her hair in his hand. Her soft face like sable brushstrokes across his cheek. The truck arrives at the ferry landing; Virginia gives James a tight hug and a kiss on the cheek, then the same to David. James is cautious and unaffectionate, not knowing how to behave. Alice gives them both a hug, and says to James she will call; she will get the number from Virginia. He is surprised. The ferry glides over the mud slick of the Mississippi and bounces into the dock at Canal Street.

James feels some satisfaction being back on this side of the river. It is a warm noon, fair and yellow, and clear. James sees David's easy, guiltless attitude. He asks him:

"What was the matter with Virginia last night?"

"When?" He does not know James was upstairs.

"Real late. She was crying," James asks without accusation.

"Oh, we got into an argument about something."

"She was only wearing a towel," he asks, and to escape any unwanted metamorphosis in David's temperament, adds, "You guys go swimming?"

"No, we had sex first, then when we started talking, we got into a fight."

"Oh," he says, a spontaneous heat binds up his chest, he quietly tries to get his breath. His cheeks tingle and he fears they've gone red.

"She was pissed because I was alone with Alice in the master bedroom."

"You were alone with Alice?"

"I told her I was just talking, but she thought more and would not believe me."

"Why not?"

"I don't know. She's very jealous, anyway. But I did do more though, but don't tell her that."

"Of course not. When would I have the occasion to tell her?"

"Well, anyway, she came down to see what I was doing."

"Alice, or . . ."

"Alice. She came into the bedroom and started asking if Virginia and I were having trouble, and we talked and everything and then I was going to go to find Virginia, but Alice said she just wanted to talk to me for Virginia's sake since they were such good friends. But I knew that was a crock of shit. Then in a few seconds, we were kissing."

"She jumped on you like that?"

"Well, no," he admits, "I kissed her, but she was so close like she wanted me to and she didn't do anything to resist."

"Wow!"

"Pretty odd, huh? But where were you?" David asks and his face is void of suspicion.

"I was upstairs with Alice and Virginia for a while and then Alice went away and Virginia started talking to me about how it was to live in the Quarter and to live with you, that it must be a nightmare, and then, almost abruptly, she said she was going to the kitchen and she never returned. But then Alice did, and she and I ended up sleeping together."

"No shit!?"

"Yeah no shit," James says, smiling and proud, but not for sleeping with Alice, rather for the genuine excitement David takes in the sensationalism, diverting the subject to a safer place. David is pumped, ready to continue the party. They're at a pay phone now:

"That's pretty fucking cool. Alice must have been pretty fucked up. Well, shit, we had dropped a couple tabs earlier. Hey man, lets get Scott over here and get some beers at Kagan's. Let me try to get ahold of him."

"No, actually, I want to get back and clean up and maybe go out to play."

"Might as well keep it rolling?"

"No, I've had enough fun, need to get back out there, you know."

"Alright, that's cool man," and David is obviously disappointed. Which is probably a good thing, under the circumstances.

VIII

Walking exhaust-blackened sidewalks back to the apartment, he examines different perspectives of the conversation. For a moment he has the feeling David knows what has happened between Virginia and himself. But he can't help feel confident that if David knew, he would have come out with it. This puts the first thought out of his head, well not completely, rather sets it to the back of his mind, silent and gangrenous. He thinks about Virginia. About her having sex with David. But then he cannot picture it clearly in his mind. Their two bodies can't approximate lovemaking. He can't even picture Virginia at all now. He tries to envision her face, but the image won't come into focus, moves around with the movement of his imagination. He needs to see her again, now, and look at her and etch an imagine of her in his mind to last forever. He worries how he will get to see her again. He hurries into the apartment, he searches David's things: corners of magazines, matchbooks, sheet music crumpled and browned and sandy on the floor near his mattress. He can call information. Virginia what? What is her address? But she is not home. Mid stream a long piss, his head full of proposed conversations with David which might get him closer to Virginia, and the phone rings. He runs to it, unshook, a drop dampening a spot on his white underpants. As he takes the receiver from the hook, he sees a number scratched in the thick latex paint on the wall, he'll soon find out it's Virginia's.

"Hello?"

"Hi, James."

"Hello," he says, not knowing who is on the other side. Is it Virginia? He cannot tell with the beating of his heart in his ears.

"Hi, it's Alice. What are you doing?"

"Nothing."

"Nothing?" playfully.

"Well, I just got here. I was going to go out."

"Were you? Do you want me to let you go?"

"No, no, that's all right. It's good that you called."

"Good, why?"

"I don't know. It is just good, because of last night."

"What about last night?"

"I don't know. *What about last night*?"

"It was crazy."

"Yeah."

They are silent. Then:

"Did you tell Virginia?"

"Why, what does she have to do with it?" Alice says, and James realizes that he doesn't know any of the rules of the game.

"Well, you know, because she was there with me, before."

"Actually she's still here. Would you like to talk to her?"

He certainly does, but he doesn't want to seem desperate, and tries to think of some plausible reason why he would need to speak to her. Unable to think of anything he says:

"Does she want to talk to me?"

"Yes, here she is."

"Hello."

"Hello, how are you?"

"Fine, very fine, beautiful day, isn't it? How are you?"

He hears her voice as if he has never heard it before. He says:

"I'm fine. Are you sick or anything?"

"No, just unbelievably thirsty."

"Drink some water."

"Actually that is supposed to make you drunk, again."

"No it isn't. It cleans you out faster."

"No, it recirculates the alcohol."

"Right."

"It's true. Are you hung over?"

"No, not at all. I really didn't drink a lot. Did you?"

"I had some shots earlier, at Bons Temps, before we picked you up."

"Tequila, I thought I might have smelled it on your breath."

Virginia says abruptly, very impersonally:

"So, what do you think about last night, the way I was?"

"You mean drunk?"

"No, I mean upstairs in Alice's room."

"Drunk."

"I was not drunk."

"Right, you were very drunk, or else you would not have acted as you did." He doesn't completely believe this, but wants to her it from her.

"No . . . yes, maybe the drinking had something to do with it happening how and when, but I really wanted to do what I did."

There is a short pause.

"Well."

"Well, so what do you think?"

"About what?"

"About last night."

"Nothing, really," he lies.

"Nothing?"

"Nothing."

"But you don't really think that it was just because I was drinking?"

"Well, I might, should I?"

"I really wanted to do what I did. I was thinking about you even before last night? What about you, were you drunk?"

"No, not the least bit."

"Then why did you sleep with Alice?"

James chokes quietly. He feels guilty and stupid. He says:

"I don't know."

"You weren't drunk?"

"Maybe a little."

"Well?"

He is desperate. He does not know how he wants to explain this. Should he explain there was no penetration? He is instantly sick with regret that he did not think of some explanation beforehand. "Well, you were all over me and I did not think that you were serious and then when Alice came . . . you know . . . I just . . ."

"Oh, right."

He is not satisfied with his response. It just came from his mouth. He continues:

"Really, you got me all worked up."

"That's sick," she says, which sounds exaggerated and ostentatious.

"Sick?"

"Yes, that's very sick, actually."

"What do you mean?"

"Do you know what Alice was doing downstairs, while we were upstairs?"

"Yes."

"You know!?"

"Yes."

"God that is sick! And then she went up and slept with you," she says, apparently Alice is no longer in earshot.

"It's not that sick."

"Yes it is."

"Well, you're no better."

"No, I wanted to kiss you. To be kissing you."

"Yes, but then you went downstairs and slept with David."

Virginia gasps; her tone becomes sterling, "I did not sleep with David! I have never slept with David!"

James is dumbfounded by this proclamation. He had heard stories, and he had walked in on them and then last night, the late night shower.

"Never?"

"Never. Ever! Ever! Oh god, that bastard," and she gags and cries in disgust. James isn't sure what to think. Is she lying? What kind of made in Hollywood drama is this?

"You did not sleep with David last night?"

"No!"

He chooses not to say anything about seeing her in the towel. (He has his own set of peculiar rules, and it would be very confrontational) He asks:

"Are you sure you weren't too drunk and can't remember?"

"No, I know, I did not. I know everything that happened. We were just making out, and he started to try to undress me and I told him not to and we got in a fight."

"Oh," he says, scarcely audible.

"He's such a bastard."

"Well."

"God this all makes me sick," she says, determinedly displaying her immaculacy, and he feels that her tone contrives to hide the whole truth, which is what is really making her sick. He tries not to think of it more and says nothing, hurrying to think of something else to talk about. Like sand escaping a closed fist, most of it will, but never all of it. Within a few minutes Virginia recovers from her distress, and they are without much to talk about. He hangs up the phone, and all that he can remember saying and Virginia saying, he replays in his mind and he sits at the kitchen table, ill, trying not to think about what he cannot stop thinking about. Not wanting to stay inside with thoughts that conspire to agitate him, nor having the interest to go out to play, he sits at the table and rests his elbows on the tabletop and scratches his oily forehead. Shiny with oil, his fingertips smell of smoke. He goes into the bathroom and draws a tub and slips into the water. He knows with great, solid disappointment he will feel sick, regretful and humiliated afterwards.

IX

In a secluded courtyard, James sits staring at the flagstones beneath his feet, late afternoon waning, pigeons coming in and out of his fixed stare, regarding him with their black, blank eyes. This would be a good place in a more entertaining novel, or at least a novel about a more entertaining person, where he would commence onto some long poignant monologue. Relate his woes to us. And we'd have great sympathy for him. Maybe laugh a moment, bittersweetly, as he makes some witty comment about his unfortunate circumstances. But this is not going to happen, now. His life is not being written for someone else's amusement, and particularly not his own, and the first draft is crude. James Buck has only a little more knowledge of the cause of his agony as the pigeons do about his feet. Is it psychological or physiological? Would his misery subside if he were better looking, or had a little more money? Would his days seem less tedious if he were among more interesting people doing exciting things, exchanging clueful opinions with competent dialogue? Would he have less time to stew in his own self-loathing, if there was a chase scene, or a fight scene, or some comedic predicament to iron out, or a match-strike-to-inferno romance to get swept up in?

Or is there nothing more the matter with him than erratic disruptions in the distribution of the chemicals squirting around his meddlesome mind? Not enough to power up this one lobe; too much burning up another. Could he pop a pill and all his problems cease to be? Wake up, medicate, masticate, fornicate, go to bed, wake up, repeat. He is not cultured enough, knows nothing of the slings, the arrows, or the seas of troubles of other men. He has not seen or read or been exposed to enough to self diagnose his torment. He is almost entirely self-educated through sight and sound, but to see and hear the self is the most challenging. The moment he identifies an emotion, singles it out, pulls it forward for better observation, it slips to another corner of his mind and appears changed. It is useless and exasperating. Is the emotion causing the pain, or is the pain causing the emotion?

His violin sits closed up in its case at his feet. He is surprised to find himself sitting in the dark, as if awakening from a trance. He walks to the apartment, which he finds empty. He is not sleepy, and before he can avoid it, he is up against the bathroom sink with his jeans off, passionately masturbating over the rim of the basin with the tap running, desperate for some relief.

X

Sunday morning, he takes a plastic bag of potatoes from the top of the icebox. He washes four under the tap and knives the eyes out and slices them into cubes. He knows David will wake hungry and cannot, but more importantly, would never *try* to cook. He puts the cubes into a skillet of hot oil and slices onion in and sprinkles with salt and pepper. The pot crackles over the fat flame and beads of water burst. While these fry, he pokes his head into the front room. David is balled up on his mattress. James takes his violin from its case back to the table. He carries the notebook and pencil as well. The potatoes cook loudly, and the smell is warm and salty. He stirs them with a wooden tablespoon.

He feels fresh and capable. If during the night he has his dreams, dreams in which he can fly and everything is in vivid color and his head is clear and feelings circulate thorough out his body smoothly, he would usually wake this way, feeling he could do anything. A quick walk outside can take this away, of course, he knows that, and so he sits back in the plastic chair and tries to hold on to it; picks up his pencil and tries to put some of it into words. He can recall the green fields and thick, solid bodies of water, soaring over tall trees, standing high in them and everything looking so beautiful from this vantage point -everything alive and healthy. The wind sweeps across his face, and he trembles with exhilaration. He, now, can remember the cool of the air against his skin as if it all had actually happened.

Some mornings there's a sedate first moment when he wakes and is unable to believe it wasn't actually real. As though in the night, while he did not need his consciousness for himself, a large bird borrowed it. He wants to write this out. Describe this. Maybe so he can carry it with him through the day, make music with it. But he can't.

David comes into the room and takes the milk jug from the icebox and tips it back, pulling out long drinks. He offers milk to James. James hands him a cup and David pours it full. James holds his slanting pencil over the notebook. David politely asks if he can take the violin from the chair so that he can sit and James nods. David gingerly removes the cased instrument from the seat and props it against the wall, there is some reverence in the ways he handles it, it must be noted.

"Kagans?"

"Yup," David replies, he's hung pretty hard.

"Drink it dry?"

"Pretty much," the pain in his head is visible all over his face.

"Remember those girls from the bowling alley, they were there."

"You hook up?"

"Sorta, the taller one. I gave her a couple bumps and she blew me in the bathroom?"

"Bumps?"

"Little nose candy," David says with irritation, sometimes James' naivety is more than he can stand. He changes the subject.

"How long will those take?" David automatically assumes there are enough potatoes for the both of them. James looks in on them, gives them a stir, says:

"About another five minutes."

"Good, I'm going to take a dump."

James stirs the lighter potatoes down. When David gets his pants down, the phone rings. James places a cover over the crackling pan, lowers the flame, goes to answer it.

"Yes?"

"Is David there?"

"Yes."

"Oh, James."

"Yes, hi."

"Hi, how are you?"

"Good, how about you? Do you want to talk to David?"

"No, not really."

"Then why did you ask for him?"

"Just in case it was *him*?"

"Oh."

"So what are you doing? Is David there, did you say?"

"Yes. He's in the bathroom."

"Oh."

"What do you want?"

"Actually, I just wanted to talk to you."

"What about?"

"Nothing, god! What's the matter with you?"

"Nothing, why?"

"Why are you like that?"

"Like what?"

"Like you are now."

"I don't know. I didn't know I was like anything." But knows what he is like, trying to desensitize himself, insulate himself.

"Don't you want to talk to me?"

James lowers his voice. "David doesn't know about that night, does he?"

"I don't think so."

"Are you still together with him in his mind?"

"I don't know."

"You don't know?"

"I guess; we haven't talked about anything."

"Why not?"

"I don't know."

"I think you should talk to him about the two of you first, then we will talk."

"God!" she says.

"Anyway, he's coming out. Do you want to talk to him?"

"Not really."

"I can't very well talk to you with him here."

"I'll just hang up."

"Who would I say called?"

"A friend."

"Do you want to talk to him or not?"

"I guess."

"Fine."

David comes out of the bathroom, and James changes his tone to a disinterested, polite one. "Well, okay, okay, yeah, David is coming out now, here he is," and he hands the phone to David, who greets Virginia in an exaggerated manner.

The potatoes are overdone, and he takes them off the burner, scoops them into equal portions onto large plates and sits them on the table. He takes the bottle of ketchup from the icebox and places it with a bounce on the plastic tabletop. He squeezes out long lines onto his breakfast and starts eating. David hangs the phone up with a clang and sits at the table.

"What did she want?" James asks casually.

"Nothing really, just wanted to see if I could come over today."

"Doing something?" James asks, wanting David's answer to reveal Virginia's intent.

"I think so, maybe go to the zoo."

The zoo! What a place to end a relationship.

"When you leaving?"

"After I eat and take a bath. What d' you got going?"

"I don't know. Might go out to the park to play."

"Nice," he grumbles, his head hung over his food as he scoops it in, his long tangled hair creating a shroud.

David eats his food, leaves the plate on the table and then bathes in a noisy hurry. He leaves the tub filthy. James swishes it out with hot, then ice-cold water, then draws a fresh, deep bath. David steps in and swabs his hairy armpits with a smacky deodorant stick and says he is leaving, pulls the door into the jamb tight.

James undresses and slides down into the tub and lies back with his eyes closed. She will probably tell him today about how she doesn't want to see him any more; probably made it sound as though they are just getting together for some fun, so that he wouldn't expect anything. He'll be pissed when he comes in, though. Or maybe not, maybe he'll be a casual as he is about everything. Something tells me he wont. It's a one sided street. Seen it before. He dips his head back and wets his hair to shampoo; his lips almost moving with the words as he thinks them. She may tell him about us. He starts brushing his teeth and rolls abstract thoughts of Virginia and David, and Virginia and himself in his head and then spits. Well, whatever happens happens, he thinks, trying to pass it off casually. He draws a cup of cold water from the spout, rinses and then lays back. Should I have a long bath? he asks himself. No, maybe a quick bath will be better. I'll get out right now. But why not have a long bath? What does it hurt? Nothing. The bath water is gray dishwater and it laps cool against the orange ring of scum around the tub. He wants to get out, but his overeager penis grows at the notion for a longer stay. And soon it is incorrigibly set on having a long bath. He is about to comply, when the phone rings. He hesitates to answer. But he thinks it might be Virginia. He jumps out and runs dripping wet into the front room with a towel in his hand.

"Hello?"

"James?"

"Yes."

"Hello, again."

"Hi."

"How are you?"

"Good."

"Good. Is David still there?"

"No, he has already left."

"Good, then you can talk."

"Yes, I can."

"So, what's your plans for the day?"

"Nothing, I'll probably go to the park."

"That's not nothing. That's good. To play, right?"

"Yes."

"I like how you can spend so much time alone like that."

"It might sound good to other people."

"It is good."

"Yes, but it's out of necessity, just as often as want."

She doesn't venture into this. "Did David say anything?"

"No, just that he was going to see you and you two were going to the zoo or something."

"Yeah," she says, not expounding.

"Are you going to tell him that you no longer wish to see him?"

"I think."

"You think?"

"It is hard."

"Yes, but you need to do it. It is not good for you to stay like you are with him."

"Yes, but let's not talk about it."

"Fine, but I don't want you calling me all the time wanting to talk when you haven't resolved everything with David."

Virginia is offended. "Fine, I think I'll go then."

"Fine, but make up your mind about what you want to do. I'll tell him if you want."

"I just want to talk to you, get to know you."

"Why?"

"I don't know. I like you. I like to talk to you."

"Really?

"Don't you like talking with me?"

"What does it matter?"

"God! Maybe I was wrong about you, you're an ass."

"I'm just serious. Are you going to tell David today?"

"What difference does it make to you?"

"Fine, none, I guess I'll go."

"Whatever makes you happy."

"All right," and he hangs the phone up, quietly. He feels his heart beat warm and fast as he sets the headset gently down, and then he starts to the bathroom and the phone rings. He determines not to answer it, but after the fourth then the fifth ring, it's metal school bell shrill impossible to ignore, he picks it up.

"Look, I'm sorry."

"Sorry?"

"Yes, It's just that I don't know what to do about David, and I was hoping you would help me cope with him and get through it."

"Well, I'd like to help you, but it seems you're taking a lot of interest in me and none in dissolving your relationship with him. I don't know David as well as you know him. I don' t know what he is capable of. Anything, if you ask me. I've seen his temper."

"He's an asshole, sometimes I'm afraid of what he might do. But I wish we could just get to know each other without dealing with him."

"Yes, but . . ."

"But nothing. I would rather talk to you," and her voice becomes low and intimate.

"David should be over there anytime, now."

"You're right. I got to get dressed."

"Well, then, I'll let you off. I've drip dried standing here and water is all over the place."

"Water?"

"I got out of the tub to answer the phone and I was dripping wet."

"You don't have any clothes on?"

"No, butt naked."

"You think I can come over there?"

He can picture her smile, her playful look. "Nope. You've got company."

"You sure?" She persists. "I could get a cab."

"No, I got to go. I'll talk to you later."

"All right, then, goodbye. Have a good day."

"I will."

"Goodbye."

"Bye."

He does not go back into the gray tub water. He puts his notebook and pencil into the box compartment in the lid of his violin case. He carries the case out with him, the pins in the handle squeaking between each step. It is a sunny, beautiful day. The sunshine springs off the green grass of Woldenburg Park, inviting his reticent spirit to dance. He has a moment of faith that everything will go well. He starts with some light-hearted Vivaldi.

XI

He works a long Monday in a thick vapor under a gray sky. The white paint on the roof deck stays tacky all afternoon, and his fingers stick together, and the brush handle sticks in his grip. They eat their lunches, swinging their legs from the tailgate of Leo's truck parked in the lawn of the big, uptown house. Leo says:

"I might have to let you off for the week, Wednesday. I've got nothing really for you to do after this and we should finish by then."

"Well, that's okay."

"I'm thinking we'll have a big job by the middle of next week."

"Sure."

"Business usually gets slow come winter, but not this early."

"Don't worry about finding work for me." He is thinking about yesterday in the park, in five hours he made eleven dollars.

"No, I'll get work, as I always get work," Leo says and then bites into his flat burger. A beautiful, young lady walks past on the sidewalk. Her hips swing, her arms glide and her breasts float on the undulation of her stride. The breeze carries the scent of her hair, sandal wood maybe, or something like it. James thinks of Virginia. Leo shakes his head slowly with mock suffering. He says:

"Oh my god! Look at that ass."

"Not too bad," James says, mentally comparing it to Virginia's.

The uncertainty of everything gnawing at his guts. Will she try to call him? Should he call her, from the safety of a pay phone?

*

David and James arrive at the apartment at the same time and climb the front steps one behind the other. The phone rings as they are opening the door and James picks it up. As he expects, it is Virginia.

"Hello?"

"James? Hi it's me."

"Hi, oh yes, he is here," James says.

"What are you saying? Is David there?"

"Okay let me get him," he says. She understands what he is doing. She says:

"I'll talk to you later, but I think you're being stupid."

"Okay, all right, bye." David is at his right shoulder.

They talk a long time, and James listens from where he sits doodling on the table, thinking how David said nothing about himself and Virginia Sunday night when he came in, nor this morning as he was leaving for work. But that was a short moment, barely long enough to get into conversation. He analyzes the things David says, but nothing seems to address the subject. He reluctantly gives up on hearing anything important and repairs to the safety of a warm bath.

In the profound silence after the running of the tub water, he can only hear murmuring. He bathes quickly, scratching off specks and scabs of paint with his fingernails and rubbing them with a hand cloth until his skin is red. He wishes they had a shower attachment for the tub fixture. He hears David's voice rise with laughter. He cleans thoroughly and climbs out and pulls on clean, broken-thread soft, faded denim jeans and sits on his mattress with his back against the wall, holding his violin in his hands, examining the tiniest cracks in the finish, looking for any structural concerns, there are none. He hears an odd tone, now, in David's voice. It suggests something. Maybe David doesn't want to tell me about it. He's hiding his feelings. I was too hard on Virginia, he thinks. He strains his ears to scrutinize the sound and the words and then a knock breaks on the front door. It is Scott. James lets him in, asks how he's doing. Scott says, with humored flagrancy:

"Well the niggers haven't got me yet."

David tells Virginia that Scott is present, and that they are about to go look at a motorcycle for sale and then he hangs up the phone. James realizes it is abrupt. This is something to think about. The three young men sit on the wood floor, fuzzy with lint. Scott says:

"If I can talk him down five hundred or six, then I'd take it."

"What I ought to do is buy a bike and not fix my car," David says.

"If you like this one . . . " Scott suggests.

"I'd have to sell my car first."

James fantasizes having a motorbike. A BMW or a Triumph, an old one, of course, steel and chrome -he so fucking sick of plastic! He could spin over to pick up Virginia; they could drive along the river under great oaks and the black cypress, past the old plantations, under the sugar cane chutes; they could ride out to the Gulf Coast, a bag of towels, lotion, sunglasses and paperback books, lay out in the sunshine; Virginia stretched out beside him in a neat little swimsuit, her brown skin drinking the sun.

"Your insurance would be a lot cheaper," Scott informs David.

"Really."

"Shit yeah."

"Well, my car was actually insured through my dad's name."

James asks, "Why?"

"Because, it would have cost thirteen hundred dollars a year for basic liability if it was in my name."

"Wow! Have you had a lot of wrecks?"

"No! That's the standard rate."

Scott says:

"I pay twelve fifty for the car I drive."

"That's absolutely ridiculous. That's more than your rent. How can it possibly cost that much? Hell, in Missouri, you can buy a different secondhand car every year for that price," James says.

"You can here too."

"It's scandalous. Why not just buy another car when, if you do, get in a wreck?"

"It's the law, you have to have insurance. It's a dick-sucking racquet is what it is!"

Scott shores it up with a "True dat!"

David and Scott ask James if he wants to come along. He says that he doesn't, wants to work on new music. They go out the door, dragging it swiftly to the threshold, another whisper of flooring swept away.

He thinks: I could drive her out to dinner, she'd hold tight to my waist with her arms wrapped around. It kind of pains him imaging the freedom he'd have. But how could he ever get that kind of money. Then gas and insurance and maintenance.

Maybe I should call her. No, I'll let her call.

He takes out a potato and washes it in the sink and jabs it with a fork, butters it with his bare hands, rubbing the butter into the skin, then folds it neatly into a sheet of foil. He puts chili on the stovetop. He sits at the plastic table with his violin. Thinks of something to compose. He thinks of the streetcar's thud, thud, thud over the buried tracks and the breeze blowing in through the windows as the car slides along swiping at the leafy branches of trees guarding the tracks. He wants to capture the atmosphere of the sweet morning ride with sounds that are light and cool and simple and invigorating. Then the phone rings:

"Hello, James?"

"Hi, yes, how are you?"

"Good."

"That's good."

"David is gone isn't he?"

"He certainly is."

"Am I disturbing you?"

"No, not at all, I just started cooking my supper."

"Do you want me to let you go?"

"No, I'm baking a potato in the oven. It'll take a while."

"Why don't you microwave it?"

"We don't have one."

"A true testament to your 'starving artist' status."

"I guess."

"I figured David would be gone by now, so I called to talk to you."

"Well, you figured right, he's gone. Went to look at a motorcycle with Scott."

"That's what he said."

"I think he wants to buy one, himself, get rid of his car."

"He'd get killed for sure."

"You don't like motorcycles, then?"

"No, it's just that David is reckless."

"Yes, he is."

"I wouldn't ride on one with him."

"Would you ride with me, if I had one?"

"I don't know, I guess. If you could drive it."

"Well, of course."

"Have you ever driven one?"

"No."

They are green lovers and so is their talk. Unlike scenes from a movie where teenage lovers exchange dialogue written by writers twice their age, they aren't saying much of anything; they are just happy to hear each other's voices. Picking the subjects of their discourse as though they were little berries from bushes in an unknown forest. When they find especially sweet ones, they gobble them up, an hour goes by quickly. James remembers he has a potato in the oven.

"Could you hold on one second, have to check my potato?"

He squeezes the potato and it gives in and he pulls it out and unwarps it and the steam heats his face as he opens it, spoons butter between the halves and salts it before spooning the chili on heavy, the moisture in the chili is burned off, it is thick. A mason jar grows green onion in the windowsill and he clips the ends off with a scissor. He goes to the phone, blowing a fork full. The butter melts into a yellow puddle in the bottom of the bowl. It's too hot. She hears the phone picked up.

"How's your potato?"

"Hot!"

"Not much of a meal."

"No it's great. It's got butter and chili and some salt and green onion. It's pretty damned delicious, and cheap. Can't see how anyone could ever starve with potatoes cheap as they are."

"You can't live off potatoes alone."

"Wanna bet?"

"You know, I don't think I've ever baked a potato. In a oven I mean."

"Really, that's interesting, because I don't think I've ever cooked one in a microwave. But I've eaten ones that have been cooked in a microwave. They're much better from the oven."

"I can't say I've ever thought about it. They all seem the same to me."

"Trust me, now that I've mentioned it, you'll be able to tell. It's subtle, but it makes a difference."

"Nobody I know ever uses the oven. It takes too long."

"Sometimes you must make the time, to do something right."

"For a potato?" she playfully chides.

"For a potato, for anything, what's the big hurry? Why does everything have to be in an instant?"

"I guess that's how I feel about David."

"What, that you should put him in the oven, but it would be quicker in the microwave?"

"You know what I mean, wise ass."

"Maybe I don't."

"I can't solve David in an instant?"

When David comes in later that night he tells James about the motorbike. Says he wishes he could buy it and go pick up 'the girl' and drive down to the coast. James is disgusted, both by David having the same fantasy and, also, the same girl in mind for the fantasy. David asks:

"Did Virginia call?"

"No," he says, knowing that Virginia will the same.

XII

The owners of the large uptown house let Leo talk them into running electric to the deck, even though he's not an electrician. He warned them about the outrageous rates the local electricians are charging these days. And nothing frightens multi-millionaires more than outrageous rates. Leo's got his truck backed onto the front lawn and they are unloading tools. James gazes long at their handiwork so impressively high atop the beautiful home, and he has the wholesome satisfaction of knowing for years it will peer down on the oak-guarded avenue. He tries to imagine what the place looks like on the inside. By the suggestion of the silver lunch tray of egg salad and tuna can sandwiches and iced sweet tea, he imagines its 99 to perfect even on the hottest day of the year. Jack pulls into the drive and climbs from his truck with his grip on three iron-heavy wrenches.

"Thought I saw a couple two-bit carpenters I recognized."

"Well, keep my wages, I'd a swore I'd never see them wrenches again, you long-legged pipe screw."

"You getting some work out this jack leg?" Jack asks James.

"A little," he replies easily. It's interesting how these young men revert, if briefly, to a tone and vernacular of several generations before them, as a form of amusement to themselves.

"Passed by yesterday and saw you guys, but didn't have time to stop," changing back to the more typical revised edition Southern lilt.

Leo puts his paint-speckled, dust-caked work boot on the welted bumper and casually rests his elbow on the tailgate.

"How's work?" Jack asks.

"Pretty slow," Leo says, looking at the big mansion with faint bewilderment.

"Yeah?"

Then Leo says:

"Looks like I might give ol' lefty here a couple days off."

"What are you doing on this place, now?"

"Running conduit to the roof deck, today. We done some repairs to it earlier and gave it a new coat of paint."

"So, you're doing electrical now?"

"Hell, I can do it all . . . and for half what them other yah-who's get."

"Yep," Jack quickens, and he takes a look over the manicured grounds, warily, changes the subject. "So, you're getting some time off?" he asks James.

"Couple days."

Jack observes:

"This is a pretty large home, you'd think they'd have work year around."

"Just about," Leo admits. "They have another big house on Magazine. Full time maintenance man between the two places. They got properties on the Gulf Coast too. Got more money than they know how to get rid of, but tighter than a rusted bolt."

They all three size up the estate: gas fueled lamppost, sago palms, furnished front porch. Leo says:

"Yeah, boys, if we had half the money these people had we wouldn't have a problem in the world. Hell you could sell this house and never work a day again in your life."

They are all quiet a moment.

"Yeah, it must be nice," Leo says, inconclusively, pending greater reflection.

For an instant James asks himself if he shouldn't apply his talent to more reliably profitable pursuits. But the question doesn't hold long, there's no doubt in his heart whatsoever. He asks Leo:

"Sure, but then what would you do with yourself?"

"Absolutely nothing, that's the point," Leo says with the wry conviction.

"Well, boys, I gotta get. I'll let you guys back to work on your dream home here."

Leo and James work into the evening, and the inhabitants never stir, if they are even home, the maid clears the lunch service.

David is sitting on the floor against the wall, smoking a cigarette and talking into the phone, when James gets home. He emits a high, artificial laugh, and James knows who reluctantly hangs on the other end. She must have called for me and he answered, he earnestly believes.

"James just came in," David explains, Virginia tells David to say hello. He is pleased but it is awkward so he says:

"Tell her hello, too," very casually and disinterestedly.

He takes a short bath. During supper, he attempts to make some notes, but finds himself gazing quietly at the television set, stewing in a lukewarm glow. As the panada grows cold and rank, he drags himself into bed. He passes another night wanting something he cannot have; wanting to write something he can not write, or play something he is likewise incapable, yet, of playing.

XIII

With a week's wages folded into his leather wallet and the long, leisurely days before him, he stands on neutral ground spirited. He gets onto an uptown car. As it chugs pleasantly along, he closely examines the area: the streets and the houses, the stores, the bars. He recognizes a gray church. He pulls on the buzzer cable to be let off the next stop. The first cross street he comes to, he turns left and walks down, slowly. He is very dirty from work and does not think for a second about going up to see Virginia, if he should find her house. He wants only to make certain he knows where it is, should ever he get invited to come visit. It might be on an occasion late in the evening, and he will want to arrive quickly and easily.

The house is a enormous, modern house. The high, steep roof slices a wound into the low, humid sky. A stain grade wood terrace sticks out like an empty shelf. It is devoid of any trance of craft from four millennia of human endeavor. It will need tearing down come its next paint job. He can clearly see the front door. He thinks about sitting back in a shrub in the odd chance Virginia might come out onto the porch. But just as he's deciding against it, the front door swings open and he falls onto the sidewalk as though a drill sergeant ordered him drop an' give 'm fifty. He kind of smacks the wind out of his chest, and he is short of breath in fear of being caught. What a psycho she would think him if she saw him now? He crawls to the front bumper of the parked car that conceals him from view and he can see the porch. A tall, dark haired, infuriatingly handsome man comes bouncing down the stairs. It is unmistakable he is very happy about something. He is coming across the street. Quickly, James gets into a crouching position, pretends he's doing something legitimate, checking the tire pressure. The car chirps and his heart nearly stops. He quickly changes to his shoelace. Just as the man comes within a foot, as soon as James is sure the guy could see his hands making the last tug on his knotted laces, he stands up. The man is in his late thirties, maybe, full head of perfect hair, gigantic, clueless smile, like a personal trainer, or a cruise ship bartender. He says hello. James nods in reply, walks on, burning up on the inside thinking whoever saw the guy off at the front door might still be watching, and, also, who is this impossibly perfectly looking guy? Who was he invisiting? His age puts him in the catbird seat exactly right between mother and daughter.

He sleeps through half of his first day off, then spends a good portion sitting at the table, slowly eating brunch, thinking about Virginia and the man leaving the house. He takes a short bath. He feels fresh and goes out with his violin.

He hikes to the public library and spends an hour listening to Itzhak Perlman; the music is quick and lively, folk polkas. He tries to imagine the mysterious man (there is only a small black and white photograph of Perlman in the tape jacket), sawing and fingering. He wants to hear the music live, to feel the sound move through the air. He switches genres to the Bing Crosby Big Band. He is toe tapping, picturing the era when musicians worked hard to find harmony, to explore the breadth of harmony, and worked harder to make it look easy, feel easy and natural. Horn blowers and guitar pickers, sweating and contorting like middle-aged men lovemaking. The early wholesome but promiscuous women dreaming of lovemaking; their bright eyes on the musicians, huge and batting, timely. He plays the cassettes of Dizzy Gillespie and Louis Armstrong and Duke Ellington.

Afterwards, he impatiently walks to a cafe in the Quarter and fishes a quarter from the bottom of his pocket to ring up Virginia. He becomes heavy with sadness listening to her mother's voice. Virginia will be out of town for several days, she says. Frozen in the phone booth, his days stretch out far now in front of him, long and empty. He tries to participate in some closing, obligatory small talk, mostly just listening to Virginia's mother say things that simply aren't heard. He sits down at a small wobbly table and hangs his head over his coffee wondering why didn't she tell him she would be going away?

The next afternoon, he shoots pool with Jack. They sit up at the bar talking. A black cloud has moved in and everything is dark and people are up to secret evil things and no one is to be trusted. Jack's a very capable pool player, and multiple defeats have soured James completely. They've been talking about the shit guys talk about when playing pool. Work, women, sports, children. James doesn't really have a job. Doesn't really have a woman. Hates sports. Plans to never have children. Can really only talk about his lack of these things.

"I guess playing the violin is kind of a obsession for me. I'm besot with it. I really don't think about other things. Maybe because I'm young and stupid? I'm just not interested in anything else."

Jack says:

"That's good man. Means you'll probably do well at it."

"I better, it's all I got."

"Don't you have family? Mom, Dad?"

"My family's not like something you have, but rather something you've *had* done *to* you, and then you're always trying to hide the scars from other people."

Jack isn't ready for this kind of announcement. Then really who ever is, especially from someone you barely know. He is confused a moment, does he laugh or offer condolence? James continues in an effort to diffuse things.

"They're a bunch of knuckle heads." Then he jams his pool stick into the clump of solids and sinks the cue ball, but adds, "except my sister, I think about her often, kind of miss her."

"That sucks man," Jack says, maybe for Buck's parents, maybe for the scratch, maybe because he misses his sister.

"I told you I was horrible at this game."

"Just takes some practice. You play much?"

"My first time."

"You've got to be kidding me."

"Nope."

"Wow."

They pull on their beers between turns. James says:

"I'm really disappointed Virginia is going to be gone the whole time I'm off."

"Yeah that sucks"

Jack says yeah that sucks to a whole lot of things, without expounding to any length thereafter.

"I don't understand why she would leave town? I told her I'd be getting some time off."

"Where'd she go?"

"Down to the coast, I guess her father lives down there; her parents are separated."

"That must suck for her, then. Maybe she didn't have a choice?"

A good point, how selfish not to think of this. You're always thinking of yourself first. Ease up on her a bit, he decides. But it doesn't take the loneliness away. He's draining off pints quickly. Patrons pour quarters into the jukebox, the tables begin to fill, and the night comes on. Five or six rounds into it and all the plans he had for his meager, and for a while, only, paycheck are washed away. He's buying Jack drinks, any girl with a pair of legs drinks, and then shots when someone spews some nonsense which when you're drunk sounds important enough to make tomorrow's front page headline.

David comes into the bar sometime after midnight with an

odd-looking, thin girl on a leather leash, with a white, pretty face, and orange and green hair and black army boots laced to her knobby knees. David is drunk and slurring his words. He says that this is his girl slave, blank blank something. James just smiles a fake, listens and watches the girl giggle and examine her new tattoo, still raw and bleeding; pinching the meat of her upper arm with her thin hand. A lot of ink in these trouble times! James earnestly despises David at this moment. With intense drunken resolve, he determines to press out a conclusion between him and Virginia, hurriedly.

He coolly asks David:

"Where's Virginia?"

"Fuck if I know."

James eyes David over the rim of his pint of beer with loathing, David doesn't even notice.

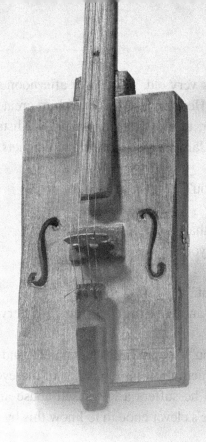

Part III

I

In the first week of October, the rendezvous begin. September seared into memory, the last of the heat abated. The first one is at Café Beignet, and James has to send the waiter away twice as he is early, and Virginia is casually late. He sits facing the street, and she draws her chair back, gently, and smiles at him with deep rose red lips and tucks a lock behind her ear with a habitual stroke. She wears a knitted, violet sweater with a low-cut collar, her chest cinnamon stick. She smells like clean clothes. Two, tiny bronzed earrings hang from her earlobes; they look very old. The tender afternoon softens the many colors of her hair. Her smooth face gives him great contentment. He wants to touch her, to cross an immeasurable distance. The waiter comes, again, and James orders coffee and beignets. Virginia is easy and calm.

"So how are you?"

"Good."

"Glad to hear that."

"And how are you?"

"Great."

"You look great."

"Thank you," and she smiles at him. He nervously tears up a paper napkin.

"And so do you," she adds, affectionately, and places her hand atop his for a moment until he looks her in the eye. It is almost as though she knows he suffers a lot of self-abuse and wants to help alleviate some. She's clever enough to know this by what she can see in his eyes?

The waiter places the coffee and beignets and water glasses upon the table. James tips the spilt coffee in the saucer back into the cup. The beignets are hot and soft and fold under their bite, and the confectioner's sugar is soft on their lips.

"My mother used to bring me here all the time when I was a little girl."

James self-consciously dabs the powdery sugar from his lips. She has gotten only the smallest hint of sugar on her top lip and casually wipes it clean with her tongue. This is not new to her. She had suggested they come here.

"We had a house on Royal Street then."

James is fascinated, and Virginia is matter-of-fact.

"It was above the antique shop that's still there."

"Why did you move?"

"My father hated it. Especially as the tourists became more of a problem. He simply hates the Quarter now."

"Really. Why?"

"He thinks it's overrun with 'faggots and tourists'," she air quotes.

"There's some truth, but it is still an extraordinary place. How long ago did you live there?"

"A long time ago, I was about eight or nine."

James is sad that she still doesn't still live in Royal Street. But he is genuinely impressed that she once had. As though, it somehow carried some significance. As though, it made her more real. As though, it made the Quarter more real.

"And then when they opened Woldenburg, we would go for walks along the river."

"That sounds lovely."

"It was very lovely," she says, taking pleasure in his choice of words.

"You must be pretty close with your mother?"

"We used to be?"

"Used to be?"

"Well you know, after the separation we just kind of drifted apart."

"Is it one of those take sides kind of things?"

"Not really. They both are kind of in their separate places right now," she says, without melodrama, matter-of-factly. She sees James has gotten powdered sugar on his nose and she leans over the table to dab it with her napkin. She says:

"Messy, huh? Trick is you hold your breath while you bite."

He would have thought he had been holding his breath this whole time. He envies her calmness, the calmness and confidence that is often found in beautiful people.

They walk along the river in Woldenburg Park. The air is cool and fresh. She stops and sits on the grass. It is surprisingly quiet. They have the park to themselves. She extends her hand to him. She sits Indian style pulling him down with her. He feels awkward sitting on his butt not knowing what to do with his legs.

"I wish we had a big blanket," she says, reclining back, planting her hands into the grass. She looks around at the park, as though it is new to her as well. She says:

"So what's it like playing violin out here?"

"Like playing in an open field to the cows."

"Really."

"Yes, there's no acoustics at all. But I'm fine with that for now. I'm not so conspicuous out here. The passersby are very indifferent. It's harder for me to play in front of one or two people, than to the general public. It's less nerving. I don't like drawing attention to myself. At least not right now. Maybe when I learn to play better."

"You play beautifully. Don't be ridiculous."

He frowns this off, but wants to believe it. He is more inclined now to believe it, than if she had told him at anytime before this day. She notices that he is struggling with this. She leans forward, staring into his downcast eyes, kisses his closed lips. She backs away a little, to examine his expression. She gives him another kiss, as a reiteration, then reclines on her hands, looking at him with her head tilted to the side.

"You're expressions are sometimes very severe."

"And I guess that's not good."

She laughs at his serious delivery.

"No."

He is splitting a blade of grass. She pushes him back and presses against him, staring intently into his eyes. She kisses him passionately several times, each time floating her lips just above his for a moment and stroking them across his like a sable brush, then pressing then firmly. She feels him grow hard against her abdomen and she rolls off, stands up and offers her hand:

"Let's walk."

They walk the river's edge. The wind picks up. Virginia clutches at his arm.

II

They are in an empty bar in Louisiana Avenue. She has suggested they go to see a movie. Virginia is searching through the Lagniappe for show times. She asks:

"So what was the last movie you saw?"

"Jaws."

"You've got to be kidding me? That was like a million years ago."

"It was not only the last movie I saw, but it was the first."

She moves across this staggering fact casually.

"Want to guess what my first movie was?"

"Hmmm," he wants to be mischievous, "Stars Wars?"

"And it was also my all time favorite movie until I was about 11."

"Definitely Stars Wars then."

"Come on be serious. See if you can guess?"

"The Muppet Movie."

"No, think about it, I bet you can guess."

"The Black Stallion."

"Nope, but I did like that movie."

"E.T?"

"Good one, but no."

"Airplane? Up In Smoke? The Shining? Tootsie? Ghostbusters? I don't know there are a billion movies."

"For someone who hasn't seen a movie since Jaws, you sure know a lot of movies."

"I thought you meant in a theater, there was no theater where I grew up, just a video aisle at the store."

"No, I didn't specify where you saw it."

"Oh, in that case, I don't know. I think the last movie I saw was Dances With Wolves. At least that was the last really good movie I saw. Lieutenant Dunbar. Stands with Fists. What was her name? Wonderful actress! Made me almost want to find a girl who couldn't speak the same language."

She punches his arm, "Heh, that's mean."

"I didn't mean it that way. I just think it was very engaging how they had to rely on non-verbal queues. A beautiful movie. It just came out on video right before I came here. I saw it at Miss Langham's house. And anything about Native Americans is interesting to me!"

"Really, I would have never guessed. I'll have to see it some time."

"I have the deepest sympathy for what happened to them. They lived in such naked balance with the land, took only as much as they needed, then were decimated by a God-loving horde of hypocrites."

"Well that's depressing."

"Yes, it is."

"You sure can spoil a moment," she says more playful than plaintive. "But come on you have to guess my favorite movie."

He tries to take her serious, now. He looks into her eyes while he flips movie titles from a decade ago, tries to remember the VHS cassette sleeve artwork. She's smiling big and bouncing a little with excitement, having complete faith he knows her well enough to guess correctly. He says:

"I think I know, considering your age and your theatric flare. I think I know..."

"What is it?"

"There's music in it, that is for sure. Dancing, maybe. Definitely a boy meets girl, girl doesn't want boy, boy wins girl, that sort of plot standard. Could it be....Grease?"

She explodes with joy, grabs his neck.

"Wow, I can't believe you guessed it."

"Me neither, but that was a very good movie."

"I probably saw it a million times."

"So what's my prize for guessing?"

"Prize? I guess that does deserve a prize. I'll buy you another beer."

"Not what I had in mind."

"What *did* you have in mind?"

"I don't know, maybe something more suitably exchanged in private."

She blows him off with playful irritation. Asks:

"Another of what you're drinking?"

"Sure."

She gets another pint from the bar. The barman doesn't ask for proof of age. Nor does anyone ever anywhere. Of the two only he is old enough to drink, just by one year, but no one ever bothers to check.

III

The next day he is in Spanish Plaza, playing automatically, looking down, contemplating vague thoughts that revolve like a carousel of ghost horses. He does not notice the brown-legged Latin American approaching until she speaks. Her delighted accent is almost comical.

"Do you accept traveler's cheques?"

"Sure, food stamps, I owe you's. It's all welcome"

"Wow, you play very good."

"Well, not really. I need a great amount of practice."

She combs her brown hair with her white nailed fingers, her smile replaced momentarily by a frown, as if he forgot his line in the scene, in which she performed her part so well. Her amiable smile returns. She says:

"You need to learn to accept compliments more gratefully."

He is not offended.

"Yes, you're probably right."

"How have you been?"

"Very well."

He lays his violin in his lap and looks up at her with great appreciation. Damarie is gorgeous in her kid glove brown skinned existence, with her tall hips and straight shoulders, her unstrapped breasts low on her chest; her hair coifed to look unfussy and uncoifed.

"And you?" James asks.

"Great. I'm trying to find a costume."

"A costume?"

"For Halloween. I want to be the sea goddess of Atlantis. I want to find sequin pants and put little gold fins on each ankle and gold cups on my breasts."

She literally exposes him to an entirely foreign and seductive world. There is nothing so frivolous and glamorous in his life. The notion to spend the day looking for a costume, at extraordinary cost (which is any cost), is otherworldly. He is fascinated.

"That will be a great costume."

"Do you really think so?"

"I certainly do."

"I might have to have it made. I haven't been able to find anything. What are you doing for Halloween?"

"Nothing, I guess."

"You should come to my party. It's going to be absolutely terrific."

"Well, I . . ."

"Yes, and you could dress like a baroque fiddler. With a red sash and a peculiar hat."

"That is a great idea."

"Please do. It would be perfect."

He nods and tries to appear enthusiastic, but panic-thinks the logistics, i.e. his financial inability. He imagines for a delicious moment, though, the dark night, the party light, the people and the excitement in the cool air.

"So, I've got to go, but here's my number." She slides a personalized card from her slender purse. Her name is pressed deeply into the pulp of the paper in new roman script. She writes out her phone number in ink. We don't need to speculate why a woman like this wouldn't already have the number printed on the card. She extends the card to him and tells him to call her if he can come. He places the card in the little compartment in his case. Virginia approaches just then, carelessly twirling the regular lock of hair. She says:

"Hello."

Damarie smiles, politely, says to James:

"Now, I've got to fly. Ciao."

Virginia doesn't even ask about Damarie. She is cheery, and apologetic for interrupting. Did she see the card change hands? She does not say anything, but James sort of wishes she would. It's a huge breathe of life into his ego.

IV

A white sun glares through the long, silver clouds. Virginia has packed a lunch, and they are spread out on a blanket in Woldenburg. It is unseasonably chilly, and they pull the corners of the blanket up over their shoulders. It has been sometime since they last were together at Spanish Plaza. Virginia has completely averted any attempt to discuss David. She is contemplative, her smile considerably subdued. She turns to him and asks:

"Do you want to go to your apartment?"

"Are you that cold?"

"No, but I feel like going back to your apartment, today," she says. He understands her. He is surprised. She has turned down many advances from him. Then she says:

"Do you have protection?"

"Well, no I don't, I . . ."

"Can we get some?"

"Sure."

"Let's then. Do you have any money?"

He feigns a search of his jeans' pockets, he knows they are empty. She pulls a crumpled bill from her back pocket and gives it to him as she stands up. She bends forward and gives him a kiss and looks him closely in the eyes and says, softly:

"Come on, let's go."

It is quiet, like there is no outside world with the singular exception of the hollow resonate chirping of birds in the courtyard. The deepening late-afternoon light validates the nakedness of the room, reveals the satin of their skin, skin softly taut from being cold. Virginia jumps when his fingers touch against her back. He unclasps her bra. Her chest expands, and he cups her large breasts into his hands, and the hardening nipples become the most remarkable thing he's ever seen. Her brassiere slides down off her arms and falls away, taking with it any uncertainty he has had about her. He is utterly submersed in this moment. He is a trillion warm molecules of collective receptivity: to her skin, to her scent, to her warmth, to her movement. He puts his hand in her crotch, and she burns through her jeans. He goes for the button fly, but she grabs his hand and stops him.

"James, I'm a virgin."

He never entirely believed her when she said she had never slept with David, but now it is impossible not to believe her. She's cautious and reckless all at the same time. She looks at him steadily. Her eyes sparkle like freshly washed gems. She asks:

"Can you be gentle?"

"Very," he whispers as he kisses her very gently, holding her face in his hands. Her eyes tear up a little.

She pulls his shirt over his head, then turns to the bed and takes him into it, and they slide under the sheets. She lies under him, staring into his eyes as deep as she can. He thumbs the button from the flyhole and she lifts herself up, as he tugs her jeans from her hips. He tries to look her naked body over slowly and meticulously, to inscribe into his mind an exact copy, that he can keep indefinitely, of the impossible rectangularness of her torso, the flat, heavy mounds of her chest, the undulation of her pelvis, the olive of her skin, the thin swatch of reddish brown hair. But Virginia is self-conscious, quickly pulls him onto her. He is so hard he can barely feel her as he enters, and she grabs him and pulls him into her. She melts inside as he goes as deep as he can go, with not even a slightest resistance, like a plane entering a cloud. Her body temperature rises a few degrees and she moans softly as she sucks his ears and neck and grabs at his back, shoulders and hips. He is slow and deliberate and intense at first and gradually quickens as she climaxes, which is disappointingly soon. But she allows him to continue. He is fast, steady and hard, now, and she climaxes again. He gets up on his hands and toes with her legs over his shoulders and is pounding and sweating and desperately trying to climax. She is building up to her third climax and is nearly wild, pulling at him, taking him, tonguing him and wiping sweat from his forehead dutifully. Twenty minutes go by, and he is still up on her slamming into her as hard as he can. She is drying up and their genitals are burning hot, and he collapses on top of her. His penis goes limp and falls from her. He is gasping for breath and sweating profusely. She is stroking the back of his shoulders and mopping his forehead. She whispers:

"Did you finish?"

"No."

"No?"

"No, I can't"

"Do you want to try again, in a little while?"

"I don't think I can."

Virginia is quiet and stares at the ceiling with a concerned look on her face. James thinks she wants to apologize to him. Maybe she does. But he says:

"I don't want you to think it was you. You were great."

He kisses her lovingly and lies back looking up at the ceiling trying not to reveal his concern. He has had sex with a virgin before and it was nothing like this. The accessibility. The moisture. The lack of blood. The fact that there was absolutely no need to be gentle. But he doesn't want to go there right now. She lays her hand on his stomach.

"Are you hungry?"

"Yes, I'm starving."

"What time is it?"

He consults his wristwatch. "Four thirty."

"Doesn't David come home around this time?"

"Yes, roughly."

"Let's go to my house, then? I'll make us dinner."

They ride out on the streetcar. Neither her mother nor her siblings are home. They eat from the icebox, standing around in the kitchen. Virginia strolls into the family room, dark and vaulted, and sits at the piano. She begins to play Sarah McLachlan's "Adia," reading from the sheet music, humming the words.

V

Damarie lives in a mauve Italianate Art Deco and presently paneled glass double doors on the second floor are thrown open onto iron balconies streaming with orange ribbons of crushed paper. Tall and dark figures occupy the balconies, smoking cigarettes and drinking from wine glasses, cocktail glasses and expensive-looking green and silver foiled beer bottles sparkling the candlelit jack-o-lanterns flickering among the potted ivies. All the windows of the second floor glow with a rich yellow in the purpling twilight. A cool breeze sizzles in the dark trees. James is nervous and excited and late because the streetcars are running full with Halloween revelers. Damarie greets him at the open apartment door. She cries rapturously:

"Oh! It's perfect. You are perfect. You've even brought your instrument. Rosa! Rosa! Come, hurry, he's perfect. He's the perfect baroque violinist."

Rosa hurries to the door. She is unmistakably Guatemalan—her powdery smooth, brown skin, the small chin, the wide-set eyes. She wears housemaid's black and whites with a neat apron. The entire aspect of her uniform immaculate, tailored. She has her shoulder length black hair pulled back, tidily, every last shiny strand. She wears smart, polished black shoes. Her quick but intense eyes are stimulated, and her huge rouge lips spread her naturally swollen cheeks wide. She says, she speaks slower than her employer:

"It is terrific. You make a great baroque fiddler. Come, come in. Make yourself at home. There's beer and wine and liquor and things to eat on the table. What would you like?"

Damarie says, shaking her tall hips—she wears a gold transparent shirt over a copper-colored brassiere and satin green panties; she rides above the room in gold high heels; she has latex rubber green fins strapped to her brown ankles:

"The party's great. I'm so glad you could come."

This is simply the finest thing she could have said. A substantial portion of his net worth went into acquiring his costume: the sash, the blouse, the embroidered pants. She takes his hands and guides him to the dining room, turning back to speak to him with a throw of her short hair and a grandiose smile like women only in dreams or commercials do:

"Do you like red wine?"

"Yes." This will be his first glass, ever.

"Are you going to play for us tonight?"

"I don't know. I guess I can be persuaded."

She pours a glass full of wine and smiles on him intently as he drinks. She is proud of him. She wants to show him off to her guests.

"Come, let's fill glasses."

The wine bottle swings from her hand by its neck, and she takes his hands and they proceed through the rooms.

Hours later. Empty wine bottles line the windowsills or roll about the shoe heel-scuffed wood floorboards. The furniture has been moved from the living room. Rosa has wrapped both legs and both arms around a tall oxford shirt with a pale, thick neck and immobile hips, a rubber Bill Clinton mask for a costume. James and Damarie, hip to hip, hands clasping over their heads, chins high, stomp, heels striking hard and in synch, in a drunken tango. He doesn't know what he's doing, but he is doing a great job. Ta ta ta dump dump, da dump, ta ta ta. When the cassette stops, Damarie steps back, her white teeth like porcelain joy, her hair tied in a scrape of silken fabric. She glistens with sweat. They have been entangled in improvised tango for almost two hours. She says, falling to his arms in exhausted theatrics:

"We need fresh air, James."

They stand out on the balcony. The night trembles. Damarie sparkles. He is using his sash, now, as a towel, drying the sweat from his chest. His blouse has lost buttons and is growing cool in the night air against his back.

"I didn't know you could dance so well."

"I didn't either."

"You dance like a Cuban."

He gratefully bows.

"Like a Cuban gangster, it's not perfect but it's full of passion."

She drinks from a glass of iced water. She offers him some. Then she asks:

"Can you play something?"

"Play something?"

"Play something on your violin for me. Serenade me, my Cuban gangster lover." For the first time, she is showing signs of intoxication. Affectionately.

"Do you know Astor Piazzolla? I can play his 'Contrabajzando.'"

"Yes, I know it." She is enchanted by the beauty in the impossibility of this.

"Then I will play it for you."

He goes into the living room to find his violin. He sees through an open bedroom door the white rump of a man humping Rosa, her legs limply swinging in the air as she is complacently pounded on. James steps quietly up to the door and pulls it closed, uncertain of Damarie' s tolerance for such a thing. He returns to the balcony. Masqueraders drift through segments dark and the lamp-lit lane, laughing, disappearing, reappearing. Damarie leans against the balcony rail, head back, basking in the moonlight. Buck puts his violin under his chin, he is warm from dance and alcohol, and he is afraid he will not be able to communicate to his hands effectively. He does not want to mess this up. This moment is more perfect than anything he has ever experienced, even better than what he has seen in movies, simply because it is real. He drags the bow across the strings, and they wake up in gorgeous vibration. It is magical. His hands orchestrate self-consciously, and the night stops in full attention. Damarie closes her eyes. James plays flawlessly. Flawlessly. Damarie moves behind him and places her hands flat on his shoulders and leans into him. He doesn't miss a note. Encouraged so, he could probably also walk tight rope. His mind races to think of what he might play for an encore, but then a digital phone rings. Damarie tries to ignore it, but it rings and rings. She runs to it.

He does not want to continue in her absence, and when she does not return in a few minutes, he grows anxious and goes back into the house and follows the sound of her voice into the bedroom. The tall door to her bedroom is ajar, and the lights are out. A small black light illuminates the ghostly undulations of the window curtains. She is saying:

"Yes everybody came. It was fabulous. Yes, oh yes, very. I know I miss you so much. Yes. It has been cool, here. It must still be warm there?"

She is sitting on the edge of the bed at an open window. She realizes his presence and turns to look at him; his teeth glow blue white when he smiles. She comes around the bed and puts a soft kiss on his cheek and whispers, without caution:

"My boyfriend." Then says into the phone. "Oh, I'm just talking to a friend of mine. He's a wonderful violinist." Then to James, again. "Get yourself something to drink. I'll be out in a minute."

James goes into the kitchen and pours Scotch into a rocks glass over a couple of melting ice cubes he scoops from a vodka tonic abandoned on the counter. There's a pack of cigarettes, and he takes these with him to the balcony. The midnight air has become damp. He smokes, carefully, and the nicotine, foreign to him, triggers the spinning in his head. He sips on the Scotch, though aware he is already very drunk. He crosses his legs and reclines in the small chair with his feet on the balcony rail. He appears calm, numb by the alcohol, but his breathing is trembling with anguish. She hasn't been dishonest. She hasn't deceived me. She has only been a friend. Don't be stupid and think anything more. This soothes him, somewhat. The cigarette is, now, effectively mellowing him. He begins to doze off.

An hour later, Damarie finds him in the heavy breathing of sleep; the rocks glass balanced in his limp, hanging fingers on one sparkling wet tangent to the balcony deck.

VI

Today they are happy and brave, and Virginia has brought one of her little books of monologues written by various melodramatic unknown authors. They are up in the large gazebo on the river's edge, and they perform for each other. It is a bold and exhilarating thing to do, and sometimes they are giddy and shy, and sometimes serious and capable.

"Because it is years later now," James baritones, reading from a short work, staring hopelessly at a low, infinite place. "Because we have forgotten all we've once said. Because we have forgotten all we've ever heard. Because we have forgotten all we've ever seen, and (he admits regretfully) because we have forgotten where we've come from."

Virginia gives out a burst of applause:

"Bravo, Bravo! Well done."

They have a knapsack full of things to eat, and they spread themselves out on their blanket, eat and drink bottled tea and read. As the sun burns itself out they pull up the corners of the blanket and cuddle close together, and Virginia confesses her love for him. He feels guilty, as though he has had absolutely no reason to ever question her sincerity. They go back to his apartment and light the oven and stovetop to heat the place, still unfurnished, rugless and drafty. They wear their socks in the bed and make love. Three or four times, one after another. Virginia places both hands on either side of his face, her fingertips on his ears, just before he is about to climax. She looks into his eyes searching for the answer to a question she hasn't yet asked. He kisses her chin and her nose, and she cries when he tells her he loves her too. When he finishes, he holds the base of the condom so that nothing will spill out and then pulls out and pulls off the hot and slippery rubber skin and discards it to the side of the bed. Virginia is still holding his face and, now, reaches with one hand for his penis and tries to re-insert it into her. The temptation is overwhelming, but James stops her.

"I'm pretty sore." Although, he is not. His mind goes racing back to their first time. He can't handle this kind of stress. He has denied the fact to himself these days since. He slides back, and it falls from her hand. He closes his eyes and wishes things weren't so.

VII

He has been playing Brahms out in Audubon Park, sitting on one end of a bench facing the pond, his case on the other end collecting very little money; the pedestrians, joggers and cyclists staying mostly on the paved coarse and seldom coming to the pond's edge. He makes several dollars. They eat lunch at Virginia' s house and then stroll out on an aimless walk and eventually, with nothing else really to do, they spread their clothes out on the levee and make love in the cool sun. And it is like love. Virginia's eyes are steady and her breath is cool and smells like grape soda. When you're young and attracted to someone, sex feels like love, and when you're young and troubled there isn't enough sex to fill the giant place where love should be. The day is spent uneconomically, and soon it is evening. They are playing at the piano. The phone rings.

"Hello. Fine, and you? Good. Nothing really. I have a recital in a few weeks. What are you doing?"

There is a long pause. Virginia gives James a look of surprise, and whispers that it is David. She listens intently, as though she is completely amazed that he has called.

"Yes, well, that's great," and she turns a lock of hair behind her ear, smiles at James, shrugs her shoulders.

"Yeah, my brother has tickets, too. That'll be a great show. Yes, sure. I don't know." A worried look crosses her face. Then a smile.

"Okay, great. Yeah. All right, then. Good bye."

She puts the phone down. To James:

"Wow, that was odd."

"What did he want?"

"Nothing, really. He said he just wanted to see how I was doing. It was kind of weird."

"How do you mean?"

"I can't say really. He did say that he was waiting for you to come home so he could give you a message."

"He asked you where I was?"

"No. I had asked him what he was doing and he said Leo had called for you and he didn't have anyway to leave you a message, so he was waiting for you to come home and while he was waiting around he just decided to give me a call."

"Why didn't you just tell him I was here?"

"Think I should have?"

"Yes, I don't see why not."

"You have told him about us?"

"No, I haven't. I didn't know if you wanted me to, yet."

"You didn't know if I wanted you to?"

"Yeah, I wasn't sure."

He is very irritated. There's no way she is being honest. He says:

"This is all very stupid. Why should there be anything wrong with us seeing each other?"

"There isn't."

"Then why don't we tell David and let it be?"

"I just don't want any problems."

"I can't see why there would be any."

"David scares me."

"What harm can he do?"

"I don't know, but I think we should wait awhile."

"Why?"

"I just do."

"Fine. Though I think maybe he already knows."

"Maybe."

James takes the streetcar and then walks to the apartment through the chilly November night. He shakes from cold in his thin shirt. He will have to do something about a coat. He didn't think to bring one when packing to leave Missouri, thinking it would not get cold in New Orleans. On the contrary, it was just as cold as home, and damp. It is warm inside the apartment, and David is on the phone, sitting back against the wall, base of the phone between his legs, one foot up on the doorjamb and the other leg sprawled out with his ashtray balanced on his knee, and a small fire burns up the plastic of his cigarette package.

He is promoting the flames with his cigarette. James steps over his leg and goes into the kitchen. He finds a triangle torn from a brown paper bag with a message scrawled onto it in ketchup. The ketchup is crusted and brown and reads:

Leo's work 8

James says:

"Nice note."

David interrupts his conversation to reply:

"I didn't have a pen."

James makes a tuna can and mustard sandwich on sliced bread, which he toasts on the top rack in the oven, watching it toast with the door ajar. David comes into the kitchen.

"I was heading out and I wanted to get the message to you. I didn't know when you'd be home."

"Thanks."

"Been out playing?"

"Yes, in Audubon Park."

"Do any good?"

"Not really."

"Kind of a far ways to go, isn't it?"

"Yes sort of, but the ride out on the streetcar is nice."

"True."

"Felt like I needed a change of scenery."

"Sure."

He knows David knows about them. He resolves to call Virginia as soon as possible and tell her David knows and they should just come out with it.

"Any tuna left?"

"In the icebox. The bread's a little old, but if you toast it in the oven, it's fine. Oven's still on."

The phone rings. David goes to answer it, and James hopes it is Virginia, but it is Scott. David talks with him and forgets to come back for his toasting bread. James puts the sandwich together for David and delivers it to him. David is very grateful. James wants to tell David about his and Virginia' s relationship, but he also feels as though he is obligated to tell Virginia he intends to do so. He tumbles through his small heap of clothing and puts together a few layers and goes out to find a payphone.

He walks the chill, dark street, his hands thrust deep into his pockets, and he breathes in hard and deep against the frequent, chilled blast of wind. The night sky black and a few stars, emerging against the city's light. His breath comes up gray, his nose waters and the top of his ears burn with the sudden cold. The cold makes everything clean and new and urgent. He comes upon a coin operator with a partial booth, and he pinches a quarter from his pocket, and it shows like a dull star. She answers, straightaway:

"Hello."

"Hi."

"Hi, how are you? Are you at home?"

"No, David is there."

"I tried calling but the line was busy."

"David is on it."

"Where are you, then?"

"At a payphone."

"A payphone? Isn't it cold?"

"Yes, it is very cold, but I wanted to call you to hear your beautiful voice."

"It sounds better in person."

"It does, but I have to get up early tomorrow."

"Working?"

"Yes."

"Good."

"Anyway, I think David either knows and is simply being cool about it or he suspects as much but doesn't want to pry. Either way, I'm going to tell him. I wanted to let you know."

"Okay," Virginia slowly articulates, as if instantly deflated, the playfulness of her mood escaping. He waits for her to speak.

"If you think so."

"I think so."

"I just don't want you to have any problems with him. You have to live with him, not me."

"I think all the secrecy is unnecessary."

"I just wanted what was best for you."

"No, I understand that, but I think it has been long enough."

"If you think so."

"I do."

"But I don't trust David. He is capable of anything. Be careful about what you say. He has an awful temper."

"Personally, I think he won't even give a damn."

Clearly she is offended by this remark. She gives a bleak;

"Well."

"Well, okay then. I'm freezing out here. I'm going to let you go." His teeth chatter together, and his nose is dripping and he wipes it on his sleeve.

"I'll call you tomorrow."

"Okay, then."

"Goodbye."

"Good night."

He hangs the receiver on the silverish claw, and night expands. He becomes insulated against the cold with difference. He feels honest now and that warms him. He strolls into the dark lane, circulating a smooth thought. How lovely to be cold and warm, huge and infinitesimal, sad and happy.

David is still chatting on the phone when he enters. He will talk with him later. David's mother had given them heavy blankets and James curls up under one in his clothes with his socks on, burrowing his cheek into the cold pillow.

*

His lips are parched from the dry heat of the stove burning all through the night. He turns all the burners off except one, which he puts a kettle over. He cracks the back door and cool air sucks in. He fills a deep ceramic bowl with cold milk and raisin and bran cereal.

He eats the cereal swiftly while the milk is cold and before the flakes can mush. He spoons coffee crystals into his cup and pours boiling water to the rim and stirs slowly. He sits in the open door, and the coffee wisps against the morning, steam dampening his face and the thin smell acidic in his nostrils.

David slaps his bare feet into the kitchen and drags back a chair. He pours cereal into the bowl James has just used, damp still with a film of milk. He smacks large spoonfuls into his mouth, holding his head just over the bowl to reduce the distance the spoon has to travel, his hair shrouding his progress. James rubs crumbs of sleep from his eyes. It is a great time for sincerity, but there is no time. He will have to get to work directly, so there is no time to have a discussion properly. He asks David why he is up so early. David continues scooping; milk dripping from his orange stubble. He shrugs his pale, bone-sharp, broad shoulders.

VIII

The owner of this Gentily house is an old man with a big nose and hound-like, liver-spotted jowls. The house is so old it probably was originally built without a bathroom. Now the tub is falling through the floor. The floor joists under it need replacing, but the house sits low to the ground, and they want to accomplish this without removing the floor tile. The dirt is packed hard, and foreign objects are half-buried in the soil, washed up under the place hurricane after hurricane. They are digging a trench to allow access to the problem area. The old man sits in a lawn chair in short pants with a Dixie and a fly swatter, although it is cool out and there are no flies. The black maid is on the back step snapping beans. Leo whispers so they can't hear him:

"I don't like the job, but it's a job, so let's tie into it and get it done quick."

They make pull shovels, large T's of 2 x 4. They creep their way under the house, quietly. By noon they are several body lengths under the house, noses inches below the damp, molded floor joists. The black maid calls them to lunch:

"Yuns kin get some dinna' nah."

She has prepared ham and olive salad sandwiches, fried okra, collard greens and fried gizzards. They eat with dirt packed under their nails and stained into the grain of their hands. They eat quietly and by themselves, the old man still out front in the lawn chair and the maid disappearing until they are done.

Inching with their elbows and heels deep under the house again, Leo says:

"Yeah, I wish I could get some steady work lined up. Get you working regular."

"I'm doing all right."

"But you've gotta start putting a little away. For when you get married and have some kids."

"I don't think I'll be doing that anytime soon."

"You never know what'll happen," he sounds twice as old as he really is.

"It won't happen. It'll never happen. There's too much burden in it all. Particularly having children."

Leo is comical in his indifference. He says:

"You'll see, the damned things just pop out of nowhere. But you're right for not wanting any. I don't think anyone really wants 'em, if you think about it. You'd have to be crazy. They aren't nothing but trouble and a mouth to feed."

"Exactly."

"You'd be smart not having any. If I were you again, I sure as hell wouldn't have any."

"Well, I don't plan to."

Quickly, Leo says:

"Your roommate says you've been screwing his old lady?"

"What?"

"S'what he says. Says you've been poking her for some time now. Sounds like you're putting yourself in a dangerous spot."

"What did he say?"

"When I called for you yesterday, he said you weren't in, that you were uptown, banging his girlfriend."

"He said 'his girlfriend'?"

"'Banging his girlfriend' those are his exact words."

"She's not his girlfriend. They had a relationship and she broke it off with him and then we started seeing each other, and also, they never had a sexual relationship."

"He didn't seem too happy about it," Leo taunts humorously. He is irritated by Leo's obtuseness. Then Leo says:

"You better watch your back."

Everything is a very different color, now, and nothing is fixed in place. There is a quiet, wholesale shifting of large pieces of memory. Things are moving by themselves from corners into better-lighted places, and some things are sliding back into halls, and the halls shrink down to fit each piece.

Soon they're at the Kodovbe house. It is dusk and cold. The damp earth has left them damp, bleary and hungry. James takes the streetcar into the Quarter and walks back to his apartment, vaguely remembering the workday, looking like a vagabond, smelling like a night crawler.

He boils elbow noodles, drains off the water and pours in a half-can of tomato juice. David comes in, and James' stomach turns and his heart beats. He experiences an unnerving sensation of rotating at the waist around the axis of his legs firmly planted. He used to get this feeling when he was very young and in great trouble. He pulls his fear out to examine it. Why am I afraid? Am I afraid? Have I created this from nowhere? David comes into the kitchen.

"What's that?"

"Tomato juice and elbow noodles."

David peers into the pot, smelling hot tomato juice and salt and pepper.

"What do you call it?"

"Tomato juice and elbow noodles."

"Got enough for two?"

"I think so."

"How was work? You look like dirt, literally."

"Yeah. Miserable work. Under a house."

"That sucks."

"Yeah. I can't wait to take a bath."

"Mind I go first?"

"No, sure."

"I'll be quick."

"That's fine. Going out?"

"Yeah. You?"

"No, too tired."

James splits the contents of the pot. They sit at the plastic table. The noodles are hot and plump and heavily peppered. James says:

"Remember that night at Alice's house?" He doesn't know why he has gone this far back. His mouth just starts speaking. David's face is blank, guiltless.

"Yeah?"

"Remember when Virginia was upstairs for a long time?"

"Yeah?"

"She was in Alice's room on the bed with me."

"Yeah, I know."

"You know?"

"I figured she was. That was why Alice was like she was."

"You knew the whole time?"

"Sure."

"Well, then, now, I feel stupid."

"How's that?"

"Well, we've been seeing each other a lot since then, secretly, thinking you might be upset."

"I kinda thought you guys were. But shit, I don't care," he chants, emptily, and James doesn't believe him, or maybe he does. Fuck it, he can't read this guy! Is he playing this along? Then David is eager to point out:

"Like when she used to call to talk to you, but if I answered she would say she was calling for me. And I wanted to tell her that I knew and she could speak to you if she wanted, but . . . " he quits.

"But what?"

"I don't know. I guess I wanted to see if she would just come out and say it."

"Really?"

"Yeah, something I never liked about her, million pound elephants in the room, she always would talk about pleasant stuff, like everything's peach cobbler. I guess I should have said something, but then, there's a point in it I wanted to make, I guess."

"Well, I'm sorry. I wanted to, but she said you'd probably go nuts."

"Hell no. I was getting sick of her anyway. I mean she's nice and all, but you know, we are two different kinds. And besides the sex wasn't all that good."

"Really? She says she never had sex with you."

"Her ass hurts! Shit, I screwed her on the living room floor while her mother was just outside the windows in the back yard."

"Wow!"

"Yeah."

David slurps the last of the tomato juice from his bowl.

"She's like that though. She told me she was a virgin, before I slept with her."

"But you don't think she was."

"Hell no. I had virgins before. She wasn't one. I don't know if you've slept with her, yet, but . . ."

"Yes, I have."

"Then you know what I'm talking about."

James doesn't know what to say to this, the very stuff of which the world is made drawn into question and leaving him almost dead with numbness. David doesn't continue. James puts their dishes into the sink. David changes the subject.

"How's your playing coming?"

"Fair enough."

"Don't get me wrong or anything, you play pretty good, but I think you should leave that old stuff alone and work on something more current. Experiment a little. Work on alternative sounds."

"I wouldn't know what to find an alternative to. I don't know the standards, well enough. You've got to know this instrument. It is an old one. Many great musicians have played it. To search for an alternative sound at this stage would be arrogant."

"Maybe, but nobody is listening to that anymore. Learn guitar. Drums. Make some real noise."

"I guess," and for the first time ever, he really wants to, blow the place apart with anger, burn the house down. But it's only a passing emotion, he is quick to turn back inward.

"Don't you want to be a part of the music of this generation?"

"A generation is a generation. Every generation thinks it is the first to go through what they are going through, it's all the same shit over and over set to different music, maybe different clothes, hairstyles. Besides this generation is as alien to me as any other."

"I don't know man, there's differences, the rag gets shittier with each wipe. But, yeah, I guess it's cool to do your own thing, though," David says, encouraging. James is provoked. What have I yet to know? How far behind am I? They fall into a long conversation about music, from Beethoven and the Beatles, Led Zeppelin to Nine Inch Nails, hip hop and techno, both of which he despises. Buck's references are limited. Classical, which he must admit, he doesn't so much listen to as quarry. Country music. They both agree old country is the best.

James is almost envious of David's carelessness concerning Virginia. He knows all this will start to break his heart later, when left alone to deal with it, when the numbness wears off. But right now he's buoyed by unconditional friendship with an unlikely character. David doesn't want anything from him and therefore, like Leo, is someone he can trust.

IX

The late November cold is quiet and damp, and compels people to stride hurriedly to their destinations. He earns little money playing out. Paper money is becoming increasingly rare, usually donated, as if, sympathetically. It isn't enough. Leo doesn't have much work for him and he looks for a job, frequently, grudgingly. He finds nothing. Every nickel matters, nothing is discretionary. Virginia feeds him regularly, and this helps to justify keeping her around until he can get over her lying to him. He doesn't like it, but he doesn't have the luxury of being sanctimonious. She pointed out a bumper sticker one afternoon on a rattle-trap automobile passing through an intersection that read: *What's a musician without a girlfriend? Homeless.* She offers he spend a couple days with her in Grand Isle at her father's during Thanksgiving. He declines, claiming he cannot afford not to play out, but really he just wants to be alone. She leaves him with some leftovers from her mother's catered pre-Thanksgiving feast. David spends two days at his parents', bitching relentlessly the day before about his obligation to go. Thus James gets two days of solitude.

Thanksgiving morning is wonderfully cool. The absence of the customary noise of the Quarter is both frightening and remarkably beautiful. He wakes early and fries potatoes in oil with chopped green onions. He stirs a couple cups of coffee crystals. He soaks in a hot tub, reading from a book a prose of such complexity it causes him to dose off several times, then he masturbates routinely, cuts his toe nails, brushes his teeth.

He plays at Presbyter for two hours and makes nothing. There aren't enough people on the street to form a small orchestra. Many of the shops are closed. Many of the bars are open, but empty. The grocer has a sign in the window to notify their intentions to close at noon. He hurries into it, and there is a quiet, scornful crowd of shoppers. He takes a small sack of groceries home.

He plays out on the back stoop until dusk. He has two plump turkey legs in the oven broiling. He boils macaroni shells, squeezes the cheese into it from the foil packet and cuts it with milk. He leaves two burners blazing against the chill of the settling evening. Each passing day he is amazed anew how cold it gets in this southern town. He eats his simple feast slowly with a glass of ice-cold milk. He pours a second glass to go with a hot slice of praline pie for dessert. He takes a fresh cup of coffee into bed and props his feet in the window, staring out at the star-pricked slate of night, bowing casually on his violin until the humming and the heat seduce him into sleep.

Next day, he goes out and it is a carnival. The streets bustle with people. The stores are like emergency rooms and buying is a part of the care process. The cafés and restaurants are inefficient cafeterias. The mass attention is to the next holiday, Christmas, as though everyone got together the day before and realized they had nothing to be thankful for and are out to buy it today. He plays until 9 p.m., and he earns seventy dollars, after which, therefore, of course, he has much forgivingness of the masses he earlier loathed for weighing upon the streets and his senses with such sweaty bulk. Thankful for the dead whale putting oil in his lamp!

It is just before noon, and it is cool; the sky is just starting to clear. James is wearing a unisex jacket Virginia has lent him. They are waiting on the stoop of a popular restaurant on Esplanade in an old paint-bare black cypress clapboard. Heat billows from the adjacent kitchen door into a column rising up over the tall house. They are waiting for Jack and Kay. Virginia is in a knitted V-neck and a leather coat, and she couldn't be more beautiful, a fact that is now bitter and sweet. She is beaming and excited to meet Jack and Kay. It is apparently a much more important event to her than to him. She stares at him as though she is proud of him for having done something very good. Jack and Kay arrive, and they are wearing matching suede bomber's jackets. Virginia is pleasant, as if this perverse pairing ritual of wearing matching jackets does not cut right into her like a piece of jagged sheet metal. She greets them eagerly:

"Hi, I'm Virginia. Thanks for asking us out for lunch."

"Jack, nice to meet you, James has told me a lot about you."

"And he has told me nothing about you," Virginia says with playful derision.

James hurriedly leads them in through the front door. It is hot in the restaurant, and they start peeling coats as they take chairs at a small table. The waitress is thin, tall as a cornstalk, her blonde hair tangled in dreads and tucked over her ears with a tuning fork. She's wearing old, browned jean shorts, thread broken and wore through in the ass. James notices her thin smooth ass immediately and can almost see her bare skin through various rents in the seams. She covers her meatless ribs and the two welts on her chest with a white blouse discolored from hard-water washing. She is a beautiful girl really, but ragged. Her skin is good, was properly nourished growing up, a small fortune spent in her teens for those perfect teeth. Her posture is angular and graceful. She hasn't been grunge long. She has fallen from someplace higher, recently, or rather leapt. James is interested in knowing something about her. He is starting to notice her kind everywhere, including David. As though a revolt were in the making. She drops menus in front of them. She isn't interested in getting to know them. She intends to be their server as long as it might take to get them fed and on their way. She already doesn't like Kay, is visibly irritated waiting for her to decide whether she will have iced tea or soda. Jack and James order beers. Virginia asks if the tea is sweet, orders it. Then she asks James, when the waitress is gone:

"Have you been here before?"

"No it was Jack's idea."

"I have heard about this place." Virginia is taking on the responsibility of moving past the hostility of the waitress. "My brother told me about it."

"It's an interesting place," Jack admits. "From the street you wouldn't even think the place is occupied, much less a restaurant, except maybe by the steam pouring from the kitchen door. It's nice inside, though."

"I love it. It reminds me of a place in Missouri, a steakhouse."

"Oh, is that where you're from?" Kay asks, as though she hadn't already asked that the first time they met.

"Yes."

"How did you end up in New Orleans?"

"Well, I..." and he is still incapable of any variety of autobiography.

It's hard, the first time, like staring directly at a 100-watt light bulb. It's slightly less difficult the second.

"He 'just thought it would be nice'," Virginia interrupts, smiling at her cleverness.

"You just packed up and took off?" Jack asks.

"He saved up five hundred dollars working at a chicken farm and then bought a one-way ticket." Virginia is proud to share her knowledge.

"Five hundred dollars? That isn't a lot of money. Weren't you concerned about things like where you'd stay and what you'd do for money once you were here."

"I intended to busk in the Quarter. I wasn't really that worried," which is only a half lie.

"Kay and I were thinking about moving to South Carolina. But it seems so difficult. Finding a job and a place to live and everything."

The waitress sits out their drinks as though she's an indentured servant, is she actually seething? The small table is perfectly intimate, and James is thinking about what a brave thing he has really done, having heard it from someone else for the first time. Jack and Kay have put it into better perspective. They don't even know the half of the story and yet they are impressed. They do not know that there is no going back if it does not work out. There is no number he can call if he needs a couple hundred to get him through. Dad won't come pick him up at the bus depot and look at him with compassionate disappointment and unwavering commitment and love.

"What did your family say about it?" Kay asks.

"Nothing, I didn't tell anyone. I just left."

Kay's jaw drops. There's no possible way in her wall-to-wall carpeted dollhouse of a world she could ever even think for a second about doing something this ruinous. Virginia puts her hand on his with prideful understanding. Jack asks:

"Do you think about them? They must be very worried."

"I do, but I never feel bad for them. It says a lot when I have recurring dreams of being able to fly and I fly off narrowly escaping their grasping fists."

"Did you not get along with them?"

"Let's just say I got along in spite of them?"

"Wow, so..." Kay is about to go on, but James interrupts.

"It was probably the smartest thing I could have ever done for myself. Trust me."

Everyone's quiet, for how can they dispute the grave confidence of this statement.

The scent of baked potatoes standing in puddles of melted butter, warm bread, flame-broiled beef, dressings, and fresh sliced tomatoes floods the dining room. It is a truly blissful moment. The conversation turns light and brisk, as they eat ravenously. They eat and drink, and when they are finished they lean back in their chairs and rub their extended stomachs and nurse fresh rounds of drinks. A good meal fixes most, at least for a little while.

They drive out to Audubon and lay down large blankets in the golden afternoon sun. They are sleepy, digesting their lunch, and they lay about staring into the azure of a Louisiana autumn as a parade of clouds go by, and they identify various persons and things: Ross Perot, Pavarotti, an archangel and a bowl of ice cream. In continental fashion, they nap intermittently for nearly two hours.

*

Virginia's mother's house is empty, dark and vast, and when they turn on the lights in the kitchen, they are in a yellowish white yelm at the center of an unoccupied world. While the espresso machine hisses, Virginia presses herself against him and kisses him passionately, as a person has never kissed him in his life. He is overwhelmed by her sincerity, and what with being properly fed, he's in love with her, for the moment, he *needs* to forgive her, maybe that's why most people do. She tells him how she has had a wonderful day. She lays her head on his chest and says, very contentedly:

"I like Jack and Kay. We should get together with them more often."

"Okay," he says and he can't actually imagine that happening.

They pour the espresso shots into tall glasses of cold milk and ice. Virginia goes to the piano, turns on the lamp, sits down and invites him join her.

"Let's sing."

"Sure."

"How about Sarah McLachlan?"

"You like her a lot?"

"She has such a great voice. And her music is beautiful."

"I really don't know much of it."

"Here let's do this one." And she keys slowly, reading from the sheet music and starts to sing the first verse. She has no range, just a breathless shrill. And she pokes at the keys the way James types. But she is gorgeous, and warm and irresistible. He slides up close to her and caresses the breast closest to him and tries to kiss her neck. She leans away and smiles and continues to sing. He takes the whole of her huge breast into his hand and presses into it deeply and tries to reach around to take the other one. Virginia stands up, not in anger, but as if struck by genius. She runs upstairs and is gone for only a moment and returns with a thick book. She takes him to the couch and they pile into it. She pulls an afghan over their legs and cracks the book. James flips through the pages of poetry, thrilled by the idea. He selects a short poem by Frost. He begins to read and reads slowly in order not to stumble and break the rhythm. He does a fair job, but it is Frost, who couldn't. He turns to Yeats. He is unsuccessful. Ties his tongue around the archaic verbiage. He does not understand a word of it. He flips over more titles, hoping by title alone he will find a good one: "Blazing in Gold and Quenching in Purple," "Out of the Cradle Endlessly Rocking," "The Lover Speaks to the Hearers of His Songs in Coming Days."

Virginia takes possession of the book. She attempts Longfellow. She reads:

Endymion
The rising moon has hid the stars;
Her level rays, like golden bars,

Lie on the landscape green,
With shadows brown between.

And silver white the river gleams,
As if Diana, in her dreams
Had dropt her silver bow
Upon the meadows low.

On such a tranquil night as this,
She woke Endymion with a kiss,
When, sleeping in the grove,
He dreamed not of her love.

Like Diana's kiss, unasked, unsought,
Love gives itself, but is not bought
Nor voice nor sound betrays
Its deep, impassioned gaze.

She quits here. Says:
"I don't like it. Let me find another one."
"What's wrong with it? It sounds good"
"It sounds sad."
"Finish reading and see. You're doing a good job."
"I don't like it."
"Well, wait a second, let me, at least, read it to myself."
He continues to read, and she sits in an air of impatience. James
reads:

It comes,—the beautiful, the free,
the crown of all humanity;—
In silence and alone
To seek the elected one.
It lifts the boughs, whose shadows deep
Are Life's oblivion, the soul's sleep,
And kisses the closed eyes

Of him who slumbering lies.

O weary hearts! O slumbering eyes!
O drooping souls whose destinies
Are fraught with fear and pain,
Ye shall be loved again!

No one is so accursed by fate,
No one so utterly desolate,
But some heart, though, unknown,
Responds into his own.

Responds,—as if with unseen wings,
An angel touched its quivering strings;
And whispers, in its song,
"Where hast thou stayed so long?"

O weary hearts! Ye shall be loved again! James is nearly moved to tears. Though, presumably, as far as he can tell, this is about some juvenescent frolicking on yonder grassy knoll, it nevertheless evokes a great, suppressed melancholy to rise to the surface to breathe. Virginia turns the page. He is irritated by this. She flips through Whitman and Tennyson. Then with an easy snap, she closes the book. She says:

"Let's go upstairs."

"Upstairs?" He thinks she means something else.

"Yes," and she climbs from the couch and takes his hand. James has already forgiven her insensitivity. He grows hard in an instant. When they enter her bedroom, she turns on the light and throws open the closet doors. She drags out several white canvasses and a shoebox of paints and brushes. She says with much animation:

"Let's paint!"

She squats on the floor and pulls him down and begins to dig out various tubes of oil and color pencils and brushes. James sits down beside her, and he is crushed. A small ball of anger starts to burn in his chest. But he extracts this from the Longfellow poem, and becomes consoled:

> *O weary heart! No one is so accursed . . .*
> *But some heart, though unknown,*
> *Responds into his own.*
>
> *Responds,—as if with unseen wings,*
> *. . . and touches his quivering strings; whispers, in song,*
> *"Where hast thou stayed so long?"*

XI

The flickering, ghostly light of the television illuminates their sleeping faces. Mrs. Gesclair pokes her head in on them. They are on the floor in a deep comforter. She pulls the door closed gently so as not to wake them. But James is awakened, and he can hear her talking in a whisper to someone as she descends the stairs. He has to piss, but waits until she is out of earshot. He slips carefully out of the warm cocoon they are bundled in and quietly makes across the landing to the bathroom. He can see the lights of the kitchen spread out into the living room below him. He pisses on the porcelain above the water in the bowl so as not to make any noise. It is a clean urination, which is good, because he doesn't want to make any noise by flushing. He lets the seat down gently and steps back out onto the landing and painstakingly steps to the rail and kneels down close to the floor. Reflected in the glass doors of the living room, he can see Mrs. Gesclair sitting at the breakfast table with a dark-haired man; it's as though watching them on a very large television screen. She has her hands laid atop his and is leaning in toward him. They are talking just loud enough that he can hear that they are talking quietly, but he cannot make out what they are saying. Nor does he care. These people don't seem to have any connection to him or Virginia. Their actions bare them few consequences. They might just as well *be* on television.

Actors acting parts in some unwatched late night drama. He crawls back to the room, amused by the crawling. He lies beside Virginia on top of the comforter, not to disturb her, and props his head up on a pillow and watches a talk show host walk a chimpanzee out across a stage and help him sit in a guest's chair. The monkey is moving his lips like he is talking, very intelligently, but only the applause from the audience can be heard with the volume of the set as low as it is.

*

They sleep into late morning. Virginia's mother gets up very early and is running around the house like a chipmunk, high on espresso, cleaning things and playing the radio and possibly being as noisy as she can in order to wake them. They ignore it for the most part, but then the smell of hot pastries permeates the cool morning air and they climb downstairs to find Mrs. Gesclair has baked croissants and apple turnovers and brewed coffee. They sit up in the couch on their bare feet and eat and drink coffee and read the newspaper. Mrs. Gesclair is happy to serve them. This is the most James has ever seen of her in all the time he has spent in the house. Virginia is very pleased. Mrs. Gesclair puts on a cute little tennis skirt and her legs are brown and beautiful for her age. She pulls a large duffel from a hall closet and hurries out, telling Virginia she won't be back until late in the afternoon.

Virginia isn't interested in the newspaper and she twirls a dark tassel of hair and stares out the tall picture windows at the soft blue above the elms and maples of the backyard.

"Do you want to do something?"

"Like what?"

"Do you want to see a matinee?"

"Do you?"

"Not really. Maybe we can go for a walk."

"I guess we can do that," James says, unenthusiastically; the thought of a fruitless walk sour in his head.

Virginia says with prevenancy:

"Maybe it will help us think of something to do?"

"Maybe."

He looks at her sitting up in the couch, warm in cotton, cool face, hair fair in the sunlight warming the tall windows. There is something he wants to do. Something more intimate than a walk. Which could be done indoors. Which he has done many times before, but could do again, and again, infinitely, and never go tired of doing it. In fact, it is so good, the more he did it, the more he had to do it. Almost nothing else is like it. Not even playing violin. Because this thing he doesn't have to question. He can feel it, and ironically, it makes him think less about her deceit concerning the very same subject with David, as absolutely absurd as that is, like the way we poke at a wound to feel the pain as though it will heal it quicker. He slides down the couch and onto her and she spreads her legs to accommodate him. He kisses her lips, chin, ears, nose, forehead and neck, and she tilts her head back. He asks softly if she wants to go upstairs. She does not say anything, her head hanging back. He asks again. She suddenly pushes him off, and he tumbles to the floor and he splays out in great, heavy frustration. She runs into a back room and comes back with his laundered shirt and tosses it on his head. He says:

"Come on, why not? No one's home."

"No!"

"Why not?"

"I just wouldn't feel right; not here."

"What?"

"Let's go for a walk."

He gives up and climbs the stairs to find his shoes and change into his clean shirt (he is wearing a t-shirt Virginia borrowed from her brother's closet). On his way back down the stairs, Mrs. Gesclair comes back into the house.

"I forgot something. You guys haven't gotten out yet?"

Virginia looks at James with a satisfied look, replies to her mother:

"We were about to go for a walk."

"It's a beautiful day outside. If you want a ride into the Quarter, I'm going that way."

Virginia looks at him and then Mrs. Gesclair looks at him. He becomes angry for a moment. Everything appears all of a sudden awfully absurd. The game everyone's playing. He says:

"It's up to Virginia."

"Sure, we'll go."

After a pleasant walk through Spanish Plaza and along the riverfront, they are at Kaldi's. It' s a big, gentle day with cool sun. They sit in the thick windows and drink iced coffees. Virginia says:

"I'm sorry about this morning."

"No, you were right."

"I wanted to, but . . ."

"I know."

The thick, double-trunked tree stands just outside their window, and it still has its leaves. A quick blow of wind loosens a small flock of sparrows. They dip low in the street and rise up in a clump and disappear over the rooftop of the market sheds.

"Maybe we can go to your apartment?"

"You want to?"

"Yes," and she smiles coquettishly.

He smiles cordially and listens to the inarticulate pretty noises that emanate from within the cafe. He smells the air rich with coffee bean, touched with sweet and cinnamon. Colors bloom behind crystal lenses, and the knowledge of his own existence expands as if he were a mere sugar crystal and everything he can feel as big as the enormous coffeehouse. His own hand lays upon the table as though miles from him. His chair gives him the sensation of rising. From a fat, cracked ceramic vase of gigantic chrysanthemum, water audibly trickles to the caramel countertop—permanent like a canyon cliff, as domestic as a kitchen table. Glass jugs of milk and cream hum in the ice chest. An arioso from the coins in the tip jar. The gentle cadence of conversation, the rattle of coffee wares and aluminum creamers; beans grinding in vats; chairs scuffing backward, forward; teaspoons tinkling in porcelain mugs; the vacuum "humph" abruptly started and abruptly stopped each time pastries are taken from under the glass dome; the front door sanding down the floor; the inescapable parley of light traffic; the wooden-bowl clop of a horse-drawn carriage, the newspapers whispering.

He feels good, peaceful. It's a very nice thing. Chemicals flow now where earlier they did not. In the midst of it, he's not to question, but to enjoy, the imbalance it suggests goes unregistered. Then Alice spots them and comes over to say hello.

"Hey guys, what's going on?"

"Hello, oh nothing, we were just about to leave," Virginia says to Alice.

"Where you going?" Alice asks, innocently.

"To his place to have sex," Virginia says. James is startled, but also amused.

"Okay, great," she replies, smiling, not knowing exactly what to say. She's not sure if there is some kind of inside joke here. "So do you have like an appointment or something?" This makes her laugh.

Virginia does not laugh, but smiles pleasantly. "Oh, no, just that's what we're going to do."

James looks at Alice. Alice looks back at Virginia, amused, says:

"I was about to go down to the thrift shop on Barracks, probably not as much fun but that's what I'm doing. I would invite you along but with plans like that..."

"Oh, thank you, I'll call you later."

"Sure, okay. I guess you're going right now, then?"

"Yeah, right now," and Virginia is mischief about it.

"Okay, well, I don't want to hold you guys up."

They all hug politely and then swing out the front door.

They walk a block without a word. A young man, about their age, is slumped against the outside wall of the bar Kagan's, on his butt, dead or unconscious (when they pass him, stepping over his legs, they can smell the stink of alcohol and piss). He has a limp, green rooster's comb. His face and hands are black, dirty and crusted. Callused, scabbed knees poke through rents in his pant legs. He doesn't look much older than James. And he's not cause for alarm. There's someone just like him passed out on the sidewalk any given day.

Back at his apartment they make love one good time, then rest;

Virginia lies in his arms. Nothing is not where it shouldn't be. She fits perfectly in his arms, her head under his chin, soft hair against his throat. The sky in the window becomes white, and an autumnal wind blows at the loose sash.

When they go out, the cold is fresh, now, and clear. James walks Virginia to the streetcar. He sits down on the curb with his elbows on his knees, with his hands together flipping mechanically a coin. The perfectness of it, how compact, and how life is impossibly without it. Virginia does not sit because the curb is cold. She leans chest forward against a lamppost. She looks into the yellow electric flame, or just beyond it at the faint appearance of stars in the vaulted sky growing dim. A streetcar rumbles from around the corner.

XII

It's December, three in the afternoon, and it is cold. He has suffered almost an hour of playing. His fingers are numb, except where the tips on the one hand mash on the stiff strings; they burn here. He wipes his running nose with his sleeve, and his nostrils are raw. How can it be so cold? He warms himself at a café. Earlier in the morning, he went looking for work in restaurants. Nothing but blank or distracted faces.

After his coffee break, he returns to his corner and finds a most unlikely thing. A clown is occupying his spot. He looks at James with his painted face, smiling lips, but dark points of anger in his eyes. He is twisting two long black and white balloons into a sword, which he gives to a small boy, and his mother slides two perfect bills from her Furla handbag. He walks to the corner of Chartres and St. Peters and stands here to play. Through a vast ceiling of gray clouds, he gets a glimmer of sunshine. It doesn't last long, but it gives him some hope and a little heat. He plays several hours in the intermittent sun sinking behind the Cabildo. He makes three dollars.

Next morning he is applying for a waiter's position. The restaurant isn't advertising a need for one, but regardless, he is applying alongside two other better-dressed applicants. A pleasant, handsome black woman, with a strong and beautiful kindness in her disposition, asks him if he would consider washing dishes. She is beautiful with her huge smile and there is nothing condescending about her. There is nothing hateful in her eyes. He says he would gladly consider it, and mostly because he is so fond of her. She pulls his applications from the pile and scratches something in the margin and tells him she will call within a few days. He so badly wants her to grant him a job in this instant that it is something of a small emotional tragedy to have to wait.

He plays out for several hours, sees nothing more than a toss of nickels. He takes a long bath in the late afternoon. A very long bath. He involves himself in the indulgence wholeheartedly. In t-shirt and jeans and a little perspiration from the steaming bath, he sits in the back door to cool. He plays a few notes on his violin, but isn't motivated to play. He is bored with every piece he knows. It is too late to go to the library. He is restless. David isn't home. He calls for Virginia, but she isn't in. There isn't anything on the television remotely interesting. He cannot stop dwelling on his irritation with everything long enough to read. He can't remember ever a time of truly being happy. Has he ever been? Shouldn't happiness stain the barrel, long after it's drunk dry? Soon he is masturbating, again. Regrets it. Hates himself. And the night isn't even close to being over.

He is in the doldrums of impoverishment. On an abandoned ship sinking slowly. He can see the huge, rusted anchor weighing heavy on the end of the long chain running deep in the murky water, and when it sinks into the deep, it tends to stay a while. He is obsessed with the chain. Can't quit pulling on it. As though it is the only thing he can do.

An entire week passes with no incremental indications of passage except passionless, but vital, intercourse with Virginia, masturbation, and spartan late-night meals of potato or red beans or packaged noodles. Then the phone rings. He is offered the job washing dishes.

XIII

Hands poached pink blubber, pant legs soaking and shirt saturated with sweat from toiling in the dish pit for eight hours; there is a palpable sense of accomplishment when his steam-chapped face meets the cool night air. Though he toiled quietly like an appliance without so much as a nod of acknowledgment from the wait staff and the prep cooks, he has the gratification of a day's wages, as meager as they are. MaryAnn, the head chef, a beautiful black woman, had walked him through the kitchen and showed him where to hang his coat. The staff aren't fond of her, she too exacting, and they are cautious around her. James loves her; she is smart, yet humble and when she smiles at him, it is sincere. Her English is perfect and with just the smallest dollop of sweet Southern accent. His only real disappointment is that she works days and he will work nights. He drags out several putrid Hefty's, and the monotonous, rapid wash cycle is over.

And then it is the next day. And then the next. The work is mindless and physical, and eight hours wash away clean. It usually begins with several towers of glasses from the lunch shift. Then a couple tubs of flatware. Then the infinite stacks of small aluminum skillets. No one offers that he take a break. He is greatly unsupervised and assumes if he needs to take one he can take one, but he doesn't order a meal or request soda, due to the hostile environment of the waiter's station. They behave as though they rather wished he did not have to exist. And he can't get food through the kitchen without a ticket from the computer, employee discount of 50%, which he really can't afford. He contents himself with ice and water and whatever edibles come back on the plates, which is quite a lot. Untouched salads and cornbread and shrimps and chunks of alligator tail.

An entire shrimp cocktail has somehow gotten back to him. He examines it for contamination, a cigarette butt or shard of glass, etc. It looks perfectly edible, and he takes it out the back door, out of sight and eats it hurriedly. David is walking by on the street adjacent and he sees James and yells out, as he turns into the alley:

"Hey man what's up?" David is amused by this chance encounter.

"Nothing," mouth full of cool, plump shrimps, a little cocktail sauce on his lips. "Snagging a little lunch."

"Cool."

David is near, now, and he is with a skinny, wobbly creature with long oil-limp tresses and an impossibly long face. James asks:

"What are you up to?"

"Have to pick up my paycheck, right now."

"On a Saturday?"

"Yeah, well, I usually get it on Fridays, but I didn't work yesterday."

"Haven't been around the apartment much?"

"Yeah, I stay over at my girl's a lot."

"Okay."

His 'girl' is very difficult to look at, as if melting right before his eyes.

"We better get, she has work in a little."

"Sure, yeah me too. Where does she work?"

"She's a stripper over at the Base." And she is proud of this, tries to look into James's eyes for the first time, now, to see how impressed *he* is. He is, but not in the way she might think.

"All right, I'll see you later, I guess?"

"Oh, how's the new job?"

"It's a job. I can't complain. And all I can eat table scraps," and he holds the cocktail glass up to validate this.

"Wouldn't eat there if it were free. Place is for tourist. Shit's over priced."

"I don't know, free tastes pretty good."

"All yours man."

They stride off in a hurry.

It is a busy Saturday night. A second dishwasher, named Clayton, comes in at 9 p.m. to help for a couple hours. He is the day washer, but he is on-call on Saturday nights. He is not pleased about it. His yellow, blood-stained eyes are contemptuous. He is reluctant to speak. The roar of the sanitizer is welcome. They work quietly and deftly on an avalanche of pots and pans and porcelain. At one in the morning, Clayton grabs the mop; James bundles up the bloated garbage bags.

In lucid dreams, he relives the night. He is in the dish room hustling, with a great anxiety to stay ahead. He wakes in cold perspiration and tries to shake himself loose from the cycle. But he falls back into it and wakes again. It is growing light out when he finally falls into sound sleep.

He dips himself into a hot bath at eleven, having buttered toast and milk for breakfast. He has the day shift today, Sunday. He is numb with fatigue. He holds himself up by the handle on the sanitizer during its cycle and falls into moments of sound sleep. The various stages of hissing, spitting, humming and knocking become subconscious. He wakes up at the very last audible indication of a finished cycle. He turns his towel over to the night washer at five. He grabs his borrowed coat and jumps on an uptown streetcar.

He isn't in a great mood, but he isn't in a bad one either. Alice and Virginia are giddy and fully charged. They dance, sing, skip and try to get him to come alive. Their reality is so outrageously different from his. They waltz. They tango. They are ballerinas on the living room carpet. James is in the couch trying to read the comics, with little success. They tower over him and flop down on him, crumpling the paper. James notices she does not have her usual scent—that of clean, freshly washed cotton. She smells of burnt rubbish.

"Get off me, you stink," and he gives her a shove.

She stands up and disposes of a guilty look in an instant. She knows James would disapprove of her smoking pot with Alice. She selects this confession:

"We've been smoking clove cigarettes. Come smoke one with us."

"Not if they smell that bad."

"Come on," and she latches both hands onto his arm, pulls him from the couch and leads him upstairs to the balcony outside the bedroom. Alice taps out leaf-wrapped brown cigarettes from a slender burgundy and gold flip-top box. The cigarettes are redolent, but aromatic like frankincense or *potpourri*, not burnt rubbish. James knows this is not what he smelt on Virginia. He thinks about his encounter with David the day before. David looked weak and partially vanished. James asks Virginia:

"Do you think David has a drug problem?"

Virginia is ironically amused. She pulls on her long brown cigarette with the corner of her mouth, head leaning away from the swirling smoke, exhales an inept jet. She looks at Alice, then at James.

"He's been using drugs for a long time, if that's what you're asking."

"Really?"

"Yes, I'm surprised you don't already know that."

"I have never seen him using anything. He smokes like a train and drinks obsessively, he's mentioned it casually, but . . . what are we taking about? Pot, or?"

"Pot, mostly, but who knows what else."

"Did he smoke around you?"

Her smile flattens, not gravely, just unenthusiastically. Alice looks guilty.

"Sometimes," and she ventures this, "it wasn't that big a deal."

He almost wants to care passionately, at least as far as Virginia is concerned, but he can do without the additional disappointment. Abandons concern. He dismisses the subject:

"I saw him with this stripper yesterday, and he didn't look too good. I was just wondering what he might be getting into. The girl he was with looked like trouble."

Virginia shrugs, "Good for him." Then becomes gleeful.

"Alice you should read one of your monologues?"

"Okay." She is eager. She's taking some sort of drama class, or something. This has become her obsession. She goes into the house and returns with two flat composition books. Virginia takes one and Alice opens the other.

"This is one I wrote last night."

She gets up on her knees, back straight, shoulders high.

"Okay, it's a middle-aged woman and she's kind of serious, but not gravely serious. I put contemplative. And she is in a kitchen kneading a piecrust on the table with a rolling pin and there is a lot of flour all over the table and on her hands and arms. There is some on her cheek and under her ear where she has rubbed her neck. All right, ready?" She adjusts herself for the delivery. She is a little nervous, because they are her words. "All right," and she tries to become contemplative.

They never usually eat the stuff. I don't know why I'm always making it. Then I end up eating it, myself. And I definitely don't need it. But the first time I don't make one they're screaming because there's not one around. Damned brats. I aunt just buy one from the Winne Dixie. They wouldn't know the difference. I could chip up the edge a little. Make it look homemade. But then Al'd be screaming how high the 'god damned fool bill' is. Like to see him cook for four kids, two of 'em boys. Hell, I'd like to see him make this pie.

(She rolls out the dough for a while, contemplative.)

We should have never had kids. He wanted them, not me. One maybe, not four. He was all talking big Christmas and a big house and big family vacation. We haven't been on vacation since we were married. He's always promising. I wish it could be like before we were married. We always went out to eat and went places. We were happy then. I don't know. I guess I wanted to get married, too. I guess it was the only natural thing to do. And the kids. Sure they mess everything up and cause us problems, but I'd do anything in the world for 'em. I guess it isn't all so bad. (She continues to knead the pliant dough, smiling, satisfied momentarily, then she picks it up from the bed of flour it lays on and tries to move it into a floured pie dish, and it breaks in two. She throws the rest down and plops down in a chair.) *Oh, who am I kidding. I hate it. I hate every minute of it. It's killing me.* (She is motionless and staring hypnotically into nothing.)

Virginia and James burst into applause. James says sincerely:

"Wow. That was very good. You wrote that last night?"

"Yes, I'm taking this creative writing class. But I think I still need to work on it."

"It is great. I like how you are left asking where the problem lies, with the family or the woman. And how fast she goes from one mood to another. Certainly can identify with that."

Alice nods with a puzzled smile, as though this wasn't her intention at all. Virginia suggests:

"Let's write some more."

The two girls are joyous, and they gather pens and paper and set up a writer' s group in her bedroom. Virginia turns the radio on and stretches out on the floor with her feet up, twirling her hair in her finger, as though she should be wearing a poodle skirt as she writes a love letter to her beau. Alice crouches in a corner with dark seriousness. James taps his pencil on the tablet, eager to write something, but not very confident. He scratches out this line: From where does the bulk of my unhappiness come? But he is incapable of continuing on. In a couple hours, he has written nothing. Alice has composed another short, interesting, though sophomoric piece.

XIV

He pulls a tall and thick hard-bound biography from a dusty shelf. He has heard of the painter before—one of the world' s most celebrated artists, but he knows very little about his life. Leafing through the glossy pages, he becomes fascinated. Oh what a gorgeous and rich world Picasso lived in! The well-lighted cafes, the Paris studios, the women, the bullfights, the Spanish villa and his gorgeous and stately last wife, Jacqueline. And the paintings! They become beautiful right before his eyes. The proliferation of work is inspiring and also daunting, spanning a century. A mythical life here evidenced in pictures. Envy at first scorching, then igniting passion. He tries to imagine how it would be if those around him inspired him instead of making him tired and feeling alone. The book is priced at thirty-five dollars. More money than he could ever justify spending on a book, but he decides to kill two birds with this stone. He can read it himself and then give it to Virginia as a Christmas present. She would love it. He doesn't have enough money at this moment. He asks the bookstore clerk if it could be held for him for a couple days. The clerk sits in a deep cave in a mountain of books, looks over the top of his spectacles with quiet frustration and studies James' s countenance a moment. He says:

"We don't put anything on hold, sorry."

"Could you bring the price down on this, I'm ten dollars shy."

He doesn't get up from his chair to examine the book, says:

"It's already a reasonable price, I couldn't sell it for less."

James can't disagree. He browses the cluttered aisles wishing he had more money, looking for something cheaper, but he must have this book. He finds a dollar-and-a-half paperback of short stories and then tucks the big book behind a tower of poetry, where no one would ever find it. He will come back when he gets his paycheck.

In several days, he gets his paycheck and is excited thinking about getting the book, hoping it will still be there, but he is horrified when he tears the perforated edge and folds open the check. It is criminally small. Thirty-five hours of minimum wage and seventeen percent in taxes. How can the vulture get any when the hunter doesn't get enough? The grocery store charges him a buck to cash the check. He puts aside the money for the book and counts out the rest for rent. He doesn't need money for food just now. He speculates his diet until his next paycheck: coffee in the morning, whatever edible scraps come back into the dish room, a potato for dinner unless he is at Virginia's house.

He devours the text of the biography, but turns each page with reverence and caution. Only one other thing has ever been so inspiring to him, and that was the catalyst, which led him to the violin. He cannot wait to give the marvelous book to Virginia. He thinks about keeping it for himself only a moment, but realizes that he will get more joy from giving it to her. He is very lucky about wrapping paper. He is walking over to the record shop to tell David the phone bill has come in, and he passes a year-round Santa Shop miraculously persevering in a narrow building on Decatur. In the Quarter, many tenants put their garbage in front, having no garbage alley. In a trash barrel overstuffed with boxes and scraps of ribbon and paper, he finds a fold of green-gold wrapping paper. It is gilt paper, and originally would have been smooth, without wrinkles, but since he finds it wrinkled in places, he crumples the rest of it gently, to create a very pleasing effect. He creases aluminum foil into flat ribbon. The end result is very professional.

Christmas plays on the gray city like a silent movie in Technicolor. Sleigh bells might be ringing, but he doesn't go into any stores to hear them. By the time he gets out of the steaming gut of the restaurant, the streets are empty, a constellation of colored lights sparkling quietly, as alien to him as the galaxies overhead. Tonight he gets out early, though, and it is beautifully cold and clear. Out on the streets, holiday shoppers are numerous and waddle along like penguins that have exchanged their smart tuxedos for a multitude of mass-produced distractions, which they carry around in expensively labeled shopping bags. There is a certain lunacy in their eyes, like people at church or a political convention. Unless they are in a long checkout line, then the vague consciousness solidifies into hate.

He's taking a streetcar out to Virginia's. His jeans are damp, but the windows are closed and it is warm. He's inside the lantern glass, next to the very thing that illuminates the oaken lane, glowing, locomoting merrily, persons in coats and furs, gathering and dispersing like moths around a traveling lamp. Everything is becoming more gorgeous than anything he has ever imagined. The stately Victorian homes modestly decorated. The giant live oaks in the intervening darkness dressed in black velvet. Specks of blinking light nesting from eave to eave like the stars of the galaxy suggesting a time for beginning. The little silver bells twinkling in the holy wreathes hanging from the lampposts. He has Virginia's book, and the excitement makes him tremble, or maybe it is his damp pants and wet socks. He gets off at her street and strides hurriedly along. He climbs the stairs in leaps and knocks on the door. He examines the package closely to make sure everything is perfect. No one answers. He knocks again. No one answers. He waits.

After one hour, he gives up. He takes the streetcar back into the Quarter. No one is going this direction, and he is alone in the car with the conductor, a big apple of a man. He notices the gilt wrapping paper.

"Awfully fancy wrappin' paper."

"Thank you. It's for my girlfriend."

"She's gonna love it just for the wrappin'."

"I hope so."

"Goin' see her."

"Yeah," James lies.

"Good for you. You get that done professionally?"

"Yes, they did it at the store where I got the gift," James lies. The lying helps to distance himself from the loneliness. But he's not sure why, he isn't even trying to do it, it's just happening.

"Very nice, she a lucky girl."

"But if you saw her, you'd see I'm the lucky one."

"Yeah-u-right," he exclaims in the rapid three-syllable way common with Cajuns. He looks back at James, laughing with admiration.

XV

He is hurtling through the starry night over snowy evergreens, the brisk air against his face. When he comes to a quiet, glowing cottage, chimney puffing, he circles a few times, descending, considering alighting on the rooftop. But there is this dreadful anxiety eating at him, from believing he is not welcome. And just as his last circle is bringing him to the roof ridge, he banks up abruptly and with great velocity launches into the sky and continues on, searching, hoping to find what he is looking for. He wakes up in a cool perspiration.

He spoons out some coffee crystals, toasts some bread, sits out on the stoop in the mild late morning playing his violin. Afterwards he draws a deep hot bath, reads a short story, sleeps a half-hour in a warm sweat. The phone starts ringing, and he is awakened. He jumps out, runs dripping wet to the phone not knowing how many rings had already sounded before he woke. It is Virginia. She explains that she was obligated to run a circuit of houses stuffed with uninterested and over interested relatives yesterday. She says she has to do dinner at one with her mother's mother in Metaire and would like to see him afterwards.

She knocks on the apartment door as it is growing dark. She has a gift for him and a Tupperware of her grandmother's food. He gives her present to her immediately. She is sparkling with excitement, meticulously separating the tape from the "expensive paper." She opens the beautiful book and reads the inscription he has written, and her eyes begin to glaze with tears.

"James, this is such a great present. I love it. He is one of my favorite painters. Thank you so very much."

She turns the thick pages slowly, caressing each powdery smooth page. She is taking her time. He is eager to see what she has gotten him. He wants to feel that same happiness.

"Can I open mine?"

"Oh, yes, but I feel bad. My gift to you is so lame."

"No, it can't be."

"Yes it is. I'm sorry. But I just didn't know what to get for you. It's as though you have everything in the world you want, but nothing you really need."

He shakes the boxes. He can hear the unmistakable slide and crumple of clothes wrapped in tissue paper. He is very disappointed, but he does not show it. She is right. He has two pairs of pants, couple shirts and a couple more t-shirts. That's her coat he is borrowing, hanging on the doorknob. He cannot be upset about it. He opens the gift, and the slack pants and shirt are nice.

*

Sex on the other hand makes for a fabulous gift. Virginia has made elaborate arrangements involving Alice in order that she can spend the entire evening in his apartment. James is very grateful for this. Even though they have sex all the time and he even stays at her house over night, she is a teenager, and technically so is he, and this will be the first time they can truly feel like adults. It even makes the sex different, better. It is frigid outside and they set the gas burners on high and open the oven door to help heat the place. They have cigarettes and wine. They make love for hours.

Sometime after midnight, and they are slipping in and out of sleep, curled into each other like hibernating animals, the front door flies open and David comes stomping in.

"David, that you?" James says from his room.

"Yeah man, sorry, did I wake you?" David asks as he's sorting through a huge pile of clothes on the floor, looking for anything long-sleeved, dirty or otherwise.

"No, not really, we were just about to doze off though."

"We," and he is just then standing in the doorway pulling on a heavy shirt. "Oh, shit, sorry man. Hi Virginia."

Virginia pulls the blanket up under her chin to better cover herself. She says, confidently:

"Hello David."

"You guys moving in together?"

"No, she's spending the night, it's Christmas."

"Sure man, that's cool. Yeah, it's fucking cold out there, too. "

David's girlfriend comes up behind him and leans on him. She is obviously drugged, smiling at some little fish of thought swimming around in her head. Virginia looks at the girl with a beautifully tolerant smile. There's not even the slightest indication that David gives one shit. Virginia then to David:

"How's everything?"

"Great . . . " which he leaves open.

"Still at the record shop?"

"Yep, got a promotion, manager now. Went to the Keys a couple weeks back, to this big boat party, pretty sweet. Shit's good."

"Wow," they both respond.

"Yeah, the owner married this guy who's fucking loaded and flew us down there."

"You and your girlfriend," Virginia ventures.

"Oh, no, this was a while back, before we started hanging out."

"Oh."

"But how's everything with you? Still taking piano lessons?"

"No, not since the end of the summer."

"Still going to go to Tulane?"

"I don't know yet."

"Cool," David says, losing all interest in the conversation in an instant. "Man, I'm thirsty." He goes to the icebox, drinks from the water jug. James can't see him doing so, but knows he is, as he always does, and because he can hear the jug breathing in and out like a plastic lung. James is irritated by this; the thought of David's lips on that girl and her lips on countless crusty cocks.

"All right, we've got to get. You guys have a great night."

Virginia rolls onto her back and stares at the ceiling, maybe disappointed by David's indifference. David shuffles out with his coked whore and slams the door.

Then Virginia looks at James. He shrugs his shoulders.

"That was a surprise. I haven't even seen him in awhile."

"He's not looking too good. And either is she."

"I'm sure it's drugs. Same story with pretty much everyone these days."

*

Three in the morning, in a galaxy far, far away, moonbeams slant in through the window in a ghost green fuzz. The open refrigerator is the landing mother ship. He pours a tall glass of water. He vaguely remembers David drinking out of it, but he is thirsty from all the wine they drank last night and drinks the water anyway. His penis is shriveled and numb. He is partially comatose from deep sleep, but he feels truly happy for a brief moment, truly happy. A moment of perfect clarity and calmness. When he climbs back down onto the mattress, Virginia re-forms herself into his mold and they sleep soundly until dawn.

When the sun breaks in through the window, it falls white and hot on their faces and heats them into consciousness. James rolls off the mattress. The floor is cool and hard, and he lies here a moment, wishing he had a shower. He goes into the bathroom and draws a warm bath. This wakes Virginia and she follows.

The warm water burns as it touches at his genitals. He sinks in slowly and lays back, and a sedate heaviness levels through his body. He wants to sleep awhile, but Virginia is in the doorway.

"God that looks good," rubbing sleep from her eyes.

"Come in."

She is wearing his T-shirt. She doesn't indict yes or no.

"Come on, there's room," and he pulls up his feet. She pulls off her panties, steps into the tub and squats down into the water.

"Aren't you going to take off that T-shirt?"

"I'm fine."

"What? You can't take a bath in a shirt."

"I'm all right." She pats the water, gently, or scoops a little over her face.

"You have to be kidding."

"I'm fine," she distractedly insists, wanting him to drop it.

He looks at her with incredulity. She knows he knows why she is wearing the T-shirt. Her breasts are large and they hang low on her chest, and her baby fat rolls when she sits and leans forward. She does not want him to see this. She never lets him see any of this. When they undress, with few exceptions, she does so under the cover of blankets. Or in a manner like that of a performer, with great posture and choreographed movement. She puts on her bra first, always, only then she will pull on her panties. She will almost be bold then, knowing how good the cut of the panties under her abdomen look, and the smooth of the silk over her butt and the gorgeous luxuriance of her cleavage—brown and deep and satiny. She's no Kate Moss. She stands up to get out, letting the water run off some, before stepping out. He is sympathetic, he knows some of it has to do with him, he's so damped critical of obesity. But this is not the same thing. He tries to be consoling:

"It's all right, I don't care, just sit down and relax."

She takes a towel from a cast-iron hook on the door.

"You don't have to get out."

"I know, you just lie back and enjoy it. I'll get a shower later."

She removes the wet shirt, her back to him, and wraps herself in the towel. Puts the shirt in the sink.

"Do you want to take a bath after me?"

"I'll get a shower later," she insists, politely.

XVI

It is warm in Kaldi's with the sun through the tall windows. They are on the raised platform by the old upright piano. Virginia washed her hair under the tap after he got out of the tub and now it is exceptionally fine and radiant. James looks at her, thinks that he truly adores her. Do I deeply love her, though? If not, why not? Because she has lied to me? Or is there more than that? Love should be easy, shouldn't it? Catching him staring, she asks:

"What?"

"Nothing."

"Want another refill?"

"Sure, but I'll get it."

At the counter, he looks into the brown, bright eyes of the countergirl. And she is beautiful! He is frightened by the possibility that beauty can produce the feeling of love. Or rather that beauty produces a feeling much like love, desire or admiration, and because he has never truly known love, then he might easily mistake one for the other. Traumatized young enough by the closet to you and you learn to distrust everything. Believe in very little. Respond only to that what moves you by any means. He moves himself down the counter to cream his strong coffee. Waiting to use the creamer, he finds himself madly in love with the slender hands of a young girl pouring cream heavy into her cup. He is charmed by her delicate fingers and the magical command she has over them. He returns to the table. Virginia says:

"I think we should go out and you can play. It is such a beautiful day."

"I guess we can do that."

"I'll even put some money in again."

"Okay."

"I think that was effective, last time."

"It could have been."

"Oh," she remembers, "are you working January second?"

"What day of the week is that?" he asks and sees an empty well bucket in his mind's eye.

"It's this Saturday."

"I always work on Saturdays," which have become synonymous with a steam-chapped face and damp clothes.

"Oh."

"Why?" He hears his voice echo down a long tunnel.

"I'm going to sing in this concert."

"Really?"

"Yes, it is nothing big, but my mother is going to take us out after."

"I might be able to get off."

"Free dinner."

"I'll see what I can do."

There is obviously something not right, just what that is, is blue prints to a carpenter ant.

*

They want to ride uptown so Virginia can check in with her mother and get a change of clothes. They wait at Canal street for the streetcar, which squeals to a stop like a brown sow, and the fat, pink piglets, tourists mostly, crush in to get at its teats. The blacks sullenly wait leaning against the exhaust-blackened wall. James holds his violin close; Virginia holds to him close. He is feverish with claustrophobia. Everyone is so alien, and ugly. The soup of harsh colognes and body odors inflame his sinuses. Elbows stab at them. Virginia presses against him, and they are pressed forward into the folding doors of the trolley.

Virginia explains to her mother how they spent the morning in the park where Alice had left them, according to the conspiracy she and Alice are maintaining, and Mrs. Gesclair does not show a hint of suspicion in her expression. Before Mrs. Gesclair dashes out for her tennis lesson, Virginia tells her they are going back into the Quarter, and Mrs. Gesclair gives her obligatory response as she pulls the door shut: *Leave a note.* Clothes stuffed into a backpack, they are back out on shady St. Charles, waiting for an inbound car. It's a most pleasant winter's day in the deep south. A note sits on the breakfast bar which reads: *Staying at Alice's again, I'll call you, love, V.*

On Woldenburg Park, James cracks open his case and begins to play. Virginia puts in five ones. It is late afternoon, by now, and the sun is vainly trying to burn through the canopy of high clouds currently sallied in. He plays a lackadaisical two hours and miraculously earns seven dollars, not including Virginia' s bait. They go back to the apartment and bake potatoes in the oven. James tunes his violin and Virginia flips channels on the television. She has it pulled around in the door, so that she can lie on his bed and not David's. He climbs onto the mattress beside her. There is a long wait for the potatoes. He slides his hand between her legs and she grabs it and smiles and says:

"Sorry, can't. I started today."

"Oh."

"Sorry."

"Well, there are other things."

He smiles mischievously. She is willing to play along. He takes her hand and places it on his swelling crotch and he lies back and she unzips him. She can almost take it all in her mouth. She sucks rhythmically and is gentle where she knows he is sore. He feels climax welling up deep in his groin, deep and potent and hot and it is climbing up and up and then the phone rings like a fire bell, shocking him out of his imminent orgasm like a bucket of cold water in the face. It is Alice. He gives the phone to Virginia. She still has him in her hand and strokes gently a couple of times while she talks, then lets go and sits up straight. She listens intently a moment. James goes limp, pulls his underwear up, sits besides her trying to follow the one-sided conversation. Virginia looks at him with bright severity. She hangs up.

"My mother called Alice's, looking for me."

"And?"

"Well, Alice said I went to the Stop 'n' Go."

"You're going to call her?"

"Have to."

She stands up. She picks up the base of the phone and rests it on her hip and dials the number, it's an old rotary so it takes a bit. Mrs. Gesclair answers immediately. Virginia listens intently, provides a series of yes and no answers and then hangs up.

"I need to go home."

"Why?"

"I don't really know. She says she needs to talk to me."

"Does she know you are not at Alice's?"

"She didn't ask."

"Really."

"I need to go, sorry," and she bends over and kisses him. "Can you walk me to the streetcar?"

They walk through the French Quarter under a heavy bruised sky. The air is clear and cold and their breath is visible. They turn onto Bourbon off Orleans with its glaring lights and the yeasty stench of a dormitory hall. They turn onto Canal and the night fills the deep street like a vodka tonic. The interior of the streetcar glows against its dark shell benevolently as it pivots off the neutral ground. It knocks and rumbles and shrieks to a halt with a smart ring of its bell and James kisses Virginia and she broads. The car moves forward, sounding like something being wound up.

He buys a six-pack of good American beer at the Royal street grocery. Buying alcohol at his age legally gives him a great feeling of responsibility. He buys the expensive stuff feeling as though he deserves the indulgence. He stretches out on the bed with his head propped up on the wall, watching the *Late Show with David Letterman*, Itzhak Perlman is the musical guests. The phone rings.

He knows it is Virginia, and he's little irritated. He takes his time reaching for the phone.

"You'll never guess what I just talked about with my mother?"

"No, what?"

"Sex! She wanted to know if I was being careful. I couldn't believe how calm she was. She was like 'be careful, use your head, make sure you use protection'. I was impressed. I think she knew I have been sleeping with you, but she never mentioned it until I told her."

"You told her?"

"Yes and she was like 'Well if you are going to with anyone I'm glad it is him'. She also asked if I wanted to get a doctor's appointment to see about birth control. I told her I would think about it. I said I would not be doing it that much. And she said, 'honey, once you have it, you'll have it all the time'. I couldn't believe she said that. I said, 'Jesus Mom, I have more self-control than that'. But she insisted that I make an appointment. I guess I should."

"I certainly think you should."

"You think so?"

"Absolutely."

"So, anyway, she said I could talk to her if I needed anything. She even offered me money for condoms."

"What? How much?"

"She just said I could have it if I needed it."

"*You need it*, take it. We really should use them all the time." The thought of Virginia becoming pregnant sobers him instantly and makes the conversation suddenly more relevant.

"I don't know, I wouldn't feel right taking money from her for condoms."

"Wouldn't feel right? Are you crazy? Take it, at least until you get on birth control."

"I don't know if I'm actually going to start taking the pill, I . . ."

"Why not. Take the pill. Take the condom money..." Shut up, grow up, he adds in his mind. She starts itemizing various reasons why she wouldn't want to start birth control, but he isn't really listening, to him it's a no brainer. He's watching Itzhak bowing wishing he can turn up the volume.

XVII

He is towel drying, feeling regretful. He has taken a short bath and although it felt good to get up from the still warm water with such resolve, he now feels as though he is missing out on something very significant. As though he is neglecting himself. This war is exhausting! But he blocks it out and hits the street, determined. By surprise, like a ray of sunlight breaking through the gloom, he feels good. In Spanish Plaza he jumps down into the sunken circle of tiled thrones around the large fountain pool. He is humming a tune of original composition. It is loose but good. He attempts to transfer it to the violin.

The fountain is dead. Then, startling him, it explodes into a complete circle of geysers erupting with great velocity. The burst of cool air inspires him and he is quick to pull some fresh notes together. He straightens his back and pinches the butt of the instrument tightly and saws on the strings, channeling his creative energy, the worn horsehair bow sawing under his nose in a blur. The melody comes and goes and he chases it around and around, falling into a trance. He is collecting all its various movements, arranging them, pairing them. Then Virginia is standing there.

"You've started without me?"

"I am just warming up."

The tune dissolves into thin air. He didn't quite have a grasp on it, yet.

"Are you going to play here?"

"Sure."

"There aren't a lot of people out here."

"Woldenburg won't be much better."

"Maybe. Let's go to the levee, then?"

He doesn't have the spit to complain. He packs up.

Past the silver Ocean Song, down a curving tree-lined path, up over the grassy levee, they come to the river's edge. They take a bench facing the river and he opens his case and tunes his instrument and pulls tangled hairs from either end of his bow, obviously not his own and he is amazed that Virginia's hair could find its way into his bow. This makes him ponder for a moment the nature of relationships. How people become intertwined in ways numerous, large and small. In ways they may not even detect for some long time. He's looking out on the river as tugs push enormous rust-red barges through the muddy water, quietly. Tugs whose propellers, by comparison to the actual size of the vessel's they push, are tiny, and yet they churn deep in the brown water with such silent furry the multi-ton barges glide along steadily. Are our lives rusting barges on muddy waters, with unlocked doors to the pilothouse, other people coming and going, adjusting the controls? Or are the doors locked, and no one's at the helm? He's rowing philosophic in a deep stream of thought.

On the levee, an old lady has been feeding seagulls, and now they play on the handrails, white and fat and staring blankly. One will land on a different segment and two will land beside it, then the first one will hop down to the next section and the other two will follow, landing precisely the same number of inches to the left of the first bird each time. They play this game all the way down the length of handrail and then race back and do it again. James is trying to remember the tune from Spanish Plaza. He is finding a few notes here and there in his mind's ear and now this promotes the collecting process again. The bird's game becomes the meter. The sun is bright behind puffs of clouds, throwing spots of shadow at times. The grass is a green blur. Each increment sings itself and he sets it into a syllabus of melody, to be fleshed out in great detail later. Virginia notices it is something new.

"What is that you are playing?"

He frowns at her for interrupting, and doesn't reply immediately.

"I like it."

"I'm just now making it up," he announces, and quickly tunes her out and opens himself up again to the music.

*

The temperature has dropped considerably. It is late afternoon. The sky is upholstered in gray velveteen. They pack up and go to a café called the Croissant d'Or. It shines in chrome and panels of mirrors. The little brunette counter girl is made of the stuff of flower petals. She is so beautiful it makes him ache just a little bit. He has her make him a turkey sandwich. Virginia asks the girl with a seemingly false, airy voice for a hot tea. They take a small table in the covered courtyard, among small trees, facing a stone fountain boy pissing into a bowl.

"Wow, it clouded over fast, didn't it?"

"Yes. It won't rain anytime soon, though."

"How do you know?"

"It looks tragic and serious and will take its time, it's not like summer rain."

"Really."

"Yes."

"You've become a weather forecaster?"

"I've watched it enough."

When he finishes his sandwich:

"Do you want to go to the apartment?"

"What for?"

He raises his brows, suggestively.

"I don't think so."

"Why not?"

"You know."

He had forgotten. But isn't dissuaded.

"What about the alternative we were working on last time, before we were so rudely interrupted."

"No, I don't want to."

"Why not."

"I just don't."

"No reason?"

"No."

"Just don't want to. You can't give me a single reason."

"That's a reason."

"That's not a reason."

"We don't have to have sex all the time, James."

"We don't? That's silly, of course we do. We're young and in love."

She's amused a moment.

"No seriously. Haven't you had a girlfriend before?"

"No, not really, nothing serious at least."

"Well, there are other things to do."

"Really? Like what?"

"I don't know. Anything."

"Fine, you make one suggestion and I'll consider it."

She doesn't answer, looks at him, challenged.

"See. Hell, I wish we had other things to do sometimes. (He doesn't really, but he knows he can make a good point with this.) There isn't a lot. Without spending money."

Virginia looks at him seriously, searching his eyes to see how upset he is. And how sincere. She finds both, it appears. She says:

"We can go back to your apartment, if you really want to."

"No that's fine. We'll do something else," he is sarcastically obstinate.

"No, really, I changed my mind. Let's go back to your place."

In the apartment, he lies back on the mattress and is satisfied a moment, as she begins. The initial wetness inside her mouth puts him at ease. But her mood becomes languid, as time passes and he is not finished. He improvises. He thrusts himself deep in her throat. Tightens the muscles in his buttocks and thighs and rams her mouth hard, holding her head. When she nicks him or lets it slip from her mouth, everything that he has built up is lost and anger wells up in its place. He becomes feverish. She can' t do anything right, he's thinking. Why am I involved with this stupid girl? Climax is near, finally, and he grabs her head with both hands and moves it for her.

She gags and tightens the muscles in her neck to slow him down, looks up at him through her hair. He is possessed. The desperation to cum is anger he needs to vent. He does not see her eyes bead with tears from almost choking. He bursts with a wave of heat and exhaustion and she swallows it and his penis throbs like an angry bone jutting from the nest of pubic hair. She rests her head on his heaving abdomen. He does not stroke her head. He's empty and burning.

XVIII

I'm ugly. That's certain. Maybe not as ugly as others, but nevertheless ugly. Big nose and little ears, which create this absurd empty space. He is looking at his profile in the mirror, as well as he can without the aid of another mirror. And my hair should've been put on a goat's ass, where it belongs. Oily and limp and not enough to go around. He tips his head to the glass, examines his high forehead. I'm fucking going bald. Look at me! I'm an ugly runt. Five foot seven and hundred and fifty-five pounds, with a gait like a wet rug in a sporadic wind. The product of two ill-matched people who hate each other. He brushes his teeth sick to death with the sight of himself.

MaryAnn notices his grave spirit when he quietly comes in through the back door and hangs up his coat. She thinks he is dissatisfied with his job. She is pleasant:

"James, how are you feelin'?"

"I'm alright."

"Look as though somethin' got you down?"

"It's nothing."

She smiles, wisely, as though she knows why he is as such, and is respectful of his humility. She offers this in the greatly improved black New Orleans dialect of hers:

"If your gettin' ty-ed a doing dishes, we can use a host up front, if your interested? More money."

He is thinking about asking David if he can take the apartment to himself. It is foolish economically, but he is tired of David's surprise visits and his downward spiral. He doesn't trust him anymore. And besides that, simply wants to be rid of him, of what he is becoming. He jumps at the opportunity. MaryAnn is happy to give this to him. She says:

"You'll need some black shoes and slackpants and a white shirt. We'll have a bow for you."

He looks all over town for the right stuff. He decides against buying his shoes at the Costless Shoes on Canal Street, because even Costless is too expensive and the shoes are crap; they look like molded vinyl. He finds a strong pair in a thrift on Decatur past Storyville. Handmade of leather in Boston. They are at least ten years old, but they are beautiful, in nearly new condition. He carries them home in a plastic grocery bag with a white shirt and slackpants. The very next day, he finds himself not in the bowels of the restaurant, but in the most forward possible, and everything is changed, except himself. The waiters introduce themselves to him as though he is newly hired. The restaurant manager speaks to him for the first time since he first set foot inside the place. A quiet, round-faced Hispanic busboy looks up to him with admiration. This all lends him moments of pleasure, but ultimately he knows he has made a mistake. Mainly in that he has to represent the establishment to the customers, as they come through the door, or call on the phone. The morning host is a fragile, pasty, Italian wafer named Penny Ruiz and when she is showing him how to do his job, she complains incessantly, but instantly chirps up and glares a smile when a pair of candied tourists waddle up to the podium. James is not capable of this kind of insincerity. He would never express his discontent to a diner, but nevertheless he can' t pretend to be overjoyed by their presence. His melancholy is thoroughly rooted, and very heavy. It weighs his face down, makes his eyelids heavy. He almost has a drugged expression. Also, to increase his displeasure, the shoes are severing his Achilles heels. Every step he takes sends a pulse of hot pain up though his leg. The first day is an eternity. He walks home in his bare feet, his heels raw and cut. Not enough money in his pocket to buy a tin of bandages. He tries to burn down the flags of leather that do the cutting with a hot butterknife, leaving the blade in the flame of the burner until it is orange, then pressing it onto the inside heel. He sets the shoes up over night with a potato in the toe and a fork and spoon working together like a shoetree.

At the end of his first week as a host he is given his tips, in a small brown envelope. His paycheck is biweekly, but he will receive his cut from the waiter's tips weekly, tabulated for some unknown reason by the bartender. His supply of food is running low and he is relieved to receive the potent little envelope. At least until he opens it, and is heated by a familiar disappointment. He no longer can eat scrapes in the dishroom, and thereby very dependent on his income. He finds eleven dollars inside. He nearly collapses, sad, hungry, angry, yet with only enough energy to walk himself home in his bare feet. He feels justified to steal a box of bandages from the grocery store, while he is buying a sack of potatoes and a tub of butter.

He bakes a potato for dinner and tries some rough arithmetic. Four or five waiters a shift. Fifty to seventy-five a waiter. By the lowest estimation it is twenty-five dollars. He has been stiffed. He brings it up to the bartender the next day, but the bartender can't be bothered, sends James away with a militant severity. He wants to walk out, but the thought of finding another job is crippling. He tells MaryAnn and she seems very disappointed with him, maybe because he doesn't stand up for himself about it. Again, he walks home barefoot, hungry, self-loathing, determined to quit.

XIX

Because he has masturbated four times since waking up at noon, and because he has a penis long enough, he is precariously balanced on his shoulders with his legs over his head. He can get about two inches into his mouth, though with much effort. He pulls himself into a tight roll with one hand on his thigh and jacks himself off with the other, balls volleying into the air off the back of his hand. He is surprised not only that he can do this, but how pleasantly flavorless he is. What discomfiture he experiences at first quickly subsides as he grows light-headed and starts to climax. Tapped dry as he is, a token squirt dribbles into his mouth, hot and mucous. It's an evil potion once it touches his lips, he is transmogrified into a hideous sexual deviant. What seemed like a good idea to pass the time, and get sexual gratification to boot, now seems a hell sure sign of grave trouble; a serious behavioral dysfunction that might require treatment. He falls over on the mattress, short of breath, head throbbing, neck hot and his shoulders and spine aching. He can't get himself up to go spit and wash out his mouth, instead spits on the floor and wipes his mouth and chin with the bed sheet. He lies in a motionless state of self-loathing and regret for what seems like an hour. Then a knock comes on the door

He jumps up as if it were the police beating on the door and he has committed some heinous crime, for that matter he thinks he truly has. He pulls on his jeans and runs into the bathroom and washes out his mouth and wets down the clown tufts of hair that are sticking up on either side of his head. He pulls on a T-shirt and then wipes up the little puddle of spittle by the bed with a sock. He is thorough. The knock comes, again. It is a gentle knock and he cannot imagine who it might be. Another knock, but this one is louder. He hollers out:

"Coming."

"It's me. Jack and Kay are with me. I'm coming in." And she starts to turn the handle and push the door in.

He panics a moment, thinking he has left some evidence of his crime unhidden. He meets them at the door.

"Hey what's up?"

"Oh, nothing. Just getting up," he confesses, as if this is what and only what he is guilty of.

"Lazy ass," Virginia laughs. The three of them are standing just inside the door.

"Yeah, tell me about it. I worked late last night."

"Work tonight?"

"Yes, at four. Here, come in. Can I offer you guys something?"

He doesn't have anything, really, coffee crystals and a contaminated jug of water. They all go into the kitchen.

"No, we're taking you out. Call in sick."

He looks at Virginia.

"Call in sick," she says. "Let us take you out. I ran into Jack and Kay today at the Riverwalk and we decided to come get you."

"Really?"

"Yeah, so you can't let us down." Kay adds.

"Everyone needs an unofficial day off," Jack says.

"Yes, but I need to work, I need the money."

"One day won't break the bank. And I'm paying for everything."

"I don't know?"

"Sure, get ready."

"I'll have to call work. What can I say is the matter?"

"You're just sick."

"No, I need something better than that. How would I explain a complete recovery tomorrow?"

"Fuck 'em," Virginia demands; she knows about his situation.

"Fuck 'em," Kay supports comically.

He looks puzzled. Studies the three visitors. Has made up his mind already, but is thinking about what to say when he calls.

"I hate this job, anyway. I'll tell them my mother has died and I have to fly to her funeral. I can get a couple days off to look for another job. And if I don't find one, then I have a job to go back to."

"Brilliant," Jack says.

"Brilliant," Virginia agrees.

Kay suggests they go to the zoo. James has never been to a zoo, which the other three find hard to believe. It isn't a busy day at the cages. At the lion's den, they wait a long time for the beast to reveal himself. It has an enormous cage with cliffs and a small forest of exotic trees. Jack speculates that it is afraid of James' ugly mug and stays hidden and James pretends to be insulted and walks the gangway to the rhino's savannah, and just then, head swinging, tail swatting, the lazy cat comes around a stone cliff. They laugh all the way to the snake's pit, dark and cold, and Virginia steals kisses from him in damp crannies. James tells her if she wanted to see a big snake they didn't even have to leave the apartment. She elbows him in the ribs and he lets out a groan which caused the motionless, yellow-eyed, horned owl, which they thought was stuffed, to turn his head and stare at them hypnotically. They slide through a clump of spectators gathered around the white alligator's tank. Back out in the rich light of late afternoon, they are hungry.

They fall into stop-and-go traffic. Jack recognizes the tail end of Leo's work truck.

"Isn't that Leo, there?"

"Looks like it."

"Let's tail him."

"We should see if he wants to eat with us?" Kay says.

"That's an excellent idea."

"You know he's not that old? About twenty-three or four," she says, a comment on his selflessness.

"I know. Exactly. He works and lives like he is forty."

They speed around a few cars and ride close on his bumper. Leo is smoking a cigarette and does not notice them. They follow him into his driveway.

"Knock off early?" Jack asks Leo.

"Yeah, they ain't nobody needs any work done," Leo says, mildly disgusted.

Everyone is climbing from Jack's car.

"So what you bunch of deadbeat 'yutes' got going today?"

"Well, we just came from the zoo," Jack begins.

"And they didn't keep any of ya?" He's got a grin in his eye like an old timer.

"Well they tried, but we managed to escape," James plays along.

"But, now we're after food," Virginia announces, boldly, wanting to be a part of the pleasantries. She has never met Leo. "You should come with us." She is warm and Leo is touched. He looks on her with genuine joy in his sunbrowned face, as though her offer has lifted some unnecessary weight from him.

"Yeah," Jack says, "Go get you some clean britches on and come with us."

"I'd have to check with that heathen, see how much of my money she hasn't got around to spenden' yet. You guys come on in, no sense standing around the yard like a pack of Jehovah's."

The house is unoccupied and the television is on. It shows dark-lit scenes of a man in an alley with a large silver gun in his hand that flashes lethally in the dark. Where the light is coming from that shines on the weapon and nothing else is anyone's guess. There's a lot of information in the tiniest of details, if looked for. Sometimes too much. Often just enough. Hollywood loves it guns! Leo stands before it, asks:

"You guys ever see this one? It's about this guy who killed his wife who he thought was cheating on him and she had this micro chip in her brain and now everyone's after him, because the chip is missing and they think he has it. But he doesn't. Turns out she was some kind of spy or something. Now he's got the cops, the FBI, the Russian mafia, and a few others after him." There are rows and rows of VHS cassettes lining the shelves under the television. Not a book anywhere.

"Wow, sounds interesting," Jack slightly exclaims. Then he asks: "Where's the wife?"

"She's upstairs somewhere, sitting on her fat ass, I reckon."

The two girls look at each other, surprised, but humored. Is he serious or is this part of his routine?

"Well, get her down here, so we can go. People are starving in this world."

"I got stuff in the fridge."

"Yes, but we want to go and sit down and let someone else wait on us."

Leo buzzes the upstairs using a small, white intercom in the wall next to the phone. He asks that his wife come down and a voice scratches up a reply and he closes with:

"And tell her to be quick about it."

She comes down shortly and she does not have the children with her. Leo explains:

"These guys want us to go out to dinner with them, so I guess we better go. So round up those monkeys and give'm to their grandma' and then get yourself ready."

"Do we have any money?"

"I reckon we have a little bit. Now get them squalling brats upstairs."

"Well they are already there," she says in the way someone might who is habitually wrong, but is for once right and wants all its worth.

"Then go get ready."

"Are you gonna put something on?"

"I don't see that I have to, I look fine."

She disappears down the hall, frustrated, but role-playing. There's a hint of social awkwardness here. James recognizes it. It is quite prevalent across rural areas where people don't encounter friendly strangers with any frequency. They don't quite know how to behave. It's annoying, but James knows he is guilty of it himself.

Jack says to Leo:

"Maybe you could get another shirt or something."

"What's wrong with this one?"

Kay and Jack raise their eyebrows. Leo says:

"I'll see what I can find."

It is quite a moment and then Leo and his wife start bickering in the back bedroom over a misplaced belt or something. Leo comes out in his socks, wearing a clean shirt, and he sits down on the couch to pull on his boots. His wife follows him out and she is wearing black denim jeans and black slippers and an oversized black blouse, elaborate with fake jewels and gold studs. Her hair is shiny, but dry and nested up atop her head. She is conspicuously and poorly overdressed, a parody of an entire generation before her, but she is modestly serious about it all. Everyone is reluctant to look at her. Leo does not think anything is unusual, pulls his work boots on, presumably the only shoes he has. James watches as Leo laces up the paint-smudged, cracked work boots. At first, they are familiar because he has worked with Leo for so long, but then they become historically familiar. He has seen them somewhere long ago, in his childhood, or somewhere, and then he falls into a moment of profoundly real déjà vu. He has experienced this exact moment before. Standing in this exact position. In this exact lighting. With these exact people. Looking at these exact boots and thinking this exact thought, which is that he has experienced this exact moment before. It's a déja vu of having déja vu. What a beautiful trick of the mind. Everything appears uncomplicated, though it is precisely just the opposite. He falls backward into himself and starts to speak, like moving his lips on the ends of long, flexible sticks:

"Are we ready to go?"

Everyone watches Leo lace up his broken boots with his callused hands and no one says anything about them. *So much depends* on a pair of broken boots.

They drive along cluttered, well-lit Veterans Memorial Boulevard, tight in the small four-door car until they pull into a franchise neighborhood restaurant. A schoolgirl waitress sits them around an enormous table. A round of drinks are ordered and no identification is requested. Virginia ostentatiously suggests:

"How about a toast?"

"To them getting that food out here quickly," Leo says, trying to be funny.

"To running into each other today."

"And to health."

"To happiness."

"To friends."

Then Leo's wife:

"To Leo," and her voice, silent until now, comes out high. It is such an innocent thing to say, but painfully intimate. To single Leo out is bizarre, but the spontaneity is beautiful. Why not? To Leo! The drinks go up and they toast all around.

The food goes fast and more drinks come to the table. The group is jolly, but James can see the large check throwing a dreadful shadow over his plate. The dead relative the waiter will wheel out on a cart. And everyone must pay respect. He can't get up from the table. He can't offer what he doesn't have. The anxiety is quantified with Leo present. He wants Leo's respect. Leo did not hear the conversation at the apartment this morning. The anxiety grips at his insides like a warm hand around a water balloon and twists and twists until it reaches the point where the balloon becomes two separate but joined spheres. Virginia is sensitive to this. She knows what he is thinking. She places her hand in his lap and he places his atop it and she opens her hand and he feels a crumpled cylinder of hard paper, the unmistakable feel of paper currency.

XX

The wind is up and he can hear it in the treetop and pushing at the loose windows. As a busker, he's become acutely aware of the weather outside, well before he goes outside. He cannot find a reason to get out of bed. The mattress has a non-negotiable gravity he's powerless to fight. There isn't anything to eat. It is too cold and windy to play out. He could look for work, but the thought is sickening to him. The way employers looked down on him, as though he is worthless, because if he wasn't worthless why wouldn't he already have a job.

Why can't I just lie in bed? What is it going to hurt? But how stupid, he murmurs aloud, with dry lips, I must get up. I'll walk around and put in some applications. They can't help the way they are. They sort through a lot of riff-raff on the receiving end of all those applications. But what if it rains? I don't have an umbrella. I'd be a fine-looking bulb-headed dude. God, I have to stop this! I need one simple job to earn a moderate income that I can live and eat and have peace of mind and free time to play. I should have never left the dishwashing job. He starts to moan, lowly, slowly, and the vibration in his throat feels good.

He's on the street. Fresh from a quick bath. He is determined to be very pleasant and smile and answer questions cheerfully and quickly. Why did he come to New Orleans? To attend college, he lies. Where? He hadn't thought that far into the lie. Well, I'm not in school, yet, I want to become a resident first, he is quick enough to reply, though not very convincingly. He doesn't lie well and he cannot make eye contact. The damage this does making a first impression is no doubt considerable. One of the numerous drawbacks of being an honest person. And, more importantly, why can't he tell the truth? He knows why. Good kids just don't run away from home. It's only the bad ones. The malcontents. The trouble-makers, when they don't get their way. The ones angry at the world, which is kind of true, he is angry at the world, and maybe for good reason, if only he thinks so.

A couple of hours of botched interviews are all he can stand. He plops face down into his pillow. He wants to fall into the deep oblivion of sleep, but the damn phone rings with a wartime fury. It is Virginia and she wants him to meet her at the streetcar. Staring out the window, his gaze locked as if he could not move his head, or if he could, his eyes would remain fixed, he goes out of himself, becomes the reflection staring back at the object. Who is this young man, tailored in sorrow, arrived here to suffer, expecting compensation in the bargaining? The rattling of the loose windows by the wind beckons him back and soon a filigree of black bones against gray comes into focus and he is staring at the bare trees of late afternoon winter.

Virginia's useless beauty is agonizing. Her hair is darker and longer. Her face smooth and clear and brown and her lips are cranberry. She wears a red cotton parka, a book sack hanging on her back. In a tight crowd on the sidewalk, she kisses him and he desperately yearns for something to pour into his emptiness, like coffee into a porcelain mug, like bourbon into a porcelain mug, like gasoline into a barrel fire, anything, but unfortunately, nothing. And he really isn't sure who's to blame. It's 'no new tale to tell', either. He heard this lyric in the Silversmith, "wish there was something real, wish there was something true." Nine Inch Nails, they are called. Could he play this on violin? no he could not, it wouldn't translate, there's a rage, there's an animalistic fury, irresponsible and unstoppable, and assault on every demon in heaven and elsewhere; he envies the music's ability to exorcise this vehement choler, he wishes he had even that. Anything other than emptiness.

"Let's get a mocha?" Virginia suggests. "I'm dying for a mocha."

"Sure," the banality is actually painful.

"How about Café Naige?"

"Sure."

"What's wrong?"

"Nothing."

"Are you sure?"

"Yes."

"No, what is it?"

"Really, it's nothing. I'm just frustrated over finding work."

"Oh, don't be. I'm sorry."

"No, it's not your fault."

"No, but I feel bad for you."

"Don't, at least one of us should be happy."

"That's not fair. I'm sympathetic. You're sadness becomes mine. You'll find something, I know you will. And besides, soon you'll be able to play out as the weather gets better."

He finds no consolation in this. She is right, but what until then?

"Hey, I brought you some food."

"Yeah?"

"I thought we would go back to your place and roll in the sack for a while, then feast."

"Like monsters, or kings?"

"We'll make love like monsters and eat like kings."

Café Naige is inside the tall, white tombstone of a skyscraper at the foot of Canal Street. They sit away from the counter and drink mochas heaped with liqueur lace whipped cream. A sparrow has gotten into the building and flies between the tables and perches on the backs of chairs and looks as though he knows more than he ever possibly could know being a bird, yet none of it affects him. His blank black eyes are intelligent, but free of the curse of an acute sentience.

He is quiet and listens to Virginia's anecdotes about this and that, but he is more interested in the bird. Maybe he can teach me a lesson about the necessities of forgetting, or the priorities of selective memory. They are scooping from the deep bottoms of their glasses. Virginia asks:

"Can I get you another one?"

She looks at him, wants to absorb his melancholy.

"No, I'm fine. This was good, though, thanks."

"Come on, let's go to your place."

The dry warmth of her skin is a drug. And the smell of her hair and her garments, especially the perfumed musk in her panties. She is melting between her legs and he falls into the warm fold. He's got his head in the pillows of her chest and she holds him tightly, until she senses he is about to ejaculate. She takes his face into her hands and stares flushed and desirous and serious into his eyes. She whispers to him:

"Don't pull out."

He is not wearing protection. He looks at her, puzzled. Has she gone mad? He slows his rhythm.

"What?"

"I want to feel you cum inside me."

"It's not safe."

"No. It's safe."

"It's never safe."

"I just want to feel you inside me."

She hugs him, gyrating under him, doing nothing to lessen the stimulation. He is about to explode. She holds him tightly. He feels it gush down the last length of the pipe and he tries to pull out. She grabs him with both arms around his neck and both legs around his waist. He struggles for a second, then hot semen explodes in her vagina and they both melt into one pulsating thing. She heaves in long, deep breaths and he rises and falls to her undulations.

He goes into the bathroom to wash himself. Virginia pulls on her panties and her parka and spreads out the blanket and makes a picnic with the contents of her backpack like a good little wife. The contents of their home a mattress and a radio, a tiny television set, foil on the antenna, a pile of tattered clothing and a violin in a blistered case.

There is fruit and small boxes of raisins and a bag of pretzel sticks and three turkey bagel sandwiches. She squeezes mustard on his the way she knows he likes it, on both sides. She waits until he returns before starting to eat and she is as happy as Kool-aid. Doesn't even try to explain, or show any trace of regret or wrong doing.

XXI

It rains all of Monday. It comes down so heavy the traffic crawls in the streets. He looks for work during breaks in the rain. The next day drizzles away. He works the next two days with Leo. They work on a house on St. Charles Ave. The old man who owns the house has known Leo's father for many years and his wife brings them gumbo and iced teas and cookies. When they finish the work and James is cleaning up, the old man goes to Leo and pays him in cash, throwing in an extra hour's pay for each of them. Leo pays James later at the house.

"You'll notice a little extra in there; the old fella liked what we did for him. It don't ever hurt to be good to old people like that, they got money piled in the bank they could never spend and when they see you do them right they'll show it in return, some of them."

James is pleased that Leo was honest about the extra hour's wage, because he would otherwise never have known it was given.

At home his food is running out. He has one hundred and eight dollars. It will not cover the rent. He lays back on his mattress, sick to death with worry. He can go back to the restaurant, but he doesn't want to. Then the phone rings, it *is* the restaurant. The manager asks how he is doing and gives his condolences for the passing away of his mother and is sorry to inform him that things are very slow and they will have to let him go. Really, he thinks, things are slow. It's slammed every night of the week. He suspects someone might have seen him out on the street, that or the fact that any number of just as desperate persons are in the ranks of the unemployed awaiting any opportunity.

Then the phone rings again. He's afraid it's the restaurant saying they changed their minds, which would be even more horrible than the first call letting him go. But it's the most delightful and unexpected person he could imagine. Damarie errupts with joy at the sound of his voice. Oh to even have the joy inside in the first place, much less find a place to express it!

"Mister James, I have the perfect thing for you! Just the perfect thing. I know you will do it. Will you do it? We should get dinner, I will tell you everything."

XXII

The house sits close to the sidewalk, which is common for these large homes in the garden district not on St. Charles Avenue. The half wall of slave made brick and black cast iron fence keep out all but the city's elite. There's gas lamps burning a tender existence at the gate, a liveried porter pulls it open at the sight of him, violin case in hand. Bursts of potted sago lead to the porch, hung with giant baskets of Tahitian bridal veil. In an alcove over grown with creeping fig, Bacchus pours from a stone amphora into a lily pool of black and red spotted koi the size of a man's forearm, making their eternal laps. The air smells of jasmine and money, generational fathoms of money. The shutters on the floor to ceiling windows are thrown open. The doubled Charleston green doors fitted with brass, and before he can knock, they open, a maidservant in smock and headdress ushers him in.

"Well good evening Mr. Buck, if you'll just follow me", in the sweetest southern accent possible, using his last name as is custom when one is not acquainted. He follows her through the enormous house. There's a Picasso on the wall in the hall. On his left a grand salon, piano and silver candelabra and hand blown Tiffany lamps, heirloom furniture, oil paintings on papered walls. On his right, through French doors of beveled leaded glass an eagle crested girandole broadcasts the crystal chandelier's white gold light over a table sit for ten on linen. From the street no one could imagine how large this home is. Through a painted six-panel door, they enter into a large library. A portly man, balding, a blue silk ascot, a salmon colored dress shirt, his jowls broke out in veins, his watery eyes green as emeralds, stands at a desk. He's on the phone, a high ball on the desk under his fingertips. Senior partner of a law firm, Damarie told him. Their families have known each other for over a century and, when her parents were assassinated by the government in her country, he was instrumental in her immigration to America. He takes a sip from the cut crystal tumbler as James Buck is introduced without a word, then immediately waves him off with a finger. She leads him to a butler's pantry. He is given white shirt and black polyester slack pants and blue bow tie. The clothes fit him well enough, but they feel unnatural, he checks himself in the mirror, unimpressed. He asks the maid to tie the tie for him, as he has never worn one much less knows how to tie one. This close to him, he can smell her. A delicious smell. Earthy, yet sweet, skillet baked cornbread with a lick of wildflower honey. Her brown skin as pecan as Christmas morning. Her black eyes gentle.

"There you go, sa," she says, looks him up and down, "'fraid those shoes will just have to do."

She guides him out into a lush courtyard. She shows him where he will stand as he plays. She informs him of when he will start and when he will end and when he will be allowed to talk a break. She puts great emphasis that whether there is anyone in the courtyard or not, he must play until instructed to stop.

"They don't most of them every come out here except to smoke, but it don't matter, Mister Paul wants you to be playing, if and when they do. And they frown on you talking to any of the guest, though they might say something to you. It's best just smile an' keep it simple, yes sa, yes ma'am. I'll come out and let you know when you can take a break, so you can use the bat' room, and what have you. They's no one here now, so you can make yourself comfortable for a little while yet. You need some water, I suppose?"

He is actually glad he is outside in the kindness of evening and gaslight. He has never felt so utterly poor and insignificant as he is in this house. There's a spoon in place setting worth more than everything he has and has ever had. Leading up to this night, he was nervous and also very excited. What a great opportunity this will be for you, Damarie encouraged him. Now he just can't wait for it to be over. Three hours, fifty dollars. He really can use the money, good money, too, he thought when asked a price. Now he realizes he could have asked triple, hell tenfold, and they would have either said no or respected him more for it.

And it comes to pass, as uneventful as that. He stood in the courtyard and played everything he knew, over and over, with some improvisation, with many mistakes, very mechanically when alone, which was most of the time. A few men came out to smoke cigars, and few elegant ladies, with dyed hair and vivid eye shadow and jewelry, jewelry like he did not know people other than royalty could own. This women wore a diamond the size of a robin's egg, almost as blue against the crepe of her breast. This another woman wore gold and jeweled wrist cuffs, and a ruby on her finger to put out an eye. Nary a word spoken to him, at most a smile, or a little nod.

Many are in the salon, he can hear their regal laughter and how their antebellum heritage still echoes in their talk. He hands the maidservant the uniform. In his own clothes now, she leads him out through the backdoor. She thanks him so very politely, hands him an envelope, which he puts in his violin case. He wishes her good night, quiet fond of her really, the unconditional kindness in her demeanor. On the streetcar, he takes it out. The paper stock is of great quality. It is not sealed. He opens it and pulls out a crisp fifty dollar bill, it hasn't seen a change of hand since it's printing. He wished it made him feel better, the possession of it. He thinks about the maidservant. Smiles thinking about her benevolent smile. She has to be at least ten years his senior.

XXIII

He's riding the bus the next day out toward City Cemetery. He is following an ad he found in the classifieds. It is a nondescript watering hole in the more residential stretch of the street. He asks to see the manager and the bartender tells him the manager is out but he can take an application. She reaches under the bar, asks:

"Do you have any experience?"

"No, but I've got an excellent memory and I can learn fast."

She was about to offer the application, but withholds it now. "Well, we don't hire inexperienced staff."

He looks around the place. The dark hides the slovenliness, only a couple neon beer signs buzzing a dim light, a shaft of sunlight pouring through a quiet storm of airborne detritus. There's a few chairs scattered around an empty table. There's an arcade-sized pool table, the felt worn through in places, delaminated in others, and a table top Pac-Man, the screen saver chomping. An accredited drunk is situated at the end of the bar. The 24-hour cable news is flashing self-importantly, a little digital, magenta *mute* in the bottom right hand corner. The irony isn't funny. His ears burn and his vision becomes blurry from the rage welling inside. He doesn't even think about the unlikeness of his even *wanting* to work in such a place.

"I'm a great self-learner," he hears himself say, as the fury swells from deep within.

She looks at him with false sympathy, says:

"It's our policy not to hire inexperienced staff."

A story as old as Jude Fawley, older, history immemorial.

He's back on the Canal Street bus in a muted rage burning throughout his body like an over-burdened fuel cell. A loud, piercing racket from the back of the bus grabs his agitated attention. A tall, black teenager is kicking on the back doors with his pristine, hundred-dollar basketball shoes. He is violently pulling on the stainless steel poles with fists of gold rings, in a shimmering sweat suit—an obscene parody of a celebrity athlete. The bus has come to a stop and the backdoors aren't opening, and he has become impatient, fighting confusion with rage. *Backdoor, backdoor*, he yells, and not just loud enough so the bus driver can hear, but even louder so he can hear himself over the violent thumping deep in his earsockets. He doesn't even bother to remove an earphone to hear a response from the bus driver, who is complacently observing the spectacle in her long rearview mirror, calmly suggesting that he push the red button to the right of the right pole. He continues to yank on the poles, looking at the bus driver as though she were the fault. James is beyond himself with disgust. He stands up and pulls one of the yellow plugs from his ear, inconceivably loud music straining from the little plastic snail, and he says with the edge of a steel blade in his voice:

"She's trying to tell you the poles are broken; push the red button, there."

The kid jumps back as if burned, hostile and ready to war, pantomiming reaching under his jumpsuit for a gun, like a scene in a John Singleton film, says:

"Fuck's up wit shoe man, don't be fuck'n putt'n yo fuck'n whitebread on my shit! I' fuck'n pop yo' ass."

"Yes, whatever. But right now we're working on trying to get you to figure out how to operate the back door. Here," and he reaches across for the button.

The kid throws his hands up, fingers twisted cryptically, pointing into his chest, like a very absurdly dressed warlock conjuring some magical power.

"You is *fucked up*, man, you better step fo' you get's yo cracker ass shot."

But the kid has no idea how furious our man is right now, at least not until he looks him directly in the eyes and maybe, then, he gets it. Either way, he reveals no sign of acquiescence.

He gives James a careless shove and bounces down off the bus and yells back.

"Consider dis yo lucky day, mother fucker."

The shove causes James to stumble back on an old nanny in a blue knit cardigan stretched thin on her thick arms. Her walking stick jabs into his back. She jumps alive as if awakened from sleep and hatefully shifts her cane to the opposite leg, riding the bus has never been easy. James goes back to his seat and he can feel the negative energy from the bus like shrink wrap, he can barely move his head, barely breath. The bus rolls forward and the black boy makes a pistol with his thumb and long, big-knuckled, middle finger and takes a shot through the window.

James is the only white person on the bus, he then realizes. He is shocked by the lack of support he receives and even more devastating is the hostility he feels. The bus driver even looks back at him as though keeping an eye on a troublemaker. Some nappyhead children run up the aisle and brazenly stare at him, sucking on sugardaddies with filthy sticks; their hippopotamus of a mother bellowing at them in entirely indecipherable Ebonics.

He turns to look out the window as the bus moves slowly in the street. There's a prolific loitering everywhere. Indoor furniture serving the same purpose outside in a blasted yard or on the sidewalk. Vacant lots wrapped in chainlink fence, buried in windswept rubbish. Decrepit shotguns listing into each other, the cypress clapboards peeling paint and gray and tagged in spray paint, the porches smashed into the dirt. Used car lots with $500 dollar Fords, because who can own a car they can't afford to insure. Unpainted corner stores with barred-up doors and walk-up windows where things are sold in small brown paper bags in broad daylight, and a hundred fold more business going on after midnight than all day long; in the hours before dawn, when not even the explosion of a firearm in the near-distance causes alarm.

It's an awful place and he knows it. The Quarter is over-run with tourists, while everything around it rots in poverty and ignorance and under-employment and racism from both directions. Anyone with money, mostly the white people, have run off into the suburbs and locked the doors and cranked up the air-conditioning. Every twenty blocks there seems to be a housing project, a.k.a. a war zone, where generations of fatherless children are weaned on hate and hopelessness. Or so it seems to a white rural Missourian who's exposure to black people is the Jeffersons on television. Where no one he's every known has ever had the luxury of *being* a tourist anywhere outside the state. Where white people didn't say disparaging things about black people very often only because there just weren't any around. There's a problem in this town and it's obvious and apparently whitey's to blame unless you're talking to whitey then it's 'them fuckin' niggers' and it isn't going to get any better anytime soon. He knows he's got to get out of town. The new is worn off. But where does he go? North, somewhere? A city, of course, I can' t make it in a small town, not without a car. New York? Too big. St. Louis? Forget it, too close. Boston? Chicago? He does the math. I can use the deposit for the February rent. I can take the bus. (He has seen various advertisements on television and billboards for Greyhound, $49 each way, anywhere in the U.S.) I can play out on every good day and night. If Leo needs me I can work for him. After a bus ticket, I'll have sixty in my pocket. I'll need about three hundred.

He climbs off the city bus and walks to the Greyhound bus terminal at Lee Circle to buy an advanced ticket. Just like that—a short wait in line in a filthy bus station and forty-nine dollars, and he's ready for what ever is next. He folds the long perforated banner of tickets into his pocket and strolls home. He actually feels better for most of the walk. But as soon as he turns on to Orleans and walks the two blocks to his apartment he begins to play host to a ballet of emotions ever swapping partners: elation with impatience, resentment with impatience, happiness with anticipation, anticipation with anxiety, anxiety with impatience.

XXIV

He's in warm, blue afternoon, soaring, soaring at escape velocity. He exits the atmosphere. He experiences an exhilarating chill. He bends his flight downward to earth, breaks clouds, and familiar landscapes come up at him rapidly—the green and golden and forested undulating country of his childhood, dotted with faces of acquaintances looking up at him, saying things he cannot hear. He can see the frighteningly hateful visages of his mother and father and they are reaching up for him and he banks up just enough degrees that he soars horrifyingly close to their fingertips, but they do not touch him. He accelerates through space and time at breathtaking velocity and where the terrain becomes less familiar, it becomes more gorgeous.

He wakes from a sound, delicious sleep, lifts his head to see the time, but the glare on the crystal obscures the small hands. His watch, lying on the floor next to his bed in a shaft of noonday sunlight pouring through the window overhead, is an extra-planetary space station immobilized in a trapezoid of starlight, illuminating a galaxy of macroscopic particles forever adrift. Outside, it is beautifully warm and sunny. When cars pass by outside, their windshields reflect spears of sunlight through the front windows that advance across the ceiling into his room. Miraculously, the trees have come to bud, as if overnight, and birds are fussing about them. The sky is an unblemished pastel blue. He gets up eager to start making arrangements for his next adventure. He boils some water and stirs in some coffee crystals. He surveys the apartment for anything he can sell right now and won't need between now and when he leaves, (not much) and after his morning coffee, he trots off to the secondhand shop on Barracks. Eighteen dollars for all of it. He got the biggest return on the black dress shoes and he is glad to see them go. He didn't sell the television, in case David wants it back, and it can be welcome company, often enough, he's grown found of Letterman.

He walks, now, along the unused tracks on the levee. Couples stroll by hand in hand, mostly same-sex couples, unless they are old. Two men walk by him and boldly, smilingly, stare him down. One has his hand in the other's shorts to the wrist, it's just wrong, heter or homo, where's the god damned decency, but what ever, he's got his own jack ass to ride. An old white-haired couple, dressed neatly, camera bag slung over shoulder, crosses the path, scold the homosexuals with stern, disapproving, shaking faces. He turns out onto the wharves at the Natchez Riverboat. Like maggots in the blood pool of a dead white whale, the people heave. Children lure seagulls to the railings with breadcrumbs, so they can throw stones at them. Harley motorbikes tear long, dense rents into whatever serenity the afternoon might possess, followed by the perpetual squeal of car alarms in their wake. A chalk-white, blockish statue of an unfinished man stands facing the river in great bewilderment, with unconcern for the city behind him. The metaphor is profoundly accurate. As if in a trance, blurthinking, he stands beside a bench and folds open his case and removes his violin and begins to play. He plays without interruption, solid and introspective, much of it improvisational. It comes from somewhere else, from the dark viscera found deep in the giant hole in his chest. In three hours, he makes nine dollars. He calls Virginia on a payphone. They arrange to meet at the Riverwalk.

He arrives well before she does and he sits in a bench under a potted ponytail palm. The noise of the long corridor of shops is slight. He contemplates playing while he waits for Virginia to arrive, but the incessant patrolling of the rent-a-cop discourages him, in a city of music, the brain surgeons that run the place have prohibited busking. When she does arrive, they walk up to the food court and she buys them slices of pizza. Her mother is at the health club in the adjacent hotel. They sit at a table under a plateglass window becoming black and cold, framing the descending night on the river. He can feel, remember, identify with the swift darkness of the river as the glass starts to mirror the two of them in the booth. Virginia asks:

"Did you look for work today?"

"No, I went out and played."

"Was it any good?"

"I made a little money."

"That's good. I'm sure you can use it."

"Yes."

"Oh! Did you get a newspaper, today?"

"No."

"I saw an ad for a bartender's position."

"Where?" he says, though not very interested.

"Someplace on Canal."

Things changed now like they are he is humored by the co-incidence.

"I don't have any experience."

"Experience. You can figure it out."

"You'd think," he says, the humor rapidly wearing off. He can't help but think how on the sit-com Cheers, Woody walks into the bar looking for a job and has some humorous encounter with Sam or Diana or the Coach and then presto he gets a job. And several other things get resolved as well, if he remembers correctly, and all in 23 minutes or less, divided into bit sized pieces between car, mattress, and check cashing service commericals. Television doesn't prepare you for the reality of life, why he's never been a big fan of it, in moderation at best.

"You sound bitter?"

"It's just very ridiculous the way things are. I can pour a drink. What fool can't or at least couldn't learn how to in a short time."

"Well, you should look into it, anyway. Just to see."

"I did. The lady looked at me like I was an idiot to think lowly me could make a drink without prior experience."

"Did you tell her you could learn, easily? You're brilliant."

"They're not looking for brilliance, just experience, and for the least the market will bare. *'It is their policy to hire only people with experience'.*"

"So how do they expect people to start?"

"Don't know, I've already pondered the whole matter. It's fucking pathetic."

Virginia is clearly startled. It is uncommon for him to use such language.

"Hey, don't get upset, there's nothing you can do . . ."

"Oh, there's something I can do. I can scratch this filthy place."

"Scratch it?"

"Yes, scratch it. Draw a line through it. Done. Pack it up. Leave."

"Leave? Leave New Orleans," she is becoming panicked, serious.

"Yes, absolutely."

"Why?"

"To make a better life. Get a job. Pay the rent. Buy a new pair of shoes and jeans. Play my violin, maybe go to school. Not have to worry every waking moment about survival."

"Is it that bad?"

"Yes," he says fluidly. "You wouldn't think it would be, with all the activity that seems to go on in this town, but yes, there's little work."

"I am sorry," and she places her hand on his and leans to him to see into his downcast gaze.

"I'm thinking about going to Chicago," he says, dryly.

"Chicago? James, why?"

"I don't know. It's North. Things are better in the North."

"How do you know?"

"It has to be, I know it. All this town has is tourists, they have to come from someplace."

She looks at him in sad disbelief.

"I'm tired of all the ignorance, the place is lethargic with it. Its overrun with hostile blacks and rednecks and drug addicts and homosexuals, and the ugly tourists come trampling over everything in hordes, clad in name-brands, clutching fists full of brochures, grease on their double chins, and they don't want to spend a dollar more than they have to on the good times they're expecting." The look of disgust on his face is impressive and dreadful.

"Well," and she isn't really prepared to reply to such a tirade.

"Well, what?"

"I don't know. Do whatever you think you have to do, I guess. I do know you have a tendency to go to absolute extremes of negativity."

He hears the low grade contempt in her tone.

"Actually, I have already bought a one-way ticket."

"James?"

"Yes."

"How long have you been thinking about this?"

"Long enough."

"Long enough? What, a day? Why didn't you say something to me about it?"

"I have."

"Not about leaving."

He doesn't respond. She says:

"What if it doesn't work out?"

"I'll make it work."

They are silent a moment, then Virginia asks:

"When?"

"Two weeks."

Her eyes are wide with astonishment.

"James, that is ridiculous!"

"How?"

"You're just going to leave? Just like that?"

"Just like what? What other way is there?"

"Not like this, in two weeks' notice."

"What then, two months, three? How long do I need? This is what I want to do. If I had the money, I'd leave tomorrow."

She is cut to pieces. Her breath escapes her. He has revealed an icy indifference. It hasn't occurred to him, until right this moment, that any of this could concern her.

"What's wrong with you? How can you say that? What about us?"

He is stupefied. What about us? How could I have not thought about us? I have never thought about us. I never imagined an *us* in the future. I'm the brain in the vat here, not you; you are one of the characters I am imagining. You are just here until I'm somewhere else and then you are no longer.

"James, look at me. Do you care about me?"

"Yes." He *half* lies.

"Don't you love me?"

"Yes." He *half* lies.

"Then how can you say that?"

"I don't know," and what he doesn't say, of course, is: I just can, it is easy. You are not the first I have had to leave behind, one can become used to it.

"You don't love me." And her voice breaks and her eyes glisten.

"Yes, I do, but I'm dying here. I can't survive."

"I can help you. I can move in with you and get a job. Or you can live with me and you wouldn't have any rent. You have to give it more time. You are giving up."

I am moving on. (Again thinking and not saying.) This book isn't finished. There are more chapters yet to be written. And you are not in them. There is nothing I can do about that.

"Can't you give it a try?"

"I have."

"You haven't."

He feels justified being angered by this:

"What the fuck do you know about it? You have everything at your fingertips. Mommy and Daddy can give you anything you want. I have shit. I have myself."

"You have me."

Her face becomes still with resolve and a tear slides down over her straight lips falling onto the table like an enormous drop of rain. Their pizza slices have gone untouched.

"I'm sorry. I wish I didn't have to go, but I have no choice."

Virginia wipes her eyes, causing the pools of tears collected here to smear, completing a truly devastated look, which penetrates his long-acquired indifference. He is beginning to have sympathy for her.

"You do have a choice. But you don't want to make it."

She is right and he almost realizes it, but won't let himself, she lost him a long time ago, with that first lie, he can't let that go. He takes a bite of pizza. After a long silence, Virginia says:

"I'm sorry for crying." The balls of her hands squeak as she wipes her damp cheeks. "I'm not mad at you, only hurt."

She grabs his hand. He kisses her because it seems like the right thing to do. Her lips are hot and then wet in the places where the streams of tears have run over them. She smiles back at him as though this has made some difference. Mrs. Gesclair finds them.

"What's the matter, V?"

"Nothing. I just," and she looks at James for approval. "James is moving to Chicago."

Mrs. Gesclair looks at James with that temepred anger only a mother can possess.

"Have you found a job there?"

"No, not really."

"Then why are you going there?" She sits down at the table, ready to take on the crisis.

"It's not going too well, here. I need work. I need more opportunities than New Orleans has to offer."

"What makes you think it will be any better in Chicago?"

"I don't know. It just has to be. There are more people there, more things going on."

Mrs. Gesclair is very visibly disappointed. She has thought James to be more sensible than this. She says, with a resignation he shouldn't be expected to have at his age:

"You'll find places are really all the same."

"They can't be," he whispers, defiantly, looking at his strong, beautiful hands. Mrs. Gesclair looks at Virginia. Virginia looks out the plateglass window into the depthless darkness beyond the yellowy reflection of herself. They are all silent a long time. Then Mrs. Gesclair says:

"Well, I'm going to go get the car. Are you riding home with me or staying here?" At this late an hour of the night, this can mean only one thing. James looks at Virginia to see what she might be thinking. But Virginia doesn't look at him and answers:

"I'll come home."

"I'll be in front then," she says, referring to the flag-stoned circular drive in front of the hotel.

When she is gone, Virginia says:

"She is very upset about you leaving."

"Well, I have to."

"No you don't, but you think you do, so I'm not going to be upset with you. I'm just going to hate to see you leave. You have to understand that people get attached to people and it hurts when they go away."

"I'm moving away, not dying."

"What's the difference?"

"I can see you again, someday. Maybe I'll be alright there and you can come visit me and who knows."

"Yes," she says, forgivingly, though she does not believe any of it.

"I'll see you tomorrow?"

"Sure," and she gives him a light kiss. Her eyes start to water, again, and she turns and walks away quickly. He is sad, now. He wished he wouldn't have told her until later, much later. But then considers whether that would have been fair to her, either.

He is flopping in his bed, dreaming vividly. He bullets through the purple night. The gleaming metropolis is approaching. A billion lights blaze all around. Laser-red arteries of every radial weave into a giant burning ribbon. He circles overhead. The columns of steam billowing from the skyscrapers warm his face. A river of yellow cabs floods the deep crystalline canyons. He alights on a cornice, and like an angel turning into a gargoyle, becomes heavy and flightless. Do I jump? Will I lose my powers of flight, forever, if I do, go hurtling to the ground? He can sense the rules of his dreams are changing.

At four in the morning, he is startled into consciousness. He can't readily remember what startled him. He can make out the time in the white film of the moonlight. He stares out the window without fear or hope of anything. He feels like he has already left this earth.

XXV

Did he arrive broken, in this life, or was he broken along the way? He wasn't a particularly boisterous child, reserved, didn't talk until he was 5. He didn't want much, so didn't ask for much, but there was never much for the asking. He feared his folks, instinctively, or so it seemed. The exact middle child in a mangy brood of heathen. Dirt poor. By the time his clothing were handed down from the two above they were rags. He wore them the best he could. There was something different about him, this innate atavistic reckoning. His mannerisms tapped from a different source. He didn't talk like the rest of them. He didn't play like the rest of them. He didn't cry like the rest of them. He took a beating like none other, barely let out a scream, unlike his brothers, they would howl and dance a wild circle around the arm by which they were held. But he was smart. He knew how to cut a switch. When the others would go for small, only to be sent back out for something more befitting a good *learning,* he would select just the right size, just the right length, something his father would be proud of, except, he would use the knife to slice just the smallest cut, a hair's breadth perforation really, unnoticeable, at a angle in the green bark, the general rule was if the switch broke the punishment was sufficient. There were times though, more than once, additional switches were harvested for the same offense.

He knew from his earliest day, he was not like them. They drank dark soda, and he drank Sprite or 7-up. They liked Snickers, while he flavored Butterfinger or a Milky Way. They liked their cornbread in a glass of milk with heaps of sugar. He liked it hot with a lick of butter. They liked to fight and argue, he liked to not come home from school and see how long he could go before someone came out after him. He liked books, they liked television. His first Susan B Anthony he spent on an World Book Encyclopedia, first book in the house other than the telephone directory. He liked to imagine what lay off beyond those wooded hills. The others like to squash frogs and torment each other. They liked to listen to records of Bob Seger and George Jones, and so did he, except he wanted to be Bob Seger or George Jones or Johnny Cash or Hank Williams Jr, until he found the violin. Worldviews collided. Here lies the collateral damage.

The difference between himself this morning and himself at 4 a.m. earlier this morning is the difference between a bungee jumper at the onset of his adrenaline rush perched over the canyon into which he will jump and a bungee jumper whose bungee snapped on the stretch and he is now crushed upon the boulders below but still alive. He has absolutely no clue as to self-recovery. Instead, instigates his suffering searching for justification for recovery. A twenty-year-old boy shouldn't have to try and shake the relentless belief that he should do something remarkable in exchange for existence—the right to breathe air and take up valuable space should *be,* as well as *feel,* like an inalienable right. But this feeling of absolute worthlessness goes back before he can remember. It has been programmed there. If he thinks it is inherent, incapable of alteration, it's because you can't see the color of a sac you're sown up in. Nor where you're being been taken.

He plays out forcibly, hoping his mood will come around. The seemingly obligatory toss of a quarter or a pinch of nickels and pennies doesn't help. Then rain comes on. He takes a long bath. He bakes a potato. He goes to bed early, but cannot sleep, flops around in bed, stares out the window, dreadfully hopeless and disappointed with himself for being in such a state. Noon the next day finds him like a shoe in a pond bobbing sluggishly just below the surface of the water, yet not enough saturation to sink to the bottom.

He makes a weak cup of coffee; his crystals are running low and he wants them to last. He isn't really hungry of late, has stopped eating breakfast. He is saving every dime for Chicago. He has a roof over his head, now; he can suffer on the food. I'll need every last cent I can get my hands on. He lets his thoughts menace him. You are foolish to go. The weather will improve soon. You've got Virginia; she loves you. You will get more work with Leo. He has been good to you. Why can't you be happy with that? You're a square sprocket. A rotten plum in the fruit bowl. This hotpressing thinking is eroding his resolve like acid. He begins to feel bound up in something hot and elastic, slowly becoming less elastic, until he is in a state of lethal immobility.

Virginia calls. Her mood is cool and unconcerned. Her lack of interest is self-interest. She invites him to go to the theatre with her and her brother and his girlfriend this evening. She's paying.

She feeds him before they go. He eats half a bowl of spicy gumbo over rice. His stomach has shrunken so much that this makes him lazy, but clearheaded. It is cold out and Virginia wears a black shawl and looks gorgeous in the bustle of people pouring into the theatre. Steinbeck's *The Grapes of Wrath* has drawn a huge crowd of every demographic. The old and bluehaired have filled much of the first, second and third rows. The back center aisles are filled with the twenty-something, careless, loud, casual, wearing ball caps and ponytails and name-brand tennis shoes and gymsuits, as though it were study hall. Middle-aged couples sit leaning into each other, talking secretively, commenting on persons they notice in the crowd; they occupy the balcony seats, in dark blues and reds of an unnatural newness and stiffness.

With Virginia at his side, they take their seats, quietly. People are chatting and filling seats and the orchestra is tuning instruments and the noise starts to settle and the lights are beginning to dim, when James notices a particular girl. She is in a smart, unpleated brown cocktail dress. Her skin is porcelain. Her hair is auburn. Her face is pale and dollish and her lips are red for the occasion. She takes a seat two rows down and an aisle over from where he is seated, with Virginia on his left. The lights go out, just as she turns her head to look around, and she, by chance, sees him, and she looks at him, a moment, and smiles affectionately. The floodlights burn up the curtains.

Drop stardust. As if by a single benevolent wave of her wand, she has alleviated him of all his torment. He comes to this epiphany: I'm young and so is Virginia. We have just begun building the relationships of our lives. There will be so many people in our lives. There is no wrong in going on. It is how the rich fabric of life is woven.

In the penumbra of the stage lights, he thinks he can make out her silhouette.

"Isn't this great?" Virginia asks.

"Yes, it is wonderful," and he really means it but he hasn't even begun to notice the performance. The cast has gathered around a dusty clapboard in theatrical flatlands. The crowd falls silent.

In the intermission, Virginia's brother and his girlfriend are red-eyed and lethargic, having slept through the first act; and you can hardly blame them. The staging is extraordinary, but the cast is mediocre by any estimation. They ask Virginia how much longer until it's over and she flips through the playbill. James scans the crowd for the girl. He spots her. She is slight of build; her dress suggests slim hips and a girlish chest. She has jewelless fingers and a small pendant around her neck. How can I meet her? I cannot, but he is not sad by this. She represents his future. That what is soon to come. She does not see him, is immersed in a crowd of acquaintances.

When the curtain falls on the last act though, and the lights come on, everything is changed. Bad acting or not, the story was still the story Steinbeck meant to tell. The grass isn't greener over yonder hill. The sun will come up tomorrow—the same way it did today. Though he realizes he isn't the reckless boy (he thinks himself more levelheaded and cautious), he still scorns his irrational behavior. Do I stay or do I go? The answer was yes in Missouri and he has yet to regret it. But he planned long and made huge sacrifices to get here and now he's here. Is leaving being too hasty?

The theatre empties rapidly. In a queue filing out on his left, the young girl is approaching. He has almost forgotten about her, wrapped up in Steinbeck's tale. Alas, the inspiration he desperately needs now. She is sidestepping around the fat ass of someone stalled in the aisle attempting to retrieve something from a seat: a wallet, a playbill, a morsel of chocolate. He stands up behind Virginia so she cannot see his desperation. The girl is near and she sees him and he sees her and he looks into her eyes and she glances away shyly. His blood runs cold. In this proximity, he can see her blemished young face. Her pale veiny neck. The split ends of her hair. Her boyish, pigeon chest. And just like that his illusion of a better life vanishes. Granted she may be an extraordinary young woman who should not be judged by her appearance, much like him self. But that isn't the point. This is allegory, a cautionary tale. Virginia takes him by the arm and they walk out into the chill, sparkling night. Their breath visible and car exhaust rising all around, as if the world sat in the smith's quench, and Virginia clings to him. She is the most beautiful person he has ever known. He puts his arm around her. In ten days, never again.

XXVI

He is playing in Woldenburg Park and it looks like rain. The days numbered each one must be squeezed of every cent. A plump, ugly man tosses him a dollar, with an air of self-admiration and distraction, a chesty blonde on his arm. She bounces alongside him in a perpetual giggle, ass jiggling in bubblegum pink spandex. The hours go by easily and a few dollars accumulate in his case. The sky grows dark. Then black. Then it breaks apart into infinite pellets of glass.

He runs like a quarterback, violin case under his arm, to Jax Brewery. He enters at Toulouse and walks along the well-lighted shops, leaving tracks of water behind. He takes a seat near the saxophone player in Café Beignet. The rain is pounding the street, they smell of detergent and the gutter water runs frothy. He watches pedestrians scramble for shelter, ducking under canopies and balconies, going into shops and cafes. This café fills up quickly. The waiter brings him coffee. The porcelain mug warms his hands. The thin acid scent of the coffee mixes with the musk of the damp air. He imagines he could get an old umbrella and strap it to his back. The bow poking at the umbrella on the upstroke. A pair of gentlemen in plaid suits will stroll by and tip their hats and toss him strange currency, as if he were, say, in England. Or a lady will stroll by, twenty silver eyes shining on her leather boots. She will unfold a colorful paper bill from her pocketbook and bend down to look into his eyes as she drops it into his hat. Her face pale and smooth and elegant. As should already be acknowledged, he is prone to wild fantasy, just not as often as relentless scrutiny.

The rain continues. He watches a woman run along Decatur Street, opposite side, her heels striking the curb hard, and she carries a black leather briefcase as though it were a dripping water pail swinging against her knee. Her umbrella has folded in half and her hair is dark from wetness. She's wrestling the broken apparatus. The metal spider' s legs folded over. She is soaked and disgusted and turns to take cover under the elegant iron railed balcony of Pontalba. He knows she will discard the accessory at her soonest convenience. He drinks the last of his coffee and dashes out across the street. At Royal and St. Ann he sees her enter the grocer, ramming the umbrella into the barrel hard on her way in. He waits for her to disappear into the store and he then takes it from the waste barrel. He walks home and doesn't see the woman come right back out with a new umbrella, pulling it from the plastic sleeve, which she throws into the waste barrel and she does not even notice that her old one is gone.

He pulls off his shoes and water pours out. He rolls off his soaked socks and wrings them out in the sink. He slaps his heavy clothes over the top of the door and pulls on dry ones. He prepares a cup of tea with a tea bag Virginia had left behind after one of her picnics, it still has potency in the second steep. He sits at the plastic table and examines the crippled instrument. Hinges on two of the eight retractable ribs have broken. He threads a few wire ties (these had always been in the kitchen drawer from a previous tenant; he and David never purchased garbage bags, used shopping bags), through the rivet holes. Slowly and simply, he threads and ties the hinges up, and with some small amount of re-bending and re-adjusting, the umbrella is repaired. He uses his belt to strap the umbrella handle to the back of his chair, to practice. It might work beautifully. Strapped to a bench back. He plays a few tunes, imagining himself in the downpour.

The phone rings; it is Virginia.

"Do you know what I did today?"

"Nope."

"Don't you remember?" she asks.

"No."

"I went to the doctor today."

"And what's the matter with you?"

"Nothing, stupid. It was the gynecologist. I'm going to start taking the pill."

"You are?"

"Yes. I think I am. He gave me the prescription. I will have to start taking them at the beginning of my next cycle."

"Next cycle? When will that be?"

"You know."

"But why will you take them then? I'll be gone."

"I'm going to take them for me."

"For you?"

"The doctor said it will make my periods milder."

This is scientific information he is not familiar with. He is suspicious. But willing to accept it, under the circumstances.

"Okay."

She senses he is unbelieving. She says:

"But, also, you might come back."

He does not reply.

"Well, I've got two weeks to decide."

"I guess even if I don't come back, it would be good for you to be safe with whoever you are with after me."

"That's not why, James."

"I know, I'm just saying."

*

Next Morning. Woldenburg Park. He mounts the umbrella with a little piece of rope to the back of the bench, though he leaves it discreetly unopened. He sets out his case and begins to play. The sky is a gray possibility of rain. This experience of busking in the streets is making quite the meteorologist out of him. He is prepared. The park is moored in the still river, isolated and abandoned. It is Tuesday, middle of February. The city is yet winterquiet.

He plays several hours. At noon, he stops to rest his hands. He is sad in that way sadness can be where it is calming and serious, but not empty and hopeless. He is rubbing his hands, slowthinking. He has earned what looks like ten or fifteen dollars. It's good money for a morning that looks like rain, in winter. His violin sits next to him, but the case is at his feet. A young man approaches:

"Yo man, look here, I bet you five dolla's I can tell you where you got your shoes."

"I already know this one, sorry."

Then without a word and quick as a fish strike, he snatches a fist full of bills and flees. It happens almost faster than comprehension. James jumps up and falls into pursuit, not thinking about what he'd actually do if he caught the thief; his strides carry him automatically and rapidly. The thief is nearly out of sight, in an instant, and he realizes the futility of continuing after him. He turns to walk back and just then another vulture swoops down to steal a share. But this one goes for the whole thing. He takes the violin, the case, the bow. With primal consciousness and the deft movements of indifference, with the impunity of the disaccorded, *I gonna get mines*, the oil-black boy is like an animal in squeaky-white basketball shoes. He grabs the instrument by the neck and folds it into the case and flees. And he runs like the cheetah, the panther, calf in mouth, taking no particular care in the catch, just the escaping with.

A wave of anger of a degree James Buck has never felt before in his entire life burns out from his heart. No person or thing has meant more to him, been more a part of his life than this violin. He is filled with a rage so fierce he could tear the creature's arms from his body and pulverize him with them and have no remorse. He is almost a hundred feet from the bench, there's no way he's going to catch up. The thief snatched and fled like a cheetah, to pursue is futile, but he bolts into a breakneck run, regardless. He doesn't even calculate the disheartening odds of catching up. He's not running on logic right now, but a surge of anger-produced epinephrine, and like those women who lift cars to save their babies, he is quite seriously flying. His feet don't much touch the ground; he could run across water, at this point. He covers an impossible distance almost instantly. The fugitive glances back, turns an impromptu corner, but with great control. His black hair shines. His white sneakers are vivid streaks. They have raced across an immense portion of the Quarter. Down from the park, through a parking lot or two, up Conti Street, onto Chartres, onto Bienville, onto Bourdon. The boy darts through the crowd like a collie among livestock, effortlessly, and he is gone.

James falls into a zombie-ish locomotion. He is emotionally numb, now. His heart explodes over and over from the exertion and he cannot get his breath, regardless how deep he breathes. He stops in the middle of the street. Hands on his hips. Gasping. He knows he has lost his violin, forever. And in this instant, like a rubber bladder, the anger comes, again, then fills him up and he bursts.

"Fucking bastards!"

He wants to get his hands on something. There isn't much, except other people, a lamppost.

"Fucking nigger bastards!" he screams aloud, and mildly amused tourists stop in their tracks and gawk.

Someone honks a horn for him to get out of the middle of the street. He looks at the driver through the windshield. A fat, bifocaled, Welcome Back Carter caricature. Do you realize you fat bastard that right now I' d just as soon strike you between the eyes with a ball peen hammer than move out of your way. Apparently, the fat bastard gets the message from the look of absolute hate in James' eyes. He doesn't honk, again. Patiently watches him cross the street.

He turns to iron as his anger solidifies, and begins cold. He strides in a suit of armor, now. Oh ugly ugly humanity, to hell with you all. A cool indifference runs up through his cheeks. If there were just a button he could push, he would end it all.

He is to meet Virginia this afternoon. He stands at the streetcar stop. It's evening rush hour for workers heading uptown. The mostly white crowd peck at each other like plucked and dressed chickens, cackling and clutching their personals in a stark hysteria. Chickens which resemble men: fat chickens with brief cases, with noses to pick instead of beaks, with glasses magnifying their blank stares. Skinny crazy chickens with crazy chicken brains, obsessing about chicken feed. How can a chicken get more chicken feed? Does that chicken have more chicken feed than I do? Where's all the chicken feed? He's nauseous by the sight of them. But there's an odd ball, a misfit that stands out in the coop like an arctic penguin chick. He is a small, wool-headed black boy, big eyed and lagging behind his mother, innocent of the race. His mother is as ugly as humanity can be, and as good as any good parody, as big as a vending machine and full of the much of same poison, a 32 ounce fountain pop in a swollen grip, yelling at the boy, vituperatively. She's wearing pink sweat pants, the lint boogered pocketliners hanging out, white t-shirt with grease stains down the front, flopping about in house slippers -her crusty gray heels crushing the back ends folded under from not ever being pulled all the way on. The boy is dressed likewise, dirty shorts and stains on his shirt, dirty fingers and scrapped knees. Brand new shoes, untied and white as marshmallow. But he is beautiful, -his skin like chocolate candy and a big soft balloon of hair. He doesn't even look like the same species as that of his mother. He looks like a small rubber toy of a man, just waiting for the world to pump him so full of hot air and hate, he'll be ready to burst before he can graduate. But now, he looks at James as though he has found something interesting about him. He looks at him with the bold innocence and wonder that only children can have. It is kind of sad, really, because as in nature, when unlike things come into contact, one will grow to be like the other. The boy stares at James, eerily like he knows something, and then is yanked out of sight and into the thick crowd. The wobbling upright walrus of a woman yelling:

"Hurry yo ass up, boy. I ain't got no time fo your shit, come on, get on up here. What's a matta' wid you?"

Passengers are pouring from the back doors. Virginia finds him immediately. She can see something is the matter. They wade through the thinning crowd boarding the streetcar; the retractable step thuds and creaks with each person, thuds and creaks with each person, thuds and creaks with each person. So many persons. The anonymous faces he a moment ago loathed, he now pities as though they were unboarding a train at Auschwitz. Pities that most are no more than the circumstances they find themselves in and the whole is less than the sum of its parts. They cross Canal onto Royal Street. Virginia buys him a coffee at the Precinct Café. She sits close at his side. He has told her about his violin and she strokes his face.

"I'm so sorry for you, James."

He hates the pitying, but doesn't know how to tell her to stop.

"You should go to the police station (which is literally next door to the cafe) and fill out a report of stolen property."

"What for? The cops aren't going to search the town for a nigger carrying a violin."

She doesn't want to instigate. Quietly looks at him. After a long silence, she realizes he isn't going to continue, she cautiously becomes cheerful.

"Guess what? This might make you feel better. It isn't much, considering all, but it's something."

"What?"

"I arranged that I can stay at your place tonight. If you want me to."

"You told your mom you were going to stay with me?"

"Not really."

"Not really?"

"I just said that I probably wouldn't be coming home this evening and she just said alright."

"That's the same thing isn't it?"

"Yes, but I'm staying the night, right? So that's good."

"Sure."

"It's not much, I know that. We can get you another violin."

Funny that she should say that, he imagines the thieves thought the same, the privilege of being white, he can just walk in a store and get whatever he wants by the fairness of his skin. But he knows she means well.

"Sure, I guess, but that violin meant everything to me."

They make love through the late afternoon and the evening, casually and comfortably and with a harmonious sense of duty, like washing a cast-iron tub with warm water; it is as much pleasure as work.

XXVII

He opens a door to an empty room. He knows there is something he is supposed to find, so he goes to the closet and opens its door and it is empty. But there is a smaller door in the back of it, which he kneels down to open and it leads to an empty room. When he enters it he is now dwarfed by the room and a large box sits before him, which he opens and finds empty. He can't help but fall into it, and continues to fall and the walls of the box expand outward and everything slows down and then they retract and the shrinking dimensions close in on him rapidly but he is never too large to get stuck, becoming smaller and smaller, until he can fit through the eye of a needle. And a pinprick of blinding white light in the absolute distance starts to grow as he falls into it and he covers his eyes with his hands and he can see right through them. Before he can reach the cold empty light, his mind wakes up from dreaming. The distance he has traveled from yesterday is immeasurable. He doesn't remember that his violin has been stolen. He stares at the empty ceiling, vast and blank, and his vision is blurry so he lifts his hand to rub his eyes. As his hand approaches his face, he begins to register a peculiar surreal sensation, and he looks at the location of the feeling presence of his arm and finds nothing there. But he trusts the feeling and continues to bring his invisible hand to his face to rub his eye. At the moment when his fingers should have touched upon the brushes of his eyelashes, he accepts the fact that his hand is not there, feeling nothing against his blinking eyes, seeing nothing. He tries to look down on the mattress to see his arm, but he cannot move his head. He tries to move the other arm. Nothing. He is in a great panic, now. He is paralyzed. His chest is heaving from his heart racing. He mentally struggles with his motor skills. But nothing comes of it. He tries to speak, but his lips barely break their seal. He pulls from deep in his throat, and he creates nothing more than an low moan, a helpless quivering of the vocal chord. This frightens him into a spontaneous spasm of head and legs and arms; in an epileptic jolt, he breaks the spell. Pops out of it in a cold sweat, startled and bewildered. He bolts up from the bed and walks into the bathroom to look for answers in the mirror.

In an instant he knows it all. He is lost. He pulls his ugly hair back off his forehead and stares deep into his eyes in the mirror. A glance at two parallel worlds from outer space, at the center of each is an impenetrable abyss, protected by a haunted emerald forest bleeding rivers of blood into the white sands surrounding. He is a plural consciousness in the deep space of sadness, anchored only by his own fixed gaze. How do I get back? The question travels at the speed of sound for several seconds to reach the various far-off outposts of self. And no answers return. His eyes fill with water as he stares at them motionlessly, until they are so full he has to blink and water floods the wells of his eyes and drips off his cheeks into the sink.

He skipped lunch and slept through the rest of the afternoon in a coma. He is walking to Virginia's house, now. He has one hundred and sixty dollars, can't afford a buck for the streetcar. His legs are growing sore. The streetcar rolls by jolly and smooth, glistening in the drizzle, which has thoroughly soaked him. His heels are raw. Virginia is home, alone, and expecting him. She is angry with him for walking. Draws him a hot bath. She puts together a supper for him while he soaks in the lavender-smelling foam. Virginia attends to his every need. Pours him a Scotch from her father' s liqueur cabinet. They make love in her bed, deep in the pillows and comforters, as if in a cloud. He dreams of playing in a dense, gray downpour. It beats on his umbrella. It drips on his legs. It is cold. His donation cup has an inch of water in it. The rainwater runs like a river around him. Then it stops, with a miraculous brightness, and people bloom like flowers from the glistening lawns. His jar fills with crisp paper currency. He wakes and remembers the color of the dream like a vibration and like a vibration it passes leaving nothing in its place.

*

Dusk is swept with yellow and blue and green. The Quarter is rumbling with festivity. The drunken stream of humanity on Bourbon Street mocks his sadness. The Lucky Dog vendor unsuccessfully solicits him, stares him off with a look of disgust. Men in sports jerseys and major league ball caps barrel through the streets with fake, plastic women dangling from their wallet pockets. The fat, pink youth of Middle America gather in numerous packs around various infamous barrooms, congesting the sidewalks, a collective, lost expression upon their pale faces, impatiently waiting to be entertained, as though entertainment would come to them the way it does on the television. Proper attire is the t-shirt. In a glance one can ascertain which rock bands toured the country this winter. What brand of shoes or sunglasses is most popular? Where a young girl is going to college. Who visited Disney Land, or at least the Warner Brothers Store? Most frequently, you are simply reminded of where you are—on Bourbon Street in the French Quarters of New Orleans, Louisiana, and Mardi Gras has just begun. Any conceivable rendering of this fact silk screened onto a t-shirt can be purchased at almost any hour of the day in any color in any size on any street.

Hurricanes are sold on the street in plastic cups, the Big Gulp of the frozen cocktail. A dairy cow digs in her hip pack for a crumple of bills. She is sucking from the drink she already has, doesn't see that she is blocking his path. He begs her pardon and she looks at him with a pair of pathetic, beady eyes clinched in rosy blubber. She is in line for a Hurricane at a sidewalk stand. She is wearing a black Nirvana t-shirt, across the back it reads HERE WE ARE NOW, ENTERTAIN US. Presumably unlicensed swag, at least he hopes so.

He has to walk in the street to continue. He takes Pirates Alley to the Esplanade. The sound of a harmonica echoes in the deep passageway. When he turns out, in front of the cathedral, he is met with a beautiful music. A couple of black men in straw hats are strumming acoustic guitars, singing:

"'Cawzz you so goooooooooood to meeeeeeeeee.

"I feel goooooooooood,

"'Cawzz you so goooooooooood tooooooo meeeeeeeeee."

And his voice fades to the chords, then:

"Tell'm how good, Drampaw."

Grandpa breathes back through the reeds of his harmonica, slaps his bare feet on the flagstone. His sweatdark straw hat pushed back, his gray eyelids squeezed tight on his yellow eyes. Grandson bounces his guitar on his knee, shakes his head with great satisfaction. There's a sweet air around them, but it's old like fresh turned soil and simple like salt.

"So tell me woman, why in the hell did you have to go and leeeeeeeee ee eeeeee eee eave meeeeeeeeeeeeee?"

A modest burst of applause cradles his waning voice. People reach in to drop money into an open drumcase. James reaches into his pocket for a bill. He gives the vocalist an appreciative nod, and turns away to Chartres Street.

Between streetlamps it is dark, and dark four-footed figures drift into side streets. A quiet crowd sits in Kueiffer's and he wishes he could go in. There's the smack of billiard balls and groups at smoking tables talking and laughing with an impossible carelessness. Several blocks down, silhouetted in streetlight, is a small crowd. He finds a seven-piece band in the center of it. They sit on bent folding chairs and paintbare wire café stools. A dirty blonde pumps an accordion. A fat man strums a weathered bass. The drummer's face shines like it's oiled with sorrow. A skeletal old man blows trumpet with bulging eyes, the legs of his gray trousers crossed, an empty hand draped over the knob of his knee. Lead guitar leans forward to sing with all the discomfort of constipation. He says, and the band nearly falls silent, except for a long note drawn from the fiddle:

"Ley's lay it all down, naw."

They produce a low, fluid noise and a quiet tapping can be heard, growing in pitch and tempo, shifting the acoustic center and the crowd's attention to a patch-work dress dancing over a sewage gate, dangling a pair of lively tapping mary janes. She is as someone possessed, almost lunatic in her abandon to the music. Orange-freckled alabaster arms flailing the woes from her world of us all. She is as ugly as a woman can be, all skin and bones, an empty nest of hair, a crop of infected insect bites on her shins. She is oblivious to the crowd around her, plugged into the band, a ragdoll pulling amps from the collective charge. Her foot-taps roll and abate in rapid series as the band dwindles and then with a hard eighth time strike on the curb the band springs back to life. So she's not just a by-stander possessed by the music, but the lead, she starts to sing with a voice as raw as the first day of your heart breaking.

James starts smooththinking. This is it. The irrepressible desire to make music, with whatever you can get your hands or feet on. To vibrate the air, whether with a voice or a hollow stick or two spoons or a barrel with a little animal hide stretched over it. It is all very simple and very necessary. To produce an affectionate noise to fill the void of consciousness. In the presence of this band, these people are peaceful, united in amicable toe-tapping, standing in the street, sitting on the curbs, leaning against the buildings, embracing the support of a lamppost. This is what I need to remember. I must hold on to this.

XXVIII

He wakes in the morning with an ancient spirit as happy as his dreams were colorful and the morning is fresh. It is as though the dreams had resolved something; something as old as his remembering is old. He climbs from bed, knowing exactly what he needs to do. He drinks his weak coffee and takes a short, cool bath. He is anxiously standing outside the doors of the second-hand instrument store as they are being unlocked from the inside.

The violins are beautiful; the new ones shine like toys, the used ones are solemn and dark. But there is no choice to be made, price dictates.

"Yes, Can I see this one at two hundred twenty-five?"

The clerk is quick to offer a bow as well. James plays several notes. The clerk is unimpressed, serious. James gives the instrument a glance over.

"Is the price negotiable?"

"I might be able to work with you"

"How about one hundred and sixty?" And he looks at the clerk earnestly.

The clerk frowns, impatiently.

"Now you have to be realistic."

"Tell me what you can do?"

"Two hundred even, with tax. That includes the bow and case and it has new strings."

James examines the instrument, now, with consternation, even though he knows he can't afford it. The clerk says:

"It is in perfect condition."

"There are some hard scars on the back, as though it has been dropped."

"But it is sound. Maybe I can consider a trade and the difference in cash?"

"I don't have a violin, anymore," he says dryly, "and I literally have only a hundred and sixty dollars, period."

"I'm sorry, I can't go that low. These second-hand instruments have very low markup as it is."

He asks if he can see the deep cherry-finished violin priced at five hundred. He examines it carefully but is un-enchanted. It is perfect and solid and light and five hundred dollars, therefore impossible and means absolutely nothing to him; in fact he detests it. He hands it back to the clerk and asks for some strings and a bow. The clerk is surprised:

"Violin strings?"

"Yes, the cheapest you have."

The clerk is uncomfortably puzzled, but doesn't pursue the matter.

He's walking the streets of the Quarter like a beggar, rummaging in garbage barrels and alley dumpsters. He gives everything an appreciative eye: a plank of wood, a vegetable crate, an old Café Du Monde coffee tin. He knows what he is looking for, or not exactly, except that when he gets his hands on it he will know. He mostly finds plastic containers: water jugs and milk jugs and juice jugs and stout detergent bottles. They are useless to him, cast and unchangeable, having no discarded potential, evoking an awful sadness imagining an ever-growing heap of packaging brought into existence for a one-time use at a rate that defies cessation and is trapped in an unusable state indefinitely, filling giant holes in the land or drifting across the oceans. In the business district, if he can get at the garbage at all, it is mostly individual-sized plastic water bottles and paper, lots of paper, as though the whole of the CBD were just stuffed full of paper. In the French Market, he finds crates constructed of a brittle poplar or nailhard hickory. He scavenges well into the Faurbourg Maringy. He finds chairs and table legs and bicycle parts and stereo consoles and lamps and typewriters and appliances and plastic toys and dogtooth-shredded shoes and lots of wire coat hangers. He begins to want to ponder over each thing, fearing he might not readily see the potential in the items he comes across, as he initially thought he would. He losing confidence, becoming desperate. Tries to calm himself. Essentially, it is the conflict between the bowhairs and the violin strings, which disturb the air, which the hollow body amplifies. I need four taut strings and a hollow body. I need resistance and an echo. Widethinking and untuned and sore of foot, he turns up Kerlerec and onto Burgundy. To wait for the good fortune of chance is a luxury I don' t have. I must make do. He finds a cigarbox. Yes! It will make an excellent body. He remembers where he can salvage a chair leg. The crude instrument starts to appear magically, displayed as a miniature tangible against a pale canvas before his mind' s eye. He turns around, staring wide-eyed. It'll work. It'll work fine. He retraces his steps in the falling dusk.

The finished instrument is curious, unrealistic, but somehow authentic. It challenges the eye to understand it. Is it some forgotten instrument from the Orient? Chopsticks serve as tuning pegs. The neck and fingerboard were once a chair leg. The body a cigar box; the lid serving as an access panel during construction, and once he gets the sound post just right he'll glue it shut with Elmer's to prevent the loss of acoustics. Hours of whittling with his Swiss Army knife and a lot of ingenuity. Drilling out holes with the leather punch and the screwdriver. Crosscuts with the saw blade. Sanding surfaces, such as the delicate bridge, on the coarse surface of the cement steps below the back door. Brad nails as string pins. F-holes drawn from memory and meticulously carved by knifepoint. Some fifty hours of crude manufacture. He's poised over completion. His back is hot. His eyes are warm and heavy but wired open. He slept a couple of hours yesterday, otherwise he has worked incessantly. He has devised a brilliant but crude method of tuning the strings; the tension of the strings pulling against the square cut holes. Pull up slightly, then twist. He becomes aware of a cold sweat sprinkled upon his forehead. He drags the bow across the strings, the acid of anxiety boiling in his stomach. The ugly noise that cries for the first time like a newborn child could not be more beautiful.

XXIX

After two days of intense experimentation, he feels as though the instrument has come to realize what he intends to do with it, and he has come to realize what it can do for him. It is unbalanced and awkward to handle. It has no range and little resonance. But it can sing!

The air smells like apples and cypress and cut grass and warm asphalt. He fords the dense, slow-moving river of tourists flowing through Bourbon Street. People stare at his strange instrument. He walks Pirate's Alley in the cavernous, sweet shade of the Cathedral. Curbpeople, young primitives, mendicants on the very edge of society, mankind even, squat on a low stoop. They eat with brown fingers from a communal, Styrofoam plate. Their long, animal manes knotted in dirty cords, decorated with a glass bead or two. Their tribal inked faces are soiled and expressionless. They have grease smeared on their chins and food particles collected in their nose rings. Or lip rings. Or eyebrow rings. Or tongue studs. A particularly poignant image is of a fragile member, trembling uncontrollably, hunkered on a high step lapping food from her small hands. Her fuzzy white-pink tongue pierced through with a silver stud. It is profound that no matter how far and long her adventures in the primitive have been, hidden in soiled men's clothes and under the indigenous bush of filthy hair, he can still clearly see the beauty of her gender, her fairness. The small slender hands. The perfect nose. The roundish features about her face. The delicate lashes. He catches a glimpse into her beautiful green eyes, sees her atrophied self-awareness. I wonder if she will be a good animal? Would she steal, not knowing stealing, only taking? Would she kill? Would she eat her offspring? Could she love someone? Could she love me? If I were the greatest violinist in the world, would she care? He turns back to look quickly at her, hunched on the transition, on the edge of an abyss. Why does she want such a gulf between herself and her fellow man? He can almost commiserate. If she does finally drown her self-awareness, will she instinctively search for it again? Is that a part of her search? Or is extracting sense futile in a world full of narcotics? Are they at the end of Kerouac's long road? He turns out the alley onto the large flagstones below St. Louis Cathedral. Humanity waddles like flightless birds, cackling flocks of turkeys and chickens, released from their cramped coops, scratching about in bewilderment, pecking morsels from paper bags, perching on benches and curbs and steps and the stone waistwall around Jackson Square. Everyone is an ugly bird without wings, except the entertainers. They each hold back a circle, great majestic eagles, all the blank birdeyes watching.

He surveys his competition with a look of lighthearted contemplation; the definite crease along either side of the mouth, but not the tense jaw, not the slanting brow. He surveys with his serious, green eyes. Tourists size him up in passing, staring at his instrument, whispering to one another with great pleasure, excited and eager to look at the strange artist, something they would not see in a hundred parades down Main Street in Sprawltown, Middle America: *Oh, honey aren't you glad we came here on vacation?* Click click goes a the cameras.

He circles in the periphery about half an hour, peering in for a piece of a bench, upon which he could stand up and begin to play. He should go in search of a bucket as many performers have, but he gets his sights on a bench end and swoops in. Grandpa and Grandma are up from Florida for the weekend and are taking a break on the opposite end, fully dressed in polyester and wearing face-covering, dark, welder's shields. James removes his cap and slides the bill into the slats of the bench, thus the crown of the cap can serve as his donation bowl. He stands up on the bench end and sits down on the thick rollover of the bench back and draws his bow down across the strings. Grandpa nearly has a heart attack at such close proximity to the source. Jumps up and donates a few obscenities before shuffling off with his bag of bones in a sunbonnet. James is impervious, plays on unfettered.

The first two to stop and behold him, accept him unconditionally, put money into his cap immediately, but stand before him curious and delighted, holding hands, wearing matching denim shorts and matching black leather hippacks and New Orleans t-shirts. Their enormous white glaring thighs choked with blue veins like some dermal ivy. Strings of colorful plastic beads collect in the deep cleavage of their breasts. He smiles at them for their generosity. He mashes out his notes, bows a beautiful tragedy. Begins to draw an audience. They watch closely. Some try to look into his eyes, searching to meet him, to understand him and his curious, but marvelous creation.

He plays an hour. Takes a short break, but doesn't leave his spot. Then two more. He has emptied his cap five or six times. People give as though he is an accredited charity. The noise he makes isn't loud, like playing a violin in a cardboard box, muffled yet echoing, more akin to the fiddle playing in Appalachia. A family gathers to watch and dad sends the fair-haired girl in with a five-dollar bill, and she nervously tucks it into his cap, grandstands, daddy videotaping the whole event. A head on a red neck pokes into the small group gathered, a Nascar cap. He puffs and snorts, drinks from an enormous plastic cup, shouts out:

"What you cawl dat damned thing?"

James knits his brows and smiles and carries on. More money fills his cap. Comments come at him, as encouragement: *Great job. Nice instrument you've made. That's pretty darned good, son. What a way to make a buck!*

The crowd that flows by is scenery outside the windows of a slow-moving train. Hour after hour, he feels like he is seeing all the world. His ass aches on the iron slats. He stands for a while, but standing this high has an ostentatious air about it. He gets down and stands beside the bench. His pockets bulge with coin and paper currency. He intends to quit at dusk, but it comes cool and raspberry over the Presbyter and compels him to continue until nine o'clock. He stops to eat.

Forty-two dollars. Eleven in quarters. Five in dimes. A buck or two in nickels and pennies, which he uses to pay the waiter at Café du Monde. He is tired but not sleepy. He hasn't eaten all day but the beignets seem to be enough. He is beautifully satisfied. Thinks about playing an hour more, but feels like he has earned a cold beer, which he takes at Kueiffer's.

In the morning, he wakes from sweet dreams, from soaring through orange and vanilla skies; he can almost taste it on his tongue. During his bath, he is delighted to relax and have no nagging need to masturbate. He reads a from a one dollar second hand paper back about man transformed into a gigantic insect. On this morning he on the other hand feels transformed into a gigantic butterfly. His spirits are high.

It is a warm morning. Foot traffic in Spanish Plaza is steady. Virginia finds him playing a foolish-looking, stringed cigarbox for a small, ever-revolving crowd. The crowd never stays long, some pause in amusement, some linger a moment in curiosity, then depart, leaving a folded dollar bill or a few pieces of silver change in his cardboard tipbox. Virginia approaches him from behind, walking on the rim of the fountain pool. She runs her fingers through his hair and bends down to kiss him, nervously.

"Wow, look at that thing," she says with feigned enthusiasm.

He stops playing.

"So what do you think?"

"It's ugly," she admits with a laugh.

"What?"

"Well, I mean, compared to a violin, but . . ."

"You don't like it?"

"No, I like it, it's just . . . very unusual. But I kind of like the way it sounds."

"It's not very loud, but it makes a very interesting sound, doesn't it?"

"Yes, I guess interesting is the best way to describe it. You made it?"

He offers it to her and she takes it into her hands and examines it, a smile slowing developing as she notices some of the apparent handiwork.

"Looks like you have made some money?"

"Yes, I seem to do very well with this."

"Good, the faster you can buy another violin."

"What's wrong with this one?"

"Nothing, but it's not a violin," she stresses, hoping he hasn't lost himself in the novelty.

"No, it isn't," he admits modestly.

She smiles, but it's empty, as she looks out towards the river. He looks at his crude instrument and it suddenly appears ridiculous. He feels a wave of heat thinking her guilty of giving him this haunt. He is visibly affected. She looks back at him.

"What's wrong?"

"Nothing."

He can see the neck is working itself loose. He will have to make adjustments to it. Virginia folds her arms and looks around the Plaza.

"How long you plan to play today?"

"I don't know."

"Are you going to play all day, a couple of hours, what?" and her tone is not spiteful, rather innocuous.

"I want to play as long as I can. Why? Do you not want me to play?"

"No, not at all . . ."

"Do you not want to be here?"

"I just needed to do some shopping today. My brother's birthday is soon."

He thinks he hears some insincerity in her voice. She rakes her hair with her thumb and index finger. She gives him a smile he hasn't seen before. It comes and goes quickly. The lip line wide and slightly upturned and the pale color of ambivalence.

"If you want to do something else?"

"No, I don't know what I want to do. I've been in a cranky mood all day."

"I was going to play here for a bit, then maybe go down to Jackson Square."

She looks back to the shops at Riverwalk, as though pondering an important decision.

"You can get your shopping done, and then come find me at Jackson Square."

"I guess I can do that." She searches his expression, but there is nothing for her to see, he has hidden it too well.

"That sounds great."

"I'll find you in a couple hours?" and she kisses him and walks across the Plaza and into the Riverwalk.

She doesn't come to find him later. He plays until he can't take the pain of the blunt instrument under his chin anymore. He makes some decent money. Gets a cheap beer and a dozen cheap oysters to indulge a craving.

XXX

The maddening silence of his apartment is enhanced each time the refrigerator kicks on, rattling its various loose metal fittings. His agitation is so accurate the duration of each second is quantified beyond itself. He doesn't have any food in the place and refrains from buying any for reasons of economy. Regrets now the oysters, they don't stick to the ribs long. If anything he's more hungry. Obviously there's nothing on the television. Nothing on the radio. He has no furniture on which to lounge, except the plastic table and chairs. He cannot bear to lay himself down on his mattress, yet again. He opens the paperback in hopes of submerging himself into another reality, but the language is not easy, though the story interesting, so each sharp-toothed turn of his agitated mind reels him back up to the surface of his banal existence. He is feverish. His genitals are sore from hours of using Virginia's vagina as a medicine cabinet, thus masturbation has no appeal. His crude instrument has left his chin and shoulder sorely bruised.

He locks up the apartment and takes off through the Quarter. Anxiety turns his shrunken, empty gut to stone. He begins a dreadful footslap along St. Charles Ave. Again, he won't waste the dollar on the streetcar, having more time than money, and he hopes the exercise might help. If Damarie isn't home, I'll ride the streetcar back, he decides. In an hour, sore of foot and lightly perspiring, he can see the lights on in the second-floor apartment.

Damarie responds to his knocking quickly, pulls the door back wearing a sleeveless rayon shirt and jeanshorts cut at an angle from her crotch, exposing the pocketliners. She looks down at him standing in tall, straw-colored heels. She is delighted to see him, exclaims breathlessly:

"Wow, what a surprise!"

"Hope I'm not disturbing you?"

"Not at all. What's up?"

"Nothing. I just thought I would visit."

"Great, come in. The apartment is a wreck. It hasn't been cleaned in a while."

"The maid on vacation?"

"Ha," she laughs breathlessly. "We need a maid." She removes a silk bathrobe from the floor and drapes it over a chairback.

"Isn't . . . What's her name? Rosa. Isn't she the maid?"

"Oh, that's so funny. You never met Rosa before, have you? You must think she really is the maid. It is perfect. I have to tell her. It is perfect."

"Wow, I'm sorry, I . . ."

"No, it is perfectly hilarious. I can't wait to tell her."

"She certainly looked the part."

"Yes, she brought a real maid's uniform."

"It was a great party. I had a great time."

"Did you? I'm glad, I felt very sad when I found you asleep on the balcony."

He looks out the glass French doors, which open onto the balcony. She says:

"I would like some wine. I'm completely exhausted. Would you have a glass with me?"

"Sure."

"God, I've had such a hectic day. We had an eleven-o'clock lunch with the graduating residents and I had to go over a stack of erroneous patient files. Then we had this long lecture on preventative safety. Was that boring."

"I can't imagine."

"Oh you never told me, how was the party at Paul's?"

He does not want to complain. He does not what to reveal his insecurities about wealth. He says:

"It was great. Easy money, and an absolutely beautiful house."

"Isn't it? And they have another one in Grand Isle and one in Aspen. You should see them," she says as though it were an option. "I'm glad I was able to arrange that for you."

"Yes, thank you. It was quite an experience."

"How about some wine, then? That would be great right now. That and a warm bath."

He feels as though he should suggest that he leave, is about to speak as she crosses the heart-of-pine floor with her heels knocking and drawing his attention to her long-legged stride. Under a transom of hand-blown glass panels, separating the living room from the dining room, she turns back and asks:

"There's a wonderful bottle of Merlot on the counter. Can you open it for us?"

"Certainly," and he involuntarily follows her into the kitchen. She reaches for wine glasses in an overhead cabinet. As he cuts the foil, he notices a photograph of her with long dark hair is taped to the kiwi green icebox, her charismatic, grandiose smile glaring out of the aged still image a currency of joy that could nearly buy her anything, the turquoise sea of another world glimmering in the back ground. It gives *him* joy just to look at her, not without a touch of envy, to be so beautiful, how differently being alive must be for her. It is the kind of smile only the truly beautiful can have, confident. She takes the wine and pours two glasses, looks at him looking at her picture.

"That's me in my country."

"You are so beautiful."

"You are sweet, but my hair was so awful."

"Who is this with you?"

"My dear best friend, Helda."

"She is beautiful, as well. You too are like super models."

"You are generous, thank you. But I miss her so much..."

"Miss her?"

"She took her life, seven years ago. I was so sad."

"That is very sad. So beautiful..."

There's a moment of involuntary silence.

"She doesn't look Venezuelan?"

"Swedish."

"We met at Tulane."

"This photo is older than seven years?"

"Can you believe it? Time just flies through the sky."

"Do you go back often?"

"That was the last time."

"Why? Because of what happened to your parents?"

"There are many reasons," she says, takes a sip, puts the glass down and starts to put some plates from the drying rack into the cabinet. Asks:

"Have you been playing a lot?"

"I've . . . well . . ." and his voice disintegrates into a warm acid in the back of his throat. The question catches him off guard. He doesn't want to bring it up, not in the context of these real tragedies. But he can't exactly lie to her, either. He starts over:

"Actually, my violin was stolen," and he takes a sip from his wine glass and immediately regrets mentioning it. He wants her admiration not her sympathy. A moment of admiration is worth all the sympathy in the world.

She grabs his hand.

"Are you serious? Do you know who stole it?"

"No, it was a pair of thieves on the street. They set me up. One ran up and snatched money from my case and like an idiot I ran after him and then the other came and took my violin, case and bow and everything."

"That is the most horrible thing I've ever heard."

He takes a glance at the photo, hardly the most horrible thing, but he understands her desire to be compassionate.

"I actually turned around in the very instant, thinking I shouldn't leave it alone, and just then I saw the other guy take it. I tried running after him, but he had too much distance on me."

"What are you going to do now? Do you have another violin?"

He does not want to say that he has made one in fear that she will not appreciate his ingenuity without first seeing it for herself. It isn't something one can easily imagine, and he believes she will not see it as an example of his industry but rather of his poverty.

"I have a make-do, for now, but I have my eye on one at the music shop."

"I'm so upset about it. Those are the evilest type of men to do such a thing. You play so beautiful. Had you had the violin long?"

"About ten years."

"It is so terrible."

"It is their lack of perception, which irritates me the most. It is obvious the instrument is worth more to me than to them. They might get thirty or forty dollars for it somewhere, if that."

"They do not realize that? They have no concern about anyone, not beauty, not anything. I've heard of many musicians getting their instruments stolen. Whole van's full. My friend, classical guitarist, gone, just like that, in a packed restaurant. It was a gorgeous instrument. Most of the time, it's drugs. It's the same people that rob their grandmothers to buy crack. It is sad."

She moves past him, turning out the kitchen light. The simple chandelier over the dining table spreads rhombi of soft light across the floor.

"So you were very young, then, when you got the violin. Did your father give it to you?"

This is another story he does not want to discuss. He has told it to very few people and each time it left him feeling empty, as if opened it up snuffed out the fire he held inside. The re-telling always sounding so implausible, how could his parents be so obdurate? He would also afterwards feel infantile. Each listener would caress him verbally, try to eradicate with a few sincerities whatever hurt he might have or have had. He hates re-living the profound feeling of helplessness of that time. He would be advised to just 'let it go, holding onto it would only hurt him continually', but he did not want to let it go, doing so would forgive the criminal, dissolve the crime, yet, he would always remain the victim. They were served no punishment for what they did to him, therefore no forgiveness.

"Actually, he didn't. It is a rather complicated story."

Before he can continue, she turns to face him, standing near the wall switch for the ceiling lamp. It makes a loud snap when she flips it down.

"Oh, really, will you tell me then?"

The streetlight pouring through windows and the balcony door floods the living room floor with pools of rippling yellow-green light. Damarie kicks off her heels and wades in with bare feet.

Reluctantly, he begins. He hopes at least in the telling she will admire him for his tenacity.

"When I was about ten, I went to the circus in St. Louis. The whole family went and we had parked a long way from the big top and had to walk by the big arch. You know the arch in St. Louis, on the river's edge, the Gateway to the West?"

She nods her head in acknowledgment.

"I saw an old man playing there under a lamppost. He just sat there playing and I watched him, as we walked by. It was mythical. The big arch climbing into the sky overhead. And he was just peacefully playing his violin all alone. I had never seen or heard anyone play like that. I mean, I knew of fiddlers, you know, in a country music group, but nothing like what he was playing. It was a music of another country, other time."

Damarie goes to each floor lamp and turns them off. She lights a few candles at the mantle and in a tall bookshelf, little flames dancing in her steady eyes. She takes a candle into the bathroom and sets it on the end of the tub and turns on the waterspout. The water quietly pours into the deep tub. He raises his voice.

"Anyway, this old man sitting there playing away, back perfectly straight, stuck with me. I was even thinking about him during the circus. Actually, I don't remember much of anything about the circus, except the panthers, and feeling sorry for the elephants and bears."

She comes to get two more candles and she lights them and takes them back into the bathroom and places them in the window. He doesn't continue thinking she is out of hear shot.

"So, what happened? Oh can you bring my wine, please."

He takes it into his hand and approaches the door.

"Thank you."

She takes a sip, sits on the edge of the tub and tests the water with her fingers. He steps back just outside the doorway.

"So, about a year later . . . " He is kind of confused. It's a long story, so how is this going to happen if she is about to climb in for a bath.

"You can come inside. Here let me move these." She removes a stack of fluffy towels from a chair under the window. He takes a seat and sips from his wine, feeling somewhat out of place.

"I can hear you better, now. So a year later?"

She opens the stiff button on her jeanshorts and they slide off her in an instant, revealing her tall hips and a small triangle of pubic hair. He tries to continue as though there isn't anything unusual about this.

"Our house burned down. The water heater caused it. There was an insurance settlement and we all got bikes, used bikes of course, but bikes none the less, as we had been promised we would while we lived about eight months in a two room shack. Not that the house was much bigger. Eight of us! No water, no indoor plumbing. So these bikes were a pretty wonderful thing. We had always been too poor for bikes. We were now among the elite. The envy of every hound-dog-chasing, lice-headed heathen for miles around."

She pulls her shirt over her head, smiling at this description. She puts her toes into the tub; a delighted expression comes over her face. She slides in. The candlelight sparkling in the water, the water wilting her pubic hair and welting like mercury on the flat of her abdomen.

"So one day, me and my brother were sent down to this junk shop, not too far from where we lived then. Margo, that's my mom's name, she had got this wild hair up her ass about making homemade ice cream and she knew there was an old ice cream maker there, the kind with the handcrank, she'd seen it in the window, and she sent us after it. That's when I saw the violin. It sat on a shelf behind the counter with a bunch of other instruments. It didn't have any strings and had dust on it so thick I couldn't tell what color it was. But it was like finding some artifact from a previous civilization, or another world that existed somewhere else, completely unknown to me, but yet somehow every familiar. If that can even make sense."

"Sure, I can understand that. Your soul recognized it, even though you didn't. Did you buy it?"

"Well, I didn't have any money. So, I went back a couple days later and traded my bike for it."

"Really. Your bike? Was that a fair trade?"

"For me it was. It was just an old Huffy Raw Hide, couldn't have been worth much. I just wheeled the bike right into the front door and told the guy what I wanted to do and he said okay, and apologized about not having any strings, even gave me five dollars to get them. But, then I took it home, and Margo . . ."

"Why do you call her by her name?"

"That's her name, why not?"

"It's unusual."

"I guess. Of course I called her Mom then, but after all the torment those people put me through growing up, I prefer not to use such affectionate nomenclature."

"That's very sad."

"Not really, there are just people to me now, and her name is Margo. So Margo, threw a fit. At first she thought I stole it and then I told her I traded it with someone, but I wouldn't tell her who. It was a small town; she figured she could hunt down the person because everybody knew everybody. I was scared out of my mind, so I just gave her this very general description, but she knew I was lying and that's what made her so mad. And, of course, I was lying, but I knew she would make me take it back. So I stuck to my story. In fact, at one point, and this woman had a horrible temper, she picked me up by the hair on my head and pulled me from the chair I was sitting in and started hitting my head against the wall, trying to get the truth out of me. 'You lying little son of a bitch, I'll beat your head in', she said" and he mimics her hateful dry voice and makes fists with his hands and pretends grabbing a hand full of hair and shaking.

"Then Bill, my dad, came home, and that's when it got bad. I held out as long as I could stand it, but then it occurred to me that they were just going to take it away anyway, so I told them where I got it, figuring I could at least get my bike back, maybe. And then the next day, they sent me back to the junk shop, by myself, which is where they made their mistake. I wasn't about to give it back, so I hid it in an old hay barn I knew about that was on my dead great uncle's land, then I went back and told them that some teenage boys had taken it from me on the way. And of course, they didn't believe me for a second. Teenage boys stealing a violin in a small town like ours. It was ridiculous. More outrageous bullshit, of course, but I was desperate. They sent me out to cut myself another switch, as I had already gone through two, and they worked on me nearly all night, all the other kids were pissed because they couldn't watch the *Dukes of Hazard* with all this going on in the kitchen. It was hours, or at least it seemed like it. But I never gave in, in fact I put up with it for a couple weeks. Every night they would interrogate me as soon as Bill came home. I couldn't sit down. I had to sleep on my stomach, from the marks on my legs and back. No one was allowed to talk to me, and they made me peel walnuts in the backyard while everyone else could play, which was great for everyone else, because under normal circumstances we all had to work all the time; Margo couldn't stand it if we were playing and not working. My hands were stained from the walnut rinds for a month. I couldn't go swimming in the creek because of the marks on my legs. It was a tough ordeal. These are hardheaded people, and it wasn't necessarily about the bike. Really it was more about me getting away with something and it killed them. It literally *killed* them. That I could hold out so long the way I did. I was possessed. They couldn't understand my desire for the violin, but most importantly my stubbornness was what set them into such a relentless rage, it was the brazen fact that I was bold faced lying and would not surrender to them, no matter the torture.

"But school was the safe haven. After some time passed, I eventually got the violin to school and I told the music teacher, Miss Langham, my situation and she promised she would help me. And she did. Although, at first she wanted to call the social services, I begged her not to because it would cause more trouble than good. She brought some strings for me, and some books, and even though she didn't know how to play the violin, she helped me as much as possible. And I just took to it. As though I had learned it in another life. She was just amazed how easily I took to it. As I got better, she would let me practice at her house after school, and she would give me money to bring home, because I would tell my parents that I was doing work for her. And I would, like cutting the grass, and washing her car. But I never told them the truth. Eventually I left home, and haven't seen them since."

"That's an unbelievable story, and when I say unbelievable, I mean ridiculous. I can't believe your parents." She washes herself with a crumple of white mesh and something lavender scented from a bottle pump.

"Well, to them it looked like a broken old instrument and they thought I was being foolish, but then when I wouldn't come clean, it became something more than the violin itself. You have to know these people to understand the full extent of their psychosis, where they lack in compassion, they exceed with an ignorant pride and a perverse sense of loyalty, which I flagrantly defied. My refusing to give in became something way bigger than the violin."

"But you were just a child."

"Yes, I was, but I don't know, at times I am very confident I was right by standing my ground, and then I tell the story and it sounds ridiculous, the whole thing. I mean your parents were assassinated, hardly seems..."

"There is no equal comparison. Even the butter knife can kill." She pulls the stopper from the drain hole by its chain, stands up as the bath water quietly drains, naked and fragrant and she kindly requests:

"Can you hand me a towel?"

He unfolds a towel from a stack and hands it to her. She has nothing to hide, nothing, she pats herself dry gently, making no effort to conceal herself.

"So where did you go, when you left home?"

"I moved into that barn; the one where I had kept the violin. It belonged to an uncle of mine. So no one really bothered me. I laid low, stayed off everyone's radar. I got a job at a poultry farm, working minimum wage. By the summer of graduation, I had about five hundred dollars and was going to buy a car, but I just couldn't stand it any more, and if I spent all the money on a car, where would I go with no money for gas. The dark sick smelling coops, all those stupid birds, just sitting there in their own shit, wings and beaks clipped, to feeble to walk much less fly. I noticed after a while that those dumb chickens started to seem like people. Those dumb, ignorant chickens, too weak to do anything, just waiting to die, inherently unable to question, to revolt, to break free from their imprisonment. So I bought a one way ticket out, and here I am, the only place I could think of that made sense at the time."

Damarie wrapped herself with the towel and went to her bedroom where the open windows turned the curtains to billowing capes. The blue moon glowed on the white walls. She climbed onto her bed and reclined the way a model might for a photographer; she hung her head back and shook her wet hair a little. Then she looked at him.

"I hope you do very well in your life, you deserve it."

"Thank you." He sits on the edge of the bed, facing her. She is as beautiful as any forbidden thing, in that it takes some courage to fully appreciate how beautiful knowing you can't have it.

"There's much cruelty in the world, we both know that. We try to make up for it. That's why I went into medicine."

He looks at his hands, and for the first time in a long long time, truly questions the decisions he's made. She sees him, looking into his palms regretfully, says:

"You must have great hands? I bet you can give a great massage?"

"I don't know, probably."

"I would love a back rub; I'd love you for it."

"Sure."

And she opens her towel and rolls onto her chest.

"I don't know how good I'll be at it."

"I'll tell you after. There's lotion on the dresser."

He puts a small welt into his palm and rubs his hands together to warm the lotion. Her skin gives easily but is taut, also. She feels like what he thinks a South American woman would feel like. Tougher than most, but if you hold tightly she give easy. He presses his fingers in deep and she gives a moan and closes her eyes.

"That is terrific. Lower, though. Right there. That's perfect."

He works the muscles out through the small of her back.

"Feel better."

"Yes, thank you very much."

"Anytime."

"Tomorrow, nine o'clock."

"Sure," he says but they know they are teasing.

She rolls over and lays back; her breasts dissolve into nothing more than brown nipples on either side of the crest of her breastplate.

"So you plan to stay in New Orleans long?"

"No, I don't."

"Why?"

"I think I might not be where I need to be."

"Where do you think you should be?"

"Someplace where I might be taken more seriously. New Orleans is a big circus. Whatever richness it might have is only noticeable in its rotting architecture. Everything else is very cheap."

"I guess it depends where you look. I don't think it is. There are a lot of people here just like you, and that's what makes it wonderfully rich with culture."

"I can't busk forever. I need to find something else."

"True, but you can find something else here. Beside I like you here as my friend."

He can trust this. She says it as matter of fact, without affectation. He feels compelled then to kiss her. Exactly because of her lack of sentimentality, her cool honesty. He leans forward and goes for her lips quickly, without looking into her eyes for permission. He kisses her open mouth and her lips are firm and dry but soft like the cellophane husks from which a new-born flying insect unfurls. Her lips follow his as though he is whispering something. He says:

"Was I out of line doing that?"

"Do you think you were?"

"Yes. But I didn't want to stop myself."

She runs her fingers into her damp hair.

"It is okay."

"It probably wasn't."

She shrugs her shoulders, makes a small effort at a smile. He sits on the edge of the bed, feels enormous.

"It's pretty late. I better let you get to sleep."

It isn't that late. He thinks he can go further with this, but won't because going further would be incongruous to the way he is feeling. He is very content to leave with this. She looks at him curiously.

"Okay?"

"You look tired."

"Yes. I can go right to sleep. Thank you for the back rub."

"No trouble, anytime."

"I'll be looking forward to it."

"I'll come visit, again, sometime?"

"Yes, please do."

"I can let myself out."

"Ciao, and thank you."

When he is on the shattered tiles of the entrance hall, he sees an expensive automobile pull to the curb, and Rosa climbs out. He does not want to talk to her and walks across the grass, before she can see him.

XXXI

His excursion uptown and his marvelously rich dreams have left him anesthetized this morning. Another version of the events with Damarie played out in his mind with such reality, he is now obligated to separate fact from dream with some small effort. She didn't rise up on her elbows and kiss you a second time and say to you, you are a beautiful man. You dreamed that part. But you did kiss her and she wasn't resistant.

He is in Jackson Square playing the St. Ann corner and morning sunlight has washed everything in bronze and softened all the hard surfaces. The drug of last night hasn't completely worn off. Oh, how beautiful the world can be when you feel this way. As beautiful as anything in Hollywood or hindsight. The streets are a deep flood of sunlight and pleasant noise. Every balcony is a lush terrace of blooming potted vines and wrought-iron furniture. The air smells of the collective breakfast of coffee and fried sausage and hot syrup. He has a remote visual image of himself: a black, sweat-salted ball cap shading his eyes, sun bleached tennis shirt, the collar tea stained from constant sweat, cut-off Dickies, and dirty canvas shoes with dry rotted laces knotted in the places where they have broken. Playing his ugly instrument, he couldn't be otherwise dressed, everyone should understand this. He's got a proper tip bucket, today. Doesn't take long to get the first donation.

*

The forenoon gone, the crowd is now a mob. The dull pain in his elbow and shoulder has now become sharp and hot. He mashes out his notes with a grimace. He takes a break and calculates his earnings. They are good. Mardi Gras! He can feel the anticipation in the air. He can hear it. A city preparing for war. Preparing for a coronation. Both at the same time. A discernible chant steady rising up out of the Ninth Ward, ByWater, Holy Cross. A giant is approaching, the city trembles upon his distance steps ever so slightly, eliciting dread in some, jubilation in others. He doesn't know what to expect, except expect big. Gargantuan. Then compound it to the next order of magnitude. As so he's been told. Let it come then, he thinks. I'll play till my head falls off. I need to get another violin. I need money for Chicago. Someone passing by folds a five-dollar bill into his bucket. It is bittersweet. And more bitter than sweet.

At four o'clock, he has a pocket full of paper currnecy. His aches have abated for the time being. He is dying of thirst. He's in a great spot and knows he will lose it if he leaves. He tries to get the attention of a young boy, to persuade him to run and buy him something to drink. The boy looks at him with disdain, doesn't even reply, and walks on. He entreats a couple of young teenage girls, and the girls become quiet and serious and look at him with much suspicion and are in a great hurry to keep moving. He begs pardon of a middle-aged man, obviously not a tourist, and the man won' t even look him in the eye. What has become of everyone? It seems as though, if he is not playing his instrument, then he is nothing more then a beggar, someone to ignore, or someone to fear. Then a woman approaches:

"Can I help you?"

She has boy's haircut, looks like she could be middle thirties or better. She is a small woman, dollish and not unpleasant to look at, except for a lazy eye, which flops around to look at him, now. He is a little startled, understandably. It takes him by surprise.

"I sawr you trying to get that man's attention."

"Yes. Thank you. I'm trying to persuade someone into bringing me something to drink. I don't want to lose this spot."

"Yeah, of course. Sure. What would you like?"

"Anything would be good, but not soda or anything syrupy."

"Sure."

"Here is some money. There is a store down this street."

"Okay, but I'll get it, don't worry about it," she says, insisting he not give her any money with a gentle push of her hand.

"No, take a couple dollars, really."

"No, it's okay."

"Well, thank you."

"I'll be back in a second."

He sits on the curb, rubbing out the cramped muscles in his hands. She is back in only a couple of minutes. She hands him a small brown paper bag then sits on the curb next to him, folding her arms atop her knees.

"Thank you very much."

"I thought bottled water would be best. Also there's a candy bar in there." There's a Butterfinger in the bag. This makes him smile.

He opens the water bottle and drinks from it. She examines his instrument, cautiously.

"That's a really interesting instrument."

"It isn't a prototype or anything that special. I just made it out of desperation, really. My violin was stolen and I just got a wild idea and went with it. It's silly, really."

"No, not at all. You have done an amazing job. I think it is great, and it makes such a peculiar sound. I like it."

"It certainly gets people's attention. Both positive and negative."

She asks if she can pick it up.

"I play guitar in the tunnels in Boston, I'm very familiar with the way people respond to street performers. Some love you and then some look at you with irritation, a lot don't even realize you are there."

"In the tunnels, huh?"

"The acoustics are great, and people are always on the platforms waiting for trains. A lot of people take the T. I have been playing in this one spot for a couple years, on the Red Line."

"Isn't it noisy in the tunnels?"

"When the trains are coming or going, but then it is dead quiet."

"Interesting."

"So do you live here?"

"Yes, I do."

"It must be a great place to be a street performer, with all the nice weather and the people all around. And the city is absolutely gorgeous."

"Well," he shrugs and looks around with uncertainty. "The Quarter is beautiful. And uptown is nice. And the weather is pretty nice. It's incredibly hot in the summer, but . . . " but he does not want to continue into the bad stuff.

She looks around to try to see it as a local, not a tourist. She wears athletic shorts with an orange hem and four-colored running shoes and a blue shirt with the shoemaker's logo on the chest. She has a black hip pack around her waist. She is a tourist and she dresses like the rest of them, as if the planet became one giant exercise facility. When she looks back at him her wayward eye remains aimed somewhere off into the Square. She offers a forgiving smile.

"It never wants to keep up."

"As long as it catches up eventually, though?"

"It just wants a good last look."

"Sure, that's reasonable."

"Well I better let you get back to playing."

He doesn't want her to leave.

"No rush. I need a break."

"How long have you been out?"

"Since this morning."

"You certainly have perseverance. I usually only play a couple hours. Do you always play out for such a long time?"

"It depends. The weather has just started to get better. And, also, I need the money to buy another violin."

"You seem to be doing alright with your creation."

"Sure, but, you know, a violin would be much better."

She isn't convinced, or at least doesn't want to be. There is too much glorious novelty in the way it is for her to want it differently. She couldn't get that excited about meeting just another violin player, but this—this is invaluable filler for a postcard to mom. You can hardly blame her. We all want to come upon something for the first time and be amazed by it.

"Oh, I'm Natalie, by the way," and she extends her hand. He shakes it.

"James, nice to meet you. Visiting then?"

"Yup."

"First time?"

"Technically?"

"Is there some other way?"

"True, no I was born here."

"Really? No accent?"

"Too young, don't reminder any of it."

"Parents headed up north."

She looks around, then back at him.

"No, foster child."

"Okay."

"Never met my parents."

"Probably for the best." He smiles. She smiles. But hers is different.

"Don't know who my father was."

"Your mother?"

"No one is sure what happened. They found her in the truck of a burnt car. Here. On the levee down in Black Pearl."

"Holy shit!" He was about to bite into the Butterfinger. Says:

"That's incredible. What were they unsure about? Isn't that pretty much self evident?"

"No sign of struggle and fire started from inside the trunk."

He looks at her. There's less sadness in her expression then one might expect. Or exactly the amount you'd expect once you accept that life tends to lean in favor of tragedy or something ever close to it. A siren can be heard in the distance, (from anywhere).

"Is that why you're here?"

"Maybe. I think at some level. Isn't like there's answers to be dug up now. I was just crazy enough to think I would just kind of hear it.

As though the city itself would whisper it to me. I know that's pretty far out there. But I don't know, maybe not in words."

"Maybe not in words, I can agree with that."

"Oh hey, sorry, I shouldn't have just plopped that into your lap like that."

"No, it's okay. It's probably a lot to carry, got to put it down sometime."

"Yeah, though I only recently found out."

"You think that was for the best?"

"Sometimes. And by sometimes, I mean often. I guess there's really no right time really. Kind of wish I could go back to not knowing."

"Ignorance is bliss."

"Yeah"

They watch people go by minute, each whether conscious or no with one eye out for whatever threat comes next.

"Are you staying in town long?"

"Four days."

He bites off a piece of his candy bar. She takes it as a cue.

"Okay, well, I guess I'll let you take your break."

He does not want her to leave. Enjoys the company, the honesty, the shared sorrow not a thing in the world anything can be done about, aside from the accepting. But won't admit it. How could he admit it?

"Okay, maybe I'll see you again, before you go."

"I hope so. Goodbye."

"Sure, enjoy your stay."

"Thank you. I'll keep my eye out for you -pun intended. You might be on to something with that."

"Oh I doubt it. But I'll make what I can of it."

In a half-hour, he begins to play. The pain in his shoulder gets worse. He tries resting the instrument out further than is comfortable for his chin to avoid the sore spot, but this strains his neck. He endures it, though, and plays into early evening. Back in his apartment, he counts a stack of one-dollar bills several times to be certain he hasn't made a mistake. Together with some coins and what he already had, he has two hundred and twenty-nine dollars and eighty cents. He lies down on his mattress and sleeps immediately.

XXXII

As an act of kindness, and also out of curiosity, he is carrying David's television up Kerlerec, having gotten his address from the manager at the record shop. The house might actually be condemned, those inside all squatters excepting that there's electricity. Men his own age lay around on oversized sofas and in armchairs. There's pizza boxes and empties and musical equipment strewn about everywhere. The smell of marijuana like burning cane. There's a ceiling fan but no ceiling and the rafters hung with Christmas lights, blinking. Several dogs sniff his crotch and then return to their corners and lay down their long bones in boredom, their jowls pooling on the plywood floor. There's a television as long as a child's coffin and twice as high. He doesn't want to interrupt the gaming, but he does, none having even acknowledged his walking through the kicked down front door.

"David here?"

"Not sure."

"Nope," says the other, there's a car chase has their attention at the moment.

"I wanted to return his television."

Their eyes never leave the screen. "His room has the surfboard on it," a head twitch to indicate the direction. There is some navigating broken furniture and cassette tapes eviscerated, motorcycle parts weeping oil, boots and pants and belts and broken skate board decks. The walls in the hall covered in stickers and showbills and spraypaint. To a door at the end of the hall, a surfboard impaled on a fireman's axe. He pushes the door open and there's a futon mattress on shipping pallets and records and tapes and stereo and speakers and electric guitars and clothes all black and stubbed and crumpled under foot and the place smells like old dressings pulled off a deep wound.

There's a girl there on the comforter, to his surprise, so covered in ink he's initially not aware she's completely naked, but once he is, he quickly puts the television set down, and backs out slowly, so's not to wake her, if that were possible, noticing as he does so, there's a newer, larger television set in the opposite corner, complete with the requisite Nintendo gaming console. No one accords his having come, and now leaving.

*

He is working the stiffness out of his elbow in a hot bath. His clavicle is red and tender to the touch. He is thinking categorically about buying a violin, leaving Virginia, moving to Chicago, Natalie and her romantic New England, the tragic fate of her mother, her one eye that looks the other way. He dries and feels clean but sterile and vaguely unfamiliar with himself. A panicked urgency starts him into reconsidering every decision he's ever made. He gets out on the street, quickly, to out run it. Regret swells up uncontrollably, as he cuts across Orleans behind the Cathedral. He reaches a desired spot, unoccupied. He's become most uncomfortable with himself, remorseful. He sits up to play in front of the Cabildo, at a bench. He places the instrument against his shoulder and a sharp, unbearable pain radiates across his chest, setting off every nerve in its path. He cannot bear to place it here. In the last couple days he's taken to padding the butt end with a fold of hand cloth, but the initial sore spot remains. He repositions it below this spot, but this is clumsy and nearly impossible to control. Also, it is out of tune, again, or at least the sound has degraded from that which he believes is its best. The sound post has worked itself from its proper placement, but now that the case is glued shut, there's no way to adjust it. What a stupid mistake! He is mad at himself not to think of this. The only way to fix it, now, would be to break it apart. Only a few days remain, and he'll be on a bus for Chicago, there is no time. He tries to work back a tune. He can see how loose the neck has become. A split in the upper block strikes his flashpoint. He rises up from the bench and throws the instrument on the bench with disgust.

"Shit!"

He picks it up for one last re-evaluation. It isn't good. He could probably fix it, but he isn't of a mind to.

"Shit!"

It is a pathetic sight. Whatever illusion he once had about it being a legitimate instrument has now vanished. He picks it up and holds it with calm resolve.

"I guess it's time we part," he speaks aloud, and doesn't even realize he is doing so.

"You've been a good monster, but you're killing me."

He begins to remove the valuable strings.

The collection of violins at the music store has increased by one. This new addition is well worn, of a German-made variety. Once a fugitive, kept hidden in a hay barn, where the acid of pigeon shit dissolved some of its varnish. Every line and crease and furrow is now as black as ink against its finish and caramel-colored tracks are worn around the sound holes by a left-handed bow. It sits safely on the top left shelf, as if it has sought and been granted amnesty from the whole wretched mess. Its little white price tag has an awful severity, is a declaration of its new independence, a void slip to cancel out ten years of bondage to a second-rate musician. The indescribable explosion of ambivalence he is subject to at this moment burns his face; he's perspiring, trembling a bit, his vision is blurred and the auditory senses are dulled. He wants to be happy, is happy, but this fragile, fearful species of happiness is perched upon long glass straws beyond his grasp and climbing up to get at it will most certainly shatter those light transparent staves into razor-sharp shards. He doesn't dare. He tries to wait patiently, while the clerk carries on a long, repetitive conversation with a teenage boy about the various advantages of a certain electric guitar presently laid upon the counter for consideration of purchase. The clerk doesn't appear to recognize him. He is flushed the color of a newborn baby. He dreadfully knows well and now what reaction he is going to get from the clerk. He can see it in his indifferent, rat-like eyes, behind half glasses. Molten rage is pouring into him, now, unchecked, and filling whatever capacity he might have for such a thing and he is about to burst.

In undue time, the clerk turns to him, already miffed by the unsuccessful sale of the guitar.

"How can I help you?"

"Yes, that is my violin!"

The clerk could be sixty with a young man's skin and hair, or he could be thirty, of frail health. He is thin and slow and favors a silver-handled cane.

"I'm sorry?"

"Yes, that violin on the top left. It is mine. Who did you buy it from?"

"We just got it in, and I don't recall who we got it from, but I assure you it's not yours. We only buy violins with original bill of sale."

"You couldn't have. Because someone stole it from me. It' s German made, and it has water streaks in the interior wood; you can see it through the sound hole. And if you turn it over you can see the chin rest has a badly stripped screw head. Also, the case has a brown handle, gray lining, and one hinge has a nail in it to replace the lost pin. I'm telling you, it is my violin, and whoever stole it from me, sold it to you."

"Look sir, calm down, or I'll call the police."

James doesn't consider he is un-calm, given the circumstance. He realizes the clerk isn't so much guilty, as unsympathetic. James adjusts his tone, willfully.

"If you let me show you, you can see the streaks inside."

"Sir, I can assure you it's not yours. We don't buy violins from people who just walk in off the street."

"If you will just let me show you?"

"Look, I'm not going to argue with you. If you want to buy it, fine, then I'll take it down, otherwise . . ."

"Go get the case. You will see what I'm talking about."

"It's in the backroom, I can't leave the front until my assistant returns."

"I can't believe you're doing this. How could I know all this about it? Just take it down and look for yourself."

He becomes dead serious, looks at James over the top of his spectacles.

"Look kid, I don't know how you know about it, maybe you were in here yesterday and looked at it? You think this is my first day of setting up shop? Maybe you sold it to buy drugs and don't remember. I don't know. All I know is it isn't stolen, so unless you are here to buy something, I'm going to have to ask you to leave."

James can't make out the price on the tag from where he stands. Asks.

"Well," and the clerk attempts to use his best salesman's voice, brushing everything under the rug, back to business, "we're having a sale on stringed instruments. It's marked down to $199, and that includes the case and bow and new strings."

James tries to look into the clerk's dense peddle-like eyes to find compassion. There isn't any, but nevertheless he pleads:

"Look, I'm about to have a nervous breakdown here. That is my violin, and you know it. Someone stole it from me and must have pawned it?"

The clerk is angry, now.

"Unless you have some proof, even a police report, anything, then I can't consider anything. You expect I just hand it over?"

James realizes this is a statement, not a consideration, as if the clerk is perfectly confident that he has no such proof and therefore has effectively ended the dispute. He is defeated. Of course he's defeated! Whether the clerk is consciously involved in the scandal or is simply defending his vested interest is now beyond his faculty for interpretation. He has gone numb. He doesn't think to call bluff on the bill of sale. He doesn't attempt to calculate some just revenge. He does not even consider knocking the frail clerk over, grabbing the violin and running. Instead, he sinks to the bottom of himself, looking up with warm eyes, as he begins to twist into the pulp of resignation like a wood screw, steadily and tightly –tighter, tighter still, he bottoms out. As if someone else were talking, he hears these voices:

"I'll buy it."

"Do you have money?"

"Yes."

He piles everything onto the counter. The clerk doesn't touch the money, as though it is contaminated. He disappears behind the counter (and of coarse the assistant is nowhere to be seen) and then returns instantly with a black violin case with a brown handle and a finishing nail inserted into one of the hinges. The clerk puts the violin into the case along with a packet of new strings and his old bow. He has the gall to ask:

"This bow is very worn, I could throw in a new one for an extra twenty?"

"No, my old one will do for now."

The clerk restrains his expression, peers down through his half glasses at the bouquet of paper money.

"How much is here?"

"Two hundred and twenty nine."

The clerk scribbles out a sales slip, calculating the sales tax. Then he opens the register, brushes off thirteen dollars, and places the rest into the drawer.

In Jackson Square, he re-strings his violin. The world around him makes no sense, people come and go as through a fun house of distorted mirrors, disfigured, grotesque, squashed and made fat, stretched into ribbon and twisted, warped then bloated faces jeering manically. His own face hot, ears burning, eyes glassed in tears that refuse to fall away. He begins to play as a man in a desert would begin to walk, simply because he has nothing else to do, except maybe to die, which almost seems like the best choice, but there's fight in him yet.

XXXIII

"James! What's wrong? Where have you been? You look like shit."

Virginia has found him slumped against a balcony support on

Chartres Street. His face is pale and hollow and she is kneeling before him. She holds his chin up and looks into his eyes—hellish, tormented yellow eyes hopelessly snared in the bloody legs of hungry octopuses.

"I have been trying to call you. What's wrong with you? Are you hung over?"

His breath is sour and exhausted. With much concern, Virginia grabs his arms, demands:

"Com'on, get up. Let's go to your apartment."

She draws a tub of warm water. He has collapsed outside the bathroom door. She lets him sit there as she searches the kitchen. There's an empty whiskey bottle. There's a small plastic one empty in his pocket.

"This place is empty. What are you trying to do, starve yourself to death?"

He responds to the sound of the running water, goes into the bathroom. His head is warm with the liquid of exhaustion, that embalming fluid which saturates the face when deprived of several nights of sleep. He looks into the mirror and sees a sunburnt stranger, with blood-shot eyes and the meat of his face coming loose of the bone. He pulls thick folds of ones from each pocket, both front and both rear, and flops them into the sink, they break open like iceberg lettuce. He reaches a little deeper and withdraws fistfuls of coins, releasing them into a salad of paper currency, dimes and pennies sliding into the drain hole. He drops his clothes off and slides down into the warm bath water. The heavy lids of his eyes succumb to the weight of his exhaustion. His shellshocked nervous system shuts down, completely. In five minutes or five hours, how can he tell, he finds himself being helped from the tub in a twilight state of consciousness. And again, at the lapse of an indeterminate duration, he can see Virginia lying next to him in cool evening sunlight. She stares at him quietly and concernedly. He can smell cold cooking grease and the taste of tomato acid is on his tongue; apparently he has eaten something, but he can't keep his eyes open long enough to find out. She lays her soft-haired head upon his chest and he wants to stroke it, but his hand won't do it voluntarily, nor does he have the necessary strength or will to make it. At some other moment, in the blue of night, she proceeds to make love to him and the sensation of his hot semen exploding up into her and soaking his testicles under her moist gyrations is one of the most satisfying he has ever known.

Rising from twenty hours of sleep is something like coming up from a vat of warm chocolate. He won't be free from it for some time, bathe in cold water, wash his face a few times, take another cold shower at Virginia's house after breaking into a sweat lovemaking, whatever, it sticks with him a while. He is coming around, though. Virginia feeds him a tray of crawfish and spicy boiled potatoes. They drink a couple beers at a nearby college bar. His convalescence is quick. It has to be. He wants to get back into the Quarter but all the streetcars are temporarily stopped for the numerous black parades currently in progress on St. Charles. Torchlit, tractor drawn, energetic parades. Flambeaus lead the way with comets of fire in orbit. Floatsmen sow the streetsides with fake pearls and colored strings of plastic ornament. The self-segregation is unabashedly outstanding. A surprisingly conservative but yet boisterous crowd of white spectators utilize just one side of the street. A very boisterous black crowd finds acceptable accommodations in the neutral ground, on the streetcar tracks. But these *are* the black parades; that whites are present is, in and of itself, something. They have come to simply watch, to enjoy. But the family and friends of the marchers, themselves, have spread themselves out on the grass of the middle ground, much like an enormous backyard barbeque, tonight this part of the city belongs to them, and they yell and defiantly drink from beer bottles wrapped in brown paper bags, unheeding the glass container restriction, and the children run in every direction, unsupervised, chasing throws under chairs and into the trees and under people's feet with complete and wonderful abandon, something you don't see across the street. Large, very large, walnut-black women laugh in consumptive roars, slap on their huge thighs and rock back and forth in frail aluminum folding chairs, which give off a crisp groan. Tall, yellow-eyed black men stand around all but motionless, except to lift a forty to their lips or to perpetually re-adjust their genitals in their standard-issue gray, black or white sweat pants. James wouldn't mind catching a throw or two, but Virginia isn't interested; this isn't anything new or unusual to her. She isn't impressed with the haphazard marching bands, in their tattered uniforms, discolored and tight in the legs, the gilt faded. The baton twirlers are all overweight and clumsy and tar black, except this one in particular, fair skinned and thin, just now passing. She excites a roar of applause as she goes by. People call out her name, with impassioned adoration—a supermodel, a Miss America in the making.

Bringing up the rear is an impromptu jazz ensemble, the second line as it's called here. Casually dressed in sneakers and oversized shirts and dark denim pants, which they frequently pull up to keep from falling down around their knees. They gather and disperse in that way flocks of birds or schools of fish do, with an uncanny collective consciousness, though leisurely. And their music is flawless. Sublime. It is to the ear nonchalant, but at its heart highly evolved and ornately crafted, seemingly voluptuous but as Spartan as the instruments they have in their possession. Bent and tarnished and ancient. But they shine, as the black foreheads of the musicians shine with a light perspiration.

James has made his way up to the curb for a closer look. He realizes with surprise that he isn't holding Virginia's hand anymore; she stands back a bit, arms akimbo, impatiently waiting for him. He is clutching his violin case, when he catches the eye of a trumpet blower, smart and cool, noticing his case, immediately. There is a kindred sparkle in the black pearl of his eye just before he blinks and turns to flourish a note with a fellow musician. James turns back to Virginia and they make their way along the car-choked streets for her house. The passing drumbeat echoes deep into the dark neighborhood.

XXXIV

Rain falling from a blue sky is like crying and not knowing why. He is eating melon and strawberries for breakfast. Trying to read the newspaper, but you know, it really isn't of much interest, never is, makes him wonder how anyone can find it worthwhile. An enormous canvas umbrella shelters him from the crystalline sprinkle falling from the sky. It sprites the lush, expensively maintained lawn with a little joy; the cool grass under his bare feet almost takes his stress away, and the bourbon and coke helps. But to acknowledge it slipping away is to initiate its return. Then he drains the last of his cocktail from the melted cubes. Then the rain comes to an abrupt end. Then an infinite sadness overtakes him, again.

Virginia has talked him into going for a leisurely stroll; he acquiesces, but it isn't leisurely. He tortures himself quietly about not getting back into the Quarter to play. They have come to a clearing in the trees on the riverside of the levee. They lay themselves out in the grass on their clothes and make love. The sun is great on their bare skin and the breeze blows in places where it doesn't normally. A miniature airplane buzzes overhead, back and forth, but they don' t let it trouble them; the grass is tall and the operator is surely quite far away. Virginia rolls onto her elbows, peeling a spear of salt grass.

"Are you ever coming back?"

He doesn't have an answer for this. Looks into the empty sky for something, a glimpse of the future maybe, but all he finds is a little gas-powered biplane executing a chandelle. He decides to challenge her.

"Will you always love me?"

She gives him a sharp look for being unfair.

"Why James?"

"Will you?"

"I will always love you."

"Then I will come back for you."

"When?"

"When I can."

"And I am supposed to wait for you?"

He doesn't know why he is saying these things, but he cannot stop himself.

"No."

"What then?"

"I will come back for you when I can take you with me. If it's too late, then it's too late. You live your life however."

"I want to be with you."

"Then I don't see why you couldn't be."

"That's a bunch of shit," she rolls away from him and sits up.

"What?"

"You're making yourself feel good about this. It's all crap. The fact is you're leaving because you don't want to face whatever's hurting you and you're hurting me because of it."

She pauses to let him take her seriously. Then:

"What's different between here and Chicago, James? Except me. I'm here. If you wanted to come back for me someday, then you wouldn't leave me now." She pulls her shirt over her head and then slips into her jeans, having used her panties to clean herself, throws them into the grass. She stands up and steps into her sandals and stomps off through the tall grasses. He catches up, buttoning his fly, wades alongside her.

"I can't make a living here. I'm starving to death."

"James, you just made an ass load of money . . ."

"That's an exception. I cannot depend on it."

"Why not? What will be different in Chicago?"

"I don't know, I'll see when I get there. But that is the thing. I have got to go there."

"It's just an excuse."

She strides hurriedly ahead, exactly the way a girl might if she hasn't anything left to argue. He doesn't chase after her, numbed by her audacity, sick by his own guilt. He finds her in a bench outside a neighborhood corner store. She buys a fried oyster po-boy and they share it, without speaking.

XXXV

The day parades on upper St. Charles are finished. The streetsweepers have already passed and wetswept the curbs. The Crew of Bacchus sits along Napoleon readying to roll at dusk. James has played out all morning in the Quarter and made a small fortune. He meets Virginia at Lee Circle, where the streetcar is cut short, due to the large crowd awaiting the next parade to roll through. General Lee is astride his frozen horse as if presiding over a small battalion—thousands of shuffling feet raising a dust cloud and it causes James to wonder. Would even a quarter of these people turn out into the street with such energy and enthusiasm if asked to participate in a neighborhood clean up? Pick up some litter, paint a fence or house or cover some absurdly senseless tagging. Plant a tree or some flowers. Lee's Circle is right on the foot of a wrecked area of town, an area that very much needs such an effort, and then they could enjoy the fruits of their efforts everyday. People are funny like this in what they aren't willing to organize for their own community. But suggest they might get something for nothing, even if it's absolutely nothing, and they pour out into the streets in floods, merry and eager and lively.

The air smells of yeast and sweetness and thundercloud. The concessions trailers generate the glow of carnival against dusk and the haze. Warm shafts from the setting sun burn on the white hill of the Superdome. The festivities have an innocuous noise like that of the wind in the trees or a stick drug through loose pebbles.

On the Tchoupitolas radial, a mob of youth cling to a corner bar like colorful fragments of steel to a magnet; you can move them around but not away. They restrict the flow of pedestrians on the sidewalk. Hundreds of bodies press in for the door, but the door receives no one. James and Virginia walk sideways to make a path. Politely at first, but it becomes futile. Without great effort and determination, you cannot proceed. Waiting patiently for an opening is inconceivable. And they aren't even trying to get into the bar, just down the street. They press forward and young men leer down their oily noses as Virginia' s breasts press across their chests or their arms, as if she were doing it exclusively for their pleasure. Likewise, in one instant, James finds himself pinned in the rack of an enormous pair of fake tits, cool and firm, nipples hard and clearly visible under a thin cotton wife-beater. They make their way to the parade route.

Little women with glossy hair are perched upon the broad shoulders of their men, waiting anxiously, candy-colored panties rising above their belts as they lean forward to peer down the long, cleared avenue. Children, also, command the best views, from ladderchairs erected along the curbside. James decides an express route can be had via these contraptions, and, pulling a reluctant Virginia by the hand, walks hurriedly beneath nearly a dozen ladders, the children mostly unaware, but occasionally he encounters the scorn of a parent, or twice, is humorlessly warned of the many years of bad luck he will now have, thinking to himself, can time served apply.

Dusk falls on the crowd fast and it remains as a purple light. Hibernia's stone cupola is lit green and maroon and gold, a carnival beckon, as the crew approaches. A gargantuan floating Franciscan monk, twenty-five feet tall and robed, leads the procession, arms sweeping over the multitudes, benevolently, blessing the devout pressing into the barricades with religious zeal. And with what? A plastic cup or a shiny embossed fake doubloon or a string of 25 cent beads made in China by children working 10 hour shifts in work camps.

Bleachers are erected in front of the hotels, to give the guests exclusive access, and James and Virginia walk under these, erratic showers of blue and silver doubloons falling through the gaps. At St. Charles and Canal, the wide intersection is a sea of people, of a most awe-inspiring magnitude; glittering things cascade through the air into an undulation of waving arms. A torn bag of charms is a comet with sparkling trail, which impacts with a roar. Lights twinkle, eyes sparkle, arms and faces are dusted in glitter and everything's in an orgiastic quiver. The end float is pulling a scarlet banner:

Welcome to Mardi Gras. *Les le bon tempes rollez!*

In the wake of the parade, they run across the street, ankle deep in garbage. They zigzag between people running after the last float of the parade advancing up the street like a mythical serpent. At Royal and Iberville, they squirm through a crowd of onlookers as an army of police wrestle a heroin addict to the ground with necessary force. In the next block, there's a blue-white storm of flashes and an explosion of applause as a generously endowed woman leans out over a balcony rail and pulls her shirt over her head; perfect, swollen, brown tits bouncing, strings of beads flying up at her. Then on the opposite side of the street, on a facing balcony, not to be outdone, a stunningly gorgeous brunette turns her ass to the uplooking crowd below, pulls her dress up over her head and bends over, smiling through her ankles as she smacks her own naked ass. A rain of carnival jewels follows. And the exhibitionists aren't confined to second-story balconies; they draw frenzied circles on the street. Everyone' s got a camera and a neck full of beads to give away; even women, and on more than one occasion a penis is taken out and swung around a bit.

The dense crowd thins at Decatur. They pass a quiet bar and notice David is inside. He's propped up on the bar, his pale face hung over a beer bottle, and a cigarette burning in his long fingers. David is slow to recognize James. Then greets them:

"Hey what's up?"

"Not much, not much. You leave any beer behind the bar for me?"

"Sure, the night's just started."

"Has it? You should see Canal Street."

"I know, I know, man," a blank pause. "They'll be in here soon."

"Really?"

"Yeah, ab-so-lutely," another pause "Shit they'll be so many people in here you could lie down across 'em. Every bar" long pause "in the Quarter'll be the same."

"Looks like we got here just in time, then."

"Yep" another dead pause "So, what's up?"

"Just enjoying my last night on the town."

"No shit! You blowing this Popsicle stand?"

"Leaving in the morning for Chicago."

"Wow, Chicago. What's in Chicago?"

David is frightfully pale and his eyes are unusually glossy. And he's taking these long pauses in mid sentence. But he doesn't look drunk.

"Nothing, I just want to check it out."

Virginia finds this comment particularly irritating. She glares at him with derision.

"That's cool."

She looks at David with an empty smile.

"Hey, that reminds me, do you want your mattress or the phone?"

"No, man, you can keep them," he says, then:

"You guys want a beer?"

James looks at Virginia; she shrugs shilly-shally. David gives Virginia a pleasant smile, holds his crooked, long nailed finger slightly out. "You want one, V? How you been?"

She does not answer. James draws up a stool.

"Sure, let's have a couple, I'll get it."

"Nah, man, I got it. Hey, Mike, get me a couple over here." Two longnecked bottled beers bounce dripping wet on the counter, frost swirling up through the open mouths. They all drink. James realizes Virginia is standing and offers Virginia his stool. He stands between her and David.

"So, how's the record business?"

"It sucks, man."

"Yeah?"

"Yeah, I getting fucking sick of dealing with the little suckass weekend gutterpunks."

"Yeah?"

"They all want to be Trent or Eddie or Robert. Like it's a big fucking charade," he takes a swig of beer, "fucking Halloween for the kiddies in the 'burbs."

"Quit, shit. Find another job."

"Yeah but this one's got nice *French* benefits," he smiles, beer bottle poised at his lips, drinks again. He drinks the pilsner like water. He finishes the bottle, a beer bubble breaking on the stubble on his chin. The bartender bounces another next to it. "Hey you need another?"

"No, haven't finished this one."

"I forgot how slow you were. You still drink Scotch?"

"I hit on it occasionally."

David orders a shot. "To Chicago, man."

James tosses it into his mouth.

"You'll need it, it'll be colder than bitch ass up there."

Virginia sips gingerly on her beer. She gets up from her stool.

"I'm going to call my mother and tell her where I am."

"Why?" James asks.

David looks at her with a congenial smile.

"To let her know where I am and that I won't be home until late."

"Why?"

She is short with him. "I'll be right back."

"Shit sucks, huh?" David asks when Virginia is away.

He shrugs, ambivalent.

David's pale, white-skinned face stretches into a huge smile, his white corn teeth glaring:

"You damned right, man," as if James had said something, "You fucking smart to get out of this town." He orders another Scotch. James tosses it back; splashing a little in his eye, wipes his face with a napkin. Scott comes in the bar, gives them both a slap on the back.

"Hey asshole, where have you been?" he asks David.

"Right here getting drunk," he says.

"Yeah-you-right." Then to James:

"What's up?"

"Not much."

Then David:

"Whatever it is, it's coming down tonight. It's his last night in New Orleans."

"No shit!"

David orders another round of drinks while James tells Scott about his plans to go to Chicago. He sees David take out a long, black leather billfold. He unsnaps it and withdraws a crisp fifty. When he attempts to slide it back into his pocket, still unsnapped, it falls from his hand and yanks short of the floor on its chromium chain. A thin stack of bills fan out like a Chinese paper fan; a couple flipping to the floor. David drags up the wallet and pushes the bills in carelessly and shuts it, pressing one of the buttons together with his thumb and finger, then he leans off his pocket and slides it back. Virginia comes up behind James at this moment. James can see where the bills have side-sailed. Scott has taken Virginia's stool. James finds her another, then stands on the opposite side of David. He slides the bills to him with his foot, picturing where they lay in his mind's eye. He looks from Scott to Virginia to David, and then Scott says to Virginia:

"So, you going with him?"

"No, the little prick's leaving me." Her tone is spitefully humorous.

"Why you little prick," David turns to him, mockingly.

"You're not taking her with you?" Scott asks.

"Well shit no! I don't see how I can. She'd require first-class airfare, accommodations in the finest hotels on the magnificent mile."

"Ah come on, you have to," Scott says, but he really doesn't care either way.

"The only thing I have to do is tie my shoe and take a piss," James says, takes a drink from his beer, looks out the corner of his eye to see the bills beneath his foot and then, making sure he isn't being watched, kneels to his shoe and takes the bills into his hand, crumples them into a tight cylinder and walks to the restroom. The toilet is occupied. A man stands at the wall urinal. James looks quickly at the two bills, two fifties, pokes them into his pocket. When the toilet stall door flings open and the guy steps out, James goes in and pulls his penis out and starts a long piss. A hundred bucks! A hundred fucking dollars! The wall is a scrapbook, a billboard, for a hostile, vulgar people. Does Bush likes bush? is scratched into the painted cement block. Die Nigger Die, surrounded by swastikas in black paint marker. Will suck cock 4 $, followed by a phone number. Trent eats potato salad and likes it. Pencil drawings of erect dicks. I like to fuck ass. I fucked Samantha right here 9/6/92. Near the paper roll someone has scratched the square letters RLH + IJB. James zips up, puts the lid down, pulls out the money and sits down, smoothes out the two bills on his knee. They are foreign to him. He looks at them closely; the grain of the paper, the official stamp and watermark, Grant's disconsolate resignation. At what price has this instrument gained currency? What will it grant me, that I can't live without? What can I buy with a hundred bucks? That would justify the theft. He tries to think big. Extravagantly. This is a hundred dollars I otherwise wouldn't have. I can buy anything I want. Shoes? Well, I have shoes for now. Clothes? Maybe. But there's got to be something very important. Food, of course: I can live off this a long time. Then he thinks about Chicago. He sees himself in the big city in one of its big, beautiful parks, playing his violin. He realizes, just now, how lucky he is in this world. The realization makes him warm. He feels content, capable, unworried. He looks into his immediate future with excitement, buoyancy. He looks at the bills in his hand. This is how it begins. Like this. I want, therefore I will. And then where does it end? What big deal is a hundred dollars? If my life or death were pending on a hundred dollars, then it's an awfully cheap thing. It doesn't matter where David got it, that's just an excuse. It doesn't matter what he'll do with it: drugs and booze. This is not you. You are not a part of it, this whole fucking greedy, rat-ugly, racing mess. You want to know if you'll ever be a great violinist, then the question is will you keep this money? If you've the makings of a great violinist, or a great anything, then this isn't a necessary crime. You'd be no better than any other cock-and-ass punk that thinks he's something great, but is really nothing more than an egotist.

When he comes out the restroom, he finds that the occupants of the bar have multiplied exponentially. The front wall is all doors and they are all open and people spill out into the street. A couple of familiar young ladies have joined the group. David and Scott have all but deserted Virginia, lavishing a baby-faced girl with all their attention, buying her drinks. Her hair is cut close to the nape of her neck and parted like wings by baby-blue plastic hair clips and when she speaks or laughs at David, James can see a stainless ball bearing stuck in the center of her tongue. He remembers her from the Silversmith, what seems like a lifetime ago. Virginia sits on the other side of Scott, quietly, watching the girl with masked jealousy, smiling pleasantly. James asks her if she needs another beer and she declines and smiles at him neutrally. He stands beside David, where he had left his beer.

"Hey, you drunks need a couple more?"

"Let me show you a trick that will answer that question," Scott says, and he tips his head parallel the ground, his ear on his shoulder, twists his mouth up, and then pours beer in it from the bottle high over his head. "In other words, even after I hit the ground I can still drink."

"You want something?" he asks the girl. She isn't flattered.

"Sure, yeah, um Madris," and she lifts her plastic cup of lavender-colored icecubes.

James slides the bartender a fifty, discreetly. James passes the drinks around and the bartender puts the remainder under James' beer and James quickly, and inconspicuously, slides it under David's ashtray where he keeps his change. David, talking, does not see it. James walks around to Virginia' s side, exuberant, thirsty. He drinks from his beer proud of his accomplishment. He intends to do this little trick a few rounds later.

But many rounds later, he finds himself outside the open doors; the bar itself soaked in split beer from the three bartenders flinging drinks out as fast as they can; the barroom offers standing room only, now, and you cannot hear over the music and the roar of the occupants. He is four inches behind his vision. Sounds pass through his numb head slowly; words pass over his lips as slow. David is not there, but Virginia and Scott and the girl are. James vaguely remembers the necessity of returning the fifty bucks. Did he or didn't he? It is a novel idea, now—a neat trinket in his mind, miniature, and it provides him some amusement, he hopes he did, he'll check later. He sucks Scotch and Coke from icecubes that haven't had time to melt. He tells Virginia he wants to go in to find David. She says he has left the bar.

"I'm gonna go in to look for him."

"James, listen to me, he is gone. We saw him leave."

"He might be just over there."

"You're not getting another drink, so forget it."

He sucks the sweet liquor flavor from the icecubes in his cup, pleads with her.

"But I'm dry here and thirsty."

"Forget it, you're already drunk enough."

He starts to walk into the bar, regardless, and she grabs his wrist and twirls him around. He staggers into a side of beef with a Swedish accent. The Swede looks down on him from a considerable height. He is with a possible twin brother; they are even dressed the same. They take notice of Virginia's large breasts and forgive James of his run-in. Their enormous hands around their beer bottles make the bottles look like little vials of medicine.

"Vat is your name?" They ask Virginia.

"I'm sorry about that, he didn't see you there." She apologizes on James' behalf.

"No it ez alright. But vat is your name, ve are saying."

"Oh, um, Susan."

"Susan, oh, great to meet you. Ve are from Sweden," of course the accent, there is no need to describe it—it's easy to imagine. "Es he with you?"

"Yes, this is my husband."

James is remotely aware of her pronouncement. She puts her arm around him. He blurts out:

"Yes, isn't she the best?"

"The beast, you say? Really, that good?" the Swede says; he is amused.

"You couldn't want more."

"Eye don't guess you could."

"I say."

"And she haus nice teets, too," the tallest says, tilts back his medicine bottle. Scott becomes aware of the conversation. Virginia looks at Scott. Scott looks at her, then to the tall Swede. Then they look at James to see how he will respond. The Swede is seemingly confrontational; at least to Virginia and Scott he appears to be. But James hangs on Virginia's shoulder registering the comment with a perplexed and comical look. He says:

"Doesn't she though?" Straightens himself up with pride.

"Eye should say," returns the same Swede.

"I remark their largeness often. They're a wonderful two things, aren't they? Hell anyone can tell you that; it's obvious."

The Swede drinks from his beer, laughs condescendingly, then asks:

"Yes, but are zey reel?"

"Oh, yes, definitely. One hundred percent. It's all milk and mammary glands there, my friend. But hey, hell, don't just take my word for it, grab on to one of them and see for yourself."

Virginia flashes a fearful smile at the Swede. James smiles with comic immunity. The Swede drinks from his beer bottle, surely pondering the offer. The other Swede, who has governed the situation silently, until now, laughs out loud and hard.

"No, no, that'z okay. Dose are yours and hers to feel. We believe dat dare reel. We are only making fun with you."

"Oh yes, the real thing," James says, "The fake stuff's for the Californians."

James looks the foreigners in the eye a moment, intently, but without hostility.

"I think every man should have a pair of these hanging around the house," he suggests earnestly. Virginia couldn't be more disgusted with him.

They chuckle at the drunk and offer him a beer. Virginia declines it, tells them he has had enough and needs to be taken home. She solicits Scott's help. He takes one arm and she takes the other. James protests amicably, tries to free himself with cries of being abducted:

"But I am innocent, I tell you. I have been framed. This is an outrage. I'll need my lawyer. Someone please, help. These people have gone mad. They intend all manner of unspeakable tortures for me. Please, I beg of someone."

"Oh, shut up, you idiot," Virginia says, tugging him by his wrist.

"Okay, okay, I'm all good, I'm coming. You can let me go now."

They release him, assuming he is serious. The instant they do, he turns and runs up behind a man walking with a woman under each arm.

"Now obviously, you have more than you can handle here. It

just so happens that all my other obligations have been cancelled for the . . . " Virginia grabs him by the shirttails and drags him off. "But I'm just trying to help a fellow out."

"Come on, James, this isn't funny." And she is in no mood for him.

A block or two further, when they think he is come to his senses, they release him again. But he can't be trusted, he runs up to a lamppost, straddles it, announces loudly:

"All delicate female eyes behold the world's mightiest sex tool," and as a foot note, "For viewing pleasure at the moment, but for those desiring individual application please form a line along the curb."

Virginia is slightly amused, but also very angry by the way he is wasting their last night. She takes him by the hair and he scampers behind her, crying a little. She lets go and tries to take his wrist, but he runs to another lamppost.

"And here it is again, folks. For a limited time, as long as the law will allow. Back by popular demand. Come see it before it is banned in this country all together."

Virginia decides to take a different approach. She whispers in his ear:

"Say, what does a girl have to do to experience this mighty sex tool of yours, privately?"

He says with a corny, singsong chant:

"You just wink and smile and follow me to my parlor."

"Your parlor. Really?" and she bats her eyes in her best vaudeville manner. "Where might that be? I'd love to go."

"Then there we are headed. Come along."

He takes her by the arm and they fall into a quick stride; he marches chin high. Scott tags along. James stops the march on Orleans a moment, abruptly, and approaches a wood gate near the curb and stands as if being frisked, facing the gate, feet apart. He undoes his fly. Virginia takes his arm as a stream begins to hiss against the gate. She steps back to let him finish. An officer steps up behind him and taps him on the shoulder, without speaking, waiting for the drunk to turn his head to him. The drunk says:

"I'm sorry, you'll have to wait your turn."

The officer says:

"Alright sir, step away from the gate. That's private property."

"I'm sorry officer," Virginia says, "he's a little drunk, we're taking him to his house right now. He lives just down the street. We'll get him home very quickly. I'm . . ."

"That's alright, ma'am. You take him on, but just make sure he holds it until he gets home."

Virginia retrieves his keys from his pockets. He has fallen into a half-sleep. They drag him into the bathroom, where Virginia begins to undress him. She gets him into the tub, kneels beside him, wipes his face with a rag. The water is cool, but it doesn't revive him. She realizes it is of no use. He will pass out shortly.

They lay him out on his mattress and he falls into heavy sleep without transition. They drag the mattress to the phone pulled to its cord's length from the wall. Virginia makes preparations to his duffle; lays out clothes for him to wear the next morning; makes sure everything is packed. She gives him kisses on the lips, while Scott stands waiting in the front room. He hasn't been too happy about all this, but he is now very sympathetic watching Virginia somberly prepare him to leave her. She tells his sleeping ears how much she loves him, you 'dumb fool'. She hugs him and then gives him one last departing kiss and she walks out the apartment, not locking the front door, as she has no way to do so.

Scott walks her to the now nearly empty Canal Street. It is four in the morning and Scott offers to give her a ride on his motorcycle, but she prefers to get a cab. Scott flags one down. The cab glides along St. Charles, littered carnival route like a street in a city evacuated by war. Virginia almost begins to cry, does not, keeps herself together, smiling indifferently at the cabbie repeatedly staring at her chest in his rearview mirror. When she gets to her house, she enters noiselessly, climbing the spiraling stairs shoeless and once in her bedroom begins to cry quietly until she breaks into heavy sobbing, lies on her bed in her dark room in her enormous empty house. She confronts her part in this, regrets she didn't tell him everything about David, about her virginity, and the priest whose hands went places were the God she once believed in should have never allowed them to go. She was aged 9. This is the first time in as many years she has let herself even think about it. The pain of it so fierce it stops her tears. She curls up in a cloud of bedding as a plea for immunity.

Part IV

I

From a sound, but inadequate sleep, he is awakened by the ringing of the goddamned phone off the hook. He lifts his heavy, saturated head from the pillow and reaches into the darkness around the bed; the ringing is intolerably close. The room is dark, darkest in the corners, but a diluted, matinal blush falls in a trapezoid from the window. He claims the phone at last and clumsily handles the receiver to his ear. He speaks slowly; his mouth is pasty.

"Hel-low?"

"Good morning Sunshine! I hope you got a good night's rest?"

"Hel-LOW?"

"Hey, it's me," Virginia says, her tone becomes less cheerful. "I didn't think you'd get up, so I thought I would call."

"Huh?"

"So are you up?"

"Yeah."

"I put some clothes out for you."

"Yeah."

"Hey, you can't go to sleep, you've got a bus to catch at six forty-five."

"I know, huu . . . umm. I know. My head hurts and I am thirsty."

"Do you feel alright, considering?"

"Huh?"

"Do you . . ."

"Why don't you let me call you back?"

"Okay, but don't go back to sleep."

"Okay, I won't, goodbye."

"Alright, goodbye."

James drops the phone and it just happens to land on the pegs. He tries crawling out of bed, but he collapses, half on the floor, half on the mattress. The cool, dusty floor against his face hurts his cheekbone—his head liquid heavy; his mouth, dry and smacky, picking up particles with each breath. He talks to himself.

"I've got to do something, don't I?"

He sits up on his butt. His hair is matted to one side of his head from being put to bed wet. He sees his canvas grip leaning against the white wall gray in the dimness. A pair of pants and a t-shirt and a ball of socks lay atop. He stands up and walks toward the bag, passes it, examining it closely, thinking what a strange thing to find sitting here. He goes into the kitchen, takes out the water jug; takes a long drink. He carries the jug with him into the bathroom.

He tries to relieve himself, cannot stand without swaying, a sitting position feels more suitable. With the jug in one hand and his head in the other, he falls into sedate sleep for many minutes. His head starts to wobble, waking him when it throws him off balance. Eventually he gets up and washes his face. The cold water cleans his eyes of the crumbs of sleep, but they are still heavy. He brushes his teeth and washes his hair. The blackout on the toilet has removed Virginia's call from memory, and now, he is functioning on his own programming. He picks up his things and puts them into his bag. He looks from room to room, not really even seeing, if there was a bucket of gold there, it'd be left there. He puts on his shoes. Looks at the time. Throws his bag on his shoulder and takes up his violin case. At the door, he takes one last look, then locks the door and throws the keys into the mailslot.

He walks along Rampart Street in the direction of the bus station. He finds his bag impossibly heavy. He does not recall it being this difficult to carry when he first arrived in New Orleans, even though, with the exception of a paper back of fiction and a set of clothing, it is packed with the same things. He shakes under the strain; the bag beats against his leg like a ship against a bulkhead, bruising it, the stiff handle cutting into his hand—a blood-thin pain in his arm and shoulder. He switches bag and violin, violin and bag, to give each arm a rest. His progress is slow. At North Rampart and Bienville, he is exhausted, flags a cab. The morning air is sweet and the city quiet, murmuring about the night before, and the cab is shuttling him into a clear state of consciousness.

*

The city of New Orleans is unique in America. No place smells like it: of sugar and cayenne, of rot and fresh paint, the yeasty stench of body sweat and spilt beer. No place sounds like it: a war going on in the projects, gunshots and siren; but then again, guitar and tambourine, the rumble of a streetcar, the moan of a river-going barge in the middle of the night. Bar fight. Cat call. There's no last call. Street poet in the Marigny. Trumpet in a narrow alley. And no place tastes like it: Okra and white rice, oyster and filet gumbo. King cake and fried fishplate. A place where generational wealth and chronic poverty yield a conspicuous decadence, where everything's "indecent", but anything goes. Flock of beautiful Catholic schoolgirls giggling in plaid skirts in mother's gleaming Suburban, passing a crack whore on the curb guzzling gin, semen dripping from her chin. Old Negro mammy on her callused knees scrubbing toilets listening through an open window to smiley blacky tapdancing in the street with bottle caps on his feet. Balustered Victorians with shanties in the shadows. Bud-swilling rednecks piled into pick-up trucks flying Confederate flags with "Southern Pride", drooling pitbull on a chain, Wal-Mart shotgun in the rack. Daddy at twenty, baby's momma in the passenger seat smacking the tobacco tighter in the Camel back. Pre-teen gangsters rolling tourists in dim-lit parks in the humid night and no one is asleep and no one sees a thing. The city of New Orleans is also just like most of America, only maybe seasoned differently. Like most of America, New Orleans is too proud of the trappings of it's own heritage to see the unrealized possibilities of it's posterity.

In the last minutes before the bus backs out the long station lot, James Buck settles into the chair, his head back, watching the morning colors fade from the sky, feeling sedately content. He can picture himself in Chicago, jeweled metropolis against a lavender night—a new, big humanity bustling about, high cultured and eager to know his experience in this ancient town. It occurs to him, now, he'll never see Virginia again. Or David. Or Jack and Kay. Or Leo. And it almost doesn't matter, literally. This pains him momentarily. Is it because no one matters? Or because they don't matter? Is he become incapable of allowing anyone to matter? He thinks then of Leo. Of all the people he has meet here, he will actually miss Leo. Why? Is Leo home personified? Is Leo all that's right about his modest, working class childhood? Or is he just a good man -flawed, broken from the wear, but a good man and it is just as simple as that? He can now remember the words:

> *so much depends upon*
> *a red wheel barrow*
> *glazed in rain*
> *beside the white chickens*

II

It is a long, uncomfortable ride, punctuated by many stops. He vacillates between a mood of irritability then calm on the brink of sleep. But cannot get any sleep, an hour at the most, as the bus would rock and lurch into station along the way, flipping on the cabin lights, arousing persons from sleep while taking on persons carrying bulging luggage they noisily stow away. He slips into a tranquil half-sleep many hours after the sun is clouded over somewhere in Missouri. He lies back in his chair looking out on the horizon at weathered hay barns and windpumps on the drink, there's a remarkable semblance to harmony, enough done, no more! Enormous objects are tiny things in the distance, black under the thunderstorm sky, which again or often glows with the sermon of lightning. The patchwork farmland unduly threatened. He searches this sky and wants to talk to God, the well-intentioned decision maker that complicates all with fable, who tells him, now, you've made mistakes, there aren't many among you who haven't, yet you are too hard on yourself, and much to hard on others. I couldn't have come this far, had I not been, he replies. Yes, you've come a long way. You've made many sacrifices, but you've also sacrificed many. Being talented, or even just determined, isn't permission to be unkind. Never forget this, and he probably wouldn't ever forget it if he really believed he was talking to God, not just a remorseful superego, prone to being often only half right. It is a short talk, and ironically leaves him satisfied with the decision made, a lesson learned, another tool gained for the employ ahead. Nine hours from this moment, he is in Chicago.

III

The bus driver wakes many weary passengers from agitated sleep by quietly speaking into his cabin microphone announcing they're entering the city limits as they barrel down the expressway; the skyline of the big town is concealed in the rising smoke of morning.

The expressway traffic is heavy. The air of the bus is different, makes him anxious; it is cold and antiseptic. At the station lot, the bus unloads slowly, almost as though the passengers dreaded doing so, bracing against the chill air. James finds his bag and quickly takes two sleeved shirts out and pulls them on under his coat. Then he secures the bag and his violin in a luggage locker inside the depot. The station is on West Harrison and South Desplaines and when he steps out the front doors, he can see how far from the heart of the city he is. Along the stark, deserted street, under a dreary overpass, along boarded-up warehouses, he goes in search of breakfast. He follows an intrinsic response to what he sees, noting his turns, suspicious of the details. He finds a place lit like a kitchen and swings open the door, fearing its conditional welcome.

He eats a big breakfast that hurts him. For reasons of economy he had not eaten the length of the trip up. He has much time to kill before day will break, he takes another cup of coffee, intending to sip on it slowly and wait it out. He listens to a cop and a waitress talk with peculiar accents, quirky 'er's and flat 'at's; the cop eats quick from his plate, while he talks with mouthfuls, "dese guys over by the Kmarts", while the waitress carelessly dries glasses behind the counter, until she sees that he is watching them, comes to refill his coffee cup. He feigns preoccupation, stares intently on his empty breakfast dishes, which she does not offer to remove. Should she inquire, as she seems like the chatty type, he panics he will not know who he is or where he has come from or why he is here and where he is going; he does not want her inquisitive conversation, should she have any. But she goes away without a word, and he immediately regrets all this. What the hell's the matter with me, he thinks. He thinks about leaving, but knows it is warm in the diner and cold outside. There's a little pop music on the radio, except that it is mostly just the pitch and jingle of commercials.

He spreads out the classifieds from a day-old paper. Tears listings from the pages with advertised rooms to rent. He puts these into his pocket. The mental task of finding lodging is daunting and what with the sheer exhaustion of inadequate sleep, he begins to nod off.

His eyes are heavy. He can't read the day-old news, which could be today's news, or tomorrow-s or the news of ten years from now—only it will have different names and maybe different locales, and if there are any deaths involved they will be multiplied for inflation. With the exception that what is horrible today, will be less horrible tomorrow and maybe just mildly unpleasant when committed in the century ahead. Reading the newspaper will callous the mind, like shoveling dirt will callous the hand of the gravedigger.

At ten after five he leaves the diner. He hits the cold, gray street, without direction. Excited only for a moment, then the bitter cold cuts through his shirts, and he realizes as if for the first time he has the desperate task of finding one warm, inexpensive bed in this enormous metropolis by nightfall. He has about three hundred dollars, as it turns out, the other fifty remained on the bar.

It is too early to make calls. On the wide, cemented street the wind sweeps away any vitality he has, shakes his bones. In one direction, the long avenue disappears into the banality of West Chicago without remembrance. The streetscape does not hint a previous existence. He thinks of New Orleans. How even the most rundown of lanes reflects a bygone society. In the opposite direction, the avenue ascends to the foot of a wide, low bridge, across which the colossal city begins to burn off its damp, exhaust-gray air. The granite walls rise from the curbs into obscurity. The gray on gray on gray is continual, except where the streetlamps produce spheres of illumination. He recalls how they buried the dead in cement tombs in New Orleans, which where bolted to the ground. He remembers with a pang of regret how the shade of an oak fell over them, how the grasses grew high around the vaults, traced with footpaths; how the many hurricane floods had cracked their plaster and the humid days ate at the brick. Van Buren crosses the South Branch Chicago River on a steel-and-stone conduit; the surface of the river a muddy tarp, a suggestion that below the surface there exists an unfathomable purgatory, where suffocating death comes slowly while the cold, lead-brown water, which you cannot fight and does not fight you, replaces your last breath. With a blurring gaze, he is paralyzed by this thought, which causes his blood to course slowly and he begins to shut down with melancholy, sheer hopelessness. He has encountered no person nor obstacle in particular, other than the obvious one, himself. Has no plausible explanation for this breakdown of spirit, aside maybe alcohol poisoning. Least not that *he* can put a finger on. A blast of the cold wind pushes him on along the gray avenue.

Where there's a momentary break in the cloud that engulfs the city, he can see the buildings reaching, offering spikes, burning red embers for the blind aircraft plowing through the mist, he can hear the dinosaur howl of their engines as they power down on long final. He catches a glimpse of the Sears Tower, which he knows with some confidence simply because it climbs into the sky and disappears—an elevator shaft to corporate heaven, or hell, depending which floor, HVAC respirated with impunity, as the whole city is, it roars with it! At the corner of Van Buren and North Franklin, he passes under a glass-and-steel shaft vertically spanning the street; a foot bridge between the Chicago Board of Trade and the Chicago Board of Options. *Why did the trader cross the street? To get more money for the exact same thing.* He continues to South Michigan Avenue. Here the buildings stop abruptly, sharp-cornered and flat as if a portion of the city had been cleft off and scraped from the cityscape into the great, silent lake.

Here, under better circumstances: a winter coat, an income, a companion, the security of a home to take shelter in, he could find something beautiful. The great, seemingly infinite lake, almost mother-of-pearl under a gray canopy waning with the coming of morning. In better circumstances, a stroll along the tree-lined water's edge might be poignantly beautiful—the company of a bourbon-haired lover bundled in a thick coat, her cheeks red against the sweeping winds. But alas, the cruel business of survival makes it all bitterly hostile and irrefutably vast and indifferent, none of its beauty penetrates the agonizing reality that the cold day will be short and the long night deathly cold. He strolls up Michigan Avenue one block, the wind fighting him. He turns in at the next corner, into the jungle of concrete and glass and iron and steel. The mighty metropolis, still slumbering, steady breathing, steam rising from its complicated form like steam from a work-hot beast standing in a drizzle. In the shadows of the buildings that instantly loom over the narrow street, he freezes. The faint penetration of morning light beginning to brighten the lake-facing buildings has not yet started to creep up the narrow lane. He begins to shake, violently and uncontrollably. He thrusts his hands into his pockets deep and bends his shoulders inward, his teeth rattling like loose bolts in a small box. He realizes he is an idiot for not being prepared, walking the pre-dawn streets of Chicago in the first of March in a borrowed unisex jacket and a couple of button-down long sleeves. He is a fool, he has to contend with it.

Under the elevated train rails, he turns into Wabash Avenue. He takes this street, dark and cold and littered and wet and flanked by shops of varieties too numerous to itemize. In half a block, he realizes he is in desperate need of a restroom. The severe cold has passed the coffee straight though him, not to mention the big breakfast, which his stomach has no doubt attacked like a lion. He slips into a franchise burger shop. It smells the eye-watering stench of urine. He doesn't waste time on the toilet bowl. When he hits the sidewalk, again, with his bowels relieved, with his sinuses relieved, he feels remarkably better, though the gloom is the same as before. He looks on his surroundings with a forced curiosity and mute ambivalence.

At six forty-five, the city starts to come alive: Cars course its arteries, people shuffle along the curbs, horns pierce the monotonous hum, a traffic cop's whistle shrieks, initiating a flow of yellow cabs. On State Street, he sees in one direction the blazing marquee of the Chicago Theatre, a recognizable image. In the opposite direction, on the other side of a wide, deep divide, at the bottom of which groans the river, he sees the architectural equivalent of two cornless cobs impaled on corkscrews of parking garage, imposing towers on an imposing skyline. On the other side of the river, he turns onto East Kinzie, which affords him North Rush. Then Hubbard. Then North Michigan. On his left, rising up eighty or so stories—a black building similar to the Sears Tower, he can hear the sound of iron and glass aspiring, revolving doors repeating, a fervid orchestration of sibilant electricity, tapered, thrusting two probes into the gray sky, to suck what it can from it. Directly before him towers a multi-colored building with a Gothic attitude about its crown, the Tribune Tower. His gawking up at it compels others to look up at what surely is something extraordinary about to happen, a suicide or fire. When others see nothing out of their ordinary, they side-look at him with suspicion as they pass on. He strolls up this avenue and stops before the Wrigley building with it's clock tower, which he wonders isn't the same Wrigley that makes chewing gum. He turns his steps back down N. Michigan on the opposite side and crosses the river, again, follows West Wacker Street back to State.

He shakes less frequently, now. The tops of his ears are numb and his nose is leaking, a problem he wipes away every couple minutes with his shirtsleeve, rubbing his nostrils raw. A plentitude of pedestrians, bundled in overcoats, some under umbrellas, none friendly in countenance, hurry by. They are a constant, endless, fluid mass. He stands on the edge of a continuous stream whirling the revolving doors of a granite tower like fly cogs in a gargantuan punch clock. Glossy, polished wingtips step from gleaming yellow cabs and the coattails fall like silk robes and flow and blow about fast-moving legs. Large groups of pedestrians emerge from around corners as if they all rode in on the same wagon, or train; that they have. He watches them as they flow into the buildings, with determined expressions. How lucky they are with their overcoats, umbrellas, large cups of gourmet coffee, which they purchase without hesitation, without deliberation, for two or three or four dollars. The luxury! He envies the immunity their incomes afford. How much he could do with this sort of resistance?

He walks along West Lake Street, under the elevated tracks until he comes to Wells Street. He bends his path along the tracks, until he finds himself on West Wacker Drive, again, next to the river. He turns and follows the street to North Wacker. Walking this way, he discerns that the river forks, South Branch from the Chicago. He takes a bridge over. It is an iron bridge, picturesque. The riveted black iron trusses are familiar to him, corroded, but strong, venerable. On the other side, he immediately discerns the outdated quality of the streetscape. He walks a block and finds Canal Street. It is not like the only other Canal Street he knows, not in any respect. On the immediate corner is a diner, and he steps in out of the cold. It has just opened, and though the lights are bright, the air is still cold, smells of sanitizer and steam. He cannot afford another cup of coffee, but he is certain the clerk won't let him stay long if he does not order at least this. His request is almost incomprehensible because his lips are numb. The coffee is served in a squeaking stryofoam cup, regardless that he says he wants to stay to drink it. The clerk mashes the lid onto the cup hatefully and slides it under his nose with impatience, as though James has insulted him coming into his coffee house and only ordering a coffee. Any a world of so many, another is just another, nothing to get excited about. He takes a seat in the window next to the payphone.

He makes his first call at fifteen after eight. An Asian accent answers and knows without hesitation what she has available; lists them rapid-fire, describing them as clean and spacious, with carpet and kitchenette and shared bath, in a quiet building.

"Two with kitchenette one seven-feye week," she says, "and one at one hundred week, no kitchenette."

He interrupts.

"Well, I was looking for something, very modest, something less expensive."

"I have basement 'apatment', very small, no carpet, no kitchenette, ninety feye."

"Ninety-five a week?"

"Yes, ninetyfeye week. We require week deposit and feye dollar key deposit and when you want to leave, I ask for two week notice. You come by and see. You hurry, they don't stay 'vailable long, 'specially the cheap ones."

"Okay, thank you for your time, I will certainly keep them in mind, but I want to try a couple more numbers."

"Okay, sure, you have good day."

He focuses on the next clipping. It does not have an address, only "The Orlando" followed by the number, which he dials. A woman answers; readily denounces herself as housekeeping and says he should call back at nine thirty or ten, when someone would be in the office to help him. Slightly irritated, James hangs up the phone. It isn't anything she said, or how she said it, he simply has these three clippings. If they all fail, then what?

He crumples the first clipping; believing this will therefore magically guarantee the last two will be available to him at a price he can afford. (A little foolish superstition against the feeling of hopelessness.) He slides the third clipping under his gaze and dials the phone. An old man, slowspeaking, tells him the rates without greeting, and, as an insignificant last remark, says that he has some rooms available. His rates are sixty-five to ninety per week. James asks if he has any sixty-five-dollar situations available. The old man says that he has two sixty-fives and one seventy. He asks for directions.

He climbs off the Green Street bus. The building sits on the corner of Green and Grand. It's a dilapidated, patched-up, crack house. Columns of blonde brick and half walls of prefabricated cement on the street level, rotting wood for the upper floors, either loose clapboard or unpainted plywood. Four oriels protrude from the Grand Street facade, suggesting the building's age, but most of the windows are covered in plastic and duct-taped, or where there is a window, it is covered with aluminum foil from the inside.

He steps into a small foyer and when the door pulls itself shut, it is pitch black, and it reeks of wet carpet and animal excrement. He climbs a flight of stairs in a half-light, produced together by a window of Visqueen and a couple of 25-watt light bulbs. The landing is bare, there is not a single chair or sofa or table or plant or picture hanging on a wall. He approaches an attendant's window, on which numerous laminated signs are taped: Pay in Advance, No Guests after 8pm, Ring for Attendant. He strikes the bell gently. The desk is unoccupied, but he can hear feet shuffling behind the rear door. He waits patiently but they continue to shuffle from the same distance, with the same indifference. He hits the bell, again, but catches it off center and it clacks. The door swings open and a black man pokes his head out. His face is spread wide in a smile.

"I'd like a room," James says politely, bending to direct his voice through the hole in the window. The attendant comes into the small room behind the glass and walks up to the desk and leans forward to look at the ground around James's feet. When he sees no luggage, not even as much as a backpack, he asks:

"Got no things?" He isn't the first person to come looking for a room in this place. He takes a moment to evaluate the question, then:

"Oh, yes, I've left them at the bus station. I just got to town."

"And you want a room?" he says. "Just one night you want it?"

"No, at least a week." James answers.

"Okay, well I don't believe I've got anythin," he says, with minimal Ebonics.

"I believe I just spoke to you on the phone . . ."

"Oh yes . . . yes, I got one sleeping room left, no kitchenette."

"Sure, that's fine. May I see it?'"

"Yes, one minute," and he turns away.

"But, sir, first, I must ask what the rent is a week?"

"Well now, let me see, hold on a minute."

He turns back to the desk, stops, as if trying to remember what it is he is after. He sifts through a clutter of letters and envelops and index cards, finds an index card with BE BACK IN FIVE in purple marker written on it. He is mumbling something about a young man coming. James bends down to the hole in the window and says:

"I think I'm the young man coming. I just spoke to you on the phone. You gave me directions."

"Oh, oh yeah, you got here quick then?"

"Yes, it didn't take long."

With an unchanged expression, carrying a broom and a pail full of keys, the attendant comes from a side door, begins to lumber up the steps directly before him, head driven forward, but his shoulders fallen, carrying the broomstick like a cane pole to a fishing hole. James follows him. Each step cries out in the absolute silence. They stop at an apartment door on the third floor, the attendant props his broomstick on the wall, takes a key from the pail. #201 is the number on the door. The man inserts the key with #420 written in ink on a little tag. But it does not turn the dead bolt. He removes it and inserts another key from the same ring. No success. Tries two more. No luck. Recycled deadbolts; switched from room to room –cheaper than re-keying. The security is in the confusion. He straightens his back, contemplates the situation, swirls his enormous finger around in his nostrils, quickly. He says:

"Might have the wrong keys. I just changed this lock. It might'n be this other'n."

He takes another set from the plastic pail.

"One of these are it. Got to be."

James scrutinizes the hall. There's a large dark stain in the carpet here. The window at the end of the hall looks out at the whitewashed brick of the building across the narrow alley. The walls are patched and painted as if by a blind man. Someone's bag of garbage sits propped next to their door. There's not a sound to be heard.

The keys are not working. The attendant is kneeling now and taking keys from the bucket randomly and trying them, one at a time, patiently. He tries nearly a dozen keys. A gaunt and oily creature of a man comes racing up the hall, a man made of sour cheese and rat hair, in a long overcoat and vinyl sneakers. His voice erupts in saliva from his pasty mouth:

"What are you doing? What is this? Get away from my door. Get away. You have no right to go in there without my permission. What the hell are you up to, you old nigger?"

He barrels between James and the attendant and quickly unlocks the door and slams it shut, and there's the sound of the dead bolts striking and chain locks clashing, a bar lock rasping.

"Oh! I believe we've got the wrong apartment," he says, entirely undistrubed, and walks two doors over to an apartment numbered 210, though James thinks it should be 203, by door count. The original key opens the lock.

The small room can only really accommodate one of them. The attendant waits very patiently in the hall. The stench stifles James' sinuses, instantly. The wind snaps a black plastic trash bag taped over the window frame. Something is underneath the carpet and creates a pitchers' mound, and the shag is crusted to turf and scabbed with tar and gum and other unidentifiable substances. There is a coverlet as worn thin as gauze and it is spread over a prisoner's cot. A vinyl chair sits next to the window; it's torn and the orange foam padding is stained with rust. Tobacco-brown waterstains spot the low ceiling. The room isn't much larger than the furnishings in it. He can hardly conceal his repulsion. He is prepared to stay wherever he has to; sleeping outside is not an option in this climate. He remembers the man saying over the phone the rates were from sixty to ninety. He assumes then that this is for sixty. How can it be otherwise! The attendant is now standing in the doorway as if in way of a response. James asks:

"So the rent's sixty a week, is that right?"

"No, I haven't got any of those left. This room's seventy."

An overwhelming anxiety fries his brain in his skull and his eye wants to fall shut. He's barely able to speak:

"It is available for tonight?"

"Yes, but you'll have to sign an agreement and put down a week's deposit."

With drowned perception, he becomes vaguely aware of his surroundings and very warm, as if injected with morphine, which leaves him numb except for a tingling in his fingertips. As if someone else speaks for him, he says:

"Well, I've got a couple more options to look into before I can make a decision. Can I come back later today?"

"Oh sure, eye's be here. You just come up. But if you want a room for the night you better not wace all day."

"Oh, no, I understand. I just want to see these other options first, that's all. You understand."

"Oh, o'right, well . . . " and he turns his attention to adjusting a block of wood that has come from under one of the bed legs. James steps out into the hall, and walks a little down from the room, assuming the attendant will follow. After a quiet minute, James says:

"Well alright, I'm going to take off. Thanks for your time."

"Oh, sure. You come back if you can't find anythin'." The attendant is as contented as if he were selling vegetables on the side of the road. Which is to say, relatively content.

"Thanks," James repeats and he turns down the hall and descends the stairwell.

Outside the clouds have lifted and it is warmer. He crosses Grand Street. He is weak and needs to sit down. He is almost unable to make it across the street. He has the wherewithal to buy a bus pass at the corner store, fourteen dollars. If he rode the bus twice a day for a week, he'd spend exactly this much. He re-phones his last option. He gets an address.

The Orlando is situated on Wells between Ohio and Ontario. It's an old, narrow building -five stories tall, without much of an entrance, just a glass door. The front desk sits on the second floor, above a dry cleaner's shop. Ascending the stairs is like ascending Mt. Everest. He is about to give out. The faint sound of men talking in hidden rooms and an ancient silence fills the landing. The attendant's desk sits behind perforated plexiglass. The air is old, but warm, and the attendant's cubicle well lit. The plaster and wood are painted with so many layers of taffy white paint they appear rubberized. The floors are conspicuously clean.

James gently taps the bell. A big man's face immediately appears, smiling, wearing trifocals. There is an oily cap of brown hair parted and slicked back atop of his huge head, presently beading with perspiration. He asks, pleasantly, eagerly:

"Yes, how may I help you?"

"I just called about a room."

"Oh, yes, good. I'm glad you came quickly. They don't last long. Yes, I've got two, but . . . Did you have trouble finding the place? I guess not, you sure got here quickly."

"Yes, it was very easy. I was already on Grand Street."

"Glad you made it, I was worried that someone would come

before you got here." His face spreads impossibly wide with a smile, exposing yellow teeth. He is inexplicably pleased. He then says:

"Let me come out of here. I'll take you to see the rooms I've got open. How long will you need one? It is for yourself?"

"Yes. But I don't know how long, couple weeks or longer."

"Good. The rent is paid by the week and you can stay as long as you like and can leave anytime as long as you give me a little notice. We don't require," and he is now completely out of sight, but still easily heard, "a week's deposit but we do have a five-dollar key deposit. Is that okay with you?"

"Sure, that's great."

"We got a lot of nice people staying here. It's a very clean and quiet building. Some of the guys have been here as long as ten or eleven years -forever; they know more about the place than I do."

He comes from an adjacent hall. He stands in front of James a moment, almost overjoyed, then moves to the stairwell. He fills a huge pair of slack pants, and a huge pair of shoes. His enormous hands have long nimble fingers, incongruously delicate. He starts to climb the stairs.

"Now I've got this room, for thirty-five. I just cleaned it this morning. It's a cozy, little room, not very big, but it always stays warm. It's got a window and a little closet and a chest of drawers for your things."

James grows weary climbing the stairs, but he tries to not let it show. He can only imagine how bad the room is going to be for that little money. The attendant glistens with sweat: it beads on his upper lip and a few streaks escape from his temples. He stops, mostly for a short break, to suggest:

"Now, if you don't need the chest and want the space, we can move it out."

"No, I've got some things locked up at the bus station."

"You just get into town this morning?"

"Yes, before sunrise."

They come to a small paneled door of glossy hardwood and turn-of-the-century black hardware. The attendant, sweating profusely now, pulls his keyring to the end of a retractable coil of braided wire and inserts a key into the new, copper-faced deadbolt. He turns the key and pushes open the door. The attendant steps aside to let James enter. Maybe like Boethius, his bliss is born of resignation. Or maybe the room is almost nearly perfect. Van Gogh's bedroom at Arles. A ten-foot ceiling and fresh air breathing in through an open window. A neatly made bed sitting in the corner, headboard and footboard painted pipe iron, with long legs, elevating the mattress almost two feet from the floor. A tall, thin, white painted radiator standing at the foot of the bed, the room cherished by its heat. A narrow chest of drawers occupying a place on the opposite wall. A functional writing table sitting under the deep windowsill. There's a small closet for his things. He is inclined presently to believe it *is* perfect, all he needs to survive here in this town and keep his sanity in the doing. A clean, well-lit, warm, modest room!

"Now I've got this one for thirty-five. And I have another room on the floor above, for fifty-five, a little bigger than this one, if you want to see it."

"Oh no, this room's perfect."

Thirty-five and five is forty and fourteen and one ten for the first bus ride is fifty-five and a dime, which leaves him two hundred and forty-four and change. But a week's rent and bus fare are paid. It is evening, beautiful evening. The crisp air sparkles in the city's canyon streets as civilization scurries to burrow in from the cold, to burn yellow squares in solidarity with the moon. The elevated train appears/disappears, a muted thunder, a rattling of iron cage, *tuck-tic, tuck-tic, screech,* the sharpening of steel. The unending stream of cabs course the cold then warm avenues, barreling through columns of steam. *Clack-thump, clack-thump* over the man whole covers. The growl of internal combustion. Oiled bearings rattle and ping. Forward with a hiss, stop with a sharp bark, a squeak, a beep, go on again carping, ambient car alarms chirping, sirens wailing, *wrrp, wrrp,* a call for urgency at every intersection. Yet, still, among it all, there's cello from the quarry, flute in the fenestration, some cymbal from the beam. To the void of space an empire of iron and stone gives voice; this is its lullaby. Chicagoans are everywhere, in long coats of brown or gray, or black, like the sky has become, and they weave themselves into themselves as they hurry through glistening intersections reflecting the signal lamps, and the black pearls in their eyes follow shiny grill to shining fender to shiny bumper to a blinking pedestrian light. In two pair of trousers and three shirts under his light jacket and two pair of socks on numb feet crammed into stiff bucks, he prowls the streets searching for a grocer, shivering with cold, rattling like a one-horsepower generator burning a search lamp in a blizzard. Knowing he can take shelter from it later, he endures it with gusto, eyes on every detail, ears tuned to every sound, remembering where he turns, what establishments he passes, the sounds of alien voices, or where music leaks from cafes and shopping stores, scarce little there is. But he can only take so much. When the hour doubles since the sun fell from the sky, and the cold intensifies, and he cannot find a grocery store, and he can't afford to eat in a restaurant, more cold now than hungry, he runs himself with long strides back to the tenement. As he turns the last corner, he sees a homeless person, curled into a tight fist in the shelter of a doorway. He is nearly more incredulous than sympathetic, thinking, how can this be done, without the aide of intoxicant or insanity? Thinking, could this happen to me? I have no safety net. He puts a few quarters into an empty, coffee stained cup.

IV

Hands deep in his pockets, jaws clinched, the dry skin on his forehead cracking, he's out on the street this morning. He knows he cannot go any longer without a proper coat. There is no way he can perform out without one. What good searching for work if he caught pneumonia? He can't afford to buy a coat, but he has no choice. He finds a thrift store with rack upon squeaking rack of musty, old coats. He sorts through them with haste, the stale odor and unsettled dust inducing a sharp migraine. He pulls from a cardboard box on the floor an insulted canvas coat, creased with random folds, but virtually unused. The sleeve ends are thick elastic, which would keep out the cold, the collar is of brown corduroy. It is years out of fashion, but it is well constructed and certainly looks warm. It has no price tag; he takes it to the clerk, a weak-eyed Greek. He says:

"That's a good coat you got there. It's like new. A coat like that," and he speaks defensively, "A coat like that would sell anywhere from seventy or a hundred dollars. It ain't seen even a day's wear."

"Yes. It really is a good coat. I haven't got a lot of money right now," James says, which completely escapes from him; he did not premeditate to beg like this, "that's why I thought I'd get a second-hand coat to hold me through the winter."

"A coat like that last you fifteen winters. Those are good coats. I give it-you forty dollars."

"Forty dollars?"

"Look," and he takes the coat into his hands and examines it, turns open the lapel, turns out a sleeve, "this coat is in excellent shape. It's worth every bit of that."

"No, it is very nice, but . . . " he momentarily hesitates, realizing that forty dollars is the legitimate value of the coat. It is in perfect condition. Why should I give this man a hard time? My poverty is not his fault. He is not making his fortune here, that's for certain. I'm the moron that came up here with no money and improper outerwear. But in the same flashthought, he realizes how desperate he is, the fact that every cent counts. What's done is done, he is here, now, and he can't readily change that. He says, as matter of fact, without self-pity:

"I've just come to town and I really have made a huge mistake thinking it wouldn't still be cold. I've only got a little money to get started with. If there's anything you can do on the price? I really haven't got much to spend."

"Have you tried it on? Does it fit good?" his tone nearly hateful, but not hateful so much as disappointed. He's got his own problems, his own shortage of cash, his own story of coming to the city with nothing from some tiny place no one has ever heard of, (in his case probably some one goat village in the north of Greece forty years ago), uninvited, looking for the opportunities, rumor had it, that abounded here.

"Yes, I pulled it on to see. It's a perfect fit. I looked for the cheapest thing I could find, until I came to this and I just thought that it wouldn't be very expensive."

"It's a bargain. That coat's insulated. You can't find a coat that will keep you as warm as it. Those are made for framers and masons, men who have to work outside to make their living."

"No, I see that it is a good coat. That's why I want it, I do work outside. But I just don't have a lot of money."

"What work you do? Can you pay thirty? If you can pay thirty, then I sell-you?"

"I play the violin, busker, street performer. Are you sure you can't go down five more bucks?"

His eyes grow softer, as if setting down the great weight they always carry. He takes the coat and helps James into it again. He admires the coat. Checks the length of sleeve. The fit of the shoulders with a prideful concern. He says:

"My father, he played the violin, in our country, until the war, then one day he did not come home." He brushes lint from the lapel.

James can see his face turn to a page in history chocked so full of unspeakable suffering, his own should merit no mention, other than it *is* his own; for all the world weeps, limps forward.

"I can do forty, it's a good coat. I just..."

"It's okay, you are young man. Times they are sometimes very hard. I understand. Where do you come from?"

"Missouri, a very small town in the hills of the south."

The old Greek can't help himself, his generosity is default, he says:

"When I was your age, I made a good living. But then you get the wife and the kids, you know, and now, you know, I am too old. In other words, sometimes life is good, others not so good. But I have no regrets."

James is folding out forty dollars. The Greek pushes his hand down. He says:

"This is a good town, you will see. The summer will be hot and you will wish it is winter again. You take the coat. You come pay me when you have more money. Forty dollars not a penny less." He pats both his shoulders.

"No, I can't..."

"No, it's okay. You come back when you have pocket full of money and you pay me then, I'm not going anywhere."

"Thank you, sir, thank you, this is very kind of you. I most certainly will."

*

The idea to write a letter to Virginia comes to him as he climbs the first flight of stairs -kindness ripples out from the place it touches. The attendant is sorting mail into the pigeonholes, sweating, standing with his huge feet wide apart for weight distribution, his knees locked. He asks, referring to the sac of groceries in hand:

"Shopping?"

"Dinner."

"How do you like your room?"

"Great. It's excellent. Stays nice and warm, even with a window open for fresh air."

"That shaft is like a big thermal chimney."

"Yes, it's perfect, it nice to have warm air and fresh air."

"Good. Is there anything you need?"

"Actually yes."

The big fellow looks at him with eager, wide eyes, enormous in his murky trifocals, he asks:

"What's that?"

"Do you have any stationary? Some writing paper?"

"Goin'a write home to Mom?"

"Well, a girlfriend, actually."

There is a strange, fleeting frown over his meaty face, and then his cordial smile returns, but changed, more polite, less friendly. He places the fist of mail in his hand atop his desk and pulls the long drawer from the adjacent desk. It is filled with white bricks of notepaper, as if stocked for this purpose. He slides a pad through the plexiglass and James takes it and asks:

"How much do I owe you?"

"Oh, nothing, no charge, we've got plenty," he is discernibly less enthusiastic.

"Are you sure?"

"Definitely, you need an envelope?" dutifully.

"Sure, if you have one."

He slides one under the glass.

"Thanks."

"You're welcome. Have a good evening," he says. There is a secretion of artificial light, which imitates actual sunlight, in this portion of the building, which never changes and therefore the lateness or earliness of the day is entirely a state of mind. James ascends the stairs and the attendant says, behind him:

"Tell her hello from me."

He eats a sandwich for early supper and then another sandwich for the lunch he did not take. Then an apple. He is happy about his appetite, but also cautious. He then sits at the writing desk and takes a pencil from his violin case and starts writing out a letter to Virginia. He does this quickly, detailing his journey up from New Orleans and everything up to this moment. He does not reflect his sadness, or his loneliness, or his regret for leaving New Orleans. Amplified by the hopefulness in the story of the kind Greek and the coat, he is upbeat.

Much later, unable to sleep, he strolls out in the cold evening, to explore the bustling metropolis, glistening, steaming, gears quickly turning. He journeys into Grant Park, beautiful and dark and with a wind off the lake that strikes him directly in the face, ice cold on his cheeks. The enormity and emptiness and mysterious darkness lend him a beautiful loneness. He had grown up nurturing a feeling much like this. Alone, but strong, lost but not needed anywhere and everything dark to him and everyone silent to him; his own thoughts what he listened to. The silence was the most important thing. He played his violin against it, for it.

He experiences a strong pang of nostalgia for his old hay barn. The smell of the burning oil lamp. Sleeping with his clothes folded under the blankets to keep them warm for the cold mornings. He hadn't felt this way, in some long time. He walks with his cheeks in his collar and his hands thrust into the pockets of his gifted winter coat, no feeling in his toes and his nose running. He feels strong and brave and thousands of miles from anything he has known his in life. He feels good about having met Virginia and not sad leaving her. He misses working long hours with Leo. He thinks about Leo coming home in damp winter evening to boiled bologna wieners on stale buns as fine with it as if it were home-made apple pie. He strolls, turning out his young life's old memories, occupying himself with the images and sounds and emotions that make up this as-of-now brief existence. He begins to feel deeply cold, a cold he can't shake, as if the nostalgia burnt itself out. He turns back, and in doing so, as if turning a channel, he becomes hopelessly lonely, and the cold is painful. He realizes he is not walking back to these things he momentarily remembered but rather he is walking away from them, to an empty room, nothing more now than a capsule in a vast, far-flung galaxy, where every connection to his previous life is lost. He begins to reconsider his complete motive.

On climbing the strong risers of the first flight of stairs in the Orlando, a great agitation fevers his exhausted brain. Do I push everything away, only to know what it feels like not to have it? Is most of my misery self-chosen? He enters his room almost faint from the climb and the migraine which enflames his skull. He sits down at the desk and re-writes the letter to Virginia from beginning to end. It reads much differently, now. He is reflective, apologetic, He writes of the mighty city, beautiful at night, with effortful poetry. Tells her about his comfortable, inexpensive room. Insists she believe he will write often, he is not gone from the world.

V

He wakes without strength. He cannot lift as much as an arm in an effort to climb out of bed. He lies heavy in his bed like a weary soul trapped in a corpse. Where has my health gone? He must start eating more. I must get up. I must! After suffering a painful sense of defeat for each minute he is stuck in this purgatory, he finally rises from his bed. It is after noon. He takes a cold shower (by this hour there is no hot water left).

On the streets it is sunny, but brisk. He bundles himself against the cold in his canvas coat. He strolls with his violin to Grant Park. At this hour, he assumes there'll be many people on walks throughout the park, but on the contrary, it is nearly deserted. The wide expressway on the west side has a steady automobile traffic. A bounty of joggers zip through, mufflers over their faces and hands gloved and yellow or black headsets clamped on their heads. Once in a while an old man or a young professional will walk a dog on a retractable leash. He opens his violin case. His beautiful instrument! This and this only inspires him now. He says to himself: This beautiful instrument, this capable, beautiful instrument—if only I could put its full voice to use. If only I could make it sing as it has been created to sing. If only I could take it up and make it sing away my grief and bring me prosperity here. If only I were half as beautiful and capable as this instrument; if I could just slip myself into a cocoon of it's weaving, an impregnable womb of sound and find comfort there, of quivering vibrating strings, humming, singing, enfolding, drowning the ululations of loneliness, -to numb the ache, to fortify against not only the harms from others, but from with-in, quell my crippling self-loathing, halt this march of fascistic pessimism, ameliorate my aching for belonging and my self-sabotaging push from it. To re-unite me with the whole. To deliver me back into the world again made right. Shall I always feel this alone? In a room of two or a planet of billions? Will I never know the love of a companion? Am I an instrument broken, the sound post lost? I'm twenty, yet I am growing tired of living, the filament burning but quivering, eminent to break. Can you keep me lit, in the darkness?

The vast park has an empty and useless quality like a football stadium in the off-season. Its enormity echoes with sadness. He puts the violin under his chin, then, almost as though he hears something from behind him, he turns to look into the distance through the spacious trees. He sees a clearing, which he immediately feels he must go to. The infatuation comes to his weary spirit with great sensation. He latches the violin into its case and takes into a run through the trees. He finds a depression in the lawn and a large amphitheater, and without haste he jumps onto the stage. He looks out over the hollow grass, damp and lifeless. He knows he will have to suffer a certain bleak existence. Without friend or lover, without money or comforts, except his little room and the warmth held there. He knows, now, his life will not be easy, at times, banal and ugly but it's long to pass, and things can't always remain the same. He knows he has only himself to blame for much of his suffering. He must be witty and spontaneous. He must be ready at any moment to spin like a whirlygig for no particular reason, just to break the monotony of the gray street he must tread. He must learn to be self-sufficient with impromptu gaiety. He stands high on the stage. Takes out his violin. Begins to play a polka, sloppily, stomping a lively circle, playing, stomping. Once or twice he looks out in the lawn and finds it empty and beautiful and gigantic and tragic. He twirls and stomps and bows, playing the verse over and over. Twirling and stomping and bowing. Twirling, stomping, bowing. The sky is a blowing dairymaid's skirt, though surrogate, and only a cold dampness belongs to the city. But it can't affect him, at least not right now.

*

He strolls across the lawn of dormat grass towards what looks like an intersecting avenue, which he crosses, then traverses another length of park, diagonally. He climbs a high turnpike and crosses the river, strolls along the avenue until he comes to a narrow slope of beach below the street, which forms the armpit of a cement promenade that stretches as far away from him as he can see. Bikes peddle. Joggers bobbing. Speedwalkers gliding, ponytails swishing. Inline rollerbladers and retro rollerskaters sliding side to side. He walks down to Navy Pier. The wind sweeps over it with intermittence. He walks to its distant end and leans against the rail, looking out over the water. The gulls cry out. A pair of portly fishermen have propped seamen's poles against the railing, with line cast out like telegraph wire, waiting for a message. White five-gallon buckets sit at their feet, empty. They talk like prisoners, like petty criminals, off duty policemen, carpenters; like just about any body it seems, every other word is fuck or son-of-a-fucking, cocksucking, whore, bitch. The fishermen with an old scar of a deep plug of flesh taken by human teeth from the pumice of cheek is telling a story:

"And what that cock-sucking whore do, she goes out and ..." A gull cries out. "You believe that? Never found it, neither! So I..."

The wind occasionally wiggles their poles. And they glance at them, as if they aren't important. The story just gets more violent. James strides along the opposite side. A pair of men, thin like schoolgirls, are standing near the rail, facing each other, wearing jeans and leather loafers and plastic windbreakers, their faces clean shaven and their short hair glossy. The thinner of the two, with his arms folded and his shoulders sunken, turns in exasperation, says:

"Well, I'll tell you, I'm tired of it. I'll have the bitch thrown out if that's what it takes. I shouldn't . . . " His voice that of an angry woman. The other extends his hand and grips his arm supportively, a bright red rubber bracelet loose around his wrist. He says:

"No, you're right. If she can't keep her dick in her pants for a week, then she can't ever be trusted. No, you're right, honey, don't let that bitch..." fill in the blank. It's not his first time, alone as he often is, to eavesdropped.

He walks the remaining length of pier. Tries to tune out the transcript of this talk show. Finds it very lonely at the end, staring out into the emptiness, a somber boat plying the white caps far far out, where is he going? Leaving, where to? Canada. He turns, looks back line the skyline. Why does it have every appearance of a better world for all, yet it doesn't feel like it, nor sound like it? He heads back. At the intersection of North Fairbanks, he collides with a sharply dressed professional; she wears a gray overcoat and carries a black handbag as if it carries a bomb, her eyes set on a point in the distance—not answering to this collision, her legs like scissors—the starched hem of her coat unmoving while her scissor legs cut, cut, cut her path along the sidewalk. He stands at this intersection and he begins to preach to himself: I must focus. It is important. There cannot be this movement all the time. This vacillation. These swings. This mental soccer game. Back, forth, back forth. To never score a point. There must be fixed points for balance and composition. I can't be in continuous exile of each moment. I can't tumbleweed. I can't be so easily affected by things. I must have a design. Establish some variety of ritual—for consistency and efficiency. This thought preoccupies him through the next intersection and the length of the next block. He comes to North Michigan Avenue, where he pauses. Take the intersection you've passed. You must be more perceptive to the things that matter, not the bullshit that doesn't. That you can do nothing about. That is and probably was always. Here you are at this thoroughfare, a diseased artery glistening like split guts. You should take that previous street. Set up at it. Without second thought, with great indifference, and begin to play. Take it as a point of certainty, solely for the reason that there you can be heard. There's your reason; there's your action. You must remember how simple everything is.

He turns back and walks to the corner of Grand and North St. Clair. He turns his back on the corner building and places his violin case at his feet, feels like a bowsprit charging new waters, undulating with the boat's rhythm. He withdraws his instrument. He begins to play. The first tip comes almost immediately, as if a bird had flown overhead and dropped it into his case. Then a half-hour goes by. Then another half-hour. He's collecting some money. Then the pedestrian traffic begins to thicken. The streets flood with yellow cabs. The crowds waiting to cross at the corners bulge into the streets, bleed through the traffic itself, begin to push him back and back until he is against the wall, until he is bowing under someone's collar. Plump secretaries bump into him unintentionally, from being pressed back from the curb, as a bus plows the street. They turn their eyes away from him quickly, with irritation, without any warmth except the warmth they protect, which he can see as they glance in and then quickly out of his eyes. What is he doing here, damned fool, no place for a violin solo? At one point a fold of tall executives in blue and black shucks engulf him, faces stoic and sterile, the world is already their oyster nothing else to talk about, empty corner conversation establishes their bond at the crowded curb of nameless commuters. He is compelled to put away his instrument and slip from the tight curb corner and take along the street in the direction of least congestion, a few more dollars in his pocket then he otherwise never had. Great!

On his walk home, he stands for a moment before a franchise burger shop. A Help Wanted sign is placed in the window next to the $2.99 Spicy Chicken Sandwich advertisement. He reads it as though seeing through it. Is he to believe it suggests employment? Full/Part Time $4.35hr. In his current circumstances, the money is actually significant. But he experiences a distasteful nausea in his stomach, maybe because he is hungry, or maybe because he knows how the meat products served at such a place are derived, or maybe because it doesn't take much to imagine the mind-numbing agony of standing behind a counter in a paper hat in polyester slacks and name tag thumb tacked to your breast pocket like it really mattered. A smell in the air like that of a biology lab and an elementary school cafeteria combined. He can't make a connection between time spent in a place like this and currency. There's an impossibility to it. Is the money the same kind he has in his pocket now? If so, where's the compensation? He can see a wire-haired black woman standing at the register; the look on her smiling face is identical to suppressed anger. In contrast, he remembers the store down the street in his childhood, the owner standing behind the counter, hair pulled back, big smile—she was kinder to him than his own parents, reaching for a Butterfinger from the candy case (purchased with money he earned collecting bottles), dust on the display glass and candy boxes piled carelessly, merchandise stacked so high he couldn't always keep track of her behind the counter; the place was never clean, never orderly, but the woman clerk was always human, always happy to see a neighborhood kid, always happy to sell a fifteen-cent candy bar, or a white-bread bologna and cheese for fifty cents, a frosty bottle of soda for a dime. An old coot on the stoop ankles deep in hound dog slicing a raw turnip like an apple with a folding knife. We see the things we see through the film of the things we've seen. Franchise restaurants hadn't yet made it to his poor town; they are a new phenomenon to him. An awful thing to witness—as people are lured and then trapped in these inescapable vending machines. He can see the other three clerks, all dressed the same way, all sad and slow and lifeless, as if plugged into the same weak power source. Manning their stations. Are they told where to stand? Are they told not to talk to each other? Told what to say, what not to say? The method of an income should never be this inhumane. Such a job has the appeal of removing an infinitive number of pennies from excrement. He wants to believe that he will not be reduced to this. He tries to stop his brain from spiraling down these black holes. He wants to hold on to his sanity. These tirades accomplish nothing. But he can't help it.

He finds little to do in his room. He tries to read. Can't. He sits on the edge of the bed. Looks at his hands or out the window at the brick wall across the shaft. His attention is weak. His thoughts are unclear and agitated. He stands up and walks to the window and looks into an adjacent window. He can see a tenant laid out in bed scoop-mouthed, magazines and newspapers covering his prostrate body. He goes to the chest of drawers and puts a peanut butter sammy together and eats it sitting at the writing desk. He thinks a moment about writing a letter to someone. Who? About what? He stands up again and then sits on the bed again, removes his shoes and lies back on the mattress. A pain like a lead cap presses on his forehead. A hollow oppressive disabling pain—this is more than just boredom; it is boredom and depression and malnutrition. He has to sit up and move about. He puts his shoes back on and leaves the room.

He finds a parlor on the second floor, dark and quiet, furnished with low couches and old wobbly chairs, occupied with old wobbly men. Two men of many multiples of his age sit quietly, on the brink of death, in infinite shadow. Another two are playing cards. No one acknowledges his quiet entrance. He sits in the oriel; the tall, slender panes of glass beaded with moisture. Through them he can see the activity of Wells Street. A steak house across the street burns lamps like ship's lights moored in a cement harbor. There's a sensation of being in a watchtower, or rather a cheap rented room and it's a stakeout. No one speaks. Then a tall man with a wrecking ball of a gut barrels in and noisily draws back a chair from the table and invites himself into the card game. One of the two men playing is slumped over, half out of his wits, slightly rocking, drooling on his collar. The other man—his tongue uninterested in staying indoors, preferring lying out over his miniature chin as if it where a stoop, sits staring out the windows, eyes balls of milk blinking, his head extending out on a hook neck; he looks like a walking stick with a head carved in the handle. The big man begins to shuffle the card deck. He is dexterous and accurate with his huge hands. He says:

"There ain't no place for cards anymore since they've closed ole' *Goose's* down."

The other players nod.

"We'd get some pretty rowdy night's goin' out'n that ole' place. Kept the floors covered in wood chips all weekend. You go in there much?"

"Oh, a time and again," says the walking stick and he speaks exactly the way a walking stick might, slow and sparingly.

"They ain't no place in this city anymore. No place to eat. No place to drink. No place to get a little pussy, clean and cheap."

The old cane nods. The other player could possibly be unconscious. Walking stick pulls three cards from his hand and slides them away from him. The big man replaces them and asks:

"You gonna annie?"

Walking stick nods. Puts the three newly dealt cards into his hand and stares at them. The big man asks:

"What's it gonna be?"

He does not answer. Continues to stare at his cards, then the dealer asks the other man if he needs any from the deck. He makes no acknowledgement. The big man ignores him. Turns his attention to stickman.

"You gonna annie?" which makes no sense at all as there are no chips or instruments of exchange of any kind on the table.

He continues to stare at his cards. The big man rockets up, his chair bolting backwards. He snatches the cards from the old man's hand; smacks them on the table. He booms:

"You ignorant fart. You ain't no good for shit. Neither one of you. Your ole' brains have rotted out. Go-on back to yer droolin'." He pulls a cigarette pack from his shirt pocket and leaves the parlor, the floorboards screaming under his stride. In his departure, silence. The two men behave as though nothing has transpired. The room is cold with a funerary stillness. Within a moment James leaves, and as if turning his back on a mortician's vault, a chill causes him to shake.

There is a television room. Two lengths of couch create a right angle facing the hanging television screen. A half-dozen men sit deep in the couches, legs crossed or folded, eyes fixed evenly on the screen. These men are much younger than those in the front parlor. They look employed, maybe not better dressed, and healthier. A conservatively dressed, young man moves over a bit to provide a genuine space for James to sit. He takes it, awkwardly, and the pillow breathes out like a lung with a sweet whistle under his weight. The young man smiles. Everyone's eyes fixed evenly on the TV. No one wants to acknowledge their presence by acknowledge another's. It's like they are all here waiting for government sponsored social services. On the television is a situational comedy about a family, a family that exchange clever one-liners on the fly, even the youngest among them, never stutter, never use the wrong word in a sentence; a family where children don't start working as soon as they get home from school. A family where the children are never slapped off their feet for mouthing off.

A gargantuan tree trunk of a man sits in a wooden chair in a red bathrobe directly below the television set, center of the room. He sits in the chair, back straight, eyes behind bifocals thick as glass ashtrays, fixed securely to the boxset, as if it were, by wires, at least until it goes to commercial. In his fat hands he holds a thick paperback, which he then turns his attention to. He devours it, nose in the fold, eyes oscillating quickly, but like a pig in a trough, snorting, grunting, scratching noisily with his free hand; his nails scraping scales of dry skin from his elbow or shins, which fall to the floor like broken garlic husk. He smells like garlic. And Pert shampoo. Or at least that's the smell in the room, and he *is* in a bathrobe. Occasionally, he will laugh—a little chuckle or a ponderous, slobbery eruption. But the instant the program flicks back onto the screen, his head comes up out his paperback crime novel, his mouth gaping, saliva dripping over his glistening lips and forming a transparent guy wire anchoring the balloon of his head to the barrel of his hairy chest. The other men watch the screen passively, as if this literate silverback, this monstrous, salivating, heavy breathing creature, was not right smack dab in the middle of the room.

When laughter from the studio audience breaks timely, the crazy ape yelps out, slaps his leg, rocks back in his chair. As a punch-line draws near, he becomes nervous with anticipation, any pre-quip and he has to suppress himself, knowing the big gag is coming, but it is terribly difficult for him; the laughter wants to burst out of his mouth, little bubbles of saliva popping. When the punch line comes, he explodes. No one in the room is laughing, because there's nothing funny; it's ABC and not NBC. In a sub-plot, a small puppy is recovered. The big man gives a low, sympathetic sigh. When, after an absurdly easy conversation between father and son, the child decides to give the puppy, which was his recent birthday present, to the homeless person who has found it (the puppy is quietly given to the hunched soul who cradles it as the father and son walk away—the boy looking back smiling), the big man trembles with tears of joy, sitting on the edge of his seat. Then the commercials come on, again, and his head drops back into his paperback. Between a Hallmark advertisement and the credits, another anecdote concludes with hearty laughs and feel-good moralization: Everything that looks good is good. The big man stands, pushes his paperback into his robe pocket, picks up his chair, holding it against his swollen belly, and walks out the door, guiding his chair carefully through the doorway. Apparently it is his own special chair.

A lean, thirty-something immediately takes the remote and flips through the stations, with great relief. A little discussion starts up over what to watch, no one has any real suggestions. Then a waiter comes in, dressed in his black-and-whites. The young man on James's left greets him, using his first name. The waiter returns the same then takes an empty spot next to the man in charge of programming. He is a thin balding man with a long, smooth nose, long as a jalapeno, and a clean-shaven face. He arranges his things in his lap, an apron, a wine tool, a stainless-steel crumber with a faux ivory handle. His well-manicured fingers hanging impatiently off his knee, wanting a Menthol. He wears a small diamond stud in his earlobe. He says:

"You find work today?"

The young man the waiter is addressing leans forward to talk around James.

"No." He stares at the older man, resignedly.

"I asked around today."

"Yeah," he replies, looks at him seriously and slowly.

"Just keep at it," the waiter says, then after a moment, while they stare at each other:

"If you need anything."

"Yeah, thanks, I will. But I'm never going back to work for that other motherfucker."

"No, you shouldn't. Did Mike find you this morning?"

"No, I left early, like around five, to get in the line."

"I think your you know who came by, today? Mike asked if I'd seen you."

"No. I left very early; it was fucking freezing this morning." He leans back in the couch, withdrawing from the cold as though it were still morning.

The older man refolds his apron idly and replaces his waiter's tools upon it. He turns to James, asks:

"You just come in? I haven't seen you around."

"I just moved in."

"Where from?"

"New Orleans."

"Oh N'awlens, such a great city!"

"Sure," James replies, looks up at the television screen, not seeing a thing, the channel changes every instant. The waiter says:

"Was that your home?"

"Not really."

"Just ready trying something new, huh?"

He is reluctant to answer. When everything is wrong, were do you begin? The waiter waits for a response without anticipation. Then asks:

"Well you guys want to join me for a drink?" and he withdraws a bottle of booze from his coat. He does not remove it from the paper bag. He says to James:

"Little bourbon to warm you up?"

James is dubious, suspecting an ulterior motive, but what the hell the guys being friendly. The waiter asks the other man:

"Little drink?"

"Sure, but I don't drink it straight."

"I've got Coke and ice upstairs," he says and then to James as he stands up, "Why don't you come help me get some glasses?"

"Sure," he says. A round of drinks, in the name of good spirits, why not?

As they climb the stairs, the waiter asks:

"How long you plan to stay in Chicago?"

"I don't know."

"Why not?"

"I'm trying to see how I like it."

"I love Chicago, myself. I think it's the greatest city you can live in."

"Really?"

The waiter's face becomes sincere; he looks back on James as he ascends.

"No other city is like this. New York. LA. Frisco. You can't afford them. New Orleans you can afford, but it's a dead end. Now Chicago, you can afford and you can do anything you want. I came here for my dancing."

He withdraws his keyring, a silver figurine of a dancer hanging from it, toes pointed, pirouetting. When he pushes the door open, James only enters as far as the threshold. He can see every corner of the room except the one behind the door. It is much like the receiving room at the Salvation Army. It is furnished with heaps of clothing. A mattress and an unmatched box spring lay up on milk crates used as storage. Vinyl blinds are pulled down on the windows. There is an electric keyboard with two milk crates for a stool, also full of things, a wooden cutting board for the seat. The waiter opens a small electric icebox, burdened with designer crackers and individually wrapped dessert cakes. He withdraws an ice tray from the shoebox-sized freezer compartment. He takes two glasses from the sink. He hands them to James and begins to remove cubes from the plastic tray, which he pries free with his nails. He says:

"Yeah, I lived in the Quarter, myself. Four years. Years ago. In the Marginy, on Esplanade."

"Yes, I know that area. Lower Esplanade is a nice."

"There's a lot of great things about New Orleans, but for me, as far as my dance and my music, I play the piano, it is a dead end, there's nothing going on there."

James holds both glasses as the waiter puts cubes into them, assuming one glass would be for the man downstairs and the other for himself and the waiter would drink his straight from the bottle. But then the waiter splashes bourbon into both glasses quickly, leaving less than a quarter for Coke. He takes one of the glasses from James and stands back to sip from it. James is about to ask about bringing another glass for the man downstairs, when the waiter says:

"So what do you do?"

"Do?"

"Yeah, do you go to school?"

"No. I don't."

"Then what do you do for a living?"

"Well, whatever pays the bills, I guess? Carpentry, washing dishes, anything." James can't bear to reveal his true passion to this person, as though it would devalue from exposure.

"That's kind of like me. My true love is my dancing and my music and my art, which is a little misunderstood right now, but I feel like any day now I'll start to go with it. And I also have my writing. But, you're right, what I do for a living isn't important. I wait tables because the money is good and it gives me the freedom to do everything else I want to do. Now once things start taking off, then I'll focus more on the important things, be it my compositions and my pieces of art or my dance. Actually, I've been getting really interested in photography. You should see some of my photographs. I'm thinking about renting a small storage room to use as a dark room. In fact, I have some great pictures of N'awlens, which I want to develop in silver gelatin. What I want to do is start photographing my artwork."

James drinks from the cheap Bourbon and Coke, the cubes have melted to slivers of glass, they weren't fully frozen. He looks from wall to wall. He sees no artwork, rather just a musical poster: Steel Pier, 11 Tony Award Nominations—a black-and-white stallion leaping from the top left-hand corner and dancing girls in gold like centurions; a gangster in double-breasted suit of pinstripes with a fat chrysanthemum in the lapel, -pinky ring with four-point glare; redheaded swingers in patent-leather shoes kicking the air; a cutesy pageant queen, wrapped in a transparent shawl, curtsying, knees together, babypink fingers on her bare thighs, pink bows on her straight shoulders and hips tall, satin bow on her head the size of a magnolia bloom, dreams in her eyes. Oh the lies we glorify! He sees no photographs, no camera on a tripod anywhere. There's a pair of cardboard boxes, and a lot of plastic grocery store bags full of indiscernible things. The smell of incense and hair products can't diffuse the sour odor of denial and too many pairs of shoes. The waiter looks like a homosexual car salesman trying to sell James a '72 Datsun for the price of a '92 Mercedes. His hair receding back every moment. A hand on his hip. The little diamond stud in his ear. Sucking his bourbon quickly. His gut protruding. His eyes go to James' bourdon and Coke.

"You need filling up?"

It is obvious he does not. James says:

"No, this is strong enough. I don't drink a lot, anyway."

"Well now how much is a lot? One drink isn't a lot."

"No, but this . . . " he is going to explain how the drink isn't enjoyable because the ice has melted and the bourbon is cheap, but the waiter says:

"Four or five drinks aren't even a lot," and he wets his thirsty lips with bourbon and forms a direct smile, winks, and his eyes become hungry. James had expected this; he isn't too surprised.

"Yes, but I have to get up early tomorrow."

The waiter walks to where the bourbon bottle sits on the corner of the icebox, pours more into his glass.

"Have you got a job?"

"No, I'll be looking for work."

"Are you looking for anything in particular?"

"No, not necessarily. Anything?'

"I could ask around at my work for you. Put your name in the drawer."

"Sure," he answers with unconcern, not taking him seriously.

"It's a great place to work. You have any experience?" And he is trying to become genuine. James entertains the notion a moment. Maybe this man *could actually* be of some help. There is incentive to be at least obliging, reluctantly.

"Here let me get another ice in that drink."

"Sure." And he takes the drink from him with great delight.

"Yeah, we all make great money over there. And I know everyone; I could probably get you in. We can go over there tomorrow and I can introduce you to a few people." He drops a single cube into the glass and then pours it as full as he can with bourbon. "In fact, a lot of the guys will be out at this club tonight, we can go over there and mingle a little, you know."

He is too careless, now. He has given himself away. James is quick to give up; it just isn't worth it. The waiter hands him the cocktail.

"You know, I better just get going. Thanks for the drink, but . . ."

"Oh no, why not?" And maybe the waiter thinks James is declining in modesty, having no money to go out. He offers:

"Hey, and I can buy you a couple drinks. Sure, we're friends, and you can return the favor later, when you are working."

"No, that's okay, thanks though. Here, where should I put this?"

He extends the glass, holding it by the rim in his thumb and index finger, but the waiter does not take it.

"You can just put it down over there," referring to the small refrigerator.

James walks over to set it down, and he doesn't see the waiter immediately push the door closed. He then comes up behind him, reaches around and grabs his crotch, not violently, brazen, as if this scripted, and not absolute insanity. His mouth is right behind his ear. His voice viscous and phlegmatic:

"Or I could lick your asshole, how about that?"

Because he is only surprised by the waiter's stealth and not the action, he pushes him off with the back of his arm with calm irritation:

"What the fuck's wrong with you, man?"

As he is going for the door, the waiter grabs his arm, gingerly:

"Oh hey, look, I'm sorry, I just thought you were shy and I. . ."

He opens and then slams the door shut behind him.

He moves through the hall suspicious now what's behind every door, disgusted by this episode and the shitty bourbon. He lies back on his bed, stares at the ceiling, starts producing a hard, upward-moving kind of thinking that climbs with irrepressible urgency up an infinite steel shaft, occasionally slipping and falling back into the brain pan, but instantly restarting its climb. There's more to this place then printed in the brochure. Why do most interactions with most people end in disappointment? Not the other way around! Has the world gone sour in the pot?

VI

He wakes, now, to the sound of heat boiling in the radiator. His eyes fly open and he sits up on the edge of the bed. He feels great, his dreams have restored him, again, as they can often do. If he could only sleep through the rest of this life! Removed from it now by a good night's rest, last night has taken on a cinematic quality. He'll accept it as such. More now than ever before, he realizes he is full into an adventure, of no small scale. Complete with danger and romance and hardship and, eventually, possibly happiness. His could be the life of London, or Faulkner, of misadventures, of threats and run-in's with seedy scruffs. He finds himself in a mood to take it as it comes, for better or worse.

The window is open. All the windows on his floor are open. He rubs the crust from his new eyes. Then something small falls outside the window, lazily but swift, a scrap of paper or a pigeon feather. He gets up and goes to the window and sticks his head out. And it returns, comes up and swirls around his head and he tries to grab it, but it soars away, riding the rising thermal. It is a delightful novelty, riding the hot air, almost weightless; it is also profoundly beautiful and symbolic. He has had dreams all his life of riding the air, climbing with thermals and soaring with the wind. Being weightless and beyond anyone' s grasp. To be weightless, drifting, nothing heavy crushing downward.

He thinks he had placed his socks in the top drawer of the chest and goes to get a pair. He finds a small radio instead (the socks are in the second drawer). Flat, heavy, black. He plugs it into the wall. Voices open and break to music, to jingles, to voices, to short, familiar violin strokes: Bach, concerto in E major for violin. Da dunt da, gettie um gettie um, gettie go, lou-ou-lalalala lah, lalalala lah. He sits at the writing desk, staring out the window, thinks, Fundamentally it's somewhat dainty, complicated like a doily. It could be more serious, stronger, but if anything it shouldn't be humiliated by that damned harpsichord. He wonders if that is what

Bach intended? He sits through a few scales, then unplugs the radio and takes it down the hall to the bathroom, cord swinging, and a towel over his arm. He plugs the radio into the socket of the sconce light over the sink, notices that the pull chain has an insulating link to prevent accidental electric shock. A remarkable little detail -an exclamation of existential lucency. He jumps into the shower, washes in a fit of cold water, knuckling his toes standing in the cold iron tub. He dries standing on his jeans on the floor. He stands there a moment wide-eyed thinking wide and smooth and mother of pearl thoughts. A different piece of music has begun to play. His attention narrows in on this. It is two violins. The one of the radio he does not know, but he thinks it is much too refined. Refined of vitality. Maybe if the composer were a more stoic individual, less educated, more isolated, then he might have taken these conversations, conversations with the self, internal conversation, and given them tension and gradually balance, more conflict between the silence and the noise. It's over-ornamented. It's icing, instead of cake. The other violin playing is playing in his head, and it's everything the other lacks and more. And it is his.

The floorboards are cold on the walk back to his room. He plugs the radio in again and places it on the writing table. Turns down the volume. He is compelled to sit down and write out his ideas, in words, as he does not know how to write music, only it feels useless, the meanings in words can never stand in the place of the sounds in the notes. On second thought though he realizes how arrogant he is being, maybe just write down some footnotes then, little mental images. He begins to think wide, again. The sideoat and indiangrass swept by the wind. A fox arches into the pounce, comes up with the field mouse by its head, little feet kicking. The plow shed has collapsed under a half-century of winter's demands. All things forgotten are found by rust. Animal hair in the barbed wire. The creek runs deepest were it fights the biggest rock. The sun fools us to thinking everything will end well. A wood wasp burrows in the handle of the shovel until you need it again. The thoughts come faster than he can write with a dull pencil.

He buttons a longsleeve over a t-shirt and pulls the loosest pair of jeans over the other and he tucks in his shirttails. He pulls on his coat and pulls the door shut behind him on his way out, leaving the radio playing out of loyalty.

The day manager, and his name is Mike, the fat man with the thick glasses, the man who so eagerly invited him into this boarding house, sits behind the front desk breathing heavy as if he is exerting a great energy in the act of reading. When he sees James, he says:

"Good morning, and how's everything?"

"Great, I guess, you?"

"Great. I notice you carry that instrument case. Is that a violin?" he asks, pushing his thick spectacles with his fat fingers against his fat face.

"Yes."

"Where do you play?"

"I'm still in the learning process really, but I play what I know out on the streets."

"Wow. Exciting!" He stands up and folds his arms and bends forward to peer out through the plexiglass. He has a look of curiosity like a child. "Now, is that what you do for a living, or?"

"I have, yes, while I was in New Orleans. But I also take other work too."

The door to the adjacent parlor is open; outside the window snow is falling, contrasting vividly against the gray; almost glowing against the dark cavity of the parlor, which he is unable to see.

"It'll be great weather for that soon."

"I hope *real* soon. When does it get warmer, anyway?"

"Could be within weeks, sometimes it gets warm around this time then has one last cold snap before summer, but mostly it doesn't start to get warm until the very last of April or the first of May. Though the Spring does seems to come a little sooner each year for a few years now." He is beginning to sweat; it beads his brow, he's the kind of person sensitive to the coming of summer weather. Buck asks:

"I guess the mail hasn't come in yet this morning?"

He really does not think he should have anything; an uncontrollable pointlessness possesses him.

"No, never this early. It's usually one or two o'clock."

"Well, I guess I'll go out for a while."

"Alright," the attendant says, "You have a good one."

When he turns the corner at half descent on the stairs and he sees now the snow pour into the street with a quiet fury and just starting to slush on the glistening black surface.

He steps out and stands in the recessed portico. The snow-filled air is warm and there is a beautiful silence, punctuated by cars passing, with a rip, as the tire tread impacts the wet street. I might find someplace with shelter, he says, his lips forming the words—he's acquired this habit now of actually speaking to himself. He traverses North Wells to the elevated tracks. From iron beams overhead water streams and beats rhythmically on the street to the accompaniment of cars splashing through oil-gleaming puddles. A pedestrian bridge connects the elevated tracks to the Merchandise Mart. He stops here, under its protection, and takes out his instrument and begins to play. He experiments, playing nothing attributed to another. He doesn't over think it, or think into it, he feels for it and it comes. And the hours pass easily as he dances with it, gets to know it better, falls in love with it, gives it a name. He returns to the building in early evening with a dozen quarters and half a dozen each of dimes and nickels like a pouch of gravel in his pant pocket.

When he lands on the second floor, the young man who'd sat on the couch beside him the night before, now stands before the front desk. He is yelling. Mike stands back from the glass, frightened and, of course, sweating. The young man is yelling:

". . . stupid hog. I was here several times throughout the day. If you weren't too fucking lazy to carry your ass up the stairs. You don't fucking care 'bout nothin' but your own fat, fucking ass."

Mike is trying to interject, cautiously:

"If I'd have known you were here I would have told you he came by. You know that I don't deliver messages. You have to come ask the front desk. I thought you were out the whole . . ."

"Fuck all that, you know how important it is that I get my prescription. But you don't fucking care. Too busy doing whatever the hell it is you do all fucking day, playing with your fat little prick, shoving food in your face, getting that big fat ass of yours fucked."

"It isn't my . . ."

"Why didn't you tell someone else in case they ran into me? All you had to do was tell some of the other guys."

"It isn't my job to track you down. I'm not your secretary. I did tell Rick. Didn't you talk to him?"

"Yes, but by that time it was too fucking late."

"Well, I'm sorry 'bout that, what am I supposed to do?" His tone is submissive. As if they are quarreling lovers and he the submissive partner. The young man says:

"You are supposed to do your job, instead of sit on your fat ass all day." He glances over his shoulder and sees James. He stops short and instantly moves down the hall, and as he advances further down the length of the hall, he yells back:

"Fuck you, you four-eyed fucker. Fuck you and fuck everyone else in this fucking place. I'll fucking leave here tomorrow. I don't have to fucking put up with this shit. I can stay at my mom's place in North Brooks. I'll fucking get this rat hole shut down."

James approaches the front desk with raised brows. Mike says, low, embarrassed, sweating:

"He's needs his 'meds', I guess. (air quotes) He gets pretty volatile. He's been kicked out of every tenement in the city. We had him removed once already. I should have never let him come back in. It's just that I'm afraid it's either here or he'll be committed. Or jail. I don't know. What can you do? I can't be his mother."

"Wow."

"Yeah," Mike sorts posted mail. James peers down the hall. There is a moment of silence. He wishes there was mail for him, but sadly knows there isn't.

He tunes his radio to an evening jazz program. He sits at the desk and eats a thin sammy, the bread not nearly as moist as it had been yesterday. He wishes he could afford to go out for dinner and then a drink. He considers going out to buy a bottle of something. But he knows it is not wise. He sits and enjoys the music, comfortable and gentle to him, until one hour later. It takes a great turn. It loses its melody and begins to burst out from the radio speaker in fits and squawks and gurgles, interrupted periodically with shrieks and yelps. He is bewildered. He realizes it is some kind of modern, experimental composition. He ponders how anyone, contented or otherwise, could enjoy it. Though envies the privilege and indulgence must a person have to bring this to air. Music for the musician's ego and not the listener's ear. He can stand only so much of it. He tunes to nothing station. So many commercials! It's maddens. It's all about *the commercials*. He clicks it off. The time glows with red numerals. It is many hours before a reasonable bedtime. But he has nothing to do. He lies back on the bed and remembers reading once how Harry Houdini submerged himself in a soldered box for one and a half hours. He wonders if it wasn't a trick. He contemplates the remark Houdini made about what he did being valuable information which could help miners and divers; teach them to be patient and lay still and breathe slow and waste no energy or oxygen and be confident. Lot of gall to say such a thing, when he had thousands watching and a telephone cable connecting him to safety.

He removes his clothing. He thinks about reacquainting himself, struggles with indecision for as long as he can control it. Then it is no use. Afterwards, he lies there, breathing heavy, sad.

VII

He is convinced there will be a reply from Virginia today, Friday. He believes she has discerned his urgency and put a letter (which would have already be written) in the mail, first class, as soon as she got his address. He gets up from his bed at eleven and takes a shower and feels content to sit in his room surfing the radio stations, pulling notes from his violin. He eats the last sandwich for lunch, using the heel. He dresses and descends to the front desk. Mike is reading from a dollars worth of novel on pages the color of smoke. He says:

"And how are you today?"

"Doing good, I guess. It's always hard to say when you're in a situation you know could be much worse, but isn't anything near what you want."

Mike looks up from his book, pushes his glasses to his face, makes a dumbfounded, vaguely surprised look, replies:

"What's the matter?"

"Nothing in particular, really, just the inaction of things. Has the mail come yet?"

"Not yet. Expecting something?"

"Yes, sort of."

Mike lets his paperback close itself. He peers through the plexiglass at him with mostly vagueness, as if this sort of conversation is bewildering, yet mildly interesting.

"You going to start playing your violin soon?"

"How do you mean?"

"On the streets."

"Oh, yes," he says, idly spinning the bell pin with his fingers.

"Do you have tapes of your stuff?"

"Recordings? No."

"You should, a lot of performers do. They make tapes of their music and sell them for five and ten dollars."

"Yes, I've seen that?"

"Yes, it's very common around here."

"No, I don't have anything like that. I just play for tips."

"I've got a recorder you could use if you're interested."

He looks closely at the attendant through the plexiglass, suspicious of course, but not showing it on his face. Then he says:

"Sure, I guess it wouldn't hurt. I could sell them for two or three dollars."

"Even more then that. I've seen them selling as high as fifteen dollars."

"Well, that is a little much, a couple dollars wouldn't seem too high for someone to pay if they were interested."

"Yes, but you're barely covering cost. You have to make it worth your trouble."

James nods his head gently. Mike says:

"Come up, I'll get it for you."

They climb to the fourth floor. Mike is breathing like wet lung. He plunges his hand into his voluminous pocket and withdraws a keyring, an enormous wad of keys of every description; every key to every lock under his jurisdiction times two, plus some forgotten others are collected here. He opens the door and begins to dig his way to the further corner of the small room, through an avalanche of junk, which slides down from as high as the ceiling. The closet is jammed full and its door permanently open, pinned under a landslide of stuff. The door to the room itself can't be opened more than seventy degrees, with junk piled behind it. His bed is a small boat in this hording sea of impulse consumerism. Nearly swamped. Blankets lay across it in twisted rolls like sails and reading materials are scattered about from cannon ball strike. As Mike begins to rummage through the toys and appliances and relics of decades obscured, James casts his eye to a disorderly fan of magazines. The top magazine is turned face down, on the backside a photograph of a seven-story vodka bottle with a fashionable jewelry shop in the ground floor. This overturned magazine conceals the cover of the one below it, the lower left-hand corner kicks out a leg from under a sheet, bare, a man's leg, muscular and brown skinned, the rectangular barcode covering the foot. James focuses on the small print on the spine, as a matter of curiosity, to ascertain its name; the print is too small, but he is certain it is Playgirl, or some variation there of. Evidence of homosexuality is becoming increasingly easy to find. And though it might have once been of a great discomfort to witness, the phenomenon is now become of some anthropological interest. What is the true nature of the behavior? Is it a physiological dysfunction or psychological? Or rather a biological non-function, he thinks, because there are certain things upon which a species must rely or it would cease to be, that much is certain.

Homosexuality, therefor, cannot be a variant rather a conclusion, a genetic dead end. DNA coding its suicide. Is it a biological Population Crisis Control Committee, endeavoring to stymie a population run rampant? An epidemic no one wants to address. Nature knows itself better than we. Is it flipping switches, as it does the sheep head that becomes the male. Or in ant colonies gender determined by the abundance of a food source. Is this akin to spawning coral, or it's dipole, more tuned to the energy reflected from the moon at night than are the rest of us. All living things must multiple, except of course when it is more beneficial they shouldn't, like the cells in our bodies.

He has lost track of Mike, burrowing into the landslide, a caricature of a hippo acting like a gopher. Mike states the obvious:

"I've got more stuff than I've got room for. I really need to get in here and sort through all this."

"Yeah, I see that," he says, surveying the contents of the room in a sweeping glance, noticing a baseball in a glass box with a long, black tangled line of a signature across it; the dog-eared pages of a current *Sports Illustrated*, and not the swimsuit issue, a Nerf hoop and backboard hung on the open closet door, chocolate boxes, shoe boxes, a toaster oven still in the box, a toy fishing pole with a big red/ white floater strung on it. Mike says:

"Ah here it is."

He pulls a police interrogation-room-type recorder from a box of clothing and hangers and estranged socks. Its long black cord comes out taut like a catgut suture from a wound. He steps out into the hall where there's more room and he hands the machine over to James, says:

"Now, I haven't used it in years. I have no idea if it still works. But if it does, you are more than welcome to use it for as long as you like. Bring it back anytime. I hope it does the trick."

"Well thanks. I hope it works, too. It'll be interesting either way."

Mike makes a straight smile, confused by this optimistic pessimism.

"Sure, but definitely give it a try. I've seen it done many times."

"Again, thank you. I'll go out and get some tapes and give it a try."

"Good luck. Let me know if there's anything else I can do to help."

"Thanks. See you later."

After placing the recorder in his room, he immediately goes out for his supper and to buy cassettes. While he walks, he idly considers what life's like for a guy like Mike. So big and out of shape and just happily sitting there reading his book like the world is just hunky-dory. His room unlivable, yet he's seemingly unperturbed. He is a good person, generous, he hopes he isn't like himself, suffering quietly out of sight of others. He wouldn't wish that on anyone. By the time he returns for the evening, the night attendant has taken the desk. He sits back in his chair with his feet up watching a small television crouched in his lap like a kitten. He is sullen and pays no attention to James, except to give him a scowl.

He loads the recorder with a new cassette. He pulls out several long notes as the small, toothed wheels turn. Then he rewinds the cassette and plays it back. Nothing. He rewinds it again, presses the record button, picks the machine up and speaks directly into the small microphone.

"Check, Check, Are you listening in there? Check. La la la de da. Check. Record, you little bastard. I've already spent money on cassettes, so record!"

He rewinds and plays it back. Not a whisper.

Foolishly, he has not saved the receipt, and he's torn the wrapping plastic off without regard. He is irritated. He cannot afford to cast money to where he cannot retrieve it immediately. He's like a fur trapper in winter, literally every single thing he does has to count. He sits back in the stiff chair. He isn't compelled to do anything. But at the same time dreads with sheer horror every moment he will now sit in his small room, completely alone, with nothing to do and nowhere to go. He sits motionless, as if in paralysis. His leg falls asleep shortly and he stands up to walk it off, and then lies back on his bed. It is too early to turn in for sleep. He tries to read, but his mind can't get into the words. Within minutes, his hands idly venture below his belt. He strokes slowly; wets his hands with spit. He knows he'll be sick with guilt and defeat when he's finished, but he also knows he can't stop, not now, and therefore he desperately wants it to last as long as possible.

VIII

The next morning he carries the recorder down to the attendant to report his findings. The attendant stands over the machine as if his consternation can fix it. He says:

"Yeah, this things probably 'bout ten years old. Well, sorry." He turns it over in his hands.

"That's alright, thanks for letting me give it a try."

"Oh, you're welcome."

"I guess I'll go out and do the real thing, then."

"Oka, good luck."

"Thanks anyway, though."

"Sure, anytime."

The bright yellow world outside is bitter cold, but he does not let his first impulse turn him back into the warm building. He strides off to find a place to play. He chooses the underground platform for the subtrain, remembering the girl with the lazy eye whose name he can't remember. So sad about her mother. Wonders how her trip went. He lasts as long as his bare fingers can burn fire against the cold. He goes to a coffee house for a small brunch, and then treks to the grocer for a loaf of bread, with which he'll finish off the remaining jar of peanut butter. In early evening, he eats a thick spread sandwich, sitting at a parlor window watching the quick glistening activity of Wells street, like watching an advanced society on another planet with a high-powered telescope. Impossibly long and quiet hours later, with the distant roar of the city only a whisper in the ringing silence of his room, he removes his undershorts and licks his palms with slow, meditative distraction. Natalie, her name was Natalie.

Sunday.

A stout, middle-aged man, still wet from a shower, black hair shining, a tooth brush in his mouth and a towel wrapped tightly around his waist, stands at the front desk, receiving his mail, which judging by the size of the stack and the fact that it is Sunday, is probably several day's worth. James descends the stairs. Mike sees him and announces with a burst of excitement.

"Jorge have you met James?"

Jorge has toothpaste foaming from his mouth, can't reply, but extends an immaculately clean hand. James shakes it. Then Mike says:

"James is a violinist. He just got here from New Orleans."

Jorge's eyes grow to say what his mouth can't.

"He plans to play out in the city this spring. We were trying to get my little tape recorder to work so he could make a few tapes to sell. But the old thing has conked out. Don't you have a tape recorder?"

Jorge holds up a finger suggesting they wait a moment. He goes into the parlor and spits in the fountain, rinses, runs water over the toothpaste to wash it down and meticulously washes out the bristles of the brush; returns, his hard-soled slippers sanding the dusty floorboards. He says:

"Sure, I just get this one."

"I thought you had said something about buying a new one this year."

"Yes, I have it maybe one month."

"Would you mind if James made some tapes on it?"

"Sure, absolutely, but I can't let you take it from the room. It's pretty big, it'd be too much trouble. But you are more than welcome to come over to use it anytime."

James looks from Mike to Jorge, uneasy about imposing. He says:

"I don't want to be a bother to you."

"No, it wouldn't. I have tomorrow off in fact, if you want to come then?"

"If you are sure it won't be a problem?"

Jorge places his hand on James's arm quickly, an affirmative pat, says:

"Not at all. Just come over in the morning, we're all pretty friendly around here. Think nothing of it."

Jorge climbs the stairs out of sight. Mike says:

"He's a pretty good man. Has been staying here on and off for ten years now. His wife lives in Mexico, well his ex-wife. She has their three children, so he goes back to Mexico every year and stays for about a month to visit them. He saves all his money and goes down there with a couple thousand dollars or more and spends it all on them and then comes back here completely broke. Not to mention he sends them nice presents all throughout the year. None of them ever come here to visit him though, that makes him pretty sad, so I've never seen any of them except in pictures. He has some very handsome children, course they're pretty much grown now, I guess. He writes to them and sends them mixtapes of music they can't find in Mexico. They write back occasionally, though most of the time, it's to ask for money. He's probably the most generous father I've ever met. Definitely the nicest tenant in the building."

"That's great, sounds like a nice guy, I hope I'm not imposing on him."

"Oh, no. He's probably pretty excited about it. He loves to be able to help people. I wouldn't worry about it."

He leaves the building feeling good about the fact that the money he spent on the tapes will not go to waste. Also the story of the generous man lightens his otherwise heavy spirit. The dregs can build very rapidly in a person, the kindness in even just one person can make a clean sweep. We have become a people of increasing self-interest, of which he fells guilty and ashamed.

He eats a hamburger for lunch and strolls about the city as long as he can stand the cold. He remains in his room the rest of the evening, practicing on his instrument, or reading, or occasionally going down to the parlor for the purpose of getting out and stretching his legs and watching the alien life down on the night streets.

Monday.

He raps on Jorge's paneled door and Jorge opens the door

immediately. The room is twice the size of his. An oriel window overlooks North Wells, the room being situated directly over the front parlor. Behind the swing of the door is Jorge's bed. A wooden cabinet runs a quarter length of the opposite wall on which sits a large television set with a video cassette player atop and next to this a large stereo system, one speaker laid horizontally on the shelf below and the other in the opposite corner of the room. Over it there are old wine crates full of cassette tapes affixed to the wall. A tall, metal gym locker stands the opposite and an open stack of shelves next to it. There is a narrow piece of wall between the window and the shelves where a stack of milk crates are stacked on their sides and filled neatly with shoes and paperback books. A desk sits in the projection of the window. The room is very tidy. Jorge offers, cordially:

"Would you like something to drink?"

"No, thanks."

"I've got Cokes or a Sprite."

A short refrigerator stands beneath the sink at the foot of his bed. He swings the door open. James can see the Coke cans and a lone Sprite can and a squeezable bottle of cheese and a squat milk cartoon. He says:

"I like Sprite, but it's your last one."

"It's no problem, there are many more at the store."

He hands him the can after opening since James has his instrument case still in hand. Jorge says:

"You can put your case down on the desk there."

He turns and places the case down gently, then Jorge directs his attention to the stereo:

"So this system has everything on it, recorder, dubbing. I've got headphones. A little microphone. I make audio letters and mixtapes for my family back home. So, I know it works very good."

"Yes Mike said as much. I see you like music."

"Oh very much, there is soo much great music these days."

"Really? Seems to me it's the same 12 songs and unrelenting commercials."

"Oh no, you can't listen to the radio except for the game. You have to find it yourself. The radio is a shame for the country."

"You couldn't say it more correctly."

He steps over to the three wall mounted crates of tapes. He tries to read some spines. There are just so many.

"Maybe I can introduce you to some stuffs you might like."

"Sure. That would be great."

He notices the tapes are alphabetized. Some that catch his eye, of the hundreds here stacked. Aerosmith. Beattles. Belly. Bjork. Clapton. Chapman. The Cure. Depeche Mode. Cyndi Lauper. Gabriel. Living Colour. New Order. His finger stops at R.E.M. *Automatic for the People. Document. Fables of the Reconstruction. Green.* By the album titles alone he's drawn in with curiosity. *Life's Rich Pageant. Murmur.* He is reminded the conversation with David about Peter Buck. He regrets that he did not investigate in the record shop more. It was just that what he heard over the speakers did not pique his interest. In the 's's, the Sisters of Mercy, a lot by the Smiths, Temple of the Dog. This one was actually a favorite of David's that he played in constant rotation. *I don't mind stealing bread from the mouths of decadence,* being a lyric he now recalls. It makes more sense to him now.

"You certainly have a lot to choose from."

"I can make you a mixtape. What do you like?"

"Shit, I don't recognize most of these."

"You are kidding with me?"

"Nope, where I grew up it was country or gospel or this crappy candy pop."

"Here, let me see," and he stands next to James, a foot shorter. At the bottom, below a Yanni tape, all the spines are hand written in a perfect miniature print. He pulls one out:

"Here you should listen to this one."

"I don't have a player, just a radio."

"I have an old one. You'll need batteries. You can have it."

"What? No, that's not necessary."

He is already digging in a crate. Pulls out an old Sony with headphones, knotted and entangled in other miscellaneous audio cords.

"It is very old, but it should still work. You can have it."

"Wow, thank you. That's very generous of you."

"It is nothing, my pleasure, you are welcome. Shall we get started then?"

James takes his violin from the case and then takes a blank cassette from its case and loads the machine. Jorge sits on the edge of his bed, watching excitedly. James mashes the record button and stands back from the machine, very professionally:

"Checking record. Check Check Check," and then he whispers, "Check record, check check check."

He rewinds the cassette and plays his voice back. It is loud and clear. He says to Jorge:

"Alright, I'm going to try to play a few minutes continuously and then play it back to see how it picks up. So we're going to have to stay as quiet as possible."

Jorge nods his head eagerly, like a young boy. He sits up in his bed, knees together, back straight, obediently.

"Okay."

The recorder is on, little white-toothed wheels nervously turning. He stands back away from the machine and draws his bow hairs across the strings smoothly and falls into a slow rhythm. He plays several minutes, and then pulls the bow off with finesse, excited. He stops the recorder. He pulls a chair from the desk to the stereo and rewinds the tape. Plays it back. Jorge is excited, says:

"That was bery good. I'm impressed," he speaks quietly as if the tape is still recording. The tape begins to play back. In the first few strokes the sound is clear and pure, but then it fizzes a moment and then becomes clear, again, and then in another moment fizzes again. The microphone has picked up the sound of the passing traffic on the damp street. He turns to look out the window, which is closed. He becomes aware, now, just how loud this sound is—something the ear tunes out, but not the microphone. He sits back in his chair, puzzled. He says:

"Well shit."

"I don't think it sounds so bad," Jorge says, and he means it.

"No, I couldn't sell it to anyone with the sound of passing cars recorded in it."

"I don't think anyone will much mind."

"No, I think they will, people are accustomed to hearing recordings done so perfectly you never hear anything but music."

"Yes, but they can't expect too much from home recording."

"I don't know. I just don't like it. Maybe I can try again sometime when the streets aren't so wet."

"Sure, anytime," Jorge answers as if it were a direct question. James glances at him a moment, to study him. His behavior is naïve, but generous and guileless, much to his great pleasure, as though already they are friends. He turns to place his instrument in its case. Jorge asks:

"So do you want to try tomorrow?"

"Yes, I'd like to, if that's alright?"

"Certainly. I get off at three."

"Okay,"

Jorge stands by the television, offers:

"If you want, I've got a couple movies here, we can watch?"

He picks them up like a child would a toy in a toy store, wanting permission. James looks at the short man with sympathy, realizes how lonely he must be, from what Mike has told. He, too, could stand a little companionship and distraction. He doesn't particularly wish to watch two hours of what he knows will be unrealistic make-believe, offering no consolation or wisdom, and maybe not even entertainment, but nevertheless it sure beats going back to his room to be alone. He says:

"I guess. What do you have?"

"These one is about three brothers who are firefighters and their neighborhood is caught in the path of a great fire. And one brother is having an abear with his brother's wife and he's also the underdog of the family haunted by the death of his father, which he thinks was his fault. It sounds pretty good. Then anodder one is about a man who works for the government, the FBI, and leads a separate life until he meets this woman and falls in love for her only to learn that she is an agent for an enemy country. This one sounds really good. I like the guy who plays the main character. His movies are always really good."

"Sure."

Jorge slides the movie into the player, offers:

"I have some pretzels if you want some?"

"No, that's fine, thanks," he says and takes the chair and turns it's back to the television to use to support his arms under his chin.

Tuesday.

He checks for incoming mail at noon; there isn't any; sad, he goes out for a stroll in the continuing cold. The sun breaks only in rare, singular shafts, which can always be seen brightening a distant corner, but never the one he is on. At four p.m., after a very brief performance on a busy street corner, he walks back to his building and climbs to his room for a sandwich, then descends to Jorge's floor with his violin. He gently raps on the door and the door breathes in; Jorge is expecting him, has left the door ajar.

The air outside has turned to black ice and a steady snow falls. The streets are quiet. An occasional horn blows. Or a passing bus roars—starting as a whisper, growing, roaring, then fading to an echo. He places his violin on the desk in the window, says:

"I think we're going to have the same problem. In a few moments it'll be rush hour traffic. It will thicken and start to melt the snow and it will be very loud. Maybe I can come some other time. Are you working tomorrow?"

"Not until five."

"Really? Maybe I could come down after the morning rush, when things quiet down somewhat?"

"Sure, but are you sure you don't want to give it a try tonight?"

"I don't think it would be worth it. I can already hear the noise becoming more constant."

"That is a terrible shame." He stands with his arms folded, facing James. Then he says:

"If you want to just practice. Make some practice tapes."

"Well the pieces I plan to play I know pretty well, if I were going to practice them, I'd just as well do that in my room."

"You can practice here if you want. I'd love to hear your music."

This is very flattering. But then he isn't easily flattered by nature.

"No. I think I'll just go up and practice and come tomorrow."

"I hate to see you go," Jorge says. James is sympathetic, is thinking of something consoling to say.

"Hey, do you want to go to a movie or something?"

This bursts from Jorge, uncontrollably. As if movies were a brand new thing they should try.

"I work at the theatre. I can let someone in with me once a week. There's a really good movie playing this week, called *The Paino*. It wouldn't cost you a thing. And I think it will be good inspirations for you."

"That's good, I could use some."

"So, you want to go?"

"Why not?" Two movies in two days, not really his thing, but whatever, at least he has found a friend, and by the name he just might find some 'inspirations'.

They catch the six o'clock, the running time two hours. They come out of the theater and the snow continues, the bustling streets glistening, the snow can't stick from the streams of yellow cabs pouring through every intersection, and the skyscrapers are quietly trembling. Jorge takes him to a cafe and prepares him an ice cream cone. This is Jorge' s second place of employment. He does not want an ice cream cone, but because it makes Jorge happy to provide it, he takes it to be kind. In the time it takes for them to eat their cones, and share a few stories, the busy streets become deserted. They walk in idle discussion, talking like brothers, or father and son, or at least good friends. Then Jorge asks:

"Do you want to give it a try tonight? It already seems really quiet out here. Maybe from the snow."

"Don't you think it's late?"

"It's nine thirty. That isn't late. I'm not planning to go to bed, yet."

The street lamps glow with a cold white light. An embraced couple strides by in long overcoats. He thinks of Virginia and the night at the theatre. It seems like it is much later than it actually is.

"It seems like it is so much later than it actually is."

"Yes it does. I like it in the city when it is really quiet. It is like it belongs to just me."

The street is intelligent and in agreement. He is content to go up to his room and practice and remember this beautiful street and this quietness, not a silence, still the sounds of a city street, just with no fury. He says:

"I think I'll just go on up to my room. Maybe I can come down in the morning and make some attempts."

"That's fine, but don't you think now's a better time? You'll have morning traffic."

"If I come down early enough, there wouldn't be."

"Sure," but he is disappointed with this.

"Or if you don't want to be disturbed too early, I can come after rush hour, around nine thirty or ten."

"Sure, anytime you want, even right now, if you want to, I think it's about as quiet as you're ever going to find."

"No, I think I'll just go on up to my room."

They climb the stairs and stop at Jorge's door. He unlocks it and James gets his violin. Jorge says:

"Okay then, I'll see you in the morning, James. But if you change your mind later, you just come back down." He places his hand on his shoulder, easily and amiably.

"Sure, thanks, but I'll probably just practice and see you in the morning."

"That'll be fine. Have a good night."

"You too."

The stairs squawk loudly as he ascends to his room, where he pulls his door shut and sits in his chair before the open window, placing his feet on the windowsill. He plays for a short time, singlemindedly.

A tenant across the way has come home, goes straight to a television set and turns it on. Kicks off his shoes and lays out on his bed and start eating Chinese food. James begins to long for a view of the night street instead of his silent shaft of blackened brick, a man eating, a man still reading. He stares intently, not seeing, hearing the silence buzzing, or the weight of other tenants on their floorboards upstairs, sequestered in their quiet rooms. He begins to suffer the weight of the air on his ears, the weight of every brick that makes up the empty shaft to which his window opens. He calls the image of Virginia up from where she stills resides, he can feel her touch, smell her hair and skin, like freshly laundered cotton sheets, he hears her voice, just the slightest hint of a southern accent, and the absence of her physical presence is more than he can stand. He latches his violin into its case, goes out the room, not wanting to be alone with himself a second more, the memory of her, his regret, his unwillingness to forgive her, and now it's too late, she's a world away. He has made so many bad decisions.

He descends to Jorge's room. He knocks on the door slightly and Jorge pulls it back in a flash. He is wearing a flannel nightshirt and pajama pants. He says:

"You've a second thought?"

"I hope I haven't gotten you up out of bed?"

"No, I was just getting comfortable. I was mending my jacket."

"Should I come later, then?"

"Oh, no, come in."

"I changed my mind. You're right, it is very quiet out. I think I might as well give it a go."

"Sure, that is great, come in."

He places his violin case on the desk, gazing out the window at the desolate street, which he is pleased to see—red light reflected in long ribbons, green light spreading out like white. Vertical things glisten, horizontal things blanketed in snow. He turns the chair to face the stereo. He is satisfied with himself for coming down and not giving into self abuse.

"Alright, let's see what happens."

Jorge sits on his mattress, in slippers, hands folded in his lap, his back straight and shoulders eagerly forward. James says with a smile:

"I hate to tell a man to be quiet in his own house, but here goes..."

"Okay, but wait, let me get more comfortable."

He gathers his coattail, the hem of which he has been mending, a long thread dangling from it. He slides back against the wall, adjusts pillows.

"I'm ready. This is gonna be fun."

"You have everything you need?"

"Yes, I think so."

The tiny wheels begin to turn. He drags his bow over the strings. Jorge takes a deep breath, as if moved by this, watches wide-eyed, hands clutching his coattails. James pulls the bow over the strings slowly and a long wail breaks open, revealing an old laborer wailing in the cover of darkness for the death of his child, cradling it gently in his callused hands. Jorge's face grows long with awe. James is satisfied with this affect.

When he draws down his bow conclusively, the very air about the room is trembling and Jorge is breathless. James is exhilarated, leans forward to rewind the tape and play it back. The results are satisfactory. He says to Jorge:

"What do you think? I think it sounds very good. You can hear if you listen closely the sound of other things, the sound that exists between the instrument and the microphone."

"You are too demanding. I think it sounds prefect."

"Well, it's definitely not perfect, but I think it'll do."

"So, you are gonna tape another, then?"

"Yes."

Jorge climbs from his bed to get a cold can of soda from the icebox. James waits until he is situated before he starts again. Jorge watches him play, intently, not turning his attention to his coat until he is well into his third piece. As the minutes goes by, Jorge becomes uncomfortable in his position, tries moving about on the mattress without making any more noise than he can possibly avoid. James cautions him with a raised brow. Jorge freezes in place. Does not move a muscle for some time. Readjusts himself as a glacier might, imperceptibly retreating to the wall. Then he realizes he is needful of a seam ripper, waits patiently for a break. Indicates to James with hand gestures his request to move about and James gives him permission with a nod of his head. Jorge carefully climbs from his bed and tiptoes to the tall metal locker, the door of which he swings back slowly, and from a shoebox he withdraws a small, yellow-handled, fork-tongued tool, and then goes back to his bed. James is certain this is all being recorded, but what can he really say? He can't hit the gift burro in the mouth. He continues playing, hoping for the best. In the final notes of the piece he notices that Jorge has left the locker door ajar. Idly, he gazes into it, where he sees a variety of things: a pair of shoeboxes, various tins of shoe polish, a plastic bin of combs and brushes and scissors and clippers, stacks of clothing, a pile of socks—like a pyramid of black potatoes, a stack of *Time* magazines. On a shelf at his eye level, he sees a row of VHS cassettes. He can plainly read the print on the slender spines of their jackets: *Pleasure Recess. A Long Hard Journey into Night. And the Cock Also Rises. The Crying Game.* On some of the cassettes, it is only the glossy images of bodies engaged in all manner of debauchery. An incredible, irrepressible urge wells up in his gut. His attention slides away from him like a plane in an exaggerated yaw. His hands complete the last notes of the tune without supervision. He stops the cassette, rewinds the tape. Jorge asks:

"I hope you didn't mind that I got up to get something from the cabinet?"

"No, not at all. You were very quiet about it. I wouldn't think it picked up on the tape."

"You did a great job."

"Thanks. I'm not exactly the best violinist you'll ever hear, as you can tell, but . . ."

"No, you are a crazy. It is terrific; you're too hard on yourself."

"No, not really, I understand that there are people with not only more advantages but also more talent than I have. I can't forget that."

"You are wrong about that. You have a great talent. I think you do a great job. Are you going to play some more?"

The pornographic films are seductively murmuring to him from inside the cabinet. He tries not to listen, not to look, but he can't keep his eyes off the small cantaloupe and rice paper colored bodies captured in ever-lasting orgy. He does not immediately reply, then without control over himself, he stands up, says:

"No, I'm kind of tired." His stomach begins to quiver, with nervousness, with a surge of blood through his body. The desire now to see the tapes has complete control over him and he goes to the cabinet, saying:

"Let's see a movie, I see you have some in here."

Jorge jumps from his bed like a frightened cricket. James focuses more closely on the images on the spines, now, perceiving the homogenous gender of the entertainers. Jorge hurries to the cabinet and begins to close the door, which James stands in the way of, and he says:

"Those are not what you think they are."

"They're porno films."

"Yes, but they're not regular ones. They're . . ."

Jorge cannot close the door with James standing in it and James takes one of the tapes into his hands and says, audaciously:

"Are they all like this?"

"Yes," he says guiltily, "but I don't watch them very often. It's just for occasionally."

"Well, what the hell, let's watch one?" and he can't believe he's actually saying this.

"Are you sure?"

"Why not, it'll be interesting." He can feel the riptide, the cross current pulling against his upright position, his feet sinking into the floor as if sand as the current erodes it from under him, the tug of the current pulling at his waist, the ability to turn the tide of his powerful sex drive is well beyond him. When the tape slides into the machine an image comes on instantly. Bare feet bounce in the air over broad shoulders, while a hollow rump pounds on another, which being against the floor has the shape of a bell, and the two men groan dramatically. The moisture, the flesh, the swollen muscle has a raw appeal, in a blind physical way. Jorge stops the film to rewind the tape to the beginning. James asks him:

"Do you do this kind of stuff?"

"Yes, but I don't have to, that's not all I'm interested in," just as he pushes play, again. Several men are monkey fucking, muscles bulging, on an outdoor jungle gym. Mouths full of penis, testicles flapping, ass cheeks glistening with oils, hands gripping bars as if they were trying to bend them. James asks:

"Is that what you want to do to me?"

Jorge looks at him nervously, uncertain what response James will have to this question. He says, his voice shaking, low:

"Yes . . . but only if you want me to, if you don't, then no. I don't want to lose you as a friend."

He is transfixed on the image of lips thin and red on penis, which could be his own. He does not see male or female or chest or breast or ego or emotion. He has an erection, now, like a stone pillar, which will rip his jeans if it is not let out soon. He says:

"If you want to do that to me (referring specifically to the blowjob presently on screen, the blower standing in the sand and the blown hanging upside down from the monkey bars giving the other the same) you can."

Jorge looks at him, seriously, with indecision and caution, contemplating the inherent consequences of the act. James looks at the television scene, imagining the wet softness of a mouth on his burning penis, not looking at Jorge, but aware of his nervous presence. Jorge asks:

"It won't change things between us, will it?"

"Of course not," James says without a moment's speculation or concern.

"Okay then," and Jorge quietly, like a humble servant, kneels before his zipper and slides it down; finds an enormous, throbbing, rock-hard penis wanting to rip out of cotton underwear, stretched thin. He pulls it free and hungrily inserts it into his mouth, as much as he can fit. James does not watch him, closes his eyes and imagines a blonde in a skirt, not unlike one of the girls from the Silversmith, nipples like hard candy, her eyes bulging while she swallows his angry cock and her long slender hand in her own crotch, titillating it, probing it in preparation for him.

He does not last long. Within minutes it is over; he erupts into Jorge's mouth like a volcano, spewing all the lava in his body at once. Jorge runs over to the sink quickly to spit it all into the sink, as if it were sour milk. James is immediately sick to his stomach. Watching Jorge turn away from the sink and wipe his chin almost causes him to vomit. Abandoned, now, of all urgency, all the toxic bile expelled, overwhelmed with disgust. He buckles his belt and pulls up his fly and grabs his violin and begins out the door. Jorge tries to stop him. He pleads:

"What's wrong? Are you upset with me? Are you mad at me? What was it? You said it was alright." He speaks intensely but low.

James does not say a word. He gives Jorge a shove to the side as if Jorge is the very sickness he feels inside. He swings open the door and begins out. Jorge holds the door only as long as he can fight James's strength, says:

"Don't be upset. Are you upset with me? Talk to me. What did I do wrong?"

He does not reply and Jorge says:

"Can I see you tomorrow? So we can talk."

He ascends the stairs three a stride to flee from him self, to escape the self-loathing enclosing all around him like fire. In the silence of his room, the mute scream shatters the windowpanes. He paces the room delirious with anger. The insuperable rage burns up the walls of the cathedral of his making. All the doors are barricaded from the outside. He can either jump or burn up in the flames.

IX

In what little sleep there was, he dreamed of serpents. They came from up out of the ground in great numbers. He snatched them and tore off their heads. New heads grew back in an instant, or headless snakes sprayed him in blood like a hose without a hand to hold it. A black, rancid smelling blood. They coiled up around his legs under his pants and he tore himself out of them. The snakes smiling at him in his nakedness, just before their strike. They bit into his hands, his face, his chest, shaking like sharks do to severe the meat. He wakes up in a sweat, he can still smell the snake blood. It might be Wednesday. A knocking falls upon the door. It comes as a delightful and very real surprise. As absurdly fantastic as God or happily ever after, in an instance of unwarranted optimism, he thinks it might be Virginia; she had gotten his letter, read between the lines, hopped a red eye into town. His pulse quickens. He pulls the door back, finds Jorge here.

"Yes?" he says indifferently.

"Hey, good morning," Jorge says, shyly. "You want me to go away?"

He has sympathy for him, says, "What is it?"

"I want to talk to you. Can I come into the room? I don't want to talk outside in this hall."

"Just say what you have to say."

"Just let me step inside, please?"

James steps back from the door about a foot. Jorge takes the small space offered, eagerly. The closeness is uncomfortable, but he does not want to back up anymore and allow him further into his room. He avoids his needful gaze. Then Jorge says:

"Can you give me a hug?"

"Are you out of your mind?"

"Just a hug, one hug for me and we'll forget about last night."

"Come on," he begs, opening his arms like a friend. James moves to the open window, no longer able to stand so close. Jorge drops his arms.

"Are you hungry, I thought we could get some breakfast. I don't have to work until seven tonight."

James realizes two things. Jorge's effeminate personality has become loathsome. And he is starving.

"Come have a little breakfast, my treat."

"Fine, but I have to take a shower."

"Sure, go ahead, take your time. You can just come down to my room when you're ready."

"Alright."

"But before I go, can you just give me a little kiss?'

"Shit no! Get the hell out."

He is ravaged by hunger. He sucks down two glasses of orange juice while his mouth waters over the menu. He drinks a steady stream of creamed coffee; black coffee has since grown too strong for his stomach. When the omelets arrive with chopped greens and blackbeans and triangles of toast and slices of fruit, he goes in at it as if with a pitchfork into hay, the food almost flinging from the tines into his mouth. Jorge has the humored look of a lover. James concentrates on his plate or flagging down the waitress for coffee or glancing at a beautiful young waitress working tables across the diner. Jorge says:

"I love their omelets here."

"Uh-huh."

"Not a bad price either."

Her top lip is very striking. It turns out with a simple, bold flare. Why can't I meet someone like her? I wouldn't have the problems I do. She would be my salvation. A guardian angel to protect me from myself—my vulgar, miserable, sex depraved self. Or would she be? He stops chewing, ball of breakfast in his cheek. Maybe there isn't an outside agent capable of curing me? A sobering thought.

"Maybe we can come here again sometime?" Jorge is saying.

But it would help, he thinks, so that I don't go it alone. Her shoulders are straight and level. Her arms are slender and swing gracefully while she walks. Beating slowly, low flying, great white wings. Long-necked egret, poised like calligraphy, to where on those broad wings can you deliver me? He barely hears Jorge. He says:

"Look, Jorge, I don't think we will be doing a whole lot together. I realize you aren't friendly to me the same way a friend might be. There's a difference. What happened last night happened not because I'm like you, or want to be like you, however you want to say it, but because I have a strong addiction to sex, and you happened to be there at the time when it overtook me and I didn't really care who satisfied it. But I'm sick with disgust about it. I'm not a homosexual. It is as simple as that. And nor do I want to be your friend."

Jorge has since stopped chewing. He swallows as if it is a mouthful of brick morter. He is almost in tears. He attempts to lay his hand on James' hand. James withdraws it. Jorge tries reaching across for his other hand, which James also removes. He says, quietly:

"Don't. Don't shun me."

"I'm not. You don't need to touch me."

"Okay, I won't. But can we talk?"

"We are."

"I mean seriously. I like you. I think you are a terrific young man."

"That's precisely the point. I don't care. You aren't listening to what I'm telling you."

"Okay, fine, you don't have to love me. That's fine. I can live with that. I don't know if I am ready for a serious commitment, either."

James is bewildered. He says, almost amused by the absurdity:

"Good, that's good to hear. But you still don't get it, do you?"

"No, I understand completely. You think I'm too old for you or not good looking enough . . ."

James turns his head away from the table, exasperated.

"Don't get upset. I'm not upset. I understand. I just don't see why we can't be friends."

"Fine, we can be friends, call it whatever you like. Acquaintances. But we won't be spending any time together. Going to movies and things."

"That's fine. I just don't want you to completely forget about me, because of last night."

"I'll be trying my best."

"Oh see, don't say that. That breaks my heart to small pieces to hear you say that. I enjoyed last night. I'm glad you opened up to me and trusted me."

"Are you crazy. Listen to yourself, I didn't 'open up to you'. That was getting my dick sucked, and that was all."

Jorge leans in, lowering his voice. "Can you please lower your voice please, I come here many times."

He lowers his voice. "Nothing more. I wasn't stumbling from the closet. And I'm not now trying to let you down easy because you're not my type or not good looking and whatever. I'm not fucking gay."

"Don't get angry. Just relax. We don't have to discuss everything right now."

James is fed up. The waitress has overheard the argument and he's pissed about that too. None of this is even remotely amusing anymore. He stands up, shaking his head with disbelief. Says:

"Thanks for breakfast, but no thanks." Throws money down on the table. "I'm leaving and I don't want you to follow me or ask about me in the building."

He crosses the intersection thick with stopped traffic and disappears around the first corner, takes an alley through to a parallel street.

The city is a shrieking machine and the sky a gray foil. His self-loathing has become loathing comprehensive. He has to get out of this sunless labyrinth, stalked by ugly humanity, himself the ugliest.

X

Next morning Jorge comes knocking, again. James pulls the door open. He says:

"I told you not to bother me."

"I just wanted to apologize for yesterday. I don't want you to be angry with me."

"No apology's necessary and I'm not angry, I just want you not to bother me. It's that easy." He begins to close the door. Jorge says:

"I've brought you a present." He has a flat, brown paper bag, the mouth folded over.

"What is it?"

"A couple presents."

James he opens the bag. There's the Sony Walkman and

headphones. Also another thing. He pulls it up. It is an instrument microphone, which can be clipped onto the mouth of the soundhole. It is in its blister package and the price tag has been removed, but he can see the receipt still in the bag. He knows it is rather expensive, or at least to him, doesn't need to look at it. He pushes it back into the bag and hands it to Jorge.

"I don't want it. Take it back."

"I want you to have it. To remember me by. Please. It would make me very happy."

"I don't have any way to use it. What good would it do me?"

"You could use my stereo anytime you wanted." He says cautiously. "Or you can just hang on to it until you have your own."

"I don't want it. Good bye." He pushes the door closed. He can hear Jorge standing outside the door. After a moment's wait, he knocks again. James yells out that he should go away. Jorge says:

"Can I just say one more thing?"

"Yes, go ahead."

He does not speak for a few moments, and then he whispers:

"Can you just open the door?"

James is staring out the open window. He realizes there is a 8 inch ledge, which connects his window to every window on his floor, which might possibly have been designed for the purpose he is now about to use it. He climbs out, with some difficulty, and then carefully moves along the ledge, his back pressed against the brick, it's a much farther distance than he estimated. At the corner he leans back and looks down the shaft, becomes aware of its lethal potentiality, considers it, and this does not frighten him. In fact, it is comforting. To release all of one's suffering to the Godless ether, in just a leap. It couldn't be easier. Death isn't the worst thing that could ever happen. It's just the last. And it isn't time yet. He moves to the adjacent window, knocks on the upper portion. No one comes to it. He carefully bends down to peer inside, sees no one. The bottom half is raised and he climbs in and quietly lets him self out the door. This room is around the corner from his own, and therefore he escapes to the stairwell, unseen. Before leaving the building, he stops at the front desk to tell Mike he will be leaving this evening.

"But, I'm kind of in a hurry now, I'll square everything up before I go."

"Okay, is everything alright?"

"Yes, something has come up, I need to get back."

"I hate to see you go, though, you just barely arrived," Mike says.

"Yes, it was nice coming. Chicago's nice, but I think I've made a mistake coming."

Mike has the sense to discern James is troubled, tries to be positive.

"It's really a great city. It's a shame you aren't staying long enough to see the spring."

James frowns. Thinking there surely is something great about the place, why else would so many be here? It causes him a moment of panic, but he has to fight it down. There's business for him yet back in New Orleans. He says:

"Well maybe some other time."

As he descends the stairs, Mike says:

"When you're touring the states, maybe." James turns back and sees him smiling affectionately.

When he returns a few hours later, he finds the brown paper bag leaning against his door, with a note attached to it. He tears it off and it reads:

James, Mike told me you were leaving. I am so sad to hear it. I will miss you. I hope you are not leaving because of me. If so, that will be a terrible shame. I want you to know that I care a great deal about you. I hope you become very successful. I also want you to keep my gifts to you. Please! Goodbye, Jorge.

He is touched by both the thoughtfulness and the forgiveness. He closes himself into his room, flips the note over on the writing desk, writes:

Thank you for the gifts, you are a good and kind person, please know this has nothing to do with you, my demons are my own.

He packs his bag. He will slip the note under Jorge's door on the way out, worries that he might have to confront him. Now packed, he counts his money, there is so very little of it. He puts aside forty. It's a huge portion, but he has on choice. Outside, it has begun to rain, he hurries to the old Greeks second hand store, it is closed, dark inside. Under the portico over the door, he opens his violin case and removes a sheet of paper from his little note pad. He writes:

Your kindness will kept me warm for a long time, thank you, James Buck

He folds it into a sleeve around the forty dollars, slides it through the mail drop.

XI

There is standing room only in the bus station. It is yet another cold evening and the station doors constantly swing open. His hands are warm from lugging his duffle, but otherwise he trembles from the chill and his nerves, afraid of what reception he might find in New Orleans. He wants to be back in New Orleans, instantly. I'm no judge of love, he says to himself. What does it feel like? Could I recognize it? I never loved my mother or my father or any of my brothers, maybe just my sister, but that is a different kind of love. I might have loved Virginia? I don' t know. Am I going back for Virginia?

The long vehicle purrs as he boards, familiar; the big engine vibrates the seat, blowing heat from the vents; he settles in.

Inter-urban Chicago is prematurely dark and sprawling and gray and emits columns of exhaust. Oh, what an ugly, complicated mess we've made of this world! He will not reach open country in the light of day. He tries to imagine the open fields of his childhood; they were vast and went deep into the horizon and he used to try to imagine how long he'd have to walk to cross them, to get to what lay beyond. He knew there were places beyond them. Great places. He is pensive. Maybe I do know what love is? I loved Bare Creek, I know that, sun-scorched stones on the grassy banks, blue gill suspended in the pull of the green creek shoulder deep. The old Iron Bridge tethered to a sharp turn in the road, spit from the hillside. That first jump from the bridge when the water was deepest in spring, a rite of passage. The only place where he might see a young girl other than his sister in a swimsuit, or if she were poor and you were really lucky, in her Daisy's and a bra. He can smell hickory and dirt and wet stones just from the thinking of it.

*

They hit all the stations along the way. A constant exchange of beleaguered supplicants struggling with their bags and boxes and sacks and sadness. When the cabin lights come on, he stares outside the blackish windows, a cast-iron bench, a luggage cart with big wobbly wagon wheels, a garbage barrel fire, an exit sign burning. On the straight and gently curving freeways of lower Illinois, he is soaring. He has put on the headphones Jorge has given him and his heart swells with the beautiful sounds borne from the immaterial. Lush, nuanced, passionate. Bjork and Love and Rockets and the Smiths and a band called James, a song called Knuckle Too Far. The Cure, a song called Plainsong. Each song labeled carefully in Jorge's perfect hand. When Peter Gabriel's *Don't Give Up* fills his brain, he begins to cry, hot tears that leave him cool from the pain they release. What a monster I've been to such a man who shares this magic with others. He promises himself he will write Jorge a beautiful letter and tell him as much.

*

St. Louis, Missouri.

The ceiling is high, but the floor space is limited. People crowd in at the gates. A tall black man leans over the crowd like a preacher and makes boarding calls. Purgatory exists only in this life; and it's the bus station, where time itself is frozen and is only just now starting to melt and it smells of urine and sour water, burns the nose. Drunk vagrants, black with filth, are asleep in benches in sitting positions, sour mouths open, while ill-rested travelers stand, waiting, heads upturned to the clock. Travelers unable to stand any longer sit on their luggage or on the floor, at least those that aren't so fat that they run the risk of not getting back up. He stands near a mother thrusting her swollen hand into her child's potato chip bag, clutching fistfuls, the dimples of her knuckles greasy, crushing the chips into her face, her jaws convulsing and her lips smacking. Another child darts between legs and luggage and stumbles over James's duffel and hits the floor with a smack on the tile. The child gets back on his feet confused, uplooking, dirty faced, wearing faded polyester shorts and a filthy shirt, canvas shoes, untied. Its mother makes her way stealthily through the crowd, her leather face quivering with anger and the child begins to cower under her approach. She hoists him by the arm and the child wails out well before she begins to swat his bare legs, over and over and over, because this isn't the first time, nor will it be the last. The Heartland, the talking heads call this. Is it? Is this really the heart of America? Or is it its liver and by these samples, these symptoms and so many more, stage four cancer, eating away at the tissue? He has to step outside for fresh air, but oh, the poor, weary street! It isn't much better here. The assault to his senses is unrelenting! Everything is stripped of beauty by design, in an advanced state of disrepair, tagged with spray paint, and the garbage cans need emptied, cement and chain-linked fence, as though rabid animals need caging. A busted Cadillac drops a man in NBA athletic wear at the curb, gold chains, the bass from the stereo rattling the windows in the frame, he doesn't have a suitcase, just a small empty backpack, his long face of tallow pocked by resentment, his blonde hair in corn rows, the driver so black as if not even there behind the tinted glass, expect for the silver caps on his teeth.

He takes a newspaper from the vendor. It is an impulse to learn more about the nation. To gather facts to better articulate the necessary holocaust of eight-tenths of the population. He opens the paper, accidentally, to the classifieds; gives them a look. Notices rents are rather low. He flips to the Help Wanted, just to browse, to consider the possibility. His eye falls on this ad: Ranch Hands, hard workers, in country, room&board 555-2825. The black letters speak out to him, and he thinks, this is what I need, a hard day's work, square meals. Most importantly, I can't go back penniless. He reads the ad again, and then he goes to the nearest payphone, like another person might stand up from the television and walk to the refrigerator for a jar of pickles, drops in a quarter.

He secures his bag in a locker and leaves the station with his violin. He has an entire evening to kill. St. Louis is quiet, like an abandoned factory. He makes his way to the giant arch, pewter against the cool porcelain blue sky. He sits on a bench in the lawn and pulls out his instrument. He is smooth inside, now, and comfortable, and it's been awhile. What a full circle this has been. Here I am back at this place. This monument. And now *I am* the violinist under the arch. He remembers the old man playing here, clearly. He wore a green plaid short sleeve and every button was done. His dark trousers rode high, revealing his shins. His dress was immaculate, though outdated. His thin canvas shoes were good for summer and he wore no socks. His crown of hair was as white as oleander and short and contrasted vividly with his sunned skin. His neat, symmetric bald head shined and his eyes were deep and serious. He looked everything like the noble artist. His old wasn't feeble. His poverty wasn't to shame. His modesty wasn't of ignorance. Rather transcendence. He knew something. And he endeavored to use it, as if to say, if there is a God, he didn't entirely fuck up when he gave us this planet; listen to the sounds we can make while we are on it! Or so it seemed to a young boy who knew nothing about anything or anyone. Now, it seems more realistic that the old man was just old and had quit pursuing all the things he thought he wanted, fought all his demons (had he had any), and now found happiness in having all that he truly needed. And those are a very few things indeed.

He plays a song he knows very well, but this time he plays it better than he's ever played it before, effortlessly. He becomes tearful with joy. His hands know themselves well and they communicate fluently with the instrument. He glances down at his open case. He sees its capacity as a rich abstraction, able to hold everything in the world. There is a great beauty in the contours of its emptiness, if the emptiness is considered of itself and not of what it lacks. His neck is a little stiff and he stops to stretch it, leans back against the bench and looks into the pale evening sky. The young galaxy is empty.

*

He eats dinner at six o'clock. He takes his time. Takes great deliberation ordering it and eating it and digesting it and afterwards acting as though he is intent on his newspaper. He does not have the money to spend on a room. He plans to wait the night through in the station, which he considers a small sacrifice. Back in the station, he changes his clothes in a bathroom stall, a miserable endeavor. Nothing can be placed on the floor because it is damp and sour. There are no hooks on the backside of the door and the seat cover is the horseshoe variety. But he manages. He holds the clean jeans as he takes off the dirty. He slips his feet from his shoes one at a time, standing on the shoes once removed so as not to get his socks wet. Then he leans on his butt against the stall wall and he contrives to remove his pants without letting them touch the tile. He completes this successfully by slinging the clean jeans over his shoulder and clasping the sock and underwear in his mouth. Then he slings the dirty over his shoulder and puts on the clean.

He dreads the night ahead of him. He knows it'll be long. But the prospect of a new job in the morning is of great encouragement. The women he talked with on the phone was pleasant, spoke with a flat, dry voice, and a familiar accent. They arranged to meet in the morning. She'll drive him out to the ranch. He sits quietly and watches the zombie-like travelers, tired and sad souls desiring nothing more complicated than their comfortable beds to lay their heavy heads. He plays his violin, with a closed case, which will be his defense if security forbids busking. He plays softly, of course, and after a quarter-hour a once-tall man, broken forward, approaches him, his feet sliding on the floor. His hair is long and tangled and brown like his long, tangled beard. He holds a paper coffee cup. He says to James:

"Here's a tip jar. Put 'er out. All them othern's have 'em."

He places it at James's feet. He is mumbling something else, which James cannot understand. He big feet drag him away. The cup looks conspicuous on the floor so far out in front of him. He pulls it in next to the leg of his chair.

This works good to pass several hours of the night, and earn him three dollars, which he uses to buy a candy bar and a Sprite from a vending machine, which cost exactly that. He thinks about going out to find a place to stretch out to sleep. He steps out the front doors. It has become frigid. He decides against it. He goes back to a bench and sits and tries to be patient and worries he will get run out sometime in the night.

XII

Six a.m. Friday. Third week of March.

Breakfast is at a diner a half-mile walk from the station. A warm welcome, busy waitresses, smell of ham and eggs, yellow broken on fried potato, cup of creamed coffee, sunbeams through the window the color of brass. The whisper of each folding page of gossip. Milk, cream pies, chocolate syrup, kept in the Frigidaire at the end of the counter, humming every time the seal is broken. Standing at the register, gut full, taste of rye in his mouth, he asks for directions to Sullivan's Lumber. The clerk doesn't know, asks another man and this man says:

"Well, now they used to be at Clark and Twenty Second, but now they're out on Gravois Avenue, where Kings Highway runs up into it. What you gonna need to do is pick up Tucker about a mile from here going towards downtown, from there you can take most any street going in that direction straight to it. You wanna turn right and it's gonna turn into Gravois and when you see the big road sign with the peacock's tail, then you're at Kings Highway, and it's right at that corner. It's about four miles from here. I'll be going out that way after breakfast, if you want to follow me out?"

James does not want to confess that he does not have a vehicle and thereby impose. He says:

"Well, no I got to get over there rather straightaway and I think with your directions it won't be hard to find. Any street to Tucker, Tucker turns into Gravois, look for the peacock's tail and intersection of Kings Highway."

"That'll get you there."

"Thank you, I appreciate your time, sir."

"More'n welcome, son."

He begins by taking Market to Tucker from the station. His spirits are high. His stride strong and quick and his head high. The clouds are like cotton pulled across a cheese grate, a thin web in the blue sky.

After he accomplishes his first mile and a half, his arms start to ache and he begins to struggle with his bag. He takes breaks every block or two, growing weary progressively, sweat pouring from his head, the bag falling from his grip. Then he carefully hoists it back up. When he makes the parking lot of the lumber store, he is exhausted and satisfied to nod off while he waits.

A long-bed pick-up truck, blue and white and covered in dust, pulls into the lot and a leather-faced woman climbs out. James wakes in a cool sweat, sedate and calm. He has been soaring over rolling fields of buckwheat with an undulating flock of sparrow. She knows without hesitation that he is the man she expects to meet and maybe she has done this before and she says, dryly:

"Put your things in the back of the truck and then come on in the store and give me a hand."

He follows her down the aisles, while she throws things into a pushcart: a large orange water jug, which takes up most of the space in the cart, electrical tape, a measuring tape. She pulls a pair of gloves from a rack and gives them to James without looking, says:

"You're gonna need gloves for this work, see if these fit."

He pulls one glove over his hand and it is a snug fit.

"If you don't have any money then we'll just take it from your first check."

At the counter, she orders eight spools of barbwire and two hundred fence posts. She pulls a checkbook from her jeans pocket and begins to write out a payment, saying over her shoulder to James:

"Go out and drive the truck 'round back of the building so's they can load this stuff on."

A flat-faced boy uses a small forklift to place two neat squares of posts and then eight large spools of wire into the bed. The lady hops into the cab of the truck like a child jumping on a couch and backs out the lumberyard with haste. She begins to talk in a moderate fit of hysteria. She says:

"Seems like every time you come here, they've jacked up the prices. Hell, don't hardly seem worth coming into town anymore. Money spent on gas and the time wasted. Kind of prices they're charge'n anymore looks like they could deliver. Sure make my day a hell of a lot better. I got shit needs get done." She takes a long cigarette from a vinyl pouch. "Now, you better be willing to work when we get out there. We've got a lot of fence to put up and Bob ain't got no time for any laziness. He's a good man to work for, fair and reasonable, but he ain't got no time for any stiff leg."

Unsure how to reply, James nods intently and listens. They pick up Interstate 44 in Webster Groves; the wheel wells riding just over the tires, the back end bouncing sluggishly and once on the Interstate, they pick up speed. With the needle on eight-five they travel for two hours. First, through suburban St. Louis. Then into open country, to a town called Steelville. The ranch is a good piece out of town and it surrounds the house. They drive on narrow, smooth asphalt, then on dirt, lifting a dust cloud the entire length to the house, and it follows them up like a sand devil. A pack of dogs swarm the pickup. The clapboard stands with a nonchalant lean to the North on a grassless patch dirt. Green hills roll far out on the horizon in the South and the East Northeast.

The lady backs the truck up to a weathered shed. She jumps from the cab of the truck with a pair of wire snips in hand. Her name is Brenda. She says:

"Here take these and clip those straps so you can unload them posts into the shed. Come inside to let me know when you are finished."

She is a thin woman, wears her jeans loose, and when a gust catches her blouse, her small breasts reveal nothing more than sharp points. Her face is like leather and angular, possibly sometimes pleasant, but humorless. Hands callused and her fingers blunt. Eyes steady and blue. She wears her hair in a pony behind small, delicate ears. She disappears behind the screen door to the house.

When he is finished, he beats on the screen door with his knuckle. Sweat runs from his temples, down his back, from under his arms, in the seat of his pants, and his hands are stiff. He can see her in shadow through the screen and he says:

"I've got it all unloaded."

"Good, I see you can work. Well then," and she comes to the screen door and pushes it out. "Let me show you where the boys sleep. They're all good ole boys, don't think you'll have a problem getting along with any of 'em. We've got this trailer 'round back for the hands."

They walk a foot-beaten path across the yard. Puppies are playing in an overturned bucket, come snooping as they pass. They come to an early-seventies recreational trailer, the truck pulled, fifth-wheel variety, much like a horse trailer. It is dark inside and she flips on a light, a cord runs from the house to supply electricity. There is the smell of motor oil and wet dogs. Brenda says:

"It sleeps five easily. But there are now seven of you and Johnson has the back room. He's the year-round hand so it's more'n fair. You other'n's have the beds here. We haven't got room in the house or we'd sleep a couple of you in there. Bob put out these cots. They're pretty good sleeping, the boys say."

He does not stare long at the cots, not wanting to give Brenda the impression he has any regret coming out. She looks at him a moment. Then she says:

"We all eat inside the house, of course. We'll keep you fed. We want good work out of you, so we try to keep your stomachs full. No one's gonna go hungry."

He smiles while she looks at him. Guilty of starving *himself*.

"There's no bathroom in the trailer. You boys have to use the outhouse. I don't know if you've used one afore, but some boys come out here and throw fits about it. We used to let them come in the house, but I just couldn't keep the floors cleaned with them tracking in and out all the time. And at night, it ain't too safe leaving the doors unlocked with kids in the house. We had stealing afore too and we had to put a stop to it."

She leads him back to the house, stepping over puppies along the way, explains how she is supposed to drive him out as soon as he finishes unloading the posts, but she has decided against it; she needs some things done around the house. She says:

"I've been trying to get him to leave a man back at the house for a month now, but I can't ever get him to do it. So looks like you'll be the one. He'll just have to take it up with me when he gets in. That's all." She smiles. This makes them friends.

Dusk. A brown pick-up truck crosses a field, loaded with men. It pulls in a dust cloud, which sweeps across the front of the house, contributes to its pale shade of beige. The men disperse from the truck like crows from a tree, regrouping in rapid, loose formation at the backside of the house. A lean man with rounded features and skin the color of wet wood climbs from the driver's seat, goes into the house. Brenda introduces him to James. The man takes James' hand in greeting and strangles it slowly, steady eyes on him. He says:

"You ready to work?"

"Yes, certainly."

"Good, that's want I need. I ain't got no space for freeloaders. You got to earn your keep. You stand around here with your dick in the dirt and you'll be sent on. We've got plenty of work needs done."

The entire pack eats in the kitchen. Brenda has prepared the food in huge pots and does not serve anyone. They form a line with plates in their hands to the stove. The lucky get a chair; the rest take a long bench or a stool, at the table.

He can't get to sleep in his narrow cot. The trailer now smells the salty musk of men, and the sweetly sour odor of their boots, piled at the door. In the snake skin silence on the ranch, he can hear every sound as it is made: there's a truck on the distant road, tinkle the tags on the dog's collar as he digs a tick from his hide, is that a barn owl's wings, a horse changes positions in his stall, moth's killing themselves over the 60 watt at the back door. He can see a rectangle of night sky over the forward bunk, the stars are out. The man on this bunk has begun to snore, a steady, rhythmic snoring, punctuated with a whistle, which almost drowns the sound of snoring coming from Johnson's room in the back. James steps out into moonshine. The air is chilled. He finds his way to the outhouse, which stands in the pitch-black pool of shadow cast by the barn. The door smacks shut and he can't see a thing. He finds paper by feel alone. The dogs remain quiet, as he walks back to the trailer. He stops just short of the door. There is something far out on the rolling hills, whispering. It is familiar. He knows it well. It is night in the country. A memory becomes the present and the present is only as good as the memory has made it, because it is the oldest of all memories. There's that owl on the roof ridge, the white plate of his face turns away and he takes to wing, as if to go tell the others.

XIII

While it is still dark, Johnson turns the lights on in the trailer and breaks the silence of collective sleep with his deep, handsaw voice. He says:
"Alright, get up, breakfast."
James is ill rested, and has anxiety stirring his gut. He climbs from bed quickly and exits the trailer. The kitchen glows in the predawn purple. They find Brenda placing a baking sheet of biscuits

on the counter. They gather like surgeons and carve the corpse into equal shares, which they generously ladled bacon gravy over. Atop this they spoon three or four heaps of sugar. They eat like beasts, hurriedly and with much grunting and smacking and slurping of coffee. James smears jelly over the fluffy halves of a split biscuit. He has no appetite and eats slowly and drinks a tall, plastic cup of milk. The men look at him suspiciously.

In light growing orange on the horizon, they speed over narrow blacktop, then turn off into a shallow ditch; the men rolling about in the truck like sailors in a gigboat. The black hills are bleeding green and clumps of trees are a solid mass of black far across the field, gradually taking color. They approach the barb-wire fence at a forty-five degree angle and then ride alongside it until they come to where they had left it last evening. When the truck comes to a stop, Johnson jumps from the cab and starts yelling at the men; they bail out and get their tools, which are locked inside a large box that sits near a pile of woodposts knee-high. They file in for their weapons like bandits, not soldiers. James is the last in the line and Bob yells from the window of the truck, as he turns it around:

"You come on back to the house with me. We gotta load some more posts, we'll surely be needin' more'n we got."

James nods his head, jumps back into the cab.

It is full morning light when they return. The men broken into pairs, one man in each pair is digging a hole with a two-handled shovel that he drives into the ground with both hands, then he separates each handle, takes a plug of earth up with it. The second man rests. When the hole is dug, the observer will place a stick into it to check for accurate depth, if it is correct, then they both will move down past the forward pair of men to the next hole marker, a small flag stuck into the ground. This time the digger will be the dipstick and the dipstick, the digger. The fifth man works with Johnson stretching three lengths of wire, two barbed and one thin and smooth; this is the wire that will carry the electric current. James and Bob climb from the truck. Bob says:

"Lucian, come give this boy a hand unloadin' these posts, here."

James and the lanky man climb into the voids created by the wheel wells and begin tossing posts onto the pile. Bob joins Johnson stretching wire. At ten o'clock, Brenda brings two thermoses of coffee and a jug of iced water.

The air stays cool. The sun drifts over their heads, ineffectually, like a little yellow balloon. They eat lunch back at the house; sit around the yard in wire chairs or on overturned buckets. Brenda has brought a baking sheet of half tuna can salad and bologna sandwiches to the back step, stacked three high, and they go quick—devoured in four or five bites apiece. Two jugs of tea are dried. Once the sandwiches are gone they sit about the yard sucking their teeth or smoking cigarettes or chewing tobacco. Quietly. Then Bob gives the word and they all pile into the truck. They spread out at the work site quietly, each man going to his position, which in James's case is now stretching the story line between holes to be dug, some hundred yards or more ahead, marking each one with a flag. Work continues until six. They drive back to the house as the sun sinks into a raspberry blaze.

On the far side of the barn is a long, white, iron sink where the men wash their hands under two swan-necked faucets. They are all in a great hurry and the dirt under their feet becomes a damp puddle. Dinner is fried chicken and white beans in a ham stock with corn bread. The smell leads them to the kitchen door, their mouths watering. Hungry as he is, James sinks his teeth into a piece of chicken and the steam condenses on his nose and the heat singes the insides of his mouth. He cautiously separates the meat from the bone and blows it and then wallows the meat in his mouth loosely, letting the juices of his watering mouth cool it. The men drain a gallon jug of iced tea. Every last piece of chicken is eaten and most the pot of beans. As the dinner plates pile, they begin filling glasses with crumbled cornbread and milk. This is dessert, stirred with sugar. James does not care for any. He offers to help Brenda clean the dishes. She says:

"No, that ain't your business. You've put your day's work in, now it's time you relax."

Bob is listening, says:

"You boys going honky-tonkin' tonight?"

Johnson says:

"Well, I wasn't planning to, but if any yuns others wont to go, I might."

Bob say to James:

"They like to go up to town on Saturdays to do little drinking. I'm sure they wouldn't mind if you wanted to go along." He presents this as a statement and not a question. James looks at him and then at his hands. He says:

"No thanks. I really haven't got any money to spare."

"Well, as soon as I get up from the table I'm gonna pay you all. I usually pay everyone on Saturday night. There's a store on the way that cashes your checks for ya."

"No, I think I'll pass tonight," and everyone is quiet, almost as though he has insulted them. They look at him steadily, to figure him out. Bob says:

"Alright then, suit yourself, thought you just might want to get out and have a little fun, chase some draw'rs in town."

The men grin. James says:

"I really appreciate the offer, though."

The men clear out of the kitchen to let Brenda clean up and they make their way to the trailer, take their turns in the shower stall in the barn. James sits in the yard in the weak light. A golden pickup truck pulls into the drive. Children jump from the bed, hair windswept and tangled, wearing cut off jeans or the little girl wears striped acrylic shorts. They carry their personal things in paper bags and they run into the kitchen through the back door. The yard dogs follow them up to the door, excited, peering in through the screen, as if bewildered that the children were ever gone. James can hear the children explaining their little vacation. He sits back in a wire chair and watches the fields grow blue, satisfied with the moment.

The men cram themselves into Johnson's pickup and peel out the drive, the very sound of the truck's wheels crackling on the gravel and the roar of the engine laden with excitement. The night hides the house in the landscape, but the windows burn as things all of their own. The trailer is now empty. He sits on his cot and looks at his hands. Looking at his hands gives him confidence. He believes they are more capable now. He takes his violin and starts out across the field, bluegrass glowing in the growing moonlight. He walks carefully but quickly. The sound of his feet through the tall grass is pleasant but also haunting. He ascends a gentle knoll and then descends into a black wall of growth. He finds a stream, sparkling in long silvers and gurgling and chiming over rocks. It gives a taste to the air and a fresh smell. It is not a big stream; he could leap it without a running start. But it feels good to be near it. He squats on a flat-headed rock. He can barely see his instrument. He begins to play. There is enchantment here. The long silvers on the stream grow more vivid. The grasses radiate a ghostly blue.

Sunday morning. The dogs barking in the yard wake him. It's light out. Their day of rest, Bob had said, and it ain't on account of no church either. Man's gota rest. He can see Johnson's door closed, also one bed empty. He gets up and walks out to the shower stall. The water is ice cold, but feels great to his skin afterwards. His eyes are wide open, everything has an enhanced brilliance: the shower handles, the swan necked faucets, even the tin roof above the rabbit cages.

The oldest child is in the back yard portioning feed for the rabbits with a plastic cup. In the kitchen Brenda stands at the sink peeling cucumbers. The other children are at the breakfast table scooping cereal into their milk-wet mouths. Bob is in the living room watching the news on the television. James can see Johnson's boots on the coffee table. Brenda says:

"We're pretty casual about breakfast on Sundays. You can help yourself to what you can find. The kids are eating cereal. We've got cornflakes and raisin bran and Lucky Charms. We've got fresh eggs, too. There are some leftover sausages in the icebox you can heat. Coffee's on the stove. Don't be shy 'round here. You want something, just get it."

He pours himself a cup of coffee and a bowl of raisin bran.

By noon all the hands are gone. After lunch, sausage and sauerkraut sandwiches, Bob asked James if he wants to ride out over the field with him.

"Can you ride a horse?"

"I haven't ridden a horse in some time, but I can manage."

"Then come help me get 'em saddled."

Bob rides a lean, smoke-gray gelding, the healthiest-looking beast in the barn. James saddles an old plow horse, which the children affectionately call Mr. Bob (not after Bob, but rather by the way he bobs his head when he walks). All the children had learned to ride on Mr. Bob, Bob tells him, to assure him that he's safe to ride. They take the grass alongside the road. The enormous pasture is like an open book and the fence down the middle like a bookmarker. Bob explains:

"There was a creek dried up along here. Used to be the property line. You see when we get that fence made out yonder and brought back to the further end, then we're gonna start raising horses, again. The man that owns all this property wants to start breeding. He's just recently bought all that land otherside of where the creek used to run. Bought it from old Charley Skaggs. He wants it done by fall."

"You think it can be finished that soon?"

"Oh, certainly, we're moving slow right now, because the gas-driven digger's being fixed; when that comes back out, we'll be moving along, like we were before."

They turn in at the truck tracks, ride out to where the work stops, then beyond this over a rolling hill which descends to a modest stream. They cross the stream and ride across the back end of the pasture. They ride along the barbed wire, watching the cows, fifty or seventy-five of them, which stand about quietly, mostly unconcerned. One might rotate a thick eye, turn an ear, a tail swat, that is all. Keep munching. Their brown eyes do not look lonely. Their slow-moving mouths do not look tired, just slow. James glances at Bob. His hat is pushed back on his head. He leans over his saddlepost. His brown skin especially dry, old leather, except it's alive. And the deep creases around his mouth tell a story more than admit his age. His brown eyes like oiled pebbles, and like the cows' eyes they do not look lonely. It takes half an hour to trot back to the house.

After supper, a poker game starts in the barn. They gamble with cigarettes, since they all smoke. James sits in the opened door on an overturned bucket, watching the sky falling. The men around the poker table are quiet, until Johnson speaks. He takes James by surprise. He says:

"Mr. Buck, you should run grab that veye-o-lynn of yourn, come serenade us a while. Brenda says you played the streets down in New Orleans. Going assume you're pretty damn good, then?"

"Some people have said I can play pretty good. I think I still have a long way to go."

"Whyn't you run get it and play us sump'n, let's us be a judge."

"Sure, if you want me to?"

"Why not, these bunch of rednecks can use a little culturen."

On the walk back he tries to decide which piece he shall play. He decides on Tchaikovsky, but then decides against it, except he tells them its Tchaikovsky. He stands in the center of the barn, and he explains, feels the need to explain:

"This is a short piece. I just learned it."

"What kind of name is that, chee cough ski?"

"Russian."

"Russian?"

"From way back, before they were the enemy."

He places the bow under his chin and straightens his back. They watch him closely. He closed his eyes, something he has started to do only just within the last few days. In fact, he began while listening to the mixtape Jorge gave him. It helped him identify some of the instruments and make out some of the lyrics. It helps him now to better read his own composition. He plays. They listen. Not a man moves as much as a finger.

Half through he opens his eyes just for a second. Is surprised to find Johnson has closed his, his hands one atop the other on his hand faced down on the table in a fan. The other men rapt with admiration.

He pulls out the last note, and they pound out applause in hand claps and boot heels.

"I'll be hanged if that aint some of the best fiddling I ever did hear. You sure can saw off an arm."

Ashley, the oldest among them, supports this:

"Best I've been given to 'ear!"

"Good god damn fine playing, that is."

"Yes sir, never heard anything like it."

These are deeply felt compliments. Johnson's voice can easily be mistaken for his father's: the exact vernacular, the exact pitch and resonance. Then Johnson says:

"What'n the shit are you doing stretching fence?"

"I still have to eat."

"Well, don't give 'er up. Whyn't you play us another."

"Sure. I think you guys will like this one. It is called Capriccio Italien, or at least my best rendition of it."

"He knows Italian too," he says to the others. "Duttin that just polish apples?"

James Buck begins to play. Closes his eyes again. He moves through the piece effortlessly, as it begins its graceful, stomping march; the proud Italian pheasants marching across the sunblazed field, holding red and green and blue silken banners in air and beautiful children and women running to keep up and the wind blowing the land. In his mind's ear, drums rumble, bass and cello gallop, trumpets blow a gale, cymbals clash. In the finale, he plays with such an ease of movement, he feels as if the violin would continue to play by itself.

"Shall I play another one?"

"You keen play'm all far as yur askin."

He plays them a few more songs. They get back to the cards. Lucian asks whose deal it is. Tim pushes back his hat and says it's his. Johnson leans in to grab the deck on the table, says:

"And your dick hurts too, son, you was the last 'n to deal."

He feels smooth inside, calm. He believes he could play all night. As though that was as simple a thing to do as playing rings with a rake handle and Ball jar bands.

XIV

At dawn, Johnson wakes the men. Outside the trailer, the air is crisp, dark and fresh. In the kitchen, they heap scrambled eggs and strips of bacon and skillet-fried potatoes onto their plates and smother them with ketchup. An entire gallon of milk is drained. A loaf of bread is toasted. They drink their coffee quickly, milked and sweet At seven, the crew hits the cold dirt path through the side yard. The truck flies over the road and bounces into the pasture. They leap from the truck. Bob takes another man back to load posts. James teams up with the big-eared man named Ashley. He asks Ashley as he carries a pair of holediggers from the gang box:

"Why don't we just load the truck with posts before we leave instead of them going back afterwards?"

"That's a way they used to do it, but see early on, we had this boy come down from north of here that worked for us and fell from the truck out'n his own stupidity as we were crossing the field. He broke his shoulder bone and he's suing the fella that owns all this land as we stand here."

"I thought there was something unusual about this method."

"Yeap, he ain't sus'posed to do it that other way annie more."

James lifts the handles over his head and drives the steel lips of the digger into the ground with a sound like breaking a head of lettuce. Then he asks:

"How long have you been working for Bob?"

"O, I've been workin' on and off several years now. They ain't always got work. I was here when they put up that first stretch a fence. Then I went out to Colorado for a while. A lot of construction going on out there."

The day wears like a giant stone, hard and cool and smooth. The first break comes and James plops down in the tall grass next to the warm tire of Brenda's truck, which feels good against his back muscles. His hands are stiff and warm. But by the afternoon break, his hands are raw and hot. They have stretched almost a thousand feet of wire by quitting time. He eats supper with an arm he can barely lift and sleeps like a sack of lead shot. The next morning the climb from bed is accomplished slowly and with a pleasant pain. He stretches himself out in the yard and then consumes a huge breakfast to stroke the fire he can feel burning in his body. Four days go by in such a way. Each day the work becoming easier as he feels stronger. By Saturday, he wakes ready to work, strong and fresh, and enjoys the first sweat of the morning. He removes his shirt to let his skin brown in the steady sun.

He will not send anything to Virginia in the mail. Nor call her. He does not go over his memory of her much during the day, the difficulty of it. If he does think of her, it is at night. But it's only the image of her. Not the rest. He will think about the different colors of her hair and her brown skin. He will imagine her breasts pressing against him. The soft of her skin and the smell of it. The moisture in her lips. Or between her legs. The smell of her desire in the fabric of her underwear. But he won't let himself suffer her absence, nor the ambiguity woven there in.

He plays his violin outside the barn doors tonight, in the faint light, watching for of the first stars to light. His stomach is full and his body sedate. Then he walks to the stream, where the cows have gathered and he can hear them chewing their cud, the bull lowing, pertain and sonorous, their heavy steps tearing holes in the grassy soil, their tails swishing and thumping against their huge flanks. He can see three or four in the stream, black and brown against the purple twilight. There is a gorgeous tranquility. The proximity of the cows, the chime in the stream, the purple of the sky and a chance firefly. A balance of light and sound, together with the smell of water and earth, and the energy inherent to the shared space of different creatures. He sits on a stone and starts playing around with a piece in its earliest gestation.

XV

The engine-driven posthole digger arrives on Thursday. The work pattern changes entirely. Johnson takes on the position of supervisor, while two men run the digger. One at the controls, the other removing dirt. Another plants poles, and is working diligently to keep up. Two are stretching wire. These two have the most time on their hands. James is running the story line, again. He is about an acre ahead of them, striking each place with a red flag on a wire stake. Sinking the stay spike, walking out the length, eyeing for alignment. Bob no longer stays out in pasture with them. He drops them off in the morning, returns during their breaks, and drives them back for lunch. During lunch, the men eat with less fury. They're more finicky with the sandwich tray. The bologna is last to go and the heels aren't touched. They smoke a lot more cigarettes and there is no urgency to return to work.

Progress is quick. The fence is closing in on itself rapidly.

Friday morning, they wake to a pewter sky about as high as the distant hills. They eat oats and brown sugar and drink coffee, leisurely, and talk about the weather. Bob tells them they will work until the weather turns, if it is to do so. Out in the pasture the wind searches for rain all morning. The clouds growing darker. The grasses dance. Crows carry urgent messages along uncharted vectors. Barn pigeons seek counsel. There is now the sound of thunder in the distance. A dark anvil of head cloud bearing heavy on these foothills.

Listen as the rain begins. A soft spoken promise whispered at a distance, now granted. It turns the air cool and fragrant. Few things in nature are as beautiful as a thunderstorm. Tragic and wonderful all at once. Oppositions converge. Time broken in the strike, mended in the backstroke. Stopgaps in the struggle between heaven and earth. James Buck stands in a high place on the geography. The sound of the men working is in one direction; the sound of the thunder in the other. The men are desperate to make as much progress as they can before the storm hits, but they have little time left. Bob's truck is moving across the distant flat. There is a certain heroic quality about its quiet movement, almost magnanimous, as though some wrong would now be made right by a sort of benevolent retribution. He is overcome by a desire to lay down arms and surrender, welcome his defeat. But not quite! A thought, with all the kinetic energy of a coal-hauling freight train pushes across the landscape of his hardscrabble reasoning. What are we if not our struggle? What would shape our contours? What would cure our mixture? Hold us upright? With little resistance, a blade of grass is pierced by a steel wire with a red flag, marks for the next post, he is sensitive to it, the energy conducted there through. The same energy harnessed by the clouds above, the same energy that connects everything to everything, everyone to everyone. Amperes drawn and amperes supplied through an infinite network of invisible arcs; it unifies the known, permeates the unknown, shimmer below a mute surface.

The air smells of a fecund earth and the murmuring in the sky already suggests remediation. An ash-black thundercloud is upon him. At the next measure of pasture, he bends to mark another, plunging a needle into imponderable derma. The hair on the back of his neck stands up. He feels light of foot, weightless. Something colossal explodes, a flash of light becomes so bright he cannot see, burns so hot its cold.

The blast of the lightning bolt projected him across the hill half a dozen feet. His feet are bare. His eyes are wide open but he cannot see. He can hear the men yelling, and soon they are over him, yelling directly at him. The earth feels good against his back. He closes his eyes and momentarily falls into a dream. It feels like home, yet it is not the house he grew up in. It is empty, only it doesn't feel deserted. Afternoon sunlight pours in through the open windows and he can hear a violin playing in the yard. He opens the screen door and the sun is a blinding explosion of warmth. As soon as he can make out things, he sees a violin playing itself, just above a chair and he walks to it and sits in the chair and the violin fits under his chin and his hand falls in sync with the sawing bow as though they had never been separated. And he plays...

Bob's got his head cradled in his hands and the other men have a limb each and they are running, as though under enemy fire. They throw down the tailgate and get him laid out on the wind ragged tarps and spoils of old rope collected here. They remove their t-shirts and soak them from the water jug. They wrap his head and dab the excess water from his eyes. Bob gets his sand paper cheek as close to his mouth as he can to feel a breath, he holds his wrist to plead for any indication of a pulse, hands so callous he might not feel a thing were it even there. They proceed to wrap each limb with each a wet shirt. They are somber, silent, they understand maybe there's nothing they can do and he is gone, now and forever gone. They hardly even got to know him and he is gone, as easily as he arrived and there's only now a race to the nearest hospital, many miles away, in hopes a doctor will prove them wrong. The truck bounces off over a landscape so sad it can never know another day like this one, a landscape so subtle in its beauty, it may seem not to care.

***

Is it a week or is it a year, sunlight finds you through the blinds, it touches your face. Slumber coalesced in unconscious tears formed seals now broken, memories are dreams, dreams you are afraid you'll soon forget, lest they go untold. You get up on your elbows and maybe you are still dreaming, there sits in the armchair in the opposite corner your little sister, her straw colored hair longer than you remember, she's just then looking through the blinds at the emptiness of another afternoon, a magazine unopened in her lap. She is quick to your side when she sees that you are awake. She helps you get a pillow behind your back to sit up a little easier. She hits the call button for the nurse. You would never have believed how happy you would be to see her again. The joy of it draws fresh tears that lubricate the crust of those dried. Your arm on fire, you pull up the short sleeve of your gown, an angry fractal tendril scars the skin raw from shoulder to elbow, beautiful actually, a divaricate bantling of rubicund coral. She asks you how you feel and you feel fine, considering, and you tell her as much, but how is it that she is here, how did she find you? Brenda tracked us down, we're all here, Mom n Dad and the boys are out getting something to eat. I wanted to stay in case you woke up. They must be pretty angry, you ask. No, James, no they are not, they are very sorry about all that has happened, they want you to forgive them, they want you to come home. And you wish it were so easy. Things done undone in the stroke of a sentence, and forgiven.

The End

A very special thanks to Panagiota, there for
the best of it and the worst of it!

About the Author

Fordon James is an artist and writer residing in Seattle, Washington. He is currently at work on another fictional novel based loosely on real experiences.